CAPITAL OFFENSE

By

Kathleen A. Antrim

ISBN: 1-4033-2578-2 (e-book)
ISBN: 1-4033-2579-0 (Paperback)
ISBN: 1-4033-2580-4 (Dustjacket)

Library of Congress Control Number: 2002091587

This book is printed on acid free paper.

Printed in the United States of America
Bloomington, IN

1st Books - rev. 07/19/02

Library of Congress Cataloging-in-Publication Data

Antrim, Kathleen

Capital Offense/ Kathleen Antrim—1st ed.

Lane, Warner Hamilton (Fictitious character)—Fiction. 2.
Lane, Carolyn Alden (Fictitious character)—Fiction. 3. Lane,
Edmund (Fictitious character)—Fiction. 4. Rudly, Jack
(Fictitious character)—Fiction. 4. Rudly, William (Fictitious
character)—Fiction. 5. Seals, Katherine (Fictitious
character)—Fiction. 6. Young, Richard (Fictitious
character)—Fiction. 7. Kane, Winston (Fictitious character)—
Fiction. 8. State Troopers—Missouri—Fiction. 9. Secret
Service—Washington D.C.—Fiction. 10. White House
Cabinet and Staff—Fiction. 11. Jefferson City (Missouri)—
Fiction. 12. Washington D.C.—Fiction.

Dedicated to my grandma, Marie Kostalnick, whose unconditional love for her family lives on in each of us.

Families really are forever.

Acknowledgments

Writing is years of taking baby steps toward the goal of publishing a quality piece of work. Along the way many have held my hand and assisted me in keeping my balance. Some have taught me to crawl, walk, and run with my writing. Others have dried my tears when I fell, or pushed me forward when I hesitated. To all of you I want to give a big hug and a heartfelt thank you.

First and foremost, my husband, Jeffery, who sees the best in me even when I don't. My children, Katie and Taylor, who often wish they had a "normal" mother who didn't write, but support my efforts regardless.

A special thank you to my Mom and Dad. I'm blessed to have you as parents.

My family Chuck, Kay, Daniel, Sue, Donna-mom and Terry-dad, Chuckie and Mikey, and my extended family of friends, you know who you are, who keep me as sane as possible–not an easy task. I love you all.

No writer works alone. Many people have assisted me in my many months of research. Some of you have asked that your names be withheld for political reasons, but please accept my sincere thanks for all of your insight and information.

Doctor Daniel Kostalnick (boy--that has a nice ring to it) you've been invaluable in your constant support and research on my many questions from psychiatric profiles to how to commit murder. Suzanne Kostalnick, my first editor, who suffered through all of those awful first drafts.

I must also thank those who've taught me what it means to be a writer. Terry Brooks, an extraordinary writer who's forgotten more about the craft than I will ever know, but who graciously shares his wealth of knowledge. You are an incredible teacher, thank you for taking the time.

Elizabeth George, your unending drive for perfection, analytical mind and phenomenal writing talent are matched by your teaching skills. I count myself very fortunate to have had such an amazing instructor. Thank you.

John Saul and Mike Sack, your boot prints are firmly etched on my backside, and I'm grateful for it. Thank you for taking me under your wings, teaching me a multitude about writing, and becoming my mentors, and friends. I love you both.

Don McQuinn, your guidance has been invaluable. Love to you and Carol.

Danelle McCafferty, editor extraordinaire, we work hard, we laugh hard and nothing I write goes out without your final stamp of approval. Thank you for being my second set of eyes.

Richard Marek, thank you for taking my writing to another level.

Laura Taylor, one of my first instructors. You've stuck with me through a thick and thin, nurturing any glimpse of talent and always being supportive. You're a terrific friend. Love and hugs.

I could go on and on with this list, but would like to get on with the story, so I will simply say thank you to all of you who have assisted with this project. Your time and effort is greatly appreciated.

Patriotism is the last refuge of a scoundrel.
Samuel Johnson (1709-1784)

CAPITAL OFFENSE

PROLOGUE

March 22, 2001---San Francisco, California

"What's deadlier to a country than war?" the man asked.

"Who is this?" Jack Rudly cradled the phone against his ear. A streetlight outside his hotel room window cast a shadow of dancing leaves across the ceiling.

"What's deadlier to a country than war?"

"I don't do riddles." Jack slammed the receiver down. What was *that* about? he wondered. He watched the fluid shadows in the room dissolve into darkness, then spring back to life as gusts of wind bent the tree branches outside the window. He rubbed his eyes. The ringing of the phone had startled him awake; now he would have a hard time falling back to sleep. His mind refused to shut down. Too many projects to think about and deadlines to meet. Jack loved being a journalist, and even years of sleep deprivation didn't deter his passion.

The phone rang again.

Jack glanced at the clock and grabbed the receiver. "It's three a.m. Don't call me--"

"Does 202-555-1416 sound familiar?"

Jack sat up. The sheet fell away, and cool air hit his bare chest. He leaned forward to press the button that activated the tape recorder he routinely plugged into his phone. "Are you calling from the White House?"

"Very good, Mr. Rudly. You know a private White House telephone number."

"Who is this?" The gears of Jack's Lanier spun slowly.

"What do murder and the White House have in common?"

"Murder? That's a bit far-fetched, isn't it?"

"Only if I were making it up."

Jack could hear the man sigh.

"You got my attention by using a White House phone number," he said. "And that bought you about a minute of my time, but I don't take kindly to phone calls at three in the morning. Tell me who you are, or I'm hanging up."

"Your father would understand the morass I'm in."

Jack leaned forward. "What does this have to do with my father?"

"An honorable man, your father. The last of the honorable politicians. A great senator. He would know what murder and the White House have in common."

Jack shivered. "My father's dead."

"Shame, such a shame. He just wouldn't play, would he? And he paid the highest price." The man hesitated. "There are several good men who are dead."

"I don't know what you're talking about. My father died of a coronary. And I know he wasn't into games. So cut the crap." *What the hell am I doing? Just hang up.*

"They're going to kill me now, especially now. It'll be headline news." The man paused. "Is he the reason you became a journalist?"

"I'm not into psychoanalysis at this hour of the night. Why don't--"

"Scotch is a man's drink, you know. Your father loved scotch, especially Glenlivet."

True. Who was this man? What did he know? "Tell me who's going to kill you."

"I know what I'm saying. You're talking to a dead man." Another sigh. "We've deceived an entire nation, you know. Your father would never have done that. He's still a legend on the Hill."

Jack's stomach knotted. Another unresolved issue, Jack acknowledged, before slamming the door on his emotions. "I don't do well on this topic." Jack loathed self-pity, but he understood regret and frustration. "Why'd you call me? And how'd you get my number?"

"I can get anybody's phone number. Whenever I want. It's one of the few benefits of the job."

"That's impressive. What's your job?"

"Not important."

"I'll be back in Washington after the trade conference. Why don't you call me then?"

"I'm not on the Hill. I'm here in San Francisco, just like you."

"Where are you staying?"

"Trust me. You don't have to know my identity or my location."

"I think you've got the wrong guy." Jack's tone changed. "I'm interested in facts from credible sources, not some idea of a poor joke."

"This was a mistake," the man whispered. "You make a lousy last option." His voice rose with agitation. "I thought you'd understand. You're his son, for God's sake! Didn't he teach you anything? He cared, he truly cared. How can you dishonor his memory?"

Jack felt his annoyance spike. "Fine. If this is so damned important, then meet with me."

"That's not possible. I'll be dead soon."

"You're alive now, meet me now."

"I don't believe that would be prudent."

"Then call the next guy on your list. Like my father, I'm not into games. Good night." Jack leaned over to hang up the phone.

"Wait!" the man pleaded. "You know the lookout on the north end of the Golden Gate Bridge?"

"I can find it."

"Thirty minutes." The man paused. "Be careful, they're watching you. Try to stay alive, Jack Rudly. You've got a job to do. And revealing your father's murderer is only part of it."

Jack inhaled. *Murdered? My God, was I right?* His control shattered.

"You want to know how I know? I'm one of them. I helped. But I'm not helping any more."

"Help who? To do what?" Jack managed, but the line was dead.

BOOK I

THE EARLY YEARS

1989-1994

Kathleen Antrim

.

CHAPTER ONE

September, 1989---Jefferson City, Missouri

Judge Margaret Merrit entered the crowded courtroom at precisely 9:00 a.m. and took her seat at the bench. The murmurs of conversation escalated in the packed room, then the smack of her gavel silenced them. The bailiff opened the back door, allowing the jurors to file into the room and sit down in the chairs they had been occupying for over six weeks.

United States Senator, Warner Hamilton Lane, of Missouri, tried without success to unobtrusively take an aisle seat at the back of the courtroom. From his vantage point, he could see the honey-colored hair of his wife, Carolyn, as she sat at the prosecution table reviewing the information in front of her.

God, he had missed her, Warner thought. Juggling their two careers took its toll, especially with hers in Missouri and his predominately in Washington, D.C. He'd only flown in this morning, and now he couldn't even kiss her hello.

Carolyn rose to address the jury, her slim figure accented by the cream Chanel suit she wore. Warner knew that the intensity of her expression revealed the passion she felt for this case. That passion was her trademark.

"Ladies and gentlemen of the jury." Warner smiled as Carolyn began her closing argument. Through their phone conversations, he knew that she'd labored over her summation.

"Today, your work begins. Today, the attorneys will have their last words, and then, the case is yours. Today, you become the arbiters of justice . . ." Warner watched as she paced, gestured, and spoke with a confidence that held the jurors enthralled.

". . . Will justice be served? That's a question only you can answer. I believe it will. Because I have faith that after each of you carefully consider the facts, you will find beyond any measure of doubt, that Albert Roit is guilty on all counts." She turned to glare at the defendant, then returned her gaze to the jurors.

"As we review this case, I only ask one thing of you. Always keep in the front of your mind the thought of one person, Jessica Barnes, because she is what this case is about. The defense would like you to believe that it is about Albert Roit. But it's not. It's about the victim. A little girl whose already difficult life has been shattered."

Compassionate when necessary, angry when appropriate, and condemning when called for, Warner thought, learned from years of experience on the receiving end of injustice. At the tender age of six, Carolyn lost the only family she'd ever known, her mother, to a drunk driver.

Thrust from a loving environment, Carolyn found herself reduced to a number in the social services system. Then, as a foster child, she suffered sexual abuse and battery from her male caretaker. Warner knew that these intensely private reasons drove her to become one of the top prosecutors in the state. She treated every case as if she were prosecuting the man who'd abused her and gotten away with it. But she never revealed her source of strength, too proud to see pity on the faces of her colleagues.

Carolyn began reviewing diagrams that detailed the sexual abuse the perpetrator had repeatedly inflicted on the child. Fury resonated in Carolyn's voice as she repeated the words of the psychologist treating the thirteen-year-old deaf girl. Jessica Barnes could not speak the words herself, Warner knew, yet emotion now reverberated through

4

the courtroom in words spoken by a woman who had lived through the same pain and vowed to fight back for those who couldn't.

This case wasn't just about another foster child, Warner realized. Like all of the other child abuse cases Carolyn had tried, it was about a system that didn't work and the lives that she felt responsible to save.

"Ladies and gentlemen, the defendant, Albert Roit, became a foster parent, not because of his concern for children, not to give love and support to those who desperately need it, but because he wanted the money to buy drugs. He wanted the government subsidy issued for the care of each foster child in order to maintain his drug habit. But Albert Roit did not stop at taking little Jessica's money. No, he also stole her childhood--and her innocence." Again Carolyn stared at the defendant, condemnation and contempt in her eyes.

"Albert Roit took everything materially possible from Jessica Barnes, and when that wasn't enough, he raped and brutalized her. And in his final act, he tried to take the only thing she had left. Her life."

* * *

Carolyn's glare met the gaze of the defendant. She knew that vile look. The door on her own private hell cracked open, releasing the demons of her childhood.

Every night, just past midnight, the hulking form of her foster father, Uncle Vince, stood shadowed in her doorway. He smelled of cigarettes, dirty socks, and whiskey.

"Hush, now, hush," Uncle Vince warned, his speech low and slurred. "I just want to hold you."

She knew better than to cry. But sometimes she still cried a little, and he'd become very angry. So, she bit her lower lip to keep from whimpering.

"That's a good girl." His hands were rough under her nightgown. "Umm . . . such a pretty little girl." He pried her fingers off the blanket she clutched, and forced her hands to his body. "Yes, just like that. Uncle Vince likes that."

The judge cleared his throat.

Carolyn snapped back to the present. She turned to the jury. Rage thundered through her measured words. "It is time, ladies and gentlemen, to stop men like Albert Roit. It is time to fight back, to show Albert Roit and others like him what happens to people who abuse our children. It is time"--Carolyn's speech pattern slowed-- "to put Albert Roit in jail for the rest of his life." Her voice rose to a crescendo. "Give me a guilty verdict so I can do exactly that."

* * *

Warner swallowed hard against the lump of emotion in his throat. Carolyn had gone pale during the pause in her summation. He could only guess at the cause. He felt an overwhelming desire to draw his wife to him, to wrap her in his arms and protect her. He knew that these child-abuse trials devastated Carolyn, just as he knew that they intensified her commitment to righting the wrongs that plagued society. This case had been especially difficult because the victim was deaf. Carolyn's words on the phone last night flashed in his mind. "'The more things change, the more they remain the same,'" she had quoted.

He realized she'd been referring to her own past. To Carolyn, Jessica Barnes wasn't just an abused child; she was Carolyn herself.

He took up a small pad of paper and a pen, then wrote:

You were brilliant. The jury will come back fast. Five dollars and a bottle of champagne say we celebrate tonight.

Your Biggest Fan

* * *

Warner arrived home at nine-fifteen that evening. Carolyn's car was parked in the garage, and he knew she'd be unwinding upstairs in their bedroom. He tiptoed into the kitchen and rifled through cupboards, locating two crystal champagne flutes and a silver ice bucket.

Grasping the flutes in one hand and the Dom Perignon-laden ice bucket in the other, he made his way up the stairs. With the tip of his toe, he gently pushed open the door to the master suite.

Unaware of his presence, Carolyn sat propped up against the pillows of their four-poster bed, legs stretched out in front of her, reading. Her shoes lay haphazardly on the floor next to the bed, her suit jacket had been tossed across the nearby desk chair, and stacks of briefs and documents surrounded her.

"What's all this?" Warner asked.

Carolyn jumped. "You startled me."

"Tonight you're supposed to celebrate. You won." Warner raised his voice and the champagne flutes in unison. "Guilty on all counts-- it's all over television. Or did they forget to tell you?"

A smile lighting her dark brown eyes, Carolyn placed the brief she was reading on the pile beside her. "No, I was there. You should have seen Roit's face. And Jessica's. Thank you, sweetheart, but really the work has just begun. Now that I've got him, I want to make sure he goes away forever."

He sat by her side, opened the champagne, and filled the glasses. "Surely you can take off for a few hours." Their eyes met and held. He leaned down and kissed her. "Congratulations," he whispered against her lips.

"Thank you, again," she whispered back.

"Did I tell you how gorgeous you looked on the five o'clock news?" Warner reached over and unbuttoned her silk blouse.

"No, you neglected to mention that."

He kissed her neck. "Maybe now that the case is over, we can get down to creating the next generation of Lanes."

Warner felt Carolyn stiffen. He saw the stricken expression on her face.

"I can't do this right now. I--I really have to work." She pulled herself out from his embrace.

"What's wrong? Whenever we discuss having children, you shut down. What is it? Don't you want them?" Gone was the poised politician; he could hear the hurt and confusion in his own voice.

"I love children," she insisted as she got to her feet.

"Then what's the problem?"

"There isn't a problem. I'm just tired, and I have to get some things done before tomorrow. Can I have a rain check? Tomorrow's Friday. I'll be able to relax then, I promise." She kissed him quickly, her usual passion absent.

Warner sat up, his legs over the side of the bed, his gaze on the untouched champagne. From the moment they married she'd said she wanted children, but they'd put it off. Now it was ten years later. Warner gulped down his drink. Was he asking too much?

* * *

Warner and Dr. Forrest Muller stepped onto the green of the eighteenth hole. It was only ten-thirty, and they were almost finished. A great way to start the day, Warner thought, savoring the morning air. Freshly mowed grass scented the air. The cloudless sky held the promise of another warm, Indian summer day.

Forrest Muller was an old family friend as well as Carolyn's gynecologist. He knelt down to gauge the lay of the green. "How's Carolyn doing?" Forrest asked, as if reading Warner's mind.

"She's doing fine, a little stressed maybe. But the victory yesterday gave her a boost."

"I'm glad to hear it. I've been worried about her since her last appointment." He lined up his putt. "I had no idea how bad the scarring was until we did the hysterosalpingogram. She was so terribly upset that the damage wasn't repairable, that it left me concerned." Forrest stood and took his position beside the ball. "I know how badly she wanted children."

Warner froze. *What the hell was Forrest talking about?* Embarrassment flushed his cheeks. *When did she have a doctor's appointment?* His political instincts took over, covering his ignorance. "Both of us did. It was quite a shock."

Forrest brought his club back a few times, readying himself. "I'd like to get my hands on the son-of-a-bitch who botched that abortion. He should have his license pulled. I just wish you'd brought her to me."

Shock knocked Warner off balance. *Abortion? When? Why?* The blood drained from his face. Feeling dizzy, he dropped to a squat, leaning on his club. *Oh my God.* His mind reeled. *Why had Carolyn done this?* Bile rose in his throat. He choked it back, then spit to clear the acid taste from his mouth. Tears threatened. Closing his eyes, he fought for breath. *Their baby was dead. Dead. And she killed it.* Rage engulfed him.

* * *

Friday night. Warner sat sipping what was left of his bottle of Jack Daniels. The phone rang again; he simply stared at the answering machine on his desk. The red message light blinked unrelentingly, the LCD display showed thirteen messages. Everyone, it seemed, was looking for him. Since his golf game that morning, he'd deliberately disappeared, easily dumping his state trooper escort.

Warner stared at the whiskey bottle, then began peeling off the label. Why in God's name had she done it? he wondered. She'd made a monumental decision for them both, a decision that destroyed their child and denied their chance for another, and she hadn't even bothered to consult him. His rage rose again but didn't break the surface; he was too numbed by the drink.

No children. Not now---not ever. This thought repeated itself over and over, like the unwanted melody of a song, until he thought he'd go mad. Had this been the natural course of things he could have accepted it, but this had been deliberate. *How could she have done this? How could Carolyn have kept it from him?* The answer seemed simple: she had done it for her own selfish reasons. Otherwise, she would have confided in him. Politically, he preached that it was a woman's right to choose what to do with her body. But didn't he have rights too?

For years, his father, Edmund, had warned him. "Don't trust women. Especially smart women. Carolyn isn't the exception, she's the rule."

How stupid could he have been? He felt like a fool. Warner grasped the Waterford glass so tightly his knuckles turned white, then he threw it as hard as he could against the wall. Crystal shards showered the floor.

The door to his den burst open. "I heard a noise, sir. Are you all right?" Maria, the housekeeper, hurried over to the mess on the floor.

"I'm just fine, Maria."

"I'll clean this up for you, sir."

"Just leave it. I'll get it later."

Maria started for the door. "It'll only take me a minute. Not to worry, sir. I'll get the dust pan--"

"I said, leave it!"

"Yes, sir." Maria stopped, clearly startled by his outburst. "Everyone is looking for you. I'll call Mrs. Lane. She's been worried."

"Don't call her."

"Oh, but, sir, she's so worried."

"You heard me Maria, *do not* call her." He softened his voice. "I'll do it myself. But thank you for offering."

"Can I get you anything before I leave?"

"No, thank you. I ate out. You go home and have a nice evening. I'll call Mrs. Lane at the office. I'm sure she'll be home soon."

Maria gave him an unconvinced smile. "Good night, sir." She backed out of the room.

"Good night." Warner glanced at his watch. Eight-thirty. *Should he call Carolyn? What could he possibly say to her? Why did you do it? Why didn't I get to be a part of the decision?* He couldn't imagine a reason he could forgive. He placed his hands over his face. If only she had told him about the pregnancy. He wasn't sure he would have felt better, but he knew he wouldn't feel so betrayed.

A half hour later, he heard the door to his office open. He lifted his gaze.

Carolyn stood in the doorway, arms akimbo, a look of consternation and worry on her face. "Where have you been all day? Your office has been in an uproar. They expected you this morning. You missed a full schedule of appointments, and everyone's concerned about you."

"I needed some time alone. I just went driving. Who told you I was home?"

"No one. I came home because I was frantic. I've been worried sick all day, and all you can say is that you went for a drive?" Carolyn glanced over at the shattered glass on the floor. "What happened in here?"

Warner glared at her.

"What's wrong with you tonight?"

"None of your fucking business!"

Startled, Carolyn hesitated. "Warner, are you drunk?"

"Not drunk enough." He took a long pull from the bottle of Jack Daniels.

10

She approached his desk, her voice calm and soft. "Please, honey, tell me what's wrong. You're scaring me. You look awful. What happened?"

Warner leveled a gaze at her. "Why did you do it?"

"Do what?" She reached out to caress his face, but he pulled away. Shock showed in her features.

"Why did you kill our baby?"

The color in her face drained so quickly it would have frightened him if he hadn't been struggling so hard to control his rage. He watched a tremor run through her body, then another. She looked as though he'd struck her, but he was beyond caring. "For God's sake, Carolyn, answer me."

"I--I don't know what to say." She found a chair, her body automatically folding into it.

"You had an abortion. You don't even bother to discuss it with me, and now you don't know what to say."

"Who told you this?" Tears filled her dark eyes. She blinked them back, then swallowed convulsively.

"Does it matter? You not only destroyed our child, but any chances of having other children." *God, he hated her at this moment.*

"Of course! You golfed with Forrest today. So much for doctor-patient confidentiality." She gave a humorless laugh that ended like a sob.

Pain arced through him at her response. *When had she lost her trust in him?* "He assumed I knew. It's a natural assumption. I'm your husband."

"You need to understand--"

"I'd *like* to understand," he interrupted. "I'd like to understand a lot of things, like why did this happen? Like why didn't you talk to me about it? Damn you, this is my life too."

"I don't know what Forrest told you, but you have to know how awkward it would have been."

"Awkward, what do you mean?"

"We weren't married, or did the good doctor neglect to mention that part? My God, we'd been dating less than two months. I couldn't possibly have told you this. I was scared to death of losing you or worse, making you feel trapped into marrying me. I wanted you to love me for myself, not out of some sense of obligation. And there

11

was your political career to think of. It was the only decision I could have made, don't you see?" Tears ran unchecked down her cheeks. Her entire body shook. "Please, you have to understand. I love you. I don't want to lose you over this."

"That was twelve years ago, and you never told me. Why the hell didn't you talk to me about it? I had to find out like this. I *don't* understand, not at all. I trusted you, I trusted you with every part of myself. My God, I married you two years after this happened. You knew then that you couldn't have kids, and I'm supposed to live with that?" He swept his arm across the desk, sending the contents crashing to the floor.

"Please, please," she begged, her gaze beseeching. "You need to calm down. I know when you look at this logically, you'll understand."

"You deceived me twelve years ago, and you've kept on lying for our entire marriage." He stood and towered over her, his fists clenched. "It's unforgivable."

She huddled in her chair, looking battered and frightened. "Please, until Forrest did the testing, I didn't know I couldn't have children--"

"And I'm supposed to believe that? When were you going to tell me that you were barren? Or were you going to let me go on thinking that any day now we'd make a family? How could you do this to me? You lying, conniving--" He raised his hand.

Carolyn flinched, her tear-streaked face filled with anguish.

Her reaction stopped him. He glanced at his threatening fist. *I'm becoming my father.* He dropped his arm to his side. His heart felt like the crystal he'd shattered, betrayal cutting him deep.

CHAPTER TWO

August, 1990---Jefferson City, Missouri

Carolyn Alden Lane sat on the bed in their home. Bishop Sleeve curtains framed arched windows then pillowed on the floor of the bedroom. Dark wood furnishings stood boldly atop forest green carpeting. A cream-colored satin comforter with gold trim lay folded at the foot of their four-poster.

She glanced over at Warner, relaxed in sleep. His tousled dark hair added to his youthful appeal, taking years off his age of thirty-nine. They'd been living separate lives for a year now. Warner found many reasons to stay in Washington, even when congress recessed. Now, he lay beside her, a handsome stranger.

Senator Warner Hamilton Lane, she thought. My life with you certainly isn't what I imagined it would be. If only she could go back and change things, fix the multitude of mistakes she had made. How could a woman, she wondered, so adept at navigating her professional life be so deficient in her personal life?

13

She got out of bed and wandered aimlessly around the spacious master suite. Despite her effort to shake off the melancholy mood that haunted her, she failed. She ached from the loss she felt.

Carolyn paused in front of a baroque wall mirror and studied her reflection. The world saw a poised and elegant thirty-five-year-old assistant district attorney. She saw, however, a vulnerable woman struggling to maintain the self-assured persona expected of one of the youngest senatorial wives in the U.S. Congress and a virtually undefeated prosecutor. Everyone assumed she had it all. Only she seemed able to see the truth--she had an image built upon air.

Exhaling unevenly, she looked across the room at Warner's sport coat. Pain scissored through her heart. The evidence of his infidelity existed. Until now, she'd avoided the truth, but she knew that she couldn't any longer.

She walked toward the desk chair where the jacket hung, reached inside the breast pocket, then re-read the note.

Dear Warner-

The flowers were beautiful, the dinner marvelous, and the dessert, as you know, my favorite. (Four times! How did I get so lucky?) You truly are every woman's dream. Until next time, I'll be missing you.

Love---Cindy

She knew why Warner had done this, but his betrayal still pierced her core. She dropped the jacket and the note on the floor, then crumpled onto the desk chair. The impact of her discovery finally registered. Bending forward, she covered her face with her hands, tears wetting her cheeks and palms. She'd had the best in a man and a marriage, but she'd destroyed it all. She blamed herself.

She'd had little choice in the abortion, and although she would forever mourn the loss of the child she knew that it had been the right thing to do. Considering the child's father, to have given birth would have been selfish, and possibly subjected the child to a life as damaging as her own.

But she'd handled the situation with Warner horribly. She should have been forthright from the beginning, Carolyn thought, even if it meant losing him. Her stomach roiled with grief.

Should she tell Warner the truth, now? He hadn't accepted what little he knew of her abortion. He'd never accept the whole story. She'd only been dating him for two months and the baby *wasn't* his.

14

He'd only despise her more if he knew who the real father had been. *No, she couldn't tell him.* Abortion--the word echoed in her mind. That single event had destroyed her marriage--her life. She didn't know if their relationship could be repaired, but she vowed to try.

She stared down at the note as she walked across the bedroom. *Who was this woman? How long had they been seeing each other? Was it serious?* Warner was her entire life, her only family. *What if she lost him?* Her knees became weak, and she grasped the door casing of the closet for support. Regardless of his affair, she loved him deeply. A child would have changed everything. Her free hand came to rest on her abdomen. He would have forgiven her mistake if only she could have given him a child, but that was never going to happen.

No, he still needed her, she reassured herself. She wasn't just a wife, she was his partner, and a politician couldn't make it without a political wife. Warner had no intention of stopping at the senatorial level and she intended to help him achieve his goals.

Her thoughts turned to her father-in-law, Edmund Lane. He'd been enthusiastic about their marriage. A week before Warner proposed to her, she'd overheard their conversation. They needed her intellect and political savvy, Edmund had said, and she knew they still did.

Carolyn refused to play the role of victim, despite her familiarity with the part. She knew that, in order to survive, she couldn't afford the weakness of indulging her battered emotions. She consciously searched for the inner strength that helped make her a survivor many years earlier. Squaring her slender shoulders she wiped away her tears.

As an attorney, she knew it was always better to have all of the facts. Treat this situation as a case, she instructed herself. Be the attorney, not the client.

She couldn't divorce Warner; she wasn't capable of it, despite his betrayal. Besides, not only would her marriage be destroyed, but so would her life. Their professional lives were so intertwined with their personal lives that one didn't exist without the other.

Carolyn knew that the professional success of a politician was contingent on the public's perception of the success of the politician's personal life. She realized that that one fact would assure her place in his life. Warner couldn't leave her, not if he still wanted to be reelected to the Senate. And definitely not if he wanted the White House. He needed her, just as she needed him in order to achieve her goal of legislative reform. The nation deserved new laws on drugs, child abuse, and foster care, and she intended to have a hand in those new laws.

Her gaze fell on Warner. He was so handsome, it made her ache. They hadn't made love in almost a year. Now, she understood why.

Emotional considerations aside, his behavior was jeopardizing his future. Their future. Should she confront him with his affair? Her first impulse was to wake him up and yell and scream. Emotional, she thought, too emotional and definitely not smart. A confrontation might force a decision that would be detrimental to them both. No, she decided, her pragmatic side ruling. The subject was better left alone until she could decide on the right approach.

Carolyn took a steadying breath. She needed to make plans, to protect herself, to get beyond her anger and humiliation, and handle this situation the way she'd handle any case. It no longer mattered that she felt alone. She'd been alone before, but she'd always survived. She would this time, as well, she promised herself.

She crossed the room and snatched the offending piece of paper off the floor. Then she folded it neatly, opened the top drawer of her lingerie chest, and placed it in a tray at the back. She wasn't sure why she took the note, except that she couldn't stand the thought of him keeping it. Yet, she couldn't destroy it. If nothing else, this painful piece of evidence grounded her in reality.

Warner was a powerful man, and Carolyn knew that powerful men required special handling.

"Warner, you have to get up." Carolyn sat on the bed next to him and rubbed his shoulder.

"What?" he responded groggily.

"It's time to get up." She smoothed a lock of hair from his forehead. "We've got church this morning. We're running late. You'd better hurry."

He shrugged away from her. "I flew in late last night. Let's skip church," he mumbled.

"No way," she said. "Your father wants us in church together every Sunday that you're in town, and you wouldn't want to disappoint him. So get out of bed and get in the shower." Carolyn crossed the room to the walk-in closet. "Besides, you have to give a speech today at the opening of the State Fair. We need the press coverage. The speech is on the desk in your study. You'd better go over it before church."

"Who's going to be there?" Warner asked, suddenly alert.

"The local big-wigs, Senator Rudly, Miss Missouri. She at least should bring in a big crowd."

* * *

Carolyn watched in silence as Warner stood behind his antique desk, reading the rewritten speech. It was always this way, she realized. His staff wrote some bland text, then she would edit it, adding the fire, the voice. The staff never seemed to notice, and if they did, she concluded, they probably thought Warner made the changes himself. Regardless, the thoughts and words were hers.

Warner raised his eyes to meet hers.

"Let me hear it," Carolyn prompted, the habit of critiquing his delivery a time-honored tradition between them.

Warner began the script verbatim. He was truly amazing, she thought, nodding her approval. With his photographic memory and her writing skill, they'd already accomplished a great deal.

* * *

When they left the church, Warner took his usual spot in the front seat of the Lincoln with the State Trooper Harry Masterson from their special security detail. Carolyn sat in the back.

"Church ran over today," Warner said. "It's about an hour to Sedalia, so we're going to be late to the fair."

"Don't worry about it, they'll wait for you," Carolyn said. "Besides, I thought the sermon was excellent."

Warner ignored her statement. Why had Carolyn insisted on coming to the fair? he wondered. He'd always made these appearances on his own.

* * *

The stage of the amphitheater at the fair offered no shade and radiated the sun's glare. It was sweltering, but Warner knew he looked cool and relaxed.

He placed his hand over his eyes to block the sun and glanced at Carolyn. She dutifully stood off to the side with her politician's wife's semi-smile, her brown eyes bright, enraptured by his message. Beautiful in a light blue linen suit with a cream-colored silk blouse, Carolyn winked when she caught his gaze, then suddenly frowned. He followed her gaze into the crowd.

Warner saw his political nemesis, Patrick Dunfey, just before he heard him.

"Senator Lane, tell us about your real politics. You're not for the working man, you're for making the rich richer," Dunfey yelled.

Warner maintained his composure. Experience told him that the only way to effectively deal with a political heckler like Dunfey was to make the indirect, direct. "Mr. Dunfey, what's your specific question?"

"Why don't you explain how building an extravagant airport with the taxpayers' money will make you and your big money friends richer."

"Thank you, Mr. Dunfey, for asking that question," Warner responded. "As you all know, everything I do is always in the best interest of both the State of Missouri and her people. The new airport is a critical step toward making our state stronger economically by encouraging industry and tourism. We need to keep up with the times in order to compete in today's marketplace. The construction alone will bring twenty thousand new jobs to the area. I believe--"

"Could you tell us how having a mistress fits into your idea of personal responsibility and family values?" Dunfey interrupted.

Warner maintained a smooth smile. Carolyn walked over and took her husband's hand. Thank God for Carolyn; she knew exactly how to react, he thought. Warner dared a look in her direction. Her cheeks were flushed, she was smiling up at him, but the smile didn't reach her eyes. He hesitated then dismissed his concern.

"Mr. Dunfey, I'm happy to answer your political questions, but when you insult my wife and myself, I draw the line."

* * *

Jack Rudly, leaning against a fence pole to the side of the backstage area, saw two police officers escort Patrick Dunfey from the amphitheater. The sounds of camera shutters clicking told him what the lead story would be in the next day's paper. He turned to the stage as his father, William Rudly, the senior senator from Missouri, began his address.

His dad captured the crowd's attention with his usual enthusiasm and wit, and Jack smiled. Back in the states from a stint in Kuwait during Iraq's invasion, his schedule allowed for only a three-day visit home before heading to Iraq to try to interview Saddam Hussein.

With time so short, his father had asked him to attend the fair. Bill Rudly claimed he needed an honest opinion on how his speech would be received by the press and insisted that only Jack could give an accurate assessment. Jack knew, of course, that his dad just wanted to spend as much time as possible with his son, and would have said anything to assure his company.

The crowd applauded. The older Rudly's blue eyes radiated an intensity that Jack had often been accused of--eyes that saw the truth. Even as mischievous young men, Jack and his friends never got away with a lie where Bill Rudly was concerned.

A small scar, over his left eye, accented Jack's bad boy demeanor, the remnant of a barroom brawl. He was fit at six-feet-two-inches tall and one hundred eighty pounds. A natural athlete, he worked out regularly in an attempt to curb his overactive mind. Regardless of the physical challenges he posed for his body, however, sleep was an illusive commodity.

He swore that insomnia had forced him to become a journalist. When the rest of the world slept, he was wide-awake, keeping watch. Bill Rudly, however, didn't agree with the practicality of this notion and disapproved of Jack's career. This was the first in a long list of topics on which they disagreed.

As the son of a foreign diplomat turned senator, Jack had grown up all over the world and spoke five languages, making him not only a valuable man in the field of foreign journalism, but also a person much sought after by government intelligence agencies. For a man of Jack's talent and contacts, these careers were easily integrated. Jack didn't mind the special assignments, even though it meant that some of his stories never went any farther than Langley, but when it came to certain sectors of the world, his father objected. Iraq was one of these sectors. Jack reminded Bill that even if he wasn't on the government payroll he'd still travel to places like Iraq, to cover the news as a journalist, but his father detested the added risk to his son.

Jack had spent six years in the Middle East. He not only spoke Arabic but also knew the culture, making his visits invaluable to the intelligence community. His father, however, feared the danger. He knew that the U.S. would never tolerate Hussein's invasion of Kuwait, that war was imminent. Bill Rudly had pleaded with his son to reconsider this assignment. His pleading had turned to anger when Jack ignored him.

Jack lit a cigarette. At age thirty-five it amazed him that his father still tried to tell him what to do. Yet, here he was looking for advice. Advice, Jack thought, the real reason for his visit. He'd been offered a position in the States with the *Today* news magazine. He didn't mind giving up the extra assignments for the CIA, but he wasn't sure if he was ready to leave Associated Press. And although he knew his father would want him to take the safe option, he still needed a sounding board.

Straightening from the fence post, Jack saw Carolyn Alden Lane and Edmund Lane walking toward him. They were in an intense discussion and didn't see him as they approached. Edmund's hands were stuffed into the pockets of his suit pants. His white hair glistened in the sun.

"This can't continue to happen," the Senator's wife was saying. "Something's got to be done about Patrick Dunfey. He's making too many waves too close to the election."

"You just worry about Warner. I'll handle Dunfey," Edmund Lane said.

Jack interrupted, "Hello, Carolyn." He tilted his head toward the senior Lane, "Edmund."

Carolyn's head snapped up. "Hello, Jack," she said quickly, obviously embarrassed by the possibility of being overheard. "I'm sorry. I didn't see you standing there. How rude of me."

Edmund shook Jack's hand. "How are you, son?"

"I'm fine. Just visiting my father for a few days before heading abroad."

"How nice," Carolyn said. "It's been a long time since we've seen you here in Missouri, but I faithfully read your articles. Your coverage of the protest in Beijing was incredible. I wish I'd known you were going to be here, we could have had you speak."

"That's nice of you, Carolyn. But I really wanted to keep this trip low key." Carolyn smiled in understanding. "I wish I could stay and talk longer, but unfortunately duty calls." She extended her hand, and Jack took it. "It was good to see you, Jack." She turned to Edmund, "I'll call you later." They both watched her walk away.

"So, today we're treated to speeches from both our favorite senators," Jack said. "I see Dunfey's been giving Warner a hard time."

Edmund's eyes narrowed. "It's not your concern and certainly not the press's concern either."

"Don't worry, Edmund, this is strictly off the record," Jack reassured him, surprised by Lane's abrupt change in attitude. "I'm here for pleasure, not as a journalist."

"Don't give me that crap. You Rudlys are all alike." Edmund began to walk away. "I hope you're a faster learner than your father," he said over his shoulder.

"Sticking your nose into other people's business can be dangerous."

What was that all about? Jack thought, his curiosity piqued.

"What did he want?"

Jack turned toward the sound of his father's voice. "I'm not sure. He was fine one moment, and then I asked about Dunfey. He went ballistic. Did you have a run-in with him?"

"Just the usual politics."

"Didn't sound like the usual politics, this sounded personal. What's going on? Maybe I can help."

"Nothing that concerns you. Don't worry about it." Bill Rudly started for the car, which was parked directly behind the amphitheater in the VIP lot.

Jack followed him. "Look, either you tell me, or you know I'll do my own checking."

Bill stopped. "I don't want you anywhere near those people. Do you understand? You have no idea who you're messing with. They'll

21

not take kindly to your investigations, and I don't want you hurt. End of discussion." He swung around abruptly and continued on to the car.

Surprised, Jack paused, then caught up a moment later. "Look, either you tell me, or I'm on the case, which could cause us both some embarrassment."

Bill Rudly opened his car door and lowered himself into the seat behind the steering wheel. He'd given his driver the day off in order to have a private time with his son. "I do my best to respect your career. I expect you to respect mine. I repeat: Discussion over." He pulled the car door closed, leaving Jack to walk around to the passenger's side and get in.

"No way," Jack said angrily. "You know I respect your career, but this doesn't fall into that category. We're talking about the Lanes and a threat that was tossed in my direction. I want the whole story. Period."

Bill rubbed his forehead in agitation. "There's corruption in that family. I'm sure of it. And it's poisoning Missouri. I won't say anymore than that." He turned the key in the ignition.

"Something must have happened between you and Edmund Lane."

"Edmund knows I'm on to them. That's why he got his back up. He's told me to keep my nose out of it. I told him I wouldn't let him and his cohorts use the political system for their own agenda. He didn't like that too much."

"I'm sure he didn't. Edmund's not used to any opposition, let alone someone talking back. Why don't you give me the details? Maybe I can help."

Bill moved the gearshift to reverse and placed his arm up on the back of the seat. "I said, I'm not going to go into that now. Too much is hearsay, but when I've got something substantial I'll let you know."

"Son-of-a-bitch." Anger flashed across Jack's features. "I'm your son, for God's sake. Not some random member of the press who you have to watch your words around."

"This has nothing to do with your profession."

"Bullshit. You don't trust the press. You've made that abundantly clear, and you can't miss an opportunity to rub my nose in it."

"Believe what you want, but the truth is that I'm just not comfortable discussing this with you, or anyone, until I have concrete evidence. If I need your help, I'll ask for it. Please, let's just leave it at that." Bill backed the car out of the parking space. "I don't want to fight with you over the Lanes. They cause me enough grief as it is."

Jack met his father's gaze, hesitated, then nodded. Years of diplomatic service had ingrained his father with discretion. Jack had seen this stance before, and knew there was no point to pushing. Bill Rudly would talk when he was ready. Missouri politics had obviously heated up, Jack thought. But what the hell was going on? His father had never refused to discuss political matters with him before.

After five miles of silence, Jack spoke. "I've gotten a job offer."

"Within Associated Press or another company?" Bill asked.

"No, I'd be leaving A.P."

"Is it more sane than your current position?"

"Probably by your standards. It's with the *Today* news magazine. I'd be a senior correspondent here in the States."

"What about your special assignments for the CIA?"

"That would be over."

Bill Rudly smiled. "Take it."

"I was hoping for more of a discussion, like: Have you considered the change in lifestyle? Are you ready to settle down? Will you miss the excitement of cutting edge news?"

"Domestic issues can be cutting edge."

"You know what I mean. A.P.'s been good to me."

"Your job at A.P. was meant to prepare you for an opportunity like this."

"I know. This is a plum job, the pay's extraordinary, it's packed with prestige, and it's the right career move. But I feel like I'm selling out, leaving the front lines of journalism for a cushy position in the States."

"You're not selling out, you're growing up. With a job like this you could find a nice girl, settle down, and start a family. It's the responsible thing to do." Bill glanced over at Jack. "Whatever happened to that girl you were dating?"

"Katherine Seals?"

"That's her."

"Ancient history. It didn't work out." Pain caught in his throat. *He was surprised that losing her still hurt. Or maybe it was the circumstances that didn't sit well. She thought he was a bastard, and maybe she was right.*

"What happened? If I remember correctly, you were quite taken with her"

"You know my track record." A bitter note crept into Jack's voice. "When it comes to women, I screw up."

"Like your marriage?"

"I don't want to talk about this." Jack clenched his jaw.

"She got drunk and wrapped herself around a tree. How's that your fault?"

"Dad!"

"That was over ten years ago, it's time you got over it."

"Let's drop it." *This was not the conversation he'd envisioned. His father had a knack for digging up truths that were better left buried. Of course, he'd heard the same complaint about himself.*

"It's true. You were both just kids. You shouldn't have gotten married in the first place. And now you harbor some distorted sense of guilt."

"It was my job to help her. I was her husband, for God's sake." Jack stared out the window. *He'd been selfish. He'd been concentrating so hard on making a name for himself in journalism; he'd ignored her drinking problem. He'd let her down. And he'd never forgiven himself for it.* "Just forget it. Okay?"

"No. I won't forget it. It's time you got over it."

"Some things you never get over."

"So you chase bullets on these insane assignments." Bill shook his head.

Jack glared at his father. "There's no correlation. My guilt has not directed my career."

"The hell it hasn't. And it's about time you recognized it and got on with your life for the right reasons."

* * *

Warner mingled with the crowd. Adrenaline pumped through his veins. This was his specialty, and he savored the adulation.

He focused on the people reaching for his hand. "Thanks for coming out today. It's good to see you," Warner said, with a firm grip and a light shake.

These were people who, in their adoration, made him feel confident that he would win his bid for reelection. "Nice to meet you." Warner patted the shoulder of a young constituent.

He spotted Carolyn, then lost her in the crowd. He liked her to see his popularity with the voters. He was a star. Their star. But by God, he thought, this was just the start. He caught another glimpse of Carolyn. Accompanied by a trooper, she was talking to the Governor's wife.

Warner turned as Harry Masterson, the trooper who'd driven them to the fairgrounds, approached. Together, they made their way out of the crowd and over to the side of the stage.

"Mrs. Lane asked me to tell you that she's going home with the Governor and his wife. She said, she knows you'll want to stay longer," Harry reported.

"That's fine," Warner replied. They often split up at events. He also knew Carolyn would take this opportunity to schmooze the Governor. Politics was about relationships and no one understood this better than Carolyn. "Stay with her until she leaves."

"Certainly, sir."

Warner moved back into the crowd, shaking hands and conversing with the locals before working his way to the backstage area. The crowd dissipated, and a police officer escorted Warner to his car in the deserted VIP parking area. Warner relaxed in the front seat, leaning his head back and closing his eyes while waiting for Harry to return. He reached into the breast pocket of his sport coat. *Son of a bitch, the note from Cindy was gone.*

He heard someone try the door handle and turned to see who it was. Carolyn looked back at him.

Shit, Warner thought, big fucking shit. *Had she found the note when she laid out his clothes that morning? It would be like her to wait to discuss it.* He opened the door. "I thought you'd left."

"I did, but I came back. Your car phone isn't on. The Governor and his wife have invited us to have dinner with them this evening."

25

"Sure, sure." He looked out the rear window of the car. The parking lot was empty, except for the Governor's car which idled by the gate.

"What time is good?"

"Anytime you want." He felt like a runner in a race, his heart pounding harder with each passing second.

"Let's see." She looked at her watch. "It's five-fifteen now, and it'll take an hour to get home. I'll tell them seven-thirty." Carolyn studied his face. "Are you okay? You look a little shaken. I hope Dunfey isn't getting to you."

"No, no. Dunfey's nothing. I can handle him. I appreciated your support though. That hand-holding thing you did was perfect." *Did she know about the affair?*

"Hey, if you can't count on your wife, who can you count on?" She forced a smile.

Warner saw her emotion. Fear turned to pain and embarrassment. *She knew.*

"It's been so long since we've talked. I've changed my mind. I'll go home with you," Carolyn said. "I'll send them on without me."

"Harry's going to be awhile. He's talking to some buddies. I told him I didn't mind waiting, but I don't want to hold you up. You go on ahead, and I'll see you at seven-thirty." He ran his fingers through his hair. His hand was shaking. *He didn't want to deal with this now.*

Carolyn's gaze dropped to the ground. "I, I need to talk to you. Please."

Damn, he never dreamt that it would come to this. "Fine."

Carolyn told the driver of the Governor's car she'd changed her plans, then took the seat beside Warner.

"I found the note."

His throat constricted in pain. Words were lost.

Tears filled her eyes. "Please. Let's start over. We could get counseling. We can try harder. I'll try harder." She moved toward him and kissed his cheek.

Thrown off balance, he moved away. He'd expected screaming and rage, not pain and remorse.

"Please," she said, then kissed him again and nuzzled his neck. "It's been so long since we've been together."

As when she'd tried months ago, he felt no physical response.

26

"Let me love you," she pleaded. "Let me fix us." Tears streamed down her face.

"I can't," he choked out. He knew his body wouldn't respond. The abortion had killed his attraction to her both mentally and physically. He couldn't explain it. He didn't understand it himself. With any other woman he functioned normally, but his wife was dead to him.

Boldly she reached for him, not comprehending his meaning, refusing to be pushed aside. Desperately she kissed his lips, his neck, and moved lower.

Warner grasped her shoulders and held her from him.

She met his gaze.

Pain cut through him as he witnessed the devastation his rejection caused her. His own tears overflowed. "I can't," he whispered again.

Carolyn sat back, anguish etched in her beautiful features. "I don't understand. Do you love her? Is that why?"

His face flushed. "No." *This was torture. How do you tell your wife that you can't get it up with her?* "Do I have to spell it out?" He shook his head. "I *can't--*" his voice broke, "with you."

Carolyn stared at him, her expression first incredulous, then filled with comprehension and embarrassment. "But you *can* with her?"

He nodded.

"Or you just don't want to try?"

He shrugged.

She wiped at the tears on her cheeks, then left the car.

* * *

The Jefferson City Democrat
September 29, 1990
GOVERNMENT PROTESTER FOUND DEAD

JEFFERSON CITY---Patrick Dunfey, known for his vocal disapproval of the current state administration and what he termed as "the immoral behavior of Senator Lane," was found dead of a gunshot wound to the head, at 11:06 p.m., an apparent suicide. This comes on the heels of the drug-overdose death of his fiancée, whose body was discovered one week ago. The investigation into the cause of her death has not been concluded, but she was not a known drug user. The families are stunned by these tragic deaths.

27

CHAPTER THREE

October, 1990---Jefferson City, Missouri

Sunshine streamed through the windows, belying the crispness of the October morning. Carolyn stood in her office at the Cole County Courthouse, gazing out at the frost-glazed trees that lined the streets of downtown Jefferson City. A burst of cold air had pushed south from Canada early this year.

She couldn't believe how the last eleven months had sped by. The election was less than four weeks away. With a flick of her fingertips, she twirled her black leather desk chair, then watched it spin. When it came to a stop, she sat down, and rested her elbows on the immense cherrywood desk. On edge, she rubbed her temples, then massaged her forehead. A dull ache collected behind her brow.

"Good morning," Edmund Lane said as he entered her office and closed the door behind him.

Carolyn jumped at the sound of his voice. "You surprised me."

"There's no time for daydreaming, girl. Warner's falling in the polls, and I want to know what you're going to do about it."

"Your son--" she began.

"I don't want to hear about *my son*." He walked around her desk, taking her chin in his hand. "I want to talk about you. What are *you* going to do?"

She warily peered up at him, struggling to conceal her loathing of the man who had cost her so much. "What would you like me to do?"

"I think you know. Or have you forgotten everything I've taught you? Drastic times call for drastic measures." He dropped his hand from her chin, but his cold blue eyes bore into hers. "I expect Warner to win. It's your job to make sure of that. From what I've seen lately, you aren't holding up your end of the bargain."

Carolyn had known Edmund longer than she'd known Warner--in ways she'd rather not remember. After twelve years of marriage to his son, she knew there were few boundaries to Edmund's ruthlessness. She kept silent. Arguing with him was pointless. He was too powerful and had been in Missouri politics too long. He possessed the power to ostracize her from the state and political life forever. She reminded herself that she might have lost her husband's love, but she couldn't afford to lose anything else. Especially not as a result of Edmund's cruel machinations. She calmed herself and waited for him to continue.

"We need to discuss this. Meet me tomorrow for lunch at the Hilton. Noon. Don't be late." Edmund's voice softened. "Let me down on this, and I may forget our deal."

"You wouldn't hurt your son like that," she said, horrified by the implication of a private encounter with her father-in-law. The pain in her head intensified.

"Try me." He turned his back on her and started out the office.

Should she believe his threat? She knew better than to ignore Edmund. How much worse could her life get? she wondered. Carolyn closed her eyes and breathed shallowly. When she reopened them, he was gone and the door to her office was closed. She'd always believed that the two Lane men were different. Cold and calculating, Edmund's self-interest guided him. Warner, however, had been loving and kind. At least, until he'd learned of her abortion. She hesitated. Maybe that's what she wanted to believe, she thought. Warner's affair certainly wasn't showing any signs of abating. And now she found herself caught between two men who both tolerated her with unconcealed disdain.

Her personal life had fallen apart, and she couldn't seem to put it back together. After Warner's complete rejection, the notion that she was going to repair her marriage seemed foolish. She closed her eyes against her tears. She refused to accept defeat. Like the professional aspects of her life, failure wasn't an option. But she needed help and advice, like the kind one received from a mother or grandmother. But to whom could she turn? There was no one she could trust. She sighed, the sound equal parts frustration and pain.

The familiar pang of loneliness and isolation threatened to overwhelm her. She wiped at her tears as they overflowed, and with a practiced shove, buried the hurt. Self-pity was not her style. Somehow she'd figure this out. Somehow she'd fix it.

Well, Edmund was right on one account, Carolyn conceded. Warner *was* falling in the polls. His opponent, Jackson Green, was hammering him on the new airport project, cuts in education, and raising taxes. She needed to do something to retrieve his career. Regardless of the state of their personal life, she believed Warner to be a great man with a great future. A future she desperately wanted to be a part of. In reality, she knew that politics was all she really had left. The thought sent a chill across her heart.

She enjoyed being a prosecutor, but it was the natural precursor to a life in politics, to effecting change at a higher level and in a more sweeping and long-lasting manner. Her entire life, she thought, was dedicated to getting beyond prosecuting one case at a time and arriving at a place where she'd be making the laws, instituting real change, real justice. This was the dream she and Warner shared.

A knock on her door disturbed her thoughts. "Enter at your own risk," Carolyn called out, forcing a smile when a newly hired assistant district attorney walked in. "Yes?"

"Mark wants to know if you're interested in a domestic case." The young attorney lingered in front of her desk.

She didn't invite him to sit down. She felt too shaken, and she feared that kindness would be her undoing. All business, she asked, "What does the case involve?"

"A child who watched his parents sell and abuse drugs for years and then turned them in. Mark thought you might want to take it on."

Carolyn considered the merits of championing the case. "This kid called the police himself?"

"Looks like it. He helped the police set up a sting. It was a pretty big bust. Mark thinks there must have been some physical abuse going on."

"There usually is," Carolyn remarked softly. She mentally prepared herself for an emotional ordeal. These types of cases were a roller coaster ride through hell at times. Not only did they trigger her back to her own abusive childhood, but they kicked into overdrive her nurturing and protective instincts. If she'd been able to, she would have adopted each of the children from every case she'd ever prosecuted.

The new assistant shifted uneasily, but remained standing in front of Carolyn's desk.

"Good for him," Carolyn said. "This is a kid I have to meet. How old is he?"

"Fifteen."

Carolyn nodded. "Where's Mark now?"

"In his office."

"Tell him I'll be down this afternoon to discuss the case. Say three-thirty. If there's a problem with the time, call me."

"If you take this case, can I help? I'd really appreciate an opportunity to work with you."

She turned her attention back to the papers on her desk. "Have you handled any case work like this before?"

"No."

"Have you ever litigated anything before?"

"No."

Carolyn looked up. "I appreciate your enthusiasm, but this is a kid's life we're talking about. Everything this child has in the world just got tossed into the air like a handful of meaningless dust. So don't take this personally when I say that no one should cut their teeth on a case like this, no one. Get some experience and then we'll talk."

"Mark told me you'd say that."

Carolyn raised an eyebrow. "Yes?"

"Yeah. But I had to try anyway." The young assistant smiled.

"Well, you get an 'A' for effort."

Knowing he'd been dismissed, the assistant walked to the door, then paused briefly. "May I ask you a personal question?"

"Sure."

31

"Does being a senator's wife ever factor into these types of decisions?"

"No, it doesn't. I just want to make sure I'm the right attorney for the job." Carolyn sighed. "This is a battle I began to wage long before I met my husband." This realization made her feel ancient.

"Really?"

"Really," Carolyn said and waved him out the door. She softened her dismissal with a faint smile.

Later that day, Carolyn made her way down the corridor to Mark Dailey's office. Mark was a unique man. Intriguing, really, she thought. He was a senior assistant district attorney, like herself, and he projected a strong, moral image. He'd been with the County Prosecutor's Office for eleven years. People listened to him, and he was an excellent litigator.

Mark had tight relationships with all of the "big boys," having grown up in Missouri as the beneficiary of old family money. Edmund had taught her not to rule out anyone until she determined how he or she could help or hinder her and in Mark's case she figured it was help. Carolyn cringed at the self-serving nature of her thoughts. Edmund had taught her so many things, long before she ever met Warner. His brutal influence still remained. His agenda disgusted her, but his street smarts had carried her far. She silently cursed the man, then relegated him to the mental closet that housed the rest of her demons.

She needed Mark's help now. He just didn't know it yet.

Carolyn walked into Mark Dailey's office without knocking. The room was furnished with built-in bookcases and two square leather chairs, which faced a matching oak desk that overpowered the room

"How's Saint Mark today?" Carolyn teased as she smoothed her hair behind one ear with her right hand.

"Fine, and knock it off." His kind hazel eyes belied the serious note in his voice. "Why? It suits you. And why not enjoy the status of your celestial reputation?"

Mark laughed. "I--Oh, forget it. I know better than to get into parries and jabs with you. Let's discuss this case."

"Chicken." She sank into one of the square leather chairs facing him, kicked off her shoes, and crossed her legs. "All right, let's discuss the case. I think it's right up my alley."

"Have you considered the time element? It could tie you up from the outset. I know you've been concerned about Warner's campaign." He leaned back in his chair.

She nodded. He sounded like a master of the obvious, but Carolyn knew he couldn't help himself. He could be articulate, but within two minutes of a discussion with her, he often behaved like a blithering idiot. Did the great Mark Dailey have a crush on her? She thought so, and she was flattered by his attention, but she didn't intend to act on it. His friendship and his role as a colleague were too important to her.

"Mark, your point is sound, and yes, I have considered it."

"What about the emotional toll? I know what these cases do to you."

Carolyn hesitated, touched by his sensitivity. Her automatic defenses took over. "I have a job to do. And I know you wouldn't have brought this case to my attention if you didn't think I should take it. Am I right?" She uncrossed her legs, and slid her feet back into her shoes.

"You don't need to be tough with me. I know your record. We're alone. I'm worried about the personal impact of this case on you."

"You're wrong. I *do* have to be tough, in this office and everywhere else, for that matter. I can't let down, because if I do the bad guys will win. The only way to stay undefeated is to push everything, but the facts, aside."

"If you had all of this figured out, why the visit?"

"I couldn't resist the opportunity to bask in your saintly glow." Carolyn laughed. "Actually, I have a favor to ask."

"Sure."

"Is your wife going to the reception tonight?"

"Yes, she is. Would you like to sit with us?"

"Well, no," Carolyn hedged. "Unexpectedly, Warner's out of town, and I hoped you'd escort me. If your wife wasn't coming, of course. But since she is, I'll work it out. It was just a thought."

"Well . . . let me give her a call. She'd probably be delighted to have a night off."

"No, no, I wouldn't think of it. I'll work it out, thank you. I'll see you tonight."

"No." Mark picked up his phone. "Please wait. Let me ask her."

Carolyn sat quietly while he phoned. The reception was important. Warner was in the southern region of the state surveying flooded farmland, and Carolyn was standing in for him at party given by an elite businessmen's organization called the Pinstripe Club. She didn't have to give a speech, but with the campaign in full gear, she did need to make an appearance.

She knew that all of the major business and political players would be in attendance. These were people with whom she needed to solidify relationships. The members were more powerful than most officials already in office. Like Warner's father, they were "king makers." They made the decisions as to who won the political offices and at what price. She and Warner needed their support--and their deep pockets--in order to break through to the national scene.

Mark was the key. He'd grown up with them, and, although Warner was a senator and the Lane family was prominent, Carolyn needed Mark's help in establishing herself as a potential political force. Even though in legal circles she'd earned a reputation as a tough prosecutor, she knew that in this arena she was perceived only as the *Senator's wife*.

She'd debated whether or not to impose on Mark for his contacts, but realized that an opportunity like this, with a party of this magnitude and Warner out of town, would not present itself again. Too, she had to admit, she'd enjoy a night out with Mark, even if it was strictly business.

Mark hung up the phone. "One of the kids has an ear infection, and Sandy would love to get out of going tonight. So, I'm available."

"Are you sure you're not just telling me this so I won't feel guilty about taking you away from your wife?"

"No, honestly, she'd rather stay home with the kids. You know me, Carolyn. Would Saint Mark lie?"

"No." Carolyn laughed low in her throat. "Saint Mark would never lie."

"Great, I'll pick you up at six."

She pushed up from the chair, and left his office. Mark's concern and compassion felt good. They'd become close over the years, and he was one of the few people she trusted, although within limits. He was kind, gentle, and dedicated. A man she admired. Dangerous,

Carolyn warned herself, stopping her thoughts. Mark was married, off limits. But she couldn't help but envy his wife.

Once she returned to her office, Carolyn called in her assistant, Katherine Seals. She'd met Katherine at party headquarters. The daughter of a party leader, Katherine had quickly become invaluable and a good friend. They shared many ideals; Katherine was one of the few people in whom Carolyn had confided her dreams of social change. The belief that they could impact the lives of needy children had forged a strong bond between the two women.

Carolyn considered twenty-seven year old Katherine young, but she realized her strengths. A striking woman with an athletic figure, Katherine wore her long auburn hair in spiral curls. She didn't seem aware of her physical attributes, or chose to ignore them. Carolyn hadn't decided which. But beauty aside, intelligence was the trait Katherine had chosen to dominate her life. Maybe it was because of this common ground that their friendship had grown so quickly.

"We've got a hot case," Carolyn announced with an easy smile.

Katherine's green eyes lit up. "What's it about?" They both loved the strategizing that was required for a court victory.

"I'll brief you tomorrow. This afternoon, go to the law library and pull everything you can find on children as informants, and everything on kids who've testified against their parents. Don't limit it to Missouri, but weed through it. I only want information with teeth to it." Her gaze caught on the wall clock above Katherine's credenza. It was four o'clock.

"You want sensational stuff, as well as precedent-setting information?" Katherine asked.

"You've got the picture." Carolyn picked up her briefcase and lifted her coat off the hook behind her door. "Have it by tomorrow, and we'll review it together. I won't be back today. Make sure you lock my office when you leave."

"Of course," Katherine replied.

* * *

The reception consisted of caviar and champagne, followed by a full-course meal featuring Maine lobsters flown in that day. Heads turned when Carolyn strolled into the main room with Mark. Cut on

35

the bias, her black cocktail dress accented shapely legs and her hair moved in soft waves about her shoulders. A waiter offered them glasses of champagne, which they accepted.

"Our seats are at the head table," Mark said.

Walking through the crowd with Mark felt natural, she thought, comfortable.

Mark introduced her to a few bankers he knew. He'd begun his professional life in investment banking. The fact that he had given up such a lucrative career for the pursuit of justice, Carolyn long ago concluded, was a testament to his moral fiber. Attentive and polite, he also made her feel valued and respected, things she hadn't felt in a long time.

"I want you to meet someone special," Mark said as they finally approached the head table and found their seats.

"Carolyn Alden Lane, may I introduce you to Mortimer Fields."

Her heart raced. *Mort Fields was the most important political player and moneyman in Missouri. He could make Warner's career.* "I've heard Warner speak of you. I can't believe we haven't met before." Carolyn extended her hand. Living up to his reputation for charm, Mort kissed it.

"And I've heard of you. Your record against the drug trade is making quite an impact."

Carolyn flushed at the compliment. "Thank you."

She couldn't believe her good fortune in sitting next to him. He was not taller than five-foot-six, with a slender build, but his charisma was enormous. As the number one power broker in Missouri, he was closely tied to the International Banking Fund, which possessed seemingly limitless monetary resources. It was alleged that he alone determined the distribution of the funds. Within fifteen minutes, she and Mort were trading jokes.

After the meal began, their discussion became more serious. "Have you heard about my latest venture?" Mort asked.

"The rumor is that you're financing two computer geniuses, with some revolutionary technology, in a software company," Carolyn said.

"Essentially that's true. Interested in investing?"

"I didn't know you were looking for investors," Carolyn said as a waiter set her entrée in front of her. *This was too good to be true.*

36

"I wasn't. I certainly don't need them." Mort picked up the seafood fork and plucked a piece of meat from the claw of his lobster. "But I may make an exception for someone I like. And I like you."

Carolyn realized that he was flirting with her. "Well, thank you. I recognize an outstanding opportunity when I see one. And based on your business reputation, I'd be a fool to decline an offer to invest with you. But what would be expected in return?"

"Smart question. Could it be that the lady is a businesswoman on top of her other talents?"

She weighed her words with care. "I try. However, I find it's men like yourself from whom I can learn a great deal."

"Thank you. If you invest with me, I guarantee you'll make money. And if Warner loses the election, you may need it."

"Bite your tongue," she teased, then grew serious. "But you still haven't answered my question."

"I might possibly need your legal talents. You scratch my back, I'll scratch yours, figuratively speaking, of course."

"Of course," Carolyn said. *She'd be a fool to turn his offer down. The extra funds and Mort's support would help Warner's presidential dreams immensely. Besides, it was a chance at financial freedom. A chance to liberate herself from Edmund Lane.* "I can live with that."

Mort studied her face silently for a moment, then raised his champagne glass. "You're a lady after my own heart. Here's to new partners."

"To new partners," Carolyn agreed, and tilted her glass to his.

* * *

After the dinner was finished and the speeches delivered, the real party began. Drinks flowed freely, and band music vibrated the floor. Mort led Carolyn across the room to meet his friend, Stephan Thomas, before excusing himself. Stephan was the lead counsel for Poultry Foods. Carolyn knew that he, too, was a contact worth cultivating. They talked about many issues, including their mutual frustration in dealing with state and federal regulators.

"Call me if you're having difficulties. I may know of a way to attack the bureaucracy," Carolyn said. "We might be able to help each other."

37

Thomas grinned. "I think we could do business."

"Well, I'm interested," Carolyn responded.

By ten o'clock, she had solidified her prospects with Poultry Foods, Comco, Bounce Plastics, and other big industry donators. Usually this was Warner's game, and she stayed in the background entertaining the spouses. Now, she was finally setting up the field for her own play. Warner couldn't have done better, and she felt certain that he would be proud of her.

She sensed that she'd been welcomed into an exclusive club, a club where the payoff could be enormous. Her best new contact was Mort Fields. Besides investing in his new software company, Carolyn planned to approach him for a major contribution to their campaign. Warner's father would applaud her initiative. Yes, indeed, Edmund had taught her well. But at the thought of him, a cold chill passed over her. So far, she hadn't seen her father-in-law, although she'd expected to meet him at the gala.

Carolyn's gaze traveled over the room. She spotted Edmund in a discussion with Ron Spietzer, Adam Miles, and the other senator from Missouri, Bill Rudly. Not again, Carolyn thought, watching the heated exchange. Ron was a local businessman who was vocal in blaming Warner, Edmund, and Edmund's partner and best friend, Adam Miles, for breaking the union that he'd once headed. Bill Rudly always supported Ron and the unions. Her body tensed as she walked to the outer edge of the room, searching for Mark and steering clear of what could easily become a scene.

She found Mark at the bar. "Would you care to dance?"

"The honor would be mine."

Mark took her hand and led her onto the dance floor. She caught sight of Edmund as he and Adam Miles departed. Relaxing, she gave herself to the moment as Mark spun her among the other dancing couples. His wife was a lucky woman, she reflected somewhat wistfully.

"Want another drink?" Mark asked.

Carolyn hesitated. She'd already had her limit. "Sure. Vodka seven." *Why not? She trusted Mark, and she hadn't relaxed in months.*

"I'll get the drinks and meet you back at the table."

Carolyn took a few sips of her drink once he joined her, then carried it along as she visited other partygoers at another table. She returned with an empty glass. Mark offered to get her another. She accepted. Carolyn eventually realized her nose was numb. She felt giddy and light headed.

The lilting notes of "Blue Moon" filled the room.

"Let's dance." Carolyn took Mark's hand and led him to the dance floor. She pressed her cheek to his as he pulled her neatly against his frame. His body felt solid and comforting. Carolyn sighed contentedly. The contact felt good.

When the song ended, she brushed her lips to his ear. "Thank you for the dance."

They returned to the table, where they were left alone. Carolyn reached for her drink and spilled it over the front of Mark's pants.

"Oh, my gosh," Carolyn said, picking up a napkin. "I'm so sorry." Her face flamed with embarrassment at her clumsiness. She bent to wipe him off, gently rubbing the wet area. Carolyn looked up, and their eyes met.

She felt the current of attraction that arced between them. "Maybe we should go." *She'd had too much to drink. Mark was married--out of bounds. She'd never cheated on Warner and she wasn't starting now.*

"Yeah, I guess. Where're my keys?" he asked, his words slurred and his hands clumsy as he searched his pockets.

They got their coats, then stood just inside the lobby, waiting for the valet to bring the car around. Mark helped Carolyn into the passenger side. She dozed off as he drove to her home. At the house, he parked, then turned off the ignition.

"Wake up, sleepy head," Mark said.

"I'm sorry. How long have I been asleep?" Carolyn blinked to clear her vision. *Definitely a headache tomorrow.*

"Only a few minutes."

Mark walked her to the door. Groggy, she fumbled in her purse for her keys, dropping them on the porch. Simultaneously they bent to retrieve the keys. Their heads cracked together.

"Are you okay?" Carolyn asked as she straightened and grabbed at the doorframe to steady herself.

He rubbed her forehead. "I'm sorry."

"No, it was my fault." A flush rose in her cheeks.

He traced the side of her face with his fingertips.

Carolyn closed her eyes at the gentle gesture. When she opened them, she noticed a small cut at his eyebrow. "You're bleeding." She reached out toward the cut.

Mark grasped her hand. "I'm fine."

Feeling vulnerable, she turned away from him. "Let me get you some ice." Carolyn opened the door and led Mark to the kitchen. The house was dark and quiet.

Her awkward hands took too long to retrieve the ice cubes and place them in a towel. Carolyn couldn't seem to escape the heat suffusing her entire body. Apprehensive, she turned back to Mark and applied the ice to his injury. Her hand shook, desire and loneliness overwhelmed her emotions.

"How long have we known each other?"

"Stop it." Carolyn laughed. "You'll make me feel old."

"I'm serious." His gaze searched hers.

Involuntarily, Carolyn leaned toward him, drawn to his heat. "At least ten years."

"Have you ever thought about me, about us?"

"Mark, this is dangerous territory. Let's not go there." Over the years, her feelings for him had grown. *But what had they grown into? Love?* She swallowed hard and relinquished the towel-wrapped ice to him.

"I'll make some coffee." Carolyn turned away, but Mark grasped her hand again, and stopped her.

"You feel it too." Lightly he pulled her too him. "I need you, and you need me."

She did feel it. Had always felt it. And it was a need, a need that had to be denied. Carolyn placed her hands on his chest. "We can't." *Was it her or him? She didn't know. Was she sending the wrong message? She hadn't intended to mislead him.*

His gaze was intent and she felt as if he were searching her soul. Slowly, he lowered his mouth to hers.

Carolyn pushed against his chest. "I don't think we should do this. I can't." She could feel the warmth of his breath against her cheek. *She couldn't hurt Warner like this---fool---as if Warner cared.*

He kissed her again, stifling her protests. Desire surged within her. She found herself wrapping her arms around his neck. *No. No, this was wrong. She didn't want to hurt Mark's wife. She didn't want to hurt anybody.* But she felt weak. And she felt such staggering need. She couldn't stop. Her body betrayed her.

She heard the ice cubes hit the floor. Mark's embrace tightened, his kisses urgent. She realized her fingers were tangled in his hair. She felt engulfed by her hunger to feel and return love. *Why couldn't Warner touch her like this? Kiss her? Because Warner hates you.* Loneliness and alcohol overpowered her resolve.

She arched into Mark, starved for intimacy. The edge of the kitchen counter dug into her back. She hardly felt it. A cupboard doorknob bruised her thigh, but she ignored the pain.

Mark leaned harder into her, pulling at her dress, his breathing rapid, his eyes glazed in excitement.

Her body screamed for fulfillment. His hands ripped at her clothing. He lifted her off the ground. His foot slipped on the ice, and he grabbed the refrigerator door handle to stop their fall, almost dropping her in the process. Then he was inside her, and she felt the tremor of his climax, while her own body still pleaded for release. She moaned, the sound equal parts frustration and disbelief over her own lack of control.

Mark moved away from her, straightening his clothes. "That was different," he said with a laugh. Clearly, it was no more satisfying for him than for her.

Where was her self-control? Guilt flooded her. *Her behavior was inexcusable.* Carolyn smoothed down her dress and tried to regain her composure.

"It's getting late," he said.

Carolyn nodded. She couldn't look at him. "This shouldn't have happened." *Their carelessness could destroy Mark's marriage and devastate his wife.* Her stomach tightened and she swallowed hard.

"Come here." Mark pulled her to him. "It'll be all right."

The hall clock chimed. Two a.m.

"I'm not sorry it happened," he said. "But we need to think about this. And at the very least find better accommodations next time."

She didn't appreciate his humor or his assumption. "No, we both have too much to lose, too many people would be hurt. This is over. It can't happen again . . ." *even though I love you, she almost added, with a depth of emotion that threatened to overcome her. And she did love him, but not the way she loved Warner.* That realization, coupled with the thought of what they'd just done, made her nauseous.

"You'd better go." She still couldn't meet his gaze.

Mark tilted her face up, forcing her to meet his eyes. "I'm not sorry this happened," he repeated before heading down the hall.

She turned away, convinced it was the alcohol talking. He had a family to think of. The door clicked shut behind her. She couldn't let this happen again. She told herself that the hope of having a loving, intimate relationship, like the one she knew she could find with Mark, was forever beyond her grasp. Her heart belonged to Warner. It always would. She wasn't willing to hurt others for a temporary fix.

A tremor of fear ran down her spine as she thought of the personal and professional ramifications of an affair. The specter of Edmund Lane loomed in her mind. If her father-in-law ever found out that she'd been unfaithful to his son, he'd destroy her.

* * *

Unable to sleep, Carolyn left the house early the next morning to get a jumpstart on her next case. At the gate of their fenced community, she slowed to a stop and rolled down the window.

"Verne, what are you doing back to work so soon?" she asked the guard.

"Can't miss too much work, what with the medical expenses and all. The Mrs. is taking care of Billy."

"How's Billy doing?" Carolyn asked. Billy was Verne's seven-year-old son who had been battling leukemia for two years.

Tears welled in the man's eyes.

Carolyn felt a knot forming in her throat. "Is there anything I can do?"

Verne reached out and touched her hand. "Please continue your prayers."

Carolyn drove toward her office. Why, she wondered, did a small child have to suffer? The feeling of vulnerability shook her, a constant reminder of the untimely death of her own adoring mother, and the years of abuse she'd endured afterward. She slammed the palm of her hand against the steering wheel.

Without warning, her car bucked with a loud thud. What had she hit? Quickly, she pulled off the road and got out, running to the furry heap lying in the road.

"No," she moaned. She picked up the animal. "Poor, poor baby." The small dog stirred in her arms, its breathing shallow. "I've got to get you to a vet." She ran back to her car. She'd been so preoccupied with thoughts of Billy that she hadn't been paying attention to the road.

She placed the whimpering dog in the seat next to her and drove downtown, pulling into the driveway of a veterinarian. She laid it carefully on the front door step and prepared to leave.

"You're on your own now, so hang in there." She smoothed her hand over the dog's head, then glanced at her watch. Seven a.m. The vet should arrive any minute now. She started toward her car, then looked back at the porch and the small animal lying there helpless.

Carolyn hesitated, then returned to the front door, and gently eased the dog into her lap after she sat down on the porch step. Soft brown eyes looked directly into hers. She cuddled the dog against her. She wasn't leaving until she knew the poor thing would live.

Five minutes later the veterinarian arrived and escorted them into the office. He took the dog from Carolyn and hurried to an examination room.

"What happened?"

Carolyn couldn't stop the tears that filled her dark eyes. "I hit her with my car. She's not my dog, but she's wearing an identification tag."

The vet took a stethoscope and checked the dog's heart and lungs. "I'll need to do some X-rays. It's going to take me some time, but I think this little soul will be all right. Her heart sounds good. I'll have my assistant contact the owner."

"Please, tell them how terribly sorry I am."

"We will. Why don't you leave your phone number, and I'll call you later?"

Carolyn hesitated, not really wanting to abandon the dog. "I'll pay whatever it costs, just save the poor little thing."

"Don't worry. She's in good hands."

Carolyn left her phone number at the desk and drove to the courthouse.

Katherine was waiting for her. "I've got the information you asked for yesterday. Lots of it."

"Great," Carolyn said, her usual enthusiasm absent.

"What's wrong?" Katherine followed her into her office. "Are you all right?"

Carolyn hung her coat up on the door hook. "No, I'm not." She was embarrassed by the emotion in her voice, but knew she could trust Katherine with her feelings. "I've had a horrible morning. I'm terribly worried about a friend's sick child and then, due to my preoccupation, I ran over a--" Carolyn's voice broke "--a little dog." *She couldn't tell Katherine about Mark--she couldn't tell anyone. She'd just have to swallow the guilt and erase it from her mind.*

Katherine gave her friend a hug. "I'm so sorry."

Carolyn regained her composure. "There's nothing I can do to help the child, and that sense of powerlessness is so frustrating. I can't even imagine the pain his parents must be going through. And now I feel awful about the little dog, but the vet thinks she'll be fine. They're supposed to call me later."

"I'll make sure you get the message," Katherine said, her arm still around Carolyn. "What can I do to make you feel better?"

"Get to work," Carolyn responded as she straightened up and focused on the stack of folders on her desk. "Looks like you came up with a lot of case files."

"Sure did," Katherine answered. "A very interesting topic, I might add."

"Together we'll sift through them all. Use the Dictaphone for your notes."

"No problem."

"You'll have to start without me, though. I'm due over at the police station this morning to speak to the detectives about the case. I'm not sure how long that will take." She glanced at the stack of work growing on her desk. She was supposed to have lunch with her father-in-law that day, and she'd already gotten a late start. Did she dare cancel? It was time, she decided, to get out from under Edmund's control. "Do me a favor."

"Sure," Katherine said.

"Call my father-in-law and tell him I can't make lunch today."

Katherine's eyes widened. "Are you sure?"

Carolyn took a deep breath. "Absolutely." She left her office before anxiety overcame her resolve and caused her to back away from what amounted to an act of great courage on her part.

* * *

Warner arrived home later that night wearing the kind of smile that didn't come from surveying flooded farmland or shaking hands on the campaign trail.

"How's the flood?" Carolyn asked, needling him.

He flashed an annoyed look. "Leave me alone. Why'd you send me on that wild goose chase, anyway?"

"It was politically necessary, and you know it."

A look of doubt crossed his face.

"Besides, it was your father's idea."

Warner shrugged, as though that bit of information settled the issue.

"I thought you were going to be home this morning," she said. She expected the lie she received a heartbeat later.

"We got held up. You know how it is."

Her heart sank. *Why couldn't he find a way to forgive her? Because he doesn't want to, she realized.* She managed to conceal her frustration behind a smile.

"I'm heading up to bed," Warner said.

"I'd like to join you." The words were out before she could stop them. *If she could be with Warner, maybe she could forget her own lapse with Mark the previous night.*

"Why do you have to push?" The flush of anger rose in his face.

"I need you, Warner. I need us to be the way we used to be." She hated the pleading note in her voice. *Didn't she have any pride?* "They have counselors for sexual problems."

"Sexual problems?" he hissed, stepping closer to her.

She could smell alcohol on his breath.

"You think I have sexual problems?" Fury flickered in his eyes.

She shrank back from his volatility. "Well, I---"

He smacked her across the face.

Her head snapped to the side. Tears flooded her eyes, more from shock than pain.

"My *only* problem is you!" He stared at his red palm, then stalked out of the room.

Carolyn sank into the nearest chair. Tears rolled down her cheeks. She smoothed her fingertips over a small cross concealed beneath her silk blouse. An idiosyncrasy she'd developed as a child in the aftermath of countless beatings.

Rubbing the heirloom, she closed her eyes remembering her mother's smiling face, loving touch, and gentle words. It was her only respite. Her only avenue to control and sanity.

* * *

Two nights later, a small figure huddled in the dark beside the terminal at the Sedalia Memorial Airport. The air was still as the Asian woman silently watched the keepers of the rural airport shut down for the evening. Once the small staff left, she slipped out to a lone plane parked near the runway.

Clad in dark clothing, she stealthily moved up the left side of the Cessna 210 to the door. She pulled a thin tool from her pocket and easily picked the lock. Swinging the door open, she leaned into the cockpit, clicked on her flashlight, and verified the plane's registration taped to the visor, then popped the latch to the cargo hold. With a gloved hand, she tucked a strand of her long black hair behind an ear, then checked her watch. Minutes, she had only minutes before she ran the risk of discovery.

After shutting the door softly, she moved to the cargo hold, pulled out the portable ladder, set it by the wing, and climbed to the top. Reaching the gas tank, she opened the lid, pulled a bag of sugar from her duffel, and then poured the contents into the tank. She stuffed the empty sugar bag back into her duffel and quickly jumped off the ladder before moving to the second wing and repeating the exercise. Completing her task she neatly folded the ladder back up, set it inside the cargo hold, and locked the door.

Moving with speed and grace, she stepped to the right wing. Brandishing a number two Phillips screwdriver, she removed the inspection plate under the wing, exposing an 18 gauge galvanized aircraft wire. She pulled out a wire cutter, then squeezing it with both hands, she severed the cable controlling the right side flap deployment. Glancing around, she assured herself that she was alone before quickly replacing the inspection plate and disappearing into the night.

* * *

Moments later, Ron Spietzer and his family strolled across the tarmac of the Sedalia Memorial Airport.

"It's a beautiful night tonight. Perfect for flying," Ron said to his companions.

"Thank you for the lovely dinner." Molly reached up and kissed Ron's cheek.

Ron Spietzer, his wife Molly, and her parents, Howard and Joanne Moore, walked the remaining distance to their Cessna 210.

"Whose turn is it to fly us home?" Molly asked the others

"I will," Howard volunteered.

"Dad, you flew us here," she pointed out.

"Yeah, Howard, I remember distinctly, it's my turn," Ron replied.

"Ronny, you flew last time. It's Mom's turn," Molly said.

"Let Ronny fly the plane home. I'm tired, anyway," Joanne said.

"It's settled, I'll fly," Ron said. "Molly, sit in back with your mom. Howard, you're my co-pilot. I'll just be a few minutes while I do the pre-flight. You guys get comfortable." Ron reached for the door to the cabin and opened it for his wife. He paused. "That's strange, I was sure I locked this door."

Molly shrugged, then climbed into the backseat of the plane. She and her parents chatted while Ron walked around the plane with his flashlight, going over the checklist per standard procedure. These outings were regular events. Two or three times a month they'd get together and fly to dinner, weather permitting. All four of them were addicted pilots.

After pre-flighting the Cessna and climbing into the left seat, Ron shouted, "Clear." Then, he started the engines. With three clicks of his mike button, the runway lights illuminated, and he guided the Cessna down the path and into the air.

"Nice roll-off, Ron," Howard said as they took to the sky and the landing gear retracted. "Nothing like flying on a beautiful, starry night."

Ron smiled as they enjoyed the view.

Twenty minutes later, they were cruising at an altitude of fifty five hundred feet and following the river basin that led straight into the Jefferson City Airport.

"We're starting our descent. We should make the Jeff City Airport in about twelve minutes," Ron estimated.

"Good, it's a school night and we need to get the baby-sitter home early." As Molly spoke the plane's engine coughed and sputtered, then resumed its normal hum. "What was that?" she asked.

"I'm not sure," Ron responded while checking the gauges.

"Are we low on gas?" Howard asked.

"We can't be, I had the tanks filled before we left," Ron said.

Molly unbuckled her seat belt and leaned forward to look over Ron's shoulder.

He pointed at the gauges. "See, both tanks are near full." They all had been flying for years, but he knew she preferred to be in the pilot's seat. He often teased her that it was her compulsion for control that made her tense unless she was at the throttle. "It seems fine now. Just relax, honey."

Molly turned to her mother, "So finish your story about---"

Suddenly the engine quit, and the plane yawed to the left, slicing through the sky and dropping. Ron grasped the yoke firmly with both hands, struggling to bring the nose up and straighten the plane. "Oh shit!"

Unable to buckle her seat belt in time, Molly was thrown against her mother. Then the force of the dive tossed her up off the seat. Her head slammed into the ceiling. She fell back to the seat unconscious.

"Molly, Molly!" Joanne, shook her daughter's shoulder. "Oh my God, Molly's hurt--she's unconscious!"

Ron managed to right the plane.

Howard turned around in his seat as Joanne tried to straighten Molly's slumped figure. Joanne looked up, terror shining through the tears in her eyes. "Help me, Howard. I can't get Molly to sit up. *HELP US!*" She pulled her daughter's limp body into her arms.

"Joanne, you have to get her buckled into her seat belt," Howard shouted. "*Please, Joanne, buckle her in.*"

"Howard, the engine's frozen. It won't turn over."

Howard spun his attention back to Ron at the panicked note in his voice. "Bleed off your airspeed and maintain your altitude."

"We'll overshoot the airport if I do that. I've got to bring us down in order to land on the runway." Beads of sweat were collecting on Ron's brow. "I'm trying to get us into a solid glide."

"Try switching to the other gas tank. If the gas is contaminated, it may be gumming up the engine," Howard said.

"You do it," Ron shouted back. "I'm afraid to let go of the yoke, I barely have control now." Sweat trickled into his eyes, and he shook his head, trying to clear his vision.

With a shaking hand, Howard flipped the lever to the second gas tank, but the engine remained silent.

"Try the auxiliary pump." Ron's heart felt as if it was in his throat as he watched Howard move in what seemed like slow motion. Howard reached for the switch and moved it to the ON position. The pump started immediately.

"There we go, there we go, baby," Ron encouraged, but the engine failed to respond.

Howard leaned forward and tapped the fuel gauges. The dial on both tanks showed full.

"This doesn't make sense. Switch back to the primary tank," Ron said, fighting to hold the plane steady.

Howard switched back, but the engine was dead. "You're right, we're *too* high."

"Son-of-a-bitch," Ron said, "I'll have to slip her down. Everybody prepare for a rough ride. Joanne, how's Molly?"

"Unconscious, Ron, but I can feel a pulse," Joanne replied shakily. "She's buckled in."

"Howard, turn the radio to the emergency frequency for me, one-two-one-point-five."

Howard did as instructed.

"Mayday, mayday, Columbia Flight Service, this is Cessna three-eight-six-seven Whiskey, plane in trouble. I repeat we're in trouble!" Behind him, Ron could hear Joanne praying the Hail Mary.

"Three-eight-six-seven Whiskey, copy your mayday. Transponder code five-five-two-two and ident."

Howard leaned over, programming the Transponder and activating the identification button.

"Columbia, copy your five-five-two-two and ident," Ron radioed back.

"Three-eight-six-seven Whiskey, we do not read your Transponder. Please ident."

"Columbia, we have. It must not be working," Ron's voice rose with fear.

"Three-eight-six-seven Whiskey, can you give us your location?"

"Four to five miles from the Jeff City Airport coming in from Sedalia."

"Copy, three-eight-six-seven Whiskey, four to five miles west of the Jeff City Airport. State your emergency."

"We're in a glide without power, but our altitude is too high. I'm going to try slipping her down for a landing, and we need an ambulance." Ron felt the plane shudder as he nosed the plane downward while pushing his left foot down on the rudder pedal and applying the right aileron.

"Copy, three-eight-six-seven Whiskey. Ambulance requested. Jeff City Airport."

"You're gaining airspeed, Ron. Watch your airspeed. We're dropping too fast," Howard urged.

"I know, I know," Ron responded, his voice cracking.

"Use your flaps! Slow us down!"

The airport loomed ahead.

"We're almost there," Howard encouraged. "Just use the flaps."

Ron reached for the flap lever and gave the plane ten degrees of flaps. Suddenly, the plane rolled hard to the right.

"Ron, the flaps are split!" Howard screamed.

The stall horn sounded in the cockpit as the plane flipped and dove.

* * *

The Jefferson City Democrat
October 15, 1990
PLANE CRASH KILLS FOUR

JEFFERSON CITY---Ronald Spietzer, a prominent businessman from Morrison, Missouri, who was well known for his recent disagreements with Senator Lane about union busting during the strike at Bounce Plastics, Inc., was killed yesterday when his Cessna 210 airplane crashed.

His wife, Molly, and her parents, Howard and Joanne Moore, were also killed. All four people aboard the plane were instrument-rated pilots and flew regularly out of the Jefferson City Memorial Airport. The plane went down on the return flight from Sedalia Memorial Airport. An investigation is now underway to determine the cause of the crash.

CHAPTER FOUR

November, 1990---Jefferson City, Missouri

One week, Carolyn thought, only one week until the election. She strode purposefully into her office at the courthouse after a long day of depositions, and called campaign headquarters. "Has anyone seen Warner?" she asked.

"No, Mrs. Lane, we haven't."

Carolyn severed the connection without another word. "Damn it, where is he?"

She picked up the receiver again and phoned the troopers' office. The whole idea of security for Warner seemed ridiculous, Carolyn thought. Very few senators required protection. In this instance, she knew the taxpayers' money could be put to better use, but Edmund insisted on a permanent escort for his son. And when Edmund made a request, few elected officials would deny him.

The phone was answered. "This is Carolyn Lane. I need to find Warner."

"Is there an emergency, ma'am?" the trooper asked. "Can I be of assistance?"

"Please, find Warner and have him call me."

"Yes, ma'am."

"Thank you." Carolyn hung up. She suspected the troopers were covering for Warner, and possibly protecting her feelings. The pain of failure and embarrassment gripped her heart. *Why couldn't she be as strong and competent personally as she was professionally?*

She wondered then how many people, aside from the troopers, knew about his infidelity. *How was she supposed to live with this constant humiliation?* Publicly, she played the role of the loving wife. Personally, she died a little bit more each day.

* * *

"Good evening, ma'am," the trooper said. "Is the Senator there, please?"

"This better be good," Warner cautioned a few seconds later.

"Mrs. Lane called, sir. She's looking for you."

"Okay, okay, I'll be there in a few minutes."

Warner cursed under his breath. Carolyn knew the situation. He'd essentially been honest with her. Why couldn't she let it go? Why did she continue to force the issue? He resented the fact that she'd caused him to lose control, to act like his father, and for that he'd *never* forgive her.

Damn, he needed some relaxation. The election was days away, and he'd been working his ass off. Warner grabbed his coat.

"I've got to go, baby. I'm sorry," he said, then kissed Cindy quickly.

"We aren't done." She stretched out on the couch, naked.

"I don't have time."

"You could make it quick." She smiled.

"I'm sorry if I seemed distracted."

"Even distracted you're good."

Warner stared down at the chessboard. "All right. But if I lose, it's because you rushed me."

"Oh, no, you don't. This is just one move, I'll concede no such thing."

Warner laughed. He slid his bishop across the board. "Check."

She frowned. "Well, at least I have some time to think of a response."

* * *

He fished the keys out of his coat pocket, opened the car door, and slipped into the driver's seat. Damn it! Carolyn and Edmund were determined to blow everything he did out of proportion. Of course, Edmund only discussed politics with him. Since the day of his mother's suicide, Edmund only spoke to Warner when absolutely necessary, leaving a bewildered and lost seven-year-old boy to cope. With that rejection Warner's guilt grew. He'd spent years believing he'd caused his mother's death.

The last time he'd heard his mother's voice, she'd been crying. Years of pain rushed at Warner when he thought of that night.

Squatting at the top of the stairs, in his pajamas, Warner had squished his seven-year-old face between two balusters and listened to the voices of his parents. Edmund raged. His mother sobbed. Something shattered against a wall. Then he'd heard a smack. His mother fell in the doorway of the library across the hall. He'd wanted to run to her, to save her, but fear kept him frozen.

Edmund liked to hit, and Warner knew he would not be spared if he challenged his father. Besides, his mother had made him promise that he'd stay away whenever Edmund was angry.

Edmund's voice grew louder, clearer. "You cheating bitch." Another smack.

Warner flinched, then clenched his eyes shut. His small hands gripped the balusters.

"I know why you coddle the boy so much, and keep him from me. He's a bastard. A bastard you're going to pay for."

"No, no, please, no." His mother voice was soft and pleading.

"When were you going to tell me I'm not his father?"

Warner's eyes flew open.

"Leave him out of this," his mother sobbed. "It's not his fault."

"Yes, it is . . ."

Warner felt hands on his shoulders. Mary, their live-in housekeeper, pulled him from the stairs, and returned him to his bedroom. He lay awake the entire night, his sheets pulled up under his chin.

The next morning, Warner learned that his mother was dead. Suicide, people whispered, and he heard them. The next week, he was shipped off to boarding school.

Warner found refuge within himself. Alone. He excelled in school. But his accomplishments, both academic and athletic, only seemed to further incense Edmund.

As a young man, Warner finally understood why his mother had died and Edmund had rejected him. Warner was the product of an adulterous affair--his mother's affair. He'd confirmed this by locating Mary, who'd worked for his family for years until that ugly night. The only servant in the house during the fight, she'd been dismissed the next day.

Not even Carolyn knew that Edmund wasn't Warner's biological parent. His election to the Senate hadn't been enough to heal Warner's wounds. And after all these years, Warner wasn't sure why he cared or why he even tried to please Edmund Lane. He'd never know the identity of his biological father, and he'd never have the love of the man who raised him.

* * *

Election eve. Carolyn sipped a mug of herbal tea before she dressed for her campaign appearance. She sank down into the sofa in the living room of their mansion. Worried that they were about to lose everything they had worked so hard to achieve, she silently cursed Warner.

Carolyn gazed out the window, watching a rainstorm brew in the distance. A lightning flash startled her, and she shivered involuntarily. She got up and closed the blinds.

She thought about the most recent poll, which showed a close race between Warner and Jackson Green. Damn Warner and his ego. He'd ignored her warnings about the airport project, raising taxes, and his vote to cut spending in education. Now these issues were haunting him.

Carolyn knew that if their relationship were still whole, he might have listened to her. Perhaps she should have asked Edmund to speak to Warner about working on their marriage. No, she thought, Warner would never forgive her for dragging his father into his personal affairs. Unconsciously her fingertips brushed her cheek. She gave a short, bitter laugh, thinking of the circumstances that had all but destroyed their marriage. What difference would it have made if she had spoken to Edmund? It wasn't as if Warner would ever forgive her, anyway.

The truth, however, was that she had no intention of ever subjugating herself to Edmund Lane again. Introduced to Edmund by a law school professor, Carolyn welcomed his willingness to act as her mentor in her pursuit of an internship clerking for the Missouri State Supreme Court. Due to her inexperience and naiveté, she mistook Edmund's manipulation for kindness and fell for his polished charm.

Carolyn's stomach knotted at the thought of the painful lesson she learned from Edmund. During their brief affair, his brutal nature became apparent. A tear slid down her cheek. Edmund Lane robbed her of the ability to conceive a child when he pressured her into having what turned out to be a botched abortion. As far as she was concerned, he was the devil incarnate. Edmund would always be a threat.

She stopped her train of thought. Warner and the election had to take precedence over everything right now. She didn't have time for self-pity. She and Warner had covered a lot of ground campaigning, but recently Warner's enthusiasm and conviction were being perceived as overconfidence. This puzzled Carolyn, because Warner's ability for gauging an audience's response to him was a trait that he had perfected.

But he had recently developed a habit of disappearing after his speeches, like a ghost. She'd told him that he needed to stay longer and shake hands, make people feel they were a part of the action and essential to his success. Hell, Carolyn thought, Warner knew this stuff. Political savvy ran in his veins. Why was he so intent on sabotaging himself now? She wished she knew the real answer.

Lightning flashed through the closed blind, creating jagged images on the wall. Feeling a chill, Carolyn walked over and turned up the heater. The warmth it produced didn't help. She doubted that anything would be able to dispel her sense of impending doom.

* * *

On election night Warner strolled through the lobby of the hotel closest to campaign headquarters, a wide smile on his face. He shook hands and waved to his supporters, then he headed for the elevator. Television news crews followed his progress through the building. They'd been with him since eight that morning, when he and Carolyn had gone together to cast their votes.

After twelve and a half hours, Warner was still going strong. Excitement pumped adrenaline into his veins. He was overdue to meet Carolyn at the suite they had reserved. The polls had just closed, and he felt great. He stepped onto the elevator with Sammy, the state trooper, who punched the button for the top floor.

"Tonight's our night," Warner said.

"Yes, sir," Sammy replied.

"It's the close races that mean the most. They get the blood pumping and make the victory sweeter." Warner flashed Sammy his two-thousand-watt smile. "This victory is going to be the sweetest."

Carolyn and Edmund had been the voices of disaster lately, he mused, but he had refused to let them dampen his spirits. He realized the polls showed a close race, but he'd witnessed the faces of the crowd, the faces that affirmed his victory.

They have no faith, Warner thought. He'd never lost an election before, and he wasn't going to lose this one. He had it all under control. This was his day. Another day of glory on his way to his destiny---the White House.

* * *

By 1:00 a.m. the unofficial results were in. Warner stepped up to the microphone to give his speech. The crowd had thinned. Filled with disbelief, he glanced around at his remaining supporters. Carolyn stood off to his side, her makeup perfect, a smile affixed to her face.

Warner grasped the podium to stop his hands from shaking. Then his eyes fell on Edmund, who stood in the back of the room. Even at this distance, he could read the disgust on the old man's face. History had repeated itself, and again, Warner found himself judged unworthy of love. Rejected. A failure. The "bastard" child had shamed the great Edmund Lane once more. Warner watched him turn his back and leave.

He could feel his lips trembling as he spoke the words of his hastily thrown together concession speech. He'd seen no reason to prepare one, and now he stumbled through words of thanks, and of putting up a good fight, before cutting the speech short and excusing himself.

He knew Carolyn was behind him as he headed for the exit. Warner turned, met her sober gaze and saw the stubborn set of her jaw.

"Warner--"

He held up his hand. "Not now."

* * *

November 4, 1990--Jefferson City, Missouri

A dumbfounded Warner Hamilton Lane slumped into the chair behind his desk in his home office. It was six a.m. He'd been up all night, grappling with the final election results. He'd spent most of the night driving around aimlessly before returning to the mansion. Carolyn wasn't at home. She must have stayed in the hotel suite, he thought. He raked his fingers through his hair. *How had this happened? He'd been so sure the election was his. How had he lost it?*

Carolyn's list of campaign concerns came to mind. "The airport project will sink you," she'd warned. "Even if you get the federal funding, you'll still have to raise taxes. You voted for spending cuts in education. Green is hammering you on these fronts." Her list had gone on and on. He'd ignored her, convinced that she was overreacting, convinced he had it all under control. He'd been stupid and arrogant, and now he was out of office. A loser.

Edmund. His heart beat faster. The image of the old man leaving in the middle of his concession speech sprang into his mind, making him feel sick to his stomach. At least he hadn't had to face the old man close up. Nor had he had to endure the sneer that he knew would be on Edmund's face. It was the look that confirmed his inability to measure up. I've proven him right, again, Warner thought.

What could he do now? He wanted to hide from the entire world, but especially from Carolyn and Edmund. Disgrace draped him like a shroud. The worst part was, Warner thought, his position was indefensible. Carolyn had been right.

Once, not long ago, he could have counted on a loving and compassionate wife, but not now---not after the last year. He had to admit, that was his failing too. Granted, he'd been having an affair, but a man needed a sexual release. Initially he'd intended to hurt Carolyn, to punish her for her deceit and his sexual inadequacy where she was concerned. Hell, it was her fault. He'd never had that problem before. But now, with defeat smothering his energy, he found it impossible to conjure up the intense anger that had caused him to strike out at her.

I've fucked up, Warner thought. Everything he'd possessed that was right and good, he'd abused or destroyed.

Warner staggered to his feet, then paused. He had nowhere to go. He wanted to die. How could he have let this happen? he asked himself again. His mind spinning, he struggled to come up with a viable plan for his future and his very survival, but he could think of nothing.

He had always joked with the troopers that he'd have to stay in politics because he was too old to be a movie star. Being a politician was who he was, what he was. He garnered respect from the world and even Edmund in the political realm. If he couldn't memorize the lines and wave to the crowd, he was lost. He didn't know anything but politics, he didn't want to know anything else. Well, he had taught law for a little while, but that was just until he'd won his first election.

Carolyn selected that moment to walk into his office. "You insisted on building that airport. There wasn't enough public support for your pet project. But you still opted to please your father and his friends. And it's cost you your political career. It was obvious to the voters that you were catering to the big money men. But you thought you were being clever, and no one would smell the corruption. You were wrong, and I've had it. I'm done playing the loving wife to a man who has just single-handedly flushed his career down the toilet."

Face flushed purple he rose to his full height.

Hands on her hips, Carolyn stood her ground.

He didn't care if he deserved her wrath, he refused to take it.

"I'll be filing for divorce," she whispered.

Warner began to shake. He wanted to hit something, to unleash his frustration and failure through his fists. The defiance in her eyes stopped him, and he sat abruptly.

The full weight of her words struck him like a blow to his solar plexus. "You can't--" He looked at her, desperation seeping into his voice. "Don't---please---you can't leave me." Warner choked on the words. "We'll both be finished if you do that."

"No," Carolyn said, "you'll be finished. You *are* finished." She turned and stormed out.

Oh, my God, Warner thought. Rings of sweat soaked the underarms of his shirt. If Carolyn left him now, he'd be lost. She was his source of strength and direction. He knew that losing the senatorial race would prompt Edmund to cut him off, and without Carolyn's income, he'd be destitute. He'd never had to worry about money before, but now, he realized, his future was doomed without her.

He stood in the middle of the study feeling disoriented, not knowing where to turn or what to do. For the first time in his life, his charm meant nothing; he couldn't talk his way out of this. Convinced that destiny was self-determined, he felt his world fly off its axis. He felt on the verge of suffocation. "I can't deal with this. I just can't."

Warner walked over to a portrait that hung on a far wall of himself in cap and gown on graduation day at Harvard Law School. Edmund had not attended. He pulled the frame forward like a cupboard door to reveal a wall safe. Warner stared at the steel door behind the picture, hesitating for a moment as he tried to make some semblance of order out of his confused emotions.

He reached out and grasped the dial to the safe, his decision made. With numb fingers, he dialed the combination. The lock clicked, then the door opened.

He pulled out a .38 caliber snub nose.

He was Warner "Fucking" Lane, the promising young Senator from Missouri. On the fast track to the White House. The presidency was his lifelong goal, and the senate was a key component to reaching that goal. Shit, what did it matter? Everything was gone now.

Warner inspected the gun as it rested in the palm of his shaking hand. A sob caught in his throat.

* * *

Carolyn knew that the balance of power in her life with Warner
had shifted on the night of the election. She'd never aspired to
anything other than a full partnership with her husband, but fate had
stepped in and turned their world upside down. She'd promised
herself that same night that they would recover from defeat and
triumph again, although she would lead the team. In her own way, and
on her terms. Then, and only then, she realized, would she be able to
reform the foster care system. Then, and only then, would she be able
to salvage her dignity, despite Warner's rejection and his shockingly
self-destructive behavior. She would not fail Warner a second time, at
least not professionally.

Carolyn sat on the corner of her desk at their mansion, scribbling
notes on a yellow legal pad. The telephone rang with calls from all
over the country. High-level politicians wanted her take on what had
happened to Warner. She answered them all without really answering.
The national attention was incredible.

The phone rang again.

"May I speak to Warner, please," a baritone voice drawled.

"I'm sorry, he's not available. May I ask who's calling?"

"This is Senator Richard Young. I wanted to offer my
condolences."

Carolyn cringed. She knew that the Senator from Georgia was one
of Warner's drinking buddies in Washington. "That's very thoughtful
of you, Senator. I've heard Warner speak of you often, and I'll be sure
to tell him you called."

"Thank you, ma'am. He knows where to reach me."

"Good day, Senator." Carolyn wrote his name down on a message
slip, then tore it up. She'd be damned before she'd encourage that
friendship. Warner knew she didn't trust Young, but they were close
friends, and he obviously didn't care what she thought. Carolyn
dropped the ripped up message into the garbage can at the side of her
desk.

The phone rang again. A female voice told her to hold for the
Speaker of the House.

"Carolyn, hello." The hearty voice of Jonathan Daniels boomed
over the phone lines.

"Well, hello, Mr. Speaker. It's so nice to hear from you."

"I was very sorry to learn of yesterday's outcome."

"Yes, we're very disappointed, but we're going to re-group and come out fighting in the next election."

"Good to hear it," Jonathan said. "Is Warner around? You know my feelings about him. I still believe he has a great future in politics, and I'd like to offer my support."

"No, actually he's stepped out for the morning," Carolyn lied. "But let me thank you for him. I'll be sure to tell Warner you called to offer your support, I know it will mean a lot to him."

She hung up, reassured by this validation of her efforts behind the scenes during the previous year. In order to separate herself from her father-in-law's grasp, she'd concentrated on cultivating relationships at the national level. Obviously, she had succeeded in bringing the right kind of attention to herself and Warner. Despite this debacle of an election, she now had a strategically tight grip on the reins of their future.

In anger she'd threatened divorce, but she knew that would be counterproductive to her life--their lives. She would build on Warner's failure. Prove to him the value of their marriage.

Edmund would make it easy for her. He'd relinquish control and want nothing to do with his son, now that Warner had lost. Carolyn stopped writing and tapped her cheek with the end of the pen. "I can make this work," she said aloud, heartened that her dreams had not been completely destroyed.

Warner had always done what he wanted. All too often, he ignored her advice. Not any longer, she decided. Carolyn stood, walked to the window, and looked out onto the gardens of the old estate.

A measure of calm came with her newfound feeling of confidence. She knew that she could get Warner into the White House, but he'd have to agree to her terms. He had rejected her personally, and that pain would probably never fade, but professionally, he needed her now more than ever. And, just maybe, if she saved his career, she could heal their marriage once he succeeded in the political arena.

She sipped at her now cold herbal tea, enjoying the quiet as her mind raced with thoughts of the future. She was, after all, a survivor.

Suddenly, the sharp report of a gunshot broke the calm.

Carolyn jumped, tea spilling on her sweater, the mug crashing to the floor. She stood stock still, frozen by fear. Warner? Oh, dear God, please don't take him from me, she prayed as she dashed out of the room and ran down the hallway toward the shot.

CHAPTER FIVE

November, 1990---Washington, D. C.

Jack Rudly walked across the tarmac about ten yards behind the President of the United States. The wind whipped at his face, and the crisp morning air sent a shiver through his body. Freshly fallen leaves skipped across the ground. He looked up at the glimmer of yellow light on the horizon as it blended into shades of pale blue and pushed against the navy darkness of the night sky.

Absently, he adjusted his tie. This was his first morning covering the White House in the "tight pool." Every White House correspondent traveled in the press plane, except the tight pool. Chosen on a rotating basis, this small group spent every moment near the president on catastrophe watch, then reported anything significant to the regular press pool. Jack boarded Air Force One and found his seat. He had to admit that since joining the *Today* news organization, his accommodations had improved dramatically. But was this what he wanted? Wearing a suit and baby-sitting the president in hopes of a scoop that he'd have to share with the rest of the press population. Adrenaline had been his steady diet for years. Now his biggest rush would be when the plane took off.

Jack reached for a cigarette, then stopped himself. Air Force One had rules about such things. Damn, domestic issues just didn't hold the charm that life as a foreign correspondent had. This was success, he reminded himself, what his goal had been, a senior position with an excellent news organization.

He remembered his discussion with his father about joining *Today*. His father had been right: living on the cutting edge of life didn't bode well for any type of meaningful relationship. And his former lifestyle and passion for journalism had caused more damage to his personal life than he cared to admit.

Having learned the hard way, Jack would no longer subject a family to the nomadic and dangerous life of a foreign correspondent. Thus, after his wife died, he'd remained single and alone. The only exception had been Katherine Seals, and the ruin of that relationship proved his fears.

But high-risk investigative journalism coursed through his veins, the essence of who he'd become as a man. Had he sold out? Or had he grown up? As his father had insisted.

Jack ignored the voices of the men and women around him. Had he made the right decision to return to the United States and a safer way of living? Granted, he was sick of the loneliness and he wanted a family, but it wasn't as if he had the love of his life waiting for him. In fact, he hadn't had a real date in six months.

"Hey, Rudly, what are you doin' here?"

Thoughts broken, Jack turned toward the voice of Sam Hutton, another reporter and an old friend. "Just getting a story like everybody else."

"I thought you were off fightin' the brave fight as a foreign correspondent. You know, hard-core news, war zones, dictators, the real stuff. This seems a little tame for you. Who clipped your wings?" At Jack's glare, Sam burst out laughing. "You don't look like a happy camper, buddy. What's the deal?"

"I've decided to focus on domestic issues and stick closer to home. I'm sick of having bullets whiz past my head."

"Doesn't sound like the Jack Rudly I know."

Jack shrugged.

"So, the rumors are true. You left Associated Press and joined *Today*."

"Don't give me that rumor crap, Sam." Jack broke into a smile. "You probably knew before I did that *Today* was going to make me an offer. Shit, with your sources, you probably know how much I'm making and how many tax deductions I take."

"I appreciate the compliment, but you give me too much credit. The question is . . . will you still talk with the rest of us now that you've hit the big time?"

Jack's face grew red. "Knock it off, Sam."

"All right, all right. How long have you been with them?"

"What's today? November fifth?"

"Yup."

"One month exactly," Jack said.

"And you've already rotated into the tight pool. I'm impressed."

"Don't be. *Today* was slotted for the spot."

"Well, I suppose the rest of us can go home," Sam said.

"Why? Afraid of the competition?"

"Damn right, I am. Your reputation precedes you."

* * *

"I can't. I can't!" Sobs overtook Warner as he stared at the hole the bullet had made in the floor. He threw the gun back into the safe, slammed the door, and leaned heavily against the wall.

Two troopers, Harry Masterson and Sammy Kelly, burst into the room. "Are you all right, sir?"

"Warner, what happened?" Carolyn ran through the doorway, fear and concern on her face.

"It was just an accident. Nothing serious. I need a drink," Warner said. *My God, he was pathetic. He didn't even have the balls to end the pain.* "Where's the whiskey?" He spun around and reached for a fifth on a nearby shelf.

"We heard a shot, sir." Harry said.

"Shit, the bottle's empty. There must be another one around here somewhere." Warner waved them away.

Carolyn turned to Harry and Sammy. "You can go. It looks as if everything's fine."

Harry gave Carolyn a doubtful look.

"It's fine, Harry. Just go. I want to talk to Warner alone."

66

"Yes, ma'am," Harry said, and the two of them departed.

"What's going on?" Carolyn asked. "Why'd you have a gun out?"

Warner stared at her. There was so much he wanted to say. So much to apologize for, but the words wouldn't come. They were stuck in his throat.

Silence hung between them.

Carolyn, her expression pained, turned and walked out of the room.

Warner watched her departure. He looked up at the bookshelves and old brown paneling that lined the walls of the study. At one end of the room was a novelty bar made from a globe. Warner walked over to it, then pressed a hidden button. The continents north of the equator lifted, exposing a hidden storage area for booze.

Warner poured himself a Jack Daniels, drank it, and felt the relief almost immediately. Hell, just holding the bottle in his hand made him feel better. He clutched it to his chest, like a life preserver destined to save him from the rough seas of years of rejection and isolation. He cared less about Edmund now, and his confidence regarding Carolyn grew.

He set the precious bottle down, then mopped his face with the back of his sleeve. Thank God for the whiskey, he thought. He had to find Carolyn, had to reason with her. Her divorce announcement couldn't be real. She needed him. Her dreams of judicial and social reform were too important to her. He shouldn't have let her leave the study without an explanation and an apology. He'd seen the concern on her face. She still loved him, he was sure of it. She'd give him a second chance, and together they would make things right. Confident, Warner forged his way down the hall of the mansion to her office.

Carolyn was on the phone when Warner walked in. "I'll have to call you back," she said, hanging up.

"Who was that?" Warner asked.

"Do you want something?" Carolyn countered, standing.

Contrition filled him. "Carolyn, I know we've had a rough couple of years. And I admit that a lot of it was my fault. I'm really sorry for that, but I believe that we can put all that behind us now and start over. I'm willing to try if you are." He reached a hand out to her.

Carolyn's eyes widened, as she came out from behind her desk. "Who in the hell do you think you are?"

67

Stunned, he dropped his hand to his side. He didn't have the energy to fight.

"Do you really believe that you can inflict a life of hell on me and then just waltz in here with your poor excuse of an apology, and I'll just come running into your arms?" Carolyn's voice rose. Her fear receded. *She didn't know where the knowledge came from, but suddenly she understood that she couldn't give in. He needed to believe their marriage was over. Otherwise, she'd always be the victim.* "How convenient for you. Now that your life is in the gutter, you've finally found it in your heart to forgive me and start over." Her words trembled with rage and hurt.

"I loved you, Warner. I loved you with all my heart, and you took that love and stomped all over it--all because of a situation you refused to understand, refused to forgive. And now you have the nerve to ask me for forgiveness."

She took a step back from him. "You deliberately set out to hurt me. You didn't make a mistake, like I did. Your betrayal was intentional, and designed specifically to humiliate me. How am I supposed to forgive you or even trust you again?"

He winced visibly. "Please, Carolyn. I couldn't help myself. I'll do anything you ask. Please, we need each other . . . ."

"Just leave me alone, Warner." *Hard as it was, she forced herself to reject him. She had to for both their sakes. For the future.* Turning away from him, she moved behind her desk and reached for the phone.

Warner slouched briefly against the doorframe, steadied himself, then staggered out of the room and back down the hallway. He needed another Jack Daniels.

* * *

Carolyn recradled the telephone and folded into her chair. She turned to look at the now empty doorway. Pulling her knees up to her chest, she hugged them tightly, as years of pent-up frustration overflowed with her tears. The emotional release felt good. Carolyn didn't know how long she sat there crying, but when she rose from her chair her legs were stiff and her knuckles white from tightly gripping her legs. She walked over to the window, staring without really seeing out across the lawn.

If he still loved her, then things would be different. But he'd never mentioned love, just need. Maybe she was destined to a life without love, but that didn't mean she had to give up her ambitions. Damn him!

Their political lives were what mattered now. The only thing, she realized, that she could count on.

She picked up her note pad and reviewed her notes. Their national positioning was good, but only *if* they could retake the senatorial seat in the next election.

Carolyn thought again about Warner. She would help him resurrect his career, and, in doing so, she would facilitate her own goals of reform. It wasn't the life she'd envisioned on her wedding day, but it was a life she understood and could be proud of. Compromise, she thought, life was about compromise.

* * *

Warner woke the next morning to the sound of pounding. He couldn't tell if it came from inside or outside his head. The pain in his temples was unbearable, and his body felt stiff. He opened his eyes, trying to focus. Then he realized that the noise was coming from a downpour striking the living room windows, and that he was lying on the couch.

Memories flooded back, and he felt as if a huge weight was pressing down on his chest. Warner pushed himself up to a seated position when Carolyn walked into the room. "You look awful."

Warner just stared at her. He could barely think, let alone respond.

"Up to a conversation this morning, or are you too *tired*?"

He gave her a surprised look. She laughed ruefully.

If there were a chance she might change her mind, then he would speak to her no matter how bad he felt. "I'm fine."

Carolyn approached him. She was wearing a red cardigan that hung to mid-thigh, a cream turtleneck underneath, and pleated, navy wool pants. Her hands were jammed into the pockets of her sweater.

Warner could smell her Chanel perfume. He glanced at the window, hungry for air. His ears rang, and he felt light headed, but he managed to push himself to his feet. "What do you want to talk about?"

"Our divorce."

Warner's heart sank. "I was hoping you might reconsider."

"We both know I can do fine on my own. I have a promising law career ahead of me, and you threw away your future."

"Edmund will never allow this," he insisted.

"Do you think your father really cares what happens to us now? He'll be looking for another political horse to run. You're out. We're both out."

"That's why we need to stick together. We can do it without him. This time, it will be different. I'll be different. I promise."

"I wish I could believe you, but after all that's happened I can't."

Warner placed a hand on her shoulder. "I'm really sorry for all I've done to you. If you'll give me a chance, I promise to make it up. And--I'll listen to you."

"I don't think so." Carolyn pulled away, resisting the tug on her heart, the instinct that urged her to believe him. "You don't know how to listen. You've proven that."

He was encouraged by the soft expression that flashed briefly in her eyes. "Please, I'll agree to anything."

"We do it my way. Your father is out. I never want to deal with, or even see, him again. In fact, I don't even want his name mentioned in my presence."

"Why?" he asked, shocked.

She couldn't bring herself to answer him. "If you want this to work, you agree to my terms."

"Fine, fine." He held his palms in the air, as if to surrender. "Your terms, Carolyn."

She sat in the nearest chair, her hands still tucked into her sweater pockets. Uncertainty and fear rose in her throat, making her question her own plan. She shoved the feeling aside. This was about survival. In the courtroom, she fought to empower her clients with the courage to stand up for themselves--to face the truth. Until now, she hadn't taken her own advice.

"If we're going to make another senatorial run, I want all the facts," Carolyn said. "I can deal with anything as long as I'm prepared. I don't want any surprises derailing the next campaign. So, now's your chance, tell it all. Can you handle that?" *My God, what was she asking? Could she handle the brutal truth?* She braced herself.

"Yes," Warner said, hope rising. "Where do you want me to start?"

"At the beginning."

He felt as if his heart was being wrenched from his chest, but he knew what he had to do. His affair began shortly after he'd learned of her abortion. "I admit I wanted to hurt you. I hurt so much, myself. All I felt was anger and hurt, day after day. I needed a distraction. I met her while flying to D.C." Warner began to pace.

He forced himself to meet Carolyn's gaze. "Her name's Cindy. She's a flight attendant. She's based out of D.C., but spends a lot of time in Missouri. Her family's here. She's not what you'd think, she's a friend. I hope you can understand this, but I felt lost. I needed someone to confide in, someone to love me."

I wanted to love you, Carolyn thought, I wanted to be there for you. But she understood his pain. He'd lost trust in her, lost trust in her love. She glanced out the window, trying to contain her own pain. "Do you love this woman?" She looked back at him.

Warner stopped pacing and made his way to the couch. He swallowed hard, his face growing gray in color, perspiration beading above his upper lip. She could see the muscles working in his jaw as he clenched his teeth.

His silence screamed at Carolyn.

"I don't know." He hesitated. "I guess not enough. I'm not willing to lose you over her. I'm not willing to toss away my career. Maybe that makes me a cold son of a bitch, but I'm trying to be honest."

Warner slouched against the couch cushions. "You're a beautiful woman, Carolyn. I mean that. But you have to understand, I was so devastated by the abortion I couldn't . . . respond sexually to you. I wish I could, but I can't. I needed to find a release somewhere, to feel like a man again. I found it with Cindy."

Carolyn nodded, choking back her own grief. Emotionally she didn't want to understand, it hurt far too much. But logically, it made sense.

"I want to make us work. Please be honest with me. Have I ruined any chance of reconciliation?"

"I won't deny that this hurts me--hurts horribly. But I can't change it. If I could I would." Carolyn took a deep breath and stood. "But we both want the same things. I have dreams of reform and you have aspirations for the White House. We make a good team, professionally speaking. So, under my terms, I'll continue our marriage."

"What are your terms?"

"First, you'll give up the other woman. I'm not willing to be humiliated any longer."

Warner nodded.

"And second, I'm an equal partner. I direct your career, the campaigns, and help decide policy. If at any point, I don't feel you're living up to your end of the bargain--it's finished. I walk. I'll divorce you, and your political career will be over." *She didn't need to tell him that as a successful prosecutor, she could pursue a lesser political career on her own.*

Six years seemed like an eternity right now, she thought, but the election would come all too soon. An election that Warner had better win, or they'd both suffer the consequences.

* * *

May, 1993---Jefferson City, Missouri

Monday morning, Carolyn arrived at the courthouse well before seven. Down the hallway, she could see light shining through the doorway of Mark's office. Their one night stand, over two years ago, had not ruined their friendship. In fact, he remained a friend and confidant. She wondered if the depth of their trust came from their intimacy, or a shared secret that could harm them both. Either way, Mark regularly expressed his love and desire for her.

Every time she allowed herself serious thought on the subject, she was filled with conflicting emotions. Mark represented the only light and warmth in her life. Her logical mind gave her a multitude of reasons justifying an affair. Although they'd reached a truce, Warner never touched her. But an affair still felt wrong.

"How are things going?" Carolyn asked.

Mark met her gaze. "I didn't hear you come in."

"Sorry." She took a seat across from him. "I was wondering if you could help me with a project."

"What type of project?"

"I'll go into more detail later, but let's just say we're going to need to add a few names to our campaign payroll. Edmund once gave me a lead on some private investigators. I think it's time we employ them. I've built up a little nest egg with some investments that can be used to fund them, for now."

"What do you need investigators for?"

"You know, Mark, here in Missouri the good-old-boys run the show. And you also know, better than I, how they love to hunt. Well, I'm sick of playing the part of the hunted. It's time I turned the tables and bought myself some ammunition." Carolyn gave him a wink, then turned and walked out of his office.

* * *

Mark watched Carolyn leave and listened to her footfalls recede down the corridor outside of his office. Then he picked up the phone and dialed a number he'd recently memorized, the office of Edmund Lane.

Six months earlier, Edmund had approached him regarding the creation of an alliance of influential men who'd work to put Warner in the White House. Mark was flattered to be included in this elite group. Edmund referred to their organization as the "Council", and enticed Mark with promises of a prominent future in Washington, D.C.

Edmund answered on the first ring.

"She's making her move," Mark said. "She wants me to hire that investigative firm you told her about."

"Do as she asks," Edmund replied. "We're ready for her."

BOOK II

DEBT OF DEFEAT

1996-1999

CHAPTER SIX

April 24, 1996---Jefferson City, Missouri

Warner collapsed onto the chaise longue in the master bedroom. He had two more engagements this afternoon before the charity ball that evening. Could he keep up this pace? he wondered. His head pulsed at the thought. Carolyn was driving him hard. She insisted they attend every committee meeting, every public event. And she arranged everything, down to where he sat and whom he spoke with at the receptions and banquets.

She handed him scripts to memorize, briefing him on specific points he needed to cover with the power brokers. She often attended the social and political functions with him. As a couple they shined, although their personal relationship remained unhealed. They only shared a bed so the household help wouldn't talk. How twisted his life had become. Was it worth it?

He walked into the bathroom, tossed back two aspirin, and splashed cold water on his face.

Yes, Warner thought. He was determined to win back his senatorial seat, then take the presidency. But my God, what a price he was paying.

* * *

Birds chirped outside Carolyn's window, and a soft breeze whispered through the room. In her office of their temporary home, Carolyn dialed a number long since committed to memory. "Mark, it's me. I need to speak to you regarding Mort Fields and the equity I own in his software company."

"You have equity in Fields's cherry project?" Mark asked, sounding incredulous.

"Yes, didn't I tell you?" Carolyn knew she'd never revealed this secret to anyone. Not even Mark. "I set up a dummy corporation in order to avoid drawing attention to myself. There really wasn't much to it." As much as she valued Mark, never again would she allow one man to control her future. However, she realized that in order to enlist his help, she'd have to disclose her financial success.

"How in the hell did you manage that?"

"I'm not sure. I guess he was feeling generous when he offered me the opportunity to invest."

"Generous? Mort? What did you do, exactly?"

"I know how politics can make you queasy, so let's just leave it my little secret. All right?"

Mark hesitated. "I worry about you. Promise me you'll be careful and that you won't take any unnecessary risks."

"Mark, there are some risks worth taking, and you know it."

Carolyn heard his sigh.

"I just worry about you, that's all."

His concern warmed her. "I know, and I appreciate it. But seriously, I need some help from you."

"Like what?"

"I own about five percent of the project, and--"

"My God, you had to have made millions! That company has grown exponentially. Warner must be thrilled."

"He doesn't know," she admitted. "And I don't intend to tell him. At least not yet. For now, this is strictly between us, okay?"

"Of course. I'm just surprised. Although I probably shouldn't be. You never cease to amaze me."

"That's sweet, Mark, thank you." Carolyn smiled. "Mort sends me regular corporate updates. I believe he's being honest with me, but I need to be sure. I want you to do some follow-up work on it, look into

Mort's finances and verify the reports I'm receiving. With a privately held corporation, it's easy to play with the numbers."

"Do you think an investigation is really necessary?"

"I do. I have to be sure the projections are accurate. Mort won't admit it, but he leveraged himself substantially to fund this project, that's why he gave me the opportunity to invest. He needed investors. Now, I want to be sure the company is financially solvent."

"He's one of the richest men in the state."

"On paper that's true," Carolyn said. "But even rich men can leverage their assets. Mort may over finance this company to start his next venture. He's built his entire empire that way. It's not a problem for him because he has cash flow from other businesses, but I can't afford to tie up my funds long-term. I need the money from this project for Warner's campaign."

"I don't like this, Carolyn." Mark's voice was tense.

"It won't hurt to check out his future projects to be sure he can cover his bets. If it looks like he's overextending himself, I want to sell my equity."

"How do you propose I do this without Fields knowing? He's not the kind of man you play around with."

"You should know by now that I don't play around," Carolyn said. "I've got a lot of money on the line here, and I need to protect it. I'm sure Fields has run checks on me. It's the way things are done."

"I'm not comfortable with this, and I don't understand why I should be involved."

Carolyn softened her tone. "Because I need your help. I trust you, and I certainly hope you trust me."

There was a pause. Carolyn guessed that he didn't know how to respond, so she continued, "We'll use Winston Cain's investigative firm."

"You want to use *Cain* to investigate Mort Fields?"

"Of course," Carolyn said, startled by his defensive tone. "Contact him and hire more of his people. Oh, and Mark, make sure they're thorough. I don't want any surprises. Just use the campaign account to hire the resources we need."

"Carolyn, I---"

"Please."

"First of all," he said, switching into a tone of reasonableness, "we can't use campaign funds. You know it's illegal. And second, what if Fields finds out you're investigating him? I'm sure he'd be offended, to say the least."

"Does this assignment offend you, Saint Mark?"

"Yes, it does. It's just not right."

"But it's not wrong, either. I'm trying to protect myself, and I need your support. Mort won't find out, and if he does, it'll come back to me, not you, and that's a risk I'm willing to take. Warner's future depends on my ability to anticipate problems and to deal with them effectively." She respected Mark's integrity, but she was sure that if he truly understood the situation he'd side with her.

"I'm still not comfortable with what you're suggesting," Mark insisted.

Carolyn was surprised by his obstinacy. He rarely questioned her. "Look, I know he's a friend of yours, but this is a necessary part of politics. It's reality. Besides, Cain's excellent. He's not your run-of-the-mill investigator; he's got access to a highly trained workforce. Edmund's used him extensively. Years ago, he gave me Cain's name. Mort will never find out about it. And as for using the funds to hire more investigators, well, technically this is a campaign expense, so I'd argue that it's perfectly legal." She replaced the receiver and sank back in her chair.

"Damn it," she whispered. She hadn't expected such strong opposition from Mark. Was he jealous of her commitment to Warner's success? Probably, but she had to get around his emotions.

Mark, she knew, was the key to her escape from Edmund Lane's control. He'd solidified her position with the big-money men in Missouri. Then, she'd demonstrated her ability as a savvy political player, by influencing local government officials to accommodate their professional needs and concerns. So far she'd delivered on all requests, applying subtle pressure on the pulse points necessary to motivate people to cooperate with her wishes. Now, those same power brokers sought her out, assuring her that they supported Warner for the Senate and possibly for higher office.

She and Warner were going to have to continue to prove their political value to these people, but Carolyn looked forward to the opportunity to do just that. It was how the game was played, and she liked the game. Liked it a lot.

* * *

Mark sat with the phone to his ear. Edmund Lane answered the call himself.

"This is Mark," he said without waiting for a greeting. "We've got some problems. Mort Fields included Carolyn as an investor in his software company."

"*What?*"

Mark expected the outburst. "That's the investment she's alluded to, but until now I didn't have any details. She owns five percent and holds it in a dummy corporation. But that's not the worst part. She wants me to hire Cain to investigate Mort. I tried to discourage her, but she wouldn't listen."

"Don't worry about Cain. I'll handle him," Edmund said, then hesitated for a few seconds. "Mort Fields is another matter. The Council chose him because he could help put Warner in the White House, but he should have revealed his partnership with Carolyn. I don't like secrets."

"Or surprises," Mark interjected.

Edmund continued as if Mark hadn't spoken. "If he'd been honest with us, we could have planned accordingly. Now, we've been caught off guard."

"Mort has also compromised our control."

"A problem we can contain. We may need Carolyn as a first lady, but she can't be allowed into our alliance. She'd demand too much from us in return. But we've got to be careful, we can't afford a power struggle with her, either."

"Should we call a meeting to discuss the situation?"

"No," Edmund said. "That's not necessary."

"What about Carolyn?"

"Do as she asks. For the most part, she's playing nicely into our plans."

"Let's just hope that Mort doesn't tell her anything about our existence," Mark said.

"He wouldn't be that stupid. If he did, our plans to use her as a cover would be jeopardized."

"Should we update the others?"

"Let's just keep this between us. We still need Mort, and this may work to our advantage."

Mark replaced his receiver. *How far was he willing to go for a Cabinet post in Washington?* He wasn't sure, and he prayed that his limits wouldn't be tested.

* * *

The White Cross Charity Ball, held each year on the last Saturday of April in Missouri's capital, was the biggest and most important social event of the year. Carolyn and Warner arrived promptly at 8:00 p.m.

"We'll be sitting with Governor Radcliff and his wife," Carolyn said. "Senator Rudly, and of course, Senator Green and his wife. Meet me there right before dinner." They paused at the entrance to the ballroom and were announced.

"Did you hear me?" she quietly asked.

Warner glared at her.

"It took me four phone calls to obtain these prominent seats," she said. "You could show some appreciation."

"Whatever." He didn't like her tone. As far as he was concerned, she didn't have anything to complain about. He was keeping up his end of the deal. He campaigned endlessly, gave speeches to civic clubs all over the state, and sang in the friggin' Baptist church choir so that he would be seen on television every Sunday next to the preacher. He had even agreed to a series of thirty-second television commercials, feeling like an idiot as he confessed all of the mistakes he'd made as a senator. Then, he asked the good people of Missouri for their forgiveness. Now that had taken balls, he thought.

"You had better smile at me before someone notices us," she said.

He responded by giving her a flash of even white teeth. God, he felt like he was balancing on one foot, on a banana peel, with a noose around his neck. "I see Edmund." Warner gestured to the left. "He's over there talking to Bill Rudly. I think I'll go say hello."

Carolyn's face flushed, but her voice remained calm. "Don't push me, Warner. I mean it, that's a non-negotiable part of our arrangement. I'm history if you involve your father in our lives ever again."

Dinner was announced, and they took their seats. The governor and his wife were introduced to the attendees. Arriving late, Senator Jackson Green and his wife followed the governor's entrance. Typically rude, Warner thought. The clueless couple seemed oblivious to the etiquette that was required of them.

A ball of rage flamed in Warner's chest. His field of vision narrowed to just the Greens, and the man who'd beaten him. The man responsible for the state of his life now. Get control of yourself, Warner told himself, attempting to dowse his anger with a cool head. This was not the time to show weakness. In fact, Warner thought, it was a moment to show up the old farmer who possessed no more finesse than the backside of a sow. The muscles in his square jaw worked as he fought back his resentment. Jackson Green was nothing but a two-bit political hack from the Missouri backwoods.

Warner pasted a smile on his face, stood up and excused himself. Carolyn shot him a quizzical glance. Warner whispered to her that he was going to the restroom, then exited the ballroom with a confident stride.

Inside the men's room, he leaned forward on the sink, staring into the basin. Finally he was angry, and the anger felt good. He lifted his gaze to the bathroom mirror and stared into his own steel gray eyes. It was time to regroup. Time to channel his frustration into positive action. Just a few days ago, Carolyn had asked him where his fight had gone. He hadn't had an answer then, but now he knew it was back.

"First step," Warner said to himself, "regain my seat in the Senate."

Broad shoulders squared, he went straight to the bar in the foyer adjacent to the ballroom. What he needed was a drink. "A shot of Jack Dan--," he began, then caught himself. This was not the time to tie one on. "Make that a Perrier with a lime."

He paid the bartender, then took a long pull of his drink.

"Enjoying yourself, son?"

Warner turned slowly, meeting the older man's gaze. "I'm not your *son*."

"Watch your mouth." Edmund glanced at Warner's glass. "That's it, have another drink."

He raised his glass. "I just might. It's Perrier."

"Oh, I know you better than that. What is it, vodka or gin?" Edmund threw a ten on the bar. "Have a few on me."

"What do you want?"

"You need me, son. Don't let Carolyn continue to separate us. Join the Council. She's the one you need protection from, not us. We're behind you. I give you my word. It's your wife who likes to keep secrets. She's keeping you from your true supporters, and pulling you around by your dick. Call me when you're ready to hear the truth."

"What are you talking about?"

"Ask her about her partnership with Mort Fields. She's making deals behind your back. You tell her she'd better watch her step, or I'll enjoy watching her fall."

Warner's brow furrowed in confusion. "Mort Fields? I don't know what--"

"Enjoy your evening, *son*." The senior Lane turned and walked away.

Warner had watched those well-staged exits his entire life. He'd always hated them. He hated them even more now, just as he hated Edmund Lane. But was Edmund telling him the truth? Was he, in fact, an ally, in spite of the animosity he invariably projected to the man the world thought was his son?

* * *

Returning to the ballroom, Edmund Lane made his way between the tables until he reached his own, and took his seat just as Governor Radcliff completed his remarks.

"What did you think of the speech?" Mort Fields asked.

"I didn't really listen. Radcliff has very little to say that interests me."

"I'd agree with you there."

Edmund lowered his voice. "Mort, we need to talk." He paused. "There's something that I have to tell you, but it puts me in a bad spot. Puts you in an ugly light, too." Edmund glanced around the table. Everyone was involved in conversation or getting up to dance.

Mort took a sip of his drink, waiting for Edmund to begin.

"I've recently learned that you're the subject of an investigation," Edmund said, then waited to see Mort's reaction. There was none.

"It's not the authorities. It's a private job."

Mort cocked his head. "Who's investigating?"

"I'm getting to that. It's one of your partners in the software company."

Edmund saw Mort's jaw tighten. Even if he couldn't shoot Carolyn himself, Edmund thought, he could load the gun and hand the weapon to someone else. If he could effectively neutralize Carolyn, then Warner would join the Council and return to his control. Divide and conquer, he thought.

He'd invested too much in Warner to be cut out now. Edmund believed he had a right to share in Warner's success. A success in politics that he'd facilitated by grooming his son for years. Hell, he'd begun the Council for the boy. Pooling the resources of rich men in order to influence Warner's political future in the country was no small feat. Even though the plan was simple. As a coalition, together they'd put Warner in the White House. In return, he would reward them with powerful government posts.

Edmund had promised these men that Warner endorsed the plan. But he'd underestimated Carolyn. The bitch. After Warner's loss, she'd separated him from his true allies. Now, she dictated his campaign. The situation was intolerable, and Edmund held her responsible. He'd make her sorry she'd ever taken *him* on as an adversary.

"How do you know about the investors in the deal?" Mort asked after a moment of silence.

"My source informed me. The Council isn't pleased that you neglected to inform us of you're partnership with Carolyn. But that's not my biggest concern."

Mort's gaze locked with Edmund's. "Are you telling me that Carolyn is having me investigated?" Mort said the words smoothly, but Edmund could hear the anger building.

"I am."

"And how would you know any of this?"

"My source is the investigator."

"Why would the investigator tell you?"

"How do you think Carolyn ever came to hiring private investigators? These men were on my payroll first, and their first loyalty is still to me, and now the Council, of course."

"So, what do you suggest?" Mort asked, his eyes wary.

"The Council is going to want you to explain the situation to them. We trusted you. It looks like you've kept a secret. A very important secret. You're going to have to make things right with the other members." Edmund took a sip of water.

"I struck that deal before the Council even existed," Mort said. "She's a small investor, anyway. I was simply doing her and Warner a favor."

"You should have been forthright from the beginning. Secrets and surprises will only defeat our agenda. I talked to Warner about your little arrangement with Carolyn, and he had no idea you'd made it. She's playing both of you like fiddles, and neither of you hears the music."

Mort's eyes narrowed. "I don't like what you're implying."

"I don't give a crap what you like. It's time you wised up," Edmund said. "She's a bitch, and she's going to ruin my son's career. A career, I might add, that could benefit you greatly. But we need to focus on our agenda. Warner must get elected. To do that, he needs strong men in the background, providing solid advice. Men like you and me. He's pussy-whipped and he doesn't even know it."

"That's not what I hear," Mort remarked.

"Regardless, she could really hurt him. It's time she was shut down."

"Don't worry. I'll cut her off at the knees. And I know just the man to do it."

Edmund followed Mort's gaze across the room. "Bill Rudly? How can he help?"

"The esteemed Mr. Rudly has a suspicious nature. I think a few well-placed pieces of information will be just enough to set him on the warpath."

"Look, I don't want Warner hurt in this. Remember, our goal is to save his career, not destroy it."

Without a reply, Mort rose.

"This isn't about your fucking ego."

Mort met Edmund's glare.

"I've given you a chance to make things right here," Edmund said. "Don't make me sorry. I'd hate to have to act against you."

Mort walked away.

Edmund took a sip of his drink. "But I will," he whispered. "I will."

CHAPTER SEVEN

As Senator Bill Rudly drove home from the White Cross Charity Ball, he reviewed the night's events. The evening had been uneventful until Mort Fields had approached him for a private conversation. The dialogue had been vague, Bill thought, but if he'd been reading between the lines correctly, Mort had inferred that Warner and Carolyn had been trading political favors for high stakes. The more he analyzed the conversation, the more he realized Mort had specifically incriminated Carolyn. Did Carolyn trade for equity in one of Mort's businesses?

Bill grunted in disgust. After Warner's airport project, the fact that the Lanes were using their political positions for financial gain didn't really surprise him. But what would inspire one of Warner's allies to expose Carolyn and Warner's activities? There had to be a reason. What could possibly be motivating Mort Fields? Corruption was a real part of politics, Bill knew, but vipers sharing the same pit rarely turned on each other.

It was twelve-thirty in Missouri, which meant two-thirty in Washington, D.C. Jack would probably still be up, Bill thought as he walked into the house. His job often kept him writing late into the night. Bill made his way into the kitchen, and picked up the phone.

Jack answered on the third ring.

"Were you asleep?" Bill asked.

"No. I just finished an article on government waste. Is anything wrong?"

"Not really. Just had an odd experience at a society event. It brought up some questions I thought you might be able to help me on."

"Shoot." *What a switch, his dad coming to him for help. He liked the feeling.*

"What do you know about Mort Fields?"

"That's a loaded question. There are a million facets to that man, but he keeps a low profile. There's not a lot published about him. He's one of the richest men in Missouri--in the country, for that matter, but you know that. What are you looking for?"

"I'm not sure." Bill proceeded to relay the conversation he'd had with Fields about Warner and Carolyn. "Mort told me he'd get some paperwork to me I might find interesting. I'm worried about the ramifications to the party if the Lanes are in business with him."

"Didn't you already suspect graft?" Jack asked. "I mean, when I was home a couple of years ago, you told me you suspected they were involved in improprieties. This may be the break you were looking for."

"Forget the break. I'd rather the Lanes were clean and I could save the party the embarrassment."

"Doesn't sound likely. And you may be getting in over your head, Dad. Why don't you get some help on this?"

"No. I'm not saying anything about my suspicions until I have concrete evidence. It wouldn't be fair to the Lanes or our party. And I'll ask that you keep it confidential as well."

"Sure. But why don't you let me come down and help you? I'll call some of my sources." *He had an old friend in the CIA who'd pull up information from the databases in Langley on Fields and the Lanes.*

"No, I don't want anyone else involved. I don't want this leaked. If I get anything tangible, I'll let you know."

"It won't be leaked. My sources are solid."

"Even so, I don't want you to do anything right now."

"I'm not asking in order to get the inside track for a story. My primary concern is you. I just want to help you." *Damn, his father was stubborn. And now, if he followed up, his father would be convinced he'd gone after the story against his wishes.*

"Jack, your career is your life. I realize that fact. And I would never dangle a story in front of your nose and tell you to squelch it. At this point, there's nothing solid to report, so I don't feel as though I'm pushing your endurance. But dragging you into the middle would be unfair."

"I'm a grown man. I can handle the temptation."

"You're a journalist."

"Thanks for the vote of confidence." *Why couldn't his father trust him?*

"I don't mean it like that. Can't we change the subject?"

"Fine. When are you coming back to Washington?" Jack asked.

"I have to be back by next Thursday for a vote on the budget. Will you be in town? Maybe we could have dinner. If Mort's documents show anything substantial, I could share them with you."

"I'm afraid not," Jack responded. "I'm going to Montana on Monday to cover the Unabomber case. Why don't you let me do some checking on my own?"

"No. Don't make me sorry I discussed this with you."

"What's wrong with wanting to look out for you? Like father, like son."

"You're right. I'm sorry. It's late and I'm tired . . . I miss you." There was a pause. "And, Jack . . . ."

"Yeah?"

"I'm really proud of you," Bill said softly. "You've made quite a name for yourself. You're head and shoulders above the pack."

Silence hung on the phone line. "Thanks, Dad."

Bill cleared his throat, "Anyway, I'll send you any paperwork I get on the Lanes and Fields. Maybe you'll be able to figure out Fields's motivation for exposing the Lanes."

* * *

April 27, 1996---Jefferson City, Missouri

Carolyn Alden Lane was sitting at her desk in the Cole County Courthouse when her intercom buzzed. "Yes?"

"Senator Rudly is here to see you," Katherine said.

Carolyn glanced at her calendar. There was no appointment scheduled. *How odd.* "Send him in."

Carolyn stood when Bill Rudly entered. "Senator, what a nice surprise. What brings you here today?"

Bill shook her hand. "Quite frankly, I'm here as a professional courtesy."

Carolyn motioned for him to sit, then sat herself, facing him. *Keep an open mind. Don't get defensive.*

"It's been brought to my attention that there may be some problems with Warner running for re-election," Bill said.

Carolyn frowned. "What are you talking about? I know we've gone round and round before with you on several issues. Aren't you as tired of this as we are? We belong to the same political party and should be supporting each other, not constantly fighting."

"This isn't about fighting, and it's not personal. I'd love to be able to support Warner, but my first loyalty goes to this country and the people who've elected me. If I see something questionable, I question it. So, please, don't insult me by suggesting that party loyalty should be the first course of business. It's not. And God help this country if that ever changes."

She agreed with his point; it was his delivery she found unacceptable. She smiled in an attempt to ease the tension of the moment. "I certainly didn't mean to offend you. And I didn't mean to infer that party politics should take precedence over integrity. It just seems we're often at odds, when I believe that fundamentally we share the same ideals."

"You're quite charming. But I don't agree."

If nothing else, he's direct. Stay calm, keep trying. He's a good man, there's just a communication problem. "What seems to be the problem?"

Bill leaned back. "It appears, from a conversation I've had with Mort Fields and some paperwork I've received, that you may have inadvertently put yourself and Warner in a compromising position for

91

the next election. Since this involves you, I thought it best to take it up with you directly. I'm sure it was all done innocently, but our party can't afford to put forth a candidate who may have hidden questionable business dealings. So, if Warner still insists on seeking the other senatorial seat, I'm here to tell you that I'll be requesting an investigation into these affairs. If everything's clear, it will help you. If not, then we save the party the embarrassment."

This was a problem. Carolyn sized him up. *She had to minimize the damage. Tell the truth, but let him know you're not a pushover.* "I don't know what you or Mort Fields think I've done, but I can assure you that nothing's occurred that would be considered improper. I would never jeopardize Warner's career or the party's position. Never." She tucked files into her briefcase as she spoke. The expression on Rudly's face told Carolyn that he'd already tried and convicted them. As a result, she found no point in continuing their meeting. "Unfortunately, I'm due in court in five minutes, so you'll have to excuse me."

An unruffled Bill Rudly rose. "Have a good day," he said.

* * *

Carolyn called Mark. "Mort Fields has gone south on us. I don't know how it happened, but Bill Rudly was just in here claiming he's had conversations with Mort that suggest impropriety on my part that would jeopardize Warner's pursuit of the Senate. He said he has the paperwork to back it up. He's going to request an investigation."

Mark paused. "This doesn't sound good. Are you worried?"

"Concerned, not worried. If he had anything concrete, Rudly would have said so. I think what he's got, at this point, is supposition. I doubt he's even got enough to start an investigation. But we need to check it out, hire Cain to look into it," she said. "This was a warning. What bothers me the most is Mort. I know he won't come forward himself--he would cut his own throat in the business community. No one would ever trust him again if they believed he turned on a partner. But he obviously set this up through the back door." Carolyn massaged the throbbing in her temples. A migraine was the last thing she needed right now.

"What can I do to help?"

"Put Cain on Rudly, and call Fields. I don't care if he's angry with me. I'm still a partner in his company. Tell him I want out. He's obviously lost faith in our deal, so he can buy me out. Otherwise, I'll offer my shares on the open market. He's not going to want an unknown on board, so he'll ante-up. Do we have a recent summary of value?"

"Yes."

"Great. Fax it over to him. Tell him he's got until Friday--after that I sell to the highest bidder. That company's a hot commodity, so it won't be hard to sell." Carolyn took a deep breath. *She was getting used to doing battle.*

"I doubt if he's going to like the strong-arm tactics."

"He's left me no choice. Feel free to tell him that."

"I'll take care of it," Mark said. "Why don't you stop by later today?"

"I wish I could. But I have a trial starting next week and a stack of files to go through. Now this. As it is, I'll be working until midnight."

"I have to work late, too. I'll bring some Chinese food down to your office later, and you can take a short break. Deal?"

"Deal." Carolyn hung up.

Her gaze fell on the chair recently occupied by the senator. She couldn't allow an investigation! If Rudly presented these allegations to party leaders in Washington, Warner's career could be seriously damaged. No matter the cost, she wouldn't allow anyone to hurt him. Yes, she thought, this was war. And she was ready to fight.

* * *

"Mort's gone to Bill Rudly with his accusations, and Bill confronted Carolyn," Mark told Edmund on the phone. "He's going to have Carolyn and Mort's business arrangement investigated."

"The selfish bastard," Edmund said. "Mort's gone too far. I warned him. He's on his own now."

"Rudly claimed he had paperwork on the matter. This could destroy Warner."

"That won't happen," Edmund's voice was flat.

"What do you mean that won't happen? Bill wants to stop Warner from being reelected. Carolyn's dealings could provide the evidence he needs. Even though the deal wasn't improper, the wrong spin on the situation will be disastrous. Mort's causing that spin."

"The key to this matter is Carolyn. And accidents happen, Mark."

"What in the hell are you talking about? The other Council members wouldn't agree to anything illegal."

"If we take a vote, I think you'll find you're wrong. Our newest members are more driven than I. Winston Cain and Richard Young helped me devise our strategy. We've protected our interests by hiding behind Carolyn. All evidence points at the bitch. She would take the blame for any, shall we say, accidents."

"No! I won't allow it. Granted I want my place in Washington, as much as any of you, but this is going too far." *Frame Carolyn? My God, Carolyn thought he loved her. And maybe he did. The whole plan had been innocent enough--just a way to get ahead, to become a player in D.C. He couldn't do this to her.*

"You don't have to like it. Just consider the matter handled," Edmund said.

CHAPTER EIGHT

April 29, 1996---Washington, D. C.

Long, shining black hair framed the face and upper torso of the young Asian assassin hidden in a small cluster of bushes on the Washington Monument grounds. The fragrance of freshly cut grass filled the air, and the sun's unseasonably warm rays flowed over her. The assassin stretched her lithe limbs, as though to reach out and claim the light.

She was attuned to every sound and nuance around her. At six a.m. the park grounds were slowly awakening to the spring morning. Birds sang and a breeze caressed her. Hand-picked by the CIA director himself, the woman had joined the Agency as a weapons specialist. Now, she freelanced as a mercenary.

The assassin spotted her target jogging far off in the distance. She noted that the subject was predictably on time, coming up Independence Avenue toward the Washington Monument. Like most high-level officials, his routine was well documented.

Timing was critical to this mission because of the chemicals involved. A cryogenic freezing unit resembling a small, benign cooler sat next to her.

95

She marked a checkpoint and timed the subject with a stopwatch. He was moving at the expected pace. The assassin reclaimed her M21 semi-automatic rifle with a custom-made suppressor and rechecked the scope, then assured herself that the temperature on the freezer was precisely as it should be.

She knew that if the temperature inside the freezing unit rose or fell one-tenth of a degree, the chemical structure of the bullet would be altered and the mission would have to be aborted. The assassin had spent years perfecting this technique---building the needed equipment and formulating the deadly projectile.

A shiver of excitement tingled her skin. This kill was going to be particularly satisfying, she thought. The challenge of pulling off this operation in the heart of Washington, D.C. on a man of such political stature was a career maker. After this she would be able to name her price on the world market. She ceased her train of thought, knowing that she couldn't permit emotion to cloud her judgment. As easily as placing a can of soup back into a cupboard because she wasn't hungry, she set aside her feelings.

Timing was critical. She wouldn't have a second chance. She wouldn't need one, she knew, her grip firm on the weapon. The bullet she would fire contained frozen sodium azide, a metabolic inhibitor. In solid form it could be fired from a high-powered rifle.

At a muzzle velocity of 2,798 feet per second, the round would melt after precisely 100 yards. Upon hitting the target, it would penetrate the body like an injection, but leave no sign of entry. When sodium azide invaded the bloodstream, the substance blocked all of the cells' ability to produce energy; the bodily functions affected simply stopped. The key was to hit the target in the chest so that the first organ to fail was the heart, giving the appearance of cardiac arrest.

The subject veered to the left, heading toward the Tidal Basin. The assassin flipped open the cooler. She grasped the metal tongs to shift the bullet to the gun. The projectile could only occupy the chamber for a maximum of 5.2 seconds.

She kept her eyes trained on the target as he crossed the bridge and followed the road to the right. Ten . . . nine . . . eight . . . . Although excited, her hands remained steady. She'd rehearsed until her timing was ingrained. She glanced up at the target to check his progress, then down at the stopwatch. Three . . . two . . . one . . . . With the tongs, she picked up the bullet, loaded the rifle, and set the timer. She glanced again at her target, then drew in a calming breath.

The jogger passed a tree, then started up Seventeenth Street toward the White House. The end of the Reflecting Pool, at the base of the Lincoln Memorial, was designated as the kill zone. The assassin took aim. The jogger reached the zone. She discharged her weapon, the suppressor muffling the report. The subject took a stride, then collapsed onto the lawn like a child exhausted from play.

The assassin rolled onto her back in the cool grass. She felt the tension seep from her pores and drain away. She gave herself one moment of respite, then in a fluid motion, sat up and drew her lightweight woolen cape around her body.

Without looking back at the scene, she pulled the rifle and the cryogenic cooler under the folds of her cape. These items had to be disposed of according to her plan. She made her way across the lawn of the Washington Monument, crossing Constitution Avenue and strolling quickly up Fifteenth Street. Her body, tense just moments before, relaxed as she cut through Pershing Park, crossed E Street, and arrived at the Hotel Washington where her limousine waited.

* * *

The Washington Post
April 30, 1996
SENATOR DIES WHILE JOGGING
WASHINGTON, D.C.---Senator William Rudly of Missouri died yesterday morning while jogging. Preliminary reports indicate the senator had a massive coronary. His body was discovered near the corner of Seventeenth Street and Constitution Avenue by another jogger. Paramedics tried to revive him, but he was pronounced dead upon arrival at the hospital.

CHAPTER NINE

May 5, 1996--Jefferson City, Missouri

Jack crossed the tiled floor of his father's kitchen, his footsteps echoed in the stillness. He thought back over the past week. The days were blurred. All he could remember were snatches of time, glimpses of the events that had transpired. He felt as if he were on remote control. The refrigerator door swung open easily. Three cans of soda were the only contents. Jack popped the top of one of them and chugged two gulps. He hadn't been able to bring himself to eat or drink anything else all day.

He sat in a kitchen chair, and set the soda can on the table. His gaze landed on the telephone. The last time he'd spoken to his father, Jack thought, he'd probably been sitting in this very spot. Jack dropped his face into his hands and rubbed his dry eyes. The tears had yet to come. Everything felt surreal, distant and detached, as if he were watching a movie in which he was the star.

Jack noted the time, 1:35 p.m. The funeral had been that morning, followed by a reception at his father's secretary's home. She'd made all of the arrangements, and for that he was grateful.

He stood, then wandered into his father's study. The room felt cold and dead. At one time, his father's energy had radiated in the masculine air of his office, but now that atmosphere was gone. Vanished with the one person he'd loved and respected most in the world. Jack's heart ached, a tangible persistent pain that weighted his chest.

Bookcases lined the walls. The shelves were filled with books and the memorabilia of an accomplished diplomat and politician. Jack scanned the collection, his eyes stopping on pictures of his father standing next to various world leaders. On the fireplace mantel was a picture of himself, at age eight, with his mother and father. Now, Jack thought, he was all alone.

His mother had died when he was just a boy, then his wife, and now his father. Some things were beyond his control, he told himself, yet he remained unconvinced.

He made his way around his father's large oak desk, sat in his high-backed leather chair, and picked up the phone. The scent of his father's aftershave lingered on the receiver. Jack closed his eyes and swallowed hard. He paused for a few moments, then dialed his secretary.

With any luck his secretary, Maureen, would be in. No matter where Jack worked, Maureen was a constant he insisted on having.

Maureen answered on the second ring. "How are you?"

"I'm hanging in."

"What can I do to help?"

"Everything's been taken care of." Jack raked his fingers through his hair. "Right now, I just need to know what *Today* wants me to do. I can be back in Montana tomorrow."

"You need to take some time off. Take care of yourself for once." Maureen's voice was soothing.

"No, the best thing for me right now is to get back to work. Sitting around here will make me crazy."

"They've already assigned someone else to the Unabomber story."

"What?" Jack slammed his hand against the desk. "I landed the interview with Kaczynski, it's my story. Why the hell did they do that? Call those bastards and tell them I'm on it. Forget it, I'll call them myself."

"You're not thinking clearly. Your father just passed away. You need to take some time. Your head's not in the game, and you know it."

Jack leaned back in his father's chair. "My head is always in the game," he muttered. That's the problem, he almost said, but stopped. Journalism consumed him, everything else in his life took a backseat, including his wife and even his father. Now, they were gone. But everyone made choices, and his was always the career.

"Come off it. You are in no shape to cover anything."

As much as he hated to admit it, Maureen was probably right, and he just didn't have the energy to fight right now. "Who'd they assign to the story?"

"Marsha Reed." Maureen's tone was flat.

"Damn, she'll do a good job too."

"I'm sure she will, so why don't you give it a rest? Take the time you need. I'm sure there are matters you need to resolve for your father. You're needed in Missouri right now, not Montana."

Jack glanced around the study. "There's more to do here than I care to deal with," he said softly.

"Are you all right? I could fly there and help you."

"Thanks, you're a great friend. But no, I'm fine. I can handle it."

"There's just one more thing."

"What's that?"

"A package came for you on Friday."

"I'll pick it up as soon as I get back to Washington. I shouldn't be more than a few days."

"The package was from your dad."

Jack rubbed his eyes. "But my dad knew I wouldn't be there."

"I don't know his reasoning, but it's here. What do you want me to do with it?"

"Open it, I want to know what it is---no, on second thought, overnight it to me. Do you think you can still mail it today?"

"I don't know. I'll see what I can do. If not, you'll get it day after tomorrow."

"Fine. And, Maureen, thanks for everything. I'm sorry I was short with you."

"No problem. Just try to get some rest. I'll talk to you soon."

Jack swiveled the chair until he faced the window. Talking to Maureen exacerbated his confusion. *Wasn't he supposed to cry? My God, he'd just buried his father. What did this say about him?*

Had he seen so much of life that he'd become desensitized? Maybe he wasn't human anymore. He obviously wasn't capable of emotion. All he felt was a deep penetrating emptiness, a void. His shoulders slumped forward. He placed his elbows on his knees, and his chin on his fists as he stared unseeingly out the window. He'd never been one to run from life, but damn if this didn't feel like the perfect time to lace up his Nikes.

*   *   *

Jack awoke to the sound of the doorbell. He read the clock: 7:20 a.m. Bare-chested, he pulled on his jeans, stumbled down the steps and swung open the door.

"Overnight mail, sign here," the Fed Ex man said.

Good old Maureen, Jack thought, as he padded barefoot, with his package, to the kitchen. He ripped open the top of the large manila envelope and pulled out a small stack of documents and a note from his father.

Dear Jack,

Just sending these copies to you for safekeeping. At this point, I don't know if any of this information about the Lanes is valid. I haven't been able to verify anything. When you have a chance, call me and we'll discuss it. I'm not very good at investigating these types of things, so maybe you could give me some pointers.

Love,

Dad

Jack glanced at the papers, most of which were his father's notes documenting conversations, between himself, Mort Fields, and Adam Miles, Edmund Lane's best friend and business associate, regarding the Lanes and specifically Carolyn. Jack stopped reading, and considered the dynamics of these men. Mort Fields was not a friend of his father's, still it was easier to explain than Adam Miles. Not only was Adam a close friend of Edmund's, but he and Bill frequently disagreed. What would inspire Adam to turn to Bill? Jack wondered.

Jack continued reading. Bill's notes mentioned Winston Cain. Interesting. From his days in intelligence, Jack knew of Cain. Cain, a former counterintelligence agent for the CIA, owned and operated a private investigation agency rumored to be a mercenary-for-hire business. The notes referenced an employment contract with Cain, but didn't include a copy of the document. Jack seriously doubted one existed. Cain didn't make the types of agreements that one put a pen to and signed.

The rest of the papers were copies of legal forms indicating that Carolyn Lane might have done some work for Fields. The documents appeared to be from some sort of corporation or holding company, but the names of the stockholders were not disclosed. Since the papers weren't the originals, it was hard to know if they were valid.

Why would Mort Fields turn over this information? Jack wondered. The whole scenario was odd. It made no sense for Carolyn to be involved in any contracts with Mort; she was a prosecutor, not a corporate attorney. At the bottom of the last page of notes was one handwritten word--*Council*--but there was no definition or reference to this word anywhere else in the papers.

Jack knew that his father's last appointment in Missouri had been with Carolyn Lane. This too, was odd. Threads, Jack thought, these were just threads of information and certainly not enough to weave together any type of a conclusion.

The kitchen wall clock read 8:03. A realtor was due to look at the house around eighty-thirty, and Jack needed a shower. He shoved the papers back into the envelope. He had a lot to do right now, and none of it pertained to local politics. The Lanes would have to wait.

* * *

November 8, 1996---Jefferson City, Missouri

Warner Hamilton Lane escorted Carolyn through the lobby of the hotel closest to campaign headquarters. Together they started up the flight of stairs that led to the mezzanine level, then stopped on the sixth stair, turned, and waved to the crowd. Carolyn raised their clasped hands high in the air as a cheer went up from the crowd.

This was the way it was meant to be, Warner thought. Carolyn was dressed in a sea foam green suit with cream trim, and her honey colored hair flowed gracefully around her shoulders. She caught his appraisal, and her eyes locked with his. Warner squeezed her hand, then shifted his gaze back to the crowd, but his thoughts remained on her.

Indeed she was beautiful, and win or lose tomorrow, she had orchestrated his reelection campaign brilliantly. Carolyn had designed every aspect of their strategy, from policy making and critical timing, to personal appearances and commercials. She had even given up her role as a prosecutor. Granted, he'd joined the Council, but they were in the background, and he couldn't discount her efforts. If he won, it was her victory.

His smile remained fixed, but he felt a bittersweet twinge in his heart. A victory would mean the necessary step closer to the White House. With Bill Rudly's death he'd be the senior senator, positioning him perfectly. But it would also lock him permanently into a loveless marriage. He wished he could change his feelings for Carolyn, but he knew it wasn't possible.

Warner followed Carolyn as she made her way up the rest of the stairs to the mezzanine, where they headed into the elevator. Deja vu, Warner thought. Six years earlier he'd made this ride to the very same suite to watch the election results come in. The difference then had been that Carolyn wasn't by his side. Now, her presence dominated the campaign. And her popularity was undeniable. Had she made a profound difference? He was about to find out.

* * *

The Jefferson City Democrat
November 9, 1996
LANE RE-ELECTED TO THE U.S. SENATE

* * *

January, 1997---Jefferson City, Missouri

Carolyn inspected their new home in the gated community she loved so much. She surveyed the paint job in every room on the first floor, then headed upstairs to look at the master bedroom.

Satisfied, she flopped onto the bed. She felt like jumping up and down on the mattress, but she quelled the urge and contented herself with the pleasure of their victory. They'd done it on their own, without Warner's father. She filled her lungs, then exhaled slowly.

Now, Warner was the *senior* senator. As much as she had disagreed with Bill Rudly, however, she felt a sense of loss for the country. Bill had been a good man and a good senator. She knew he fought for what he believed in, and she respected that quality. Bill Rudly had been a man with an honest purpose and no favors to pay.

Carolyn remained sprawled across the bed. The sound of muted voices and footsteps echoed off the hardwood floor of the main hall as movers filled the residence with her possessions.

She reflected on Warner, aware that his behavior toward her had improved. Even if she no longer had his love, she knew that she'd regained his respect and appreciation.

Now, he held the most powerful senatorial seat in Missouri. Because of their teamwork, he was on the track to the White House.

Working as a prosecutor, she had fought for justice on a case-by-case level, but, as Warner's partner, she would be positioned to design the much needed legislative reforms in social services and drug enforcement for the entire country. The time had come for Warner to present *her* ideas as a part of his political platform, his vision for the country. They both knew that he owed her that much. And she intended to collect on that debt.

CHAPTER TEN

February, 1999---Jefferson City, Missouri

Carolyn sat next to her assistant, Katherine Seals, in front of her computer. "Internet lesson number nine-hundred-fifty-four," Carolyn said with a laugh. "Will I ever get all of this?"

"Of course," Katherine responded. "You have to remember, I've been working with computers for years."

Carolyn knew that information was the key to success. And, she had to admit, finding herself on the learning curve again was exciting.

"I know you majored in Computer Science in college, but how did you get so proficient?"

"My real education came from my old boss, Clayton Small, at the National Security Agency," Katherine said.

Carolyn paused, searching her memory. "Wasn't he part of the espionage story Jack Rudly broke? Something about trapping a German spy who tapped into our military computers."

Carolyn saw pain flash in Katherine's eyes. Why? she wondered.

"Yes. After I graduated, Clayton offered me a job at NSA in Information Systems Security. I worked for him for several years, and learned more about computers in that time than I learned in my four years at Berkeley. He's an incredible man."

"Why'd you leave?"

Katherine met Carolyn's gaze. "I had no choice. Jack Rudly saw to that."

"What happened?"

"I'd rather not go into it. Let's just say that I thought my trust was well placed, but I was wrong. Never date a journalist."

Carolyn nodded. No wonder they related so well; they both had suffered at the hands of men. Carolyn considered Katherine more than a kindred spirit. She viewed her as a strong ally for the future, because Katherine could wield her computer skills like a weapon.

* * *

September, 1999---Washington, D. C.

Life has definitely improved, Carolyn reflected, sitting next to Warner in their limousine. With Katherine running Warner's Missouri office, Carolyn spent more of her time in D.C. Since the last election, he hadn't done anything without consulting her first. Now, they were equals.

Warner stretched, then leaned his head back against the seat and closed his eyes. She studied his handsome profile. Their relationship had fallen into a comfortable rhythm. And her elevated status to confidant and consultant gave her hope that their personal relationship might be salvageable. Maybe all the ugliness was behind them.

"I've summarized some topics you might want to address with a few key players." They were on their way to a reception in the East Room of the White House with the party leadership and other dignitaries.

His eyes remained closed. "That's good. Have you written it down?"

"Of course. It's all right here." Carolyn pulled a document out of the leather portfolio next to her. "We need to push for more funding for the war on drugs. The congress talks a big game, but nobody's coming up with serious programs."

Warner took the file from her. "I agree." Within minutes, he read through the typed pages, loading the information into his brain like a computer. That skill still amazed her. She knew that even under the influence of a few cocktails, he would be able to articulate their agenda.

"Any questions?"

Warner smiled at her. "Not one. As usual you've handled it all. I'll make sure to spend time with Alex Major."

Alex Major was the chairman of their political party, and his support would be crucial to securing the nomination for president.

Warner kissed her cheek. "What would I do without you?"

His compliment warmed her. "Warner, I--"

His gaze met hers.

Could they move beyond their mistakes into a real marriage again? A warning flashed in her mind--too soon, too fast, slow down.

"Yes?"

She shook her head and gave him a gentle smile. "It's nothing."

* * *

"Can I get you a glass of champagne?" Warner asked.

"I'd like that."

"Wait here. I'll be right back."

Feeling buoyant, Carolyn turned her attention back to the party. It was imperative that she spend time mingling. There were senators, congressmen, various foreign diplomats, the most prestigious members of the press, and, of course, the President and First Lady. She mentally took notes. It wouldn't hurt to be seen on the society page attending a gala at the White House.

Carolyn saw Warner's friend, Senator Richard Young of Georgia, coming toward her. A tall man with jet-black hair cut military style and dark brown eyes, he wore a colorful cummerbund and bow tie, giving him an air of confident youthfulness. The bright blues and reds stood out against the conservative black of the tuxedo. She had to admit he was strikingly handsome.

"Hello, Carolyn," he said. "How are ya 'all?"

She smiled broadly, concealing her discomfort. Just his "Hello," put her on edge, though she wasn't sure why. "Just fine, thank you. And you and your family?"

"We're all fine. One of the kids has the flu, though. So Dixie had to stay home tonight."

"I'm sorry to hear that." Carolyn realized that regardless of Warner's friendship, being objective about Young was impossible. Whether Warner admitted or not, he was their biggest obstacle in running for the presidency.

But this was a good chance to get to know the competition, Carolyn reminded herself. She clicked through her mental catalogue of information on Young. His family had a long-standing history in politics. That fact alone gave him a serious political edge. His father and grandfather had both been senators. He had much of the party brass on his side and a great political image. Moderate in his political positioning, he and Warner shared many ideals. Their voting records in the Senate were almost identical, both supported welfare reform, cutting defense spending, increasing funds for education, environmental protection, and lower taxes for middle America.

Strategically, she had to admit, Young was the clear front-runner for the nomination. Somehow, she realized, his voter appeal needed to be neutralized, although she had no idea of how to accomplish that feat. First, she needed to know and understand more about their adversary.

As Carolyn and Young talked, they were joined by a man she'd never met. She gauged him to be about five foot nine, with dark hair slicked straight back, cold gray eyes, and sharp, angular features.

"Carolyn Lane, I'd like to introduce you to Winston Cain," Senator Young said. "It's nice to meet you, Mr. Cain." Their eyes met. They'd never been in the same room together, had never even spoken directly, but each was well versed on the other. Edmund Lane had made sure of that.

"The pleasure is mine, Mrs. Lane."

"And what do you do?" Carolyn asked, knowing his resume already. According to Edmund and Warner, Cain had some of the finest retired intelligence operatives in the world on his payroll.

"Oh, a little of this and a little of that," Winston responded, laughing. Richard laughed with him.

They're quite comfortable with each other, Carolyn noted, sensing a stronger tie between the two men then just a chance meeting at a reception. Why was Young so chummy with a man like Cain? Carolyn wondered. Was it a result of the years his family had been in politics? Or was the distinguished gentleman from Georgia more than surface charm and a flashy wardrobe?

Warner joined them, handing Carolyn a glass of champagne. "Good evening, Richard." He shook Cain's hand warmly. "Winston, how've you been?"

Winston met Warner's gaze. "Well, thank you. How's your father?"

Surprised by Warner's familiarity with Cain, Carolyn watched as the three men talked. Richard Young puzzled Carolyn, and she promised herself that she'd figure him out.

* * *

Jack ran his index finger along the inside of the collar of his tuxedo shirt, then took another sip of his club soda. Carrie Masters, a twenty-something correspondent, strolled toward him with a glass of champagne in one hand.

"Quite a party," Carrie said. "It always amazes me to see so many power brokers all in the same room. It has to be a security nightmare."

"I'd say so," Jack agreed as he surveyed the crowd, taking note of who was talking to whom. Lead stories often started with an overheard sentence or phrase.

"Did you have a tough time getting in?" Carrie asked. "Scratch that. With your family history, you probably don't have a hard time getting in anywhere."

Jack shrugged. He'd given up long ago explaining that he lived in the trenches with the rest of the media troops, scrapping for a story, spending years cultivating sources. What did it matter, anyway?

"I guess they're used to seeing me periodically." His father had nothing to do with his A-list party invitations. If anything the politicians considered him a traitor. He'd worked doubly hard to be accepted and receive invitations to most Washington functions. Now, with his journalistic reputation well established, he was rarely overlooked. "How about you?"

"My editor had to pull some strings."

Jack knew her type all too well, a pretty face with a mind like a bulldozer when it came to news. She was relatively new to the

Washington scene, but Jack had no doubt that her ambitions would take her far.

"Isn't that Senator Lane with his wife Carolyn over there?"

Jack followed her gaze. "Yes."

"I gather the Senator is on the fast track to the White House. Who are they talking with?"

"Senator Young. I'm not sure who the other guy is, though." Jack knew the man's identity to be Winston Cain, but didn't want to admit it. Why was Cain at the party? he wondered.

Carrie squinted in concentration, no doubt committing the scene to memory. "I'm going to check him out," she said distractedly.

She made a beeline toward the foursome. The direct approach, Jack thought. Interesting. He looked on as Carrie shook hands with them. The group immediately dispersed, leaving Carrie standing by herself. So much for visiting with the press, he thought with a chuckle.

Carrie sulked back over to him.

"Looks like you broke up the party," Jack said.

"Not exactly what I had in mind."

"Who's the other guy?"

"Winston Cain. Does the name ring a bell?"

"I'm not certain," Jack said, skirting the issue. It wouldn't do to admit knowing a former CIA operative like Cain.

The infamous Winston Cain, Jack thought. Plenty of rumors had floated through the intelligence network about the man. None of them flattering, he reflected.

"I can't get a scoop, so would you care to dance?" Carrie asked.

"Sure, why not." Jack took her hand, and they approached the dance floor. "You're quite a dancer," Carrie said. "Is there anything that you don't do well?"

"Kids," Jack answered.

The music ended.

"How about we go somewhere, get a drink, and something a little more substantial than hors d'oeuvres to eat?" Carrie said. "You'd still be working, and we could have some fun." She linked her arm through his. "I know the perfect spot."

"Oh really, where?"

"My place. I could whip up some pasta and I make a killer martini."

He hesitated only a moment. "Thanks, but I'll have to take a rain check. I've got a night of writing ahead of me."

Carrie pouted. "Gee, you must have seen something at this party that I missed."

Jack kissed her cheek. "Just the usual run-down. See you at the next event."

"Keep playing hard to get, and I might give up," Carrie said with a forced a laugh.

* * *

Later that night, Jack stood next to his car, enjoying a cigarette.

"I got your note," a voice from behind him said.

Jack turned. "Thanks for coming."

"I don't know how much I can tell you," Randall Kipp, a CIA counterintelligence officer, said.

"How and why was Cain at the party tonight?"

"Technically, he attended as Richard Young's guest."

"Technically?"

"Yes, only the Secret Service knew because they didn't arrive together. Young's office arranged it. It was kept very quiet."

"Why was he there?" Jack asked. *Cain was tied to his father's suspicions of the Lanes. But where did Young fit in?*

"Possibly to generate business for his firm, but we're not sure. Cain's into the social register. Maybe he just wanted to be seen at another White House function."

"Did you guys watch him?"

"Of course. We wanted him out of there, but you know how it is. The White House is the Secret Service's domain. They didn't want a scene," Kipp said.

"Who'd he talk to?"

"Cain logged twenty-two minutes with Young, fourteen with Warner, and thirty-six with Carolyn--they danced twice."

"Thorough as ever, I see," Jack said.

"We try."

"So what does it mean?"

"Beats the hell out of me," Kipp said. "The election is around the corner. I hear Lane and Young are both contenders. *If* there's any correlation, that may be it."

Jack took a final hit off his cigarette. *Thirty-six minutes with Carolyn Lane. Cain's attendance meant something. But what?*

* * *

The next morning, Jack Rudly shook Winston Cain's hand as he entered Cain's office. "It's been a long time."

"Yes, it has," Jack said, taking a seat across from Cain's desk.

An Asian woman lounged in an overstuffed leather chair across the room. A long stem red rose lay across her lap. She appeared to be reading, but Jack felt her cold gaze sweep over him. Cain did not introduce her.

"I hope you've come looking for employment. My agency could use your skills."

"Maybe," Jack responded.

Cain smiled. "Good."

"I'm interested in your project with the Lanes and Young."

Cain pressed his intercom. "Mr. Rudly is leaving now. Show him out."

The Asian woman stood, her dark eyes alert and intense.

"That was a quick interview," Jack said. "Do I get the job?"

Cain glared at him.

Two well-dressed men entered the office. The woman nodded toward Jack.

Jack stood. "We didn't even discuss salary."

* * *

Carolyn felt the plane taxi down the runway, then lift off the ground as they flew to Missouri. Washington was growing on her. It seemed that being away was not only good politically, but also personally. She and Warner had shone at the party, drinking champagne and dancing long into the night. Warner's arms around her as they glided across the dance floor had felt good. It was a night to savor.

She had finally gone back to their townhouse for some sleep. Warner, however, had stayed on for conversations with the party leadership. It wasn't uncommon for him to stay up all night. She glanced over at her husband. He'd been out so late he hadn't changed, and they'd had to race to make their early flight.

Did she dare hope that they might one day be a real couple again? What was life without hope? she thought.

Suddenly feeling restless, she got up from her seat and began pacing in the aisle. So much planning to do, strategy to develop, so many critical areas that required her attention.

She glanced at Warner, who had fallen asleep. Even in a first-class seat, he looked cramped and uncomfortable. His seat wasn't reclined, she realized. Carolyn pressed the button on the arm of his seat, pushing on the back until it reclined.

Warner adjusted his body to the new position. His arms relaxed, allowing his jacket to fall open. A note fell out of his breast pocket.

Carolyn picked it up and read it. Her face flushed red. Pain sliced through her, knocking the wind from her chest. She held the back of the seat for support as she waited for her body to relax and respond at will. She'd been a fool, yet again. Fool, fool, fool. The words pounded in time to the headache that now throbbed.

She re-read the note.

Dear Warner,

*I'm glad we had one last night together. I understand that, for now, we must say good-bye. But remember, I love you, and will be waiting for your return. Good luck, **my** future Mr. President.*

Love,
Cindy

Humiliation rocked Carolyn. Getting her bearings, she lowered herself into her seat. Warner certainly had a talent of putting things into perspective for her. A perspective that he would pay for, she thought, and pay for dearly.

BOOK III

DAMNED BY VICTORY

2000-2001

"The world breaks everyone and afterward many are strong at the broken places."
--Hemingway, A Farewell to Arms

Kathleen Antrim

CHAPTER ELEVEN

January, 2000---Jefferson City, Missouri

"Drugs are killing our children! Crime is overtaking our streets! Global warming is destroying our environment! Hunger and homelessness are out of control. We are the greatest nation on Earth, yet we are plagued by problems. And I ask, why?" Warner squinted from the glare of the spotlights.

He continued his speech. "Then I look at the current administration. And I begin to understand. Billions are spent every year on defense, in a world we already dominate. Billions that could help correct these problems. But Washman won't cut defense spending, for these are his friends. And when he raised your taxes, and still didn't balance the budget, he gave tax cuts to these same friends. Well, I say enough! It's time to take back our country. It is time to correct these wrongs!" Warner pounded the podium with his fist.

Strobes flashed, a signal to the crowd, who whistled and applauded.

"This is why I feel it is my duty to pursue the office of President of the United States of America."

The crowd roared.

Carolyn stood behind him, her hands folded neatly in front of her. Energy and excitement bubbled under her skin, but she acted serene and composed. She enjoyed the crowd's response, and she felt pride in her husband. This was Warner at his best, making eye contact with those in the front rows, gesturing for emphasis, and carrying the crowd along on his passionate rhetoric.

She glanced over at Nick Creed, Warner's deputy campaign manager. He was deep in conversation with Jack Rudly. An interesting match, Carolyn thought, watching the intense exchange. Nick's wit against Jack's dogged persistence.

Nick emanated high energy, radiated intelligence. His lean runner's build matched his quick movements. Everything he did was fast, from his speech patterns to his thought processes. His answers were always direct and immediate, his social skills finely tuned, his smile filled with charm. At thirty-three, he exuded the competence of a more mature man. Clever enough to handle just about anything and anyone, she thought, he was patently Jack's equal.

In the glare of the overhead lights, Carolyn could barely make out Matt Carson and Ernie Weiland, Warner's political consultants, standing at the back of the hall. Both were engaged in conversations with members of the press corps. Spinning the message, Carolyn thought with satisfaction.

She turned her attention back to Warner. His powerful stage presence still startled her. He built enthusiasm to a crescendo. Carolyn watched, yet again, the transformation of the faces in the audience. Of course many in attendance were already sold on the Lane agenda, and made their excitement known at the outset. But others initially appeared reticent and wary. Then, as Warner spoke, their commitment increased.

Warner's skill as an orator didn't necessarily come from his word choice, Carolyn knew--after all, these were her words--but from that elusive quality that Hollywood producers referred to as "star power." That unexplainable magnetism that caused crowds to follow. Warner not only possessed it, he knew how to exploit it.

He turned toward Carolyn. "Ladies and Gentlemen, let me introduce to you my partner, my teammate, and the woman I love, Carolyn Alden Lane." He took a few steps toward her, clasped her left hand and kissed her cheek.

The crowd surged to their feet with another roar.

This was not part of the script. Shocked, Carolyn veiled her surprise. She smiled and waved to the audience.

Warner waited for his supporters in the hall to quiet and retake their seats. "As many of you already know, this dynamic woman wages our most effective war on drugs--single-handedly. In the courtrooms of Missouri, she has sent more drug dealers to prison than any other prosecutor in the state."

"It is time for all of us to fight for tougher laws, and changes in the social services system that will take our nation forward. Carolyn Alden Lane is already fighting those battles. She is my partner, and I say we join her. Together, we can rebuild America. Together, we can overcome the plague of drugs, hunger, homelessness, and hardship. Together, we can again become the greatest nation on earth."

The crowd cheered and clapped their hands high in the air. A group began chanting, "Warner, Warner . . ."

Warner held out his hand to stop the applause. "But tonight I come to you for a special purpose, because I truly need your help. I need your permission to pursue this office. I gave you my word that I would finish my term as senator before running for the presidency. So I come to you now and ask that I be relieved from that commitment. If you say no, I will respect your wishes. If you say yes, then it's on to the White House."

The crowd roared, "Lane for President, Lane for President . . ."

Warner flashed a big neon grin. Strobes exploded. Carolyn walked forward with Warner. They raised their clasped hands high in the air. The audience surged to their feet, again, clearly enthralled. Together they stood on the edge of the stage beaming, pointing and waving to familiar faces below in the crowd. They had their answer.

* * *

Pleased with the successful launch of Warner's candidacy, Carolyn called a meeting the next day to discuss strategy for grooming their candidate for the primaries. Matt and Ernie, who clearly understood that Carolyn was the guiding force behind the man employing them, addressed Warner's communication skills.

Ernie met Warner's gaze. "They're adequate for Missouri, but not for a man who wants to be president," he explained. "Your accent needs to be toned down. In effect, your voice inflection needs to be homogenized so as not to ring any discordant bells with the voters."

Like a tag team, Matt continued where Ernie left off. "The northern states will notice any type of accent. Everywhere Warner goes, we want him to appear as if he's a hometown boy. We want people to relate to him, and the best way to do that is to have him look and sound like one of them. Of course, a polished version of them. So, I've taken the liberty of hiring a voice trainer."

Ernie took up the strategy. "There's an interpersonal communication technique called 'matching' that we'll key in on. It's effective in all types of interpersonal interaction, but especially politics. Often, a politician will use region-specific jargon or a mannerism common to the group he's addressing. This works on the subconscious, although people rarely realize why they feel so comfortable. Simply put, people like what's familiar to them."

"For example," he continued. "In some parts of the country people will say soda when asking for a carbonated beverage. In other regions they order pop. Both terms mean the same thing, but they're demographic specific. It's our job to make sure you ask for a pop in the right places and a soda elsewhere."

"We sure are paying you two a hell of a lot of money to tell me how to ask for a Coke," Warner said.

They all laughed.

"Warner's already a master of sustained eye contact while speaking to a crowd," Nick commented. "So he doesn't need much practice with that."

How true, Carolyn thought. His gaze seemed to penetrate the soul.

"Our most critical secret weapon, however, is Warner's memory. He remembers names and details of people he's met by the thousands, and he's able to make these people feel they're of critical importance to him. I've watched you do it, Warner. Very impressive." Matt slapped him on the back.

Warner preened.

"Our other secret weapon is Carolyn. She's a woman of our times, and the voters like her willingness to support her husband's goals.

Carolyn accepted the compliment with a warm smile. A lot of political savvy had gotten them to this point, Carolyn thought. But political favors aside, she and Warner had the social expertise to cajole supporters out of buckets of money at fund-raisers.

She waited for a lull in the conversation. When it finally came, Carolyn got to her feet. "I think we need to confront a potentially difficult issue--Richard Young." She looked at Warner. "I know he's your friend, but we can't afford to ignore the threat he poses to your nomination."

"I'll handle Richard. You just concentrate on how to make me a better candidate," Warner said, his tone so terse that everyone in the room glanced at him.

"We can't afford to be naive. Young will demolish us in the primaries. We need to neutralize him, or we can kiss the nomination good-bye." She saw the muscles in Warner's jaw flex in anger, but she continued to meet his gaze. She wouldn't let him sabotage himself out of some misplaced sense of loyalty to a colleague.

"You heard what I said, 'I'll handle it.'"

"Warner, he might be your friend, but he's also an adversary."

"End of discussion." Warner rose from his seat.

Carolyn shrugged to conceal her dismay and began to gather up the files she'd brought to the strategy session. Somehow, she had to protect Warner from himself. "I guess we're adjourned, gentlemen."

* * *

The next morning Carolyn left early for the courthouse, aware that she needed to catch Mark before he became too involved with his work.

His face brightened when he saw her. "This is a pleasant way to start the day," he said, setting his newspaper on his desk.

She took the chair across the desk from him. She'd taken the moral high road where Mark was concerned, in spite of his frustration with her behavior and her own loneliness.

"Don't look so bleak," she said.

"Why not?" he asked, sounding unexpectedly terse. "I'm used to seeing you at least twice a week. Now, I'm lucky to get a glimpse of you on television."

"You aren't being fair, Mark."

"I'm sorry, I just miss you."

Carolyn suddenly felt very sad. She'd hurt Mark, although that hadn't been her intention. She cared deeply for him, and she valued his friendship. And she believed he loved her. But she couldn't knowingly contribute to the destruction of his family.

"Me, too," she said. "It's just that things are crazy right now, trying to get the staff and organization in place for the primaries."

"I know, I know. Can't you take a few hours off for an old friend?"

"You know I can't," she said. "I need your help."

"Sure, what can I do?" .

"It's time to collect the last payment from Mort. He's going to be sorry he pulled his support." She shook her head as if in disgust. "Once we have that money, we don't need him anymore. I'm going to use the funds for a special project I want you to set up. If there's a way to delay paying taxes, that's the route we need to take. Pull strings if you have to."

"What's this project about? Is it for the campaign?" Mark sat back in his chair, tapping one finger on the barrel of the pen in his hand.

"Of course it's for the campaign. Remember the firm we used for Rudly and Fields?"

"Sure." He gave her a wary look.

"It's time to set up a permanent staff to investigate possible candidates for the nomination." Carolyn stood and began pacing. "After that's accomplished, the investigative staff will come in handy for the big campaign, in order to gather ammunition against President Washman and any of his advocates. I want you to set it up."

"You need to be careful about this," Mark warned. "It could ruin Warner if anyone found out."

Concern nibbled at her. She understood that she was bending the law. "Which is why I trust you to handle everything for us. I want the best. Contact Winston Cain again. He can get us ex-FBI and ex-CIA agents. We'll need a lot of money to pay for the best, but I want them on retainer for us, and strictly us. Can I count on you to do this for me?" she asked quietly.

"Of course, but . . ."

"No buts." She straightened. "Start right away. Call me if you have any problems. By the way, I've set up a private meeting room on the Internet. Here's the address." Carolyn handed him a piece of paper with Cleopatra1600.com written on it. "The password is Caesar. Make sure Winston Cain has it, but no one else. Either of you can leave me a message anytime, I check it frequently."

"Since when did you start using the Internet?"

"Since I discovered that Katherine Seals is a computer whiz. The girl's absolutely brilliant. She can access anything. Which reminds me--I had her pull up Warner's accounts." She started pacing again. "What's left of his investment portfolio won't carry us far, but it's a place to start. We'll use my money when it becomes necessary, but until then we can tap into campaign funds. I have some overdue political favors that should generate funding, and I intend to call in those markers now."

Carolyn paused and faced him. "Mort Fields has pulled his support, but I know we can count on the Poultry Foods people for a steady supply of cash. We saved them millions by pushing through some regulations that would have taken years to enact without our support."

"You can't risk misappropriating campaign funds. We've talked about this before."

"I don't intend to do anything improper, and I know you'll use sound judgment every step of the way. We're just creatively using campaign funds."

Mark frowned as he got up from his chair and approached Carolyn.

"Please do this for me," she said.

"All right."

"Is anyone using my old office now?"

"Of course not. You're supposed to be coming back from your leave of absence, remember?"

Carolyn smiled. "I'll need to extend it indefinitely, I'm afraid. I'd understand if you gave my office away."

"I'll save it for you as long as I can. Right now, it's still yours."

Carolyn brushed his cheek with a platonic kiss. "Good. Then, I'm going to my office to put together some notes on the possible candidates. Let me know who Cain has on line already, so we can get these investigations underway. I want to start with a thorough report on Richard Young."

* * *

After Carolyn left his office, Mark shut off the tape recorder Edmund had built into his desk. He opened the pencil drawer and popped out the tape. He twirled it between his fingers, and sat for a moment considering his options. He knew that Edmund would want to hear what Carolyn planned, but Warner also had a right to know. He owed Warner that much, Mark thought, as he dialed the phone.

Warner's secretary put the call through.

"Hi, Mark. How are you?"

"Fine, Warner, fine. But this isn't a social call, it's about Carolyn."

"Okay. What's up?"

"I could have called Edmund, but I felt you had a right to know first hand. Carolyn asked me to hire Cain to investigate your primary opponents. She's going to focus on Richard."

"Don't worry. Young and I have discussed it. We've got Cain set up to handle her inquiries."

"Good, but that's not why I called. She's had her assistant, Katherine Seals, pull up your financial accounts."

Warner chuckled. "Edmund and I figured she might snoop around. Most of my assets have been taken out of my name, so relax. She can't link me to Edmund, so I doubt she found much of anything worth worrying about."

"No, she didn't. I just thought I'd better warn you."

"Thanks, buddy. I won't forget you for this. Loyalty like yours is hard to find. When I get to the White House, I'm taking you with me. In the meantime, let Carolyn do what she wants. We can take care of her."

Mark hung up, satisfied with the outcome of the conversation. When Warner won, he was sure a Cabinet post would be his.

It bothered him a little that Carolyn might end up a casualty, but not enough to tell her the truth. Turnabout was fair play, he rationalized. She'd brushed him off as if nothing had ever happened between them, coldly rejecting his love. And that rejection would cost her.

* * *

Carolyn stopped in the kitchenette and made herself a cup of tea before going on to her old office. The desk once occupied by her assistant, Katherine, sat vacant. Carolyn stepped past it and into her former domain. She sat down behind her desk. Although, it felt good to be back, this office represented her past--a past she had no desire to revisit.

She turned her attention back to the campaign, and pulled a legal pad from her top desk drawer. President Washman and Vice President Dexter would be dealt with later. For now, she needed to focus on the primaries.

Her biggest concern was Senator Richard Young. What puzzled her was Warner's relaxed attitude about the man. Young was, by far, the most serious potential presidential candidate aside from Warner.

His Boy Scout public image, however, frustrated her. She grasped the mug of steaming tea and held it between her two hands, taking tiny sips.

Other than a weakness for women, Young's only other vulnerability was his devotion to his children. While this genuine love for his family aided him with the voters, she sensed that it might be the key to slowing down his momentum. Carolyn pondered the possibilities and concluded that, whatever it took, they would give Richard Young the fight of his political life.

She considered their other adversaries. Martin Gaston from New Hampshire and Frank Landon were both contenders. She'd heard rumors that Bradley Davis of California was on the verge of declaring, but she knew he'd be an easy target. Nebraska Senator David Taylor posed a more viable threat, she realized.

Carolyn decided to concentrate her energy on Taylor's personal past. He had to have ghosts, she concluded. Ghosts that the voters needed to be aware of when deciding the country's leadership.

She had met him once. David Taylor was an eloquent, charismatic speaker. His record included a Medal of Honor in the Vietnam War, and he could be legitimately touted as a war hero. Carolyn knew that

Warner's lackluster military record was a great deficit when compared to Taylor's. She tapped the pencil against the bridge of her nose. Her glance fell on the stack of mail in her basket that had yet to be forwarded on to her home. Carolyn set aside her pencil. Most of it was junk or periodicals. She picked up the most recent issue of *Today* and began leafing through it.

"Just what we need right now," she muttered as she read the bold-print header of the article.

ALLERGY CLAIM KEEPS LANE FROM COMBAT DUTY

Senator Warner Hamilton Lane, a rising star in politics, appears to have made a miraculous recovery from his severe allergies, the malady that kept him out of combat during the Vietnam War.

Carolyn skimmed the text.

Medical records, from Lane's personal physician, claim that his condition worsened during the war forcing him to maintain a desk post in Hawaii. Remarkably, however, the allergies seem to have disappeared. In medical records released by the Senator himself, during his last campaign, he was given a clean bill of health and no mention was made of the severe sensitivity.

Carolyn turned the page, finding the byline--*by Jack Rudly.*

How in the world had Rudly acquired confidential medical and military records? Carolyn wondered. This was typical of his silent, but deadly, attack style. Like a shark, he came out of nowhere, his prey clenched between his jaws.

Carolyn checked the date. No wonder, Carolyn thought, the conversation between Nick and Jack had been so intense. Nick must have known about this article. Carolyn snatched up the phone, her fingers shaking as she dialed.

"Nick, why didn't you tell me about Rudly's article?" She didn't wait for his response. "Nothing, and I mean--nothing--goes on in this campaign without my knowledge. I thought you understood that. Now, please find out how Rudly got his information, then shut it down. We've got friends at that magazine--call them."

"Edmund Lane called me about this," Nick said. "He told me he and Warner had handled it."

"Say that again," she instructed ever so softly.

"Edmund said he'd handle it because he was afraid he'd caused the problem for Warner. Since they obviously have some pull with the magazine, they assured me it would never happen again."

"Nick, I want to make something very clear to you right now. Edmund Lane is not part of this campaign." Her voice trembled with barely suppressed anger.

"Not according to Warner. I'm sure you can appreciate my position."

Carolyn reigned in her emotions. "I repeat: *nothing* goes on without my knowledge."

"I understand, but I think you should know that Edmund is worried about Young's position. We discussed the situation and agreed that something has to be done. And soon. He feels that Warner's friendship is clouding his judgment. I tend to agree with him. As it stands now, we can't beat the guy."

"Nick, you're not listening to me. If you don't do as I ask, then I'll have to make other arrangements. Do you understand me now?" she asked, aware that he'd never been terminated from a professional position.

Nick said nothing for a long moment. Carolyn remained silent, although she felt like screaming.

"I understand, Carolyn. I just don't think Edmund's clear on it."

Carolyn severed the connection. Did she dare question Warner about Edmund? No, she thought, let them have their little secret. Fighting with them was the last thing she needed right now, but forewarned was forearmed. She had to remain focused on the campaign--a united front.

She returned her attention to the magazine. Damn the press. And damn Jack Rudly. First he'd hurt Katherine, and now he'd gone after Warner. She realized that as a journalist he had a job to do, but this felt personal. If he wanted a blood bath, she'd give him one, but it wasn't Warner's blood that was going to be spilled.

CHAPTER TWELVE

Associated Press
January 16, 2000
SENATOR YOUNG'S SON CRITICALLY INJURED
ATLANTA---Senator Richard Young's son, Bobby, age nine, was seriously injured today when hit by a car. His condition is considered serious, but stable. Witnesses say the accident was a hit and run. Bobby Young was riding his bike when a white Ford Explorer swerved around a corner, hitting the boy head on. A witness described the hit-and-run driver as an Asian female. She is wanted for questioning.

* * *

Nick walked into Carolyn's office and handed her a hotdog. "Lunch is served."

"Nutritious." Carolyn accepted.

"The path is almost clear for us," Nick said, then bit into his own hotdog as he sank down into the nearest chair.

"I think Davis and Landon are both out of it. We still have to worry about Gaston, though. He could be tough to beat since New Hampshire is his home state." Carolyn wiped mustard from the corners of her mouth with a tissue. "And I can't believe our luck.

128

David Taylor's defeating himself. I don't get it. He's got the best of
the best as far as political advisors are concerned. No offense to you,
of course, yet he appears completely disorganized."

"You're right. They haven't been able to define his campaign.
People don't know what he stands for or what he represents. He'll get
killed in the primaries." Nick waved his hotdog for emphasis.

"I'm worried about Richard Young and his family," she said.
"What a horrible accident. Not that I ever liked the man, but I can't
stand the thought of that little boy lying in a hospital bed. Thank God,
he's going to make it. Did we send flowers yet?"

Nick nodded. "Rumor has it Young is going to withdraw from the
primaries. They say the kid may never walk again."

Carolyn set aside her hotdog. "That makes me sick. I wonder if
we can help in any way. Put a call into his office and offer our
support."

"I'll do it right away. At this point, he's canceled all of his
commitments. It's a bad break for him, but we obviously benefit from
the tragedy." He shook his head. "Political reality 101."

"I don't care about how this accident has 'helped' us," Carolyn
snapped. "A little boy is horribly injured and I have no desire to profit
from such a catastrophic event. That's not what we're about here."

Nick flushed. "I understand. Forgive me for being so insensitive."

"You're forgiven."

"Good." Nick pushed up from his chair. "Onward and upward."

Once he was gone, Carolyn dialed Mark's number. "Mark, it's
Carolyn." Her tone was all business.

"How are you?"

She detected a note of discontent in Mark's voice, but chose to
ignore it. "Fine. I'm calling about the transactions you've been
handling for me. I need a total dollar figure."

Mark paused. "I'm uncomfortable about using campaign funds to
hire investigators, and delaying tax payments. I'm also worried about
my exposure. I have a family to care for."

His remark sliced her heart. "I'm aware of your commitment to
your family."

"I'm sorry. I didn't mean--"

"Let it go, Mark."

He continued, "It's just that, I spend my days in this courthouse fighting for what's right. It used to be so cut and dried, black and white. And now, I look in the mirror, and I don't know who the bad guys are anymore."

"How can you even think such a thing?" Carolyn asked. "You're one of the good guys."

"I don't know about that anymore."

What was bringing on his crisis of conscience? Certainly not hiring investigators, Carolyn thought. Mark was not naive, and none of this was illegal. Worst-case scenario was paying penalties to the Internal Revenue Service, and that was a long shot.

"What's really bothering you?" she asked, her concern growing. "You don't sound like yourself."

Mark hesitated. "It's . . . it's nothing."

"We both know who the bad guys are, Mark. You prosecute them every day. Nothing has changed, except your perception. You just aren't looking at this clearly. The only way to fight a battle is to employ the tools necessary to win. We're just arming ourselves correctly." She rubbed her eyes. "It's the same as having a weak case, but knowing the guy is guilty. You'd search for an angle and argue to use evidence even if you knew it was tainted, if that was all you had. Right?"

"This is a little different, misusing funds could be construed as improper."

"And using tainted evidence isn't? Think about this, please. There's no difference here. We're just bending the rules within the law. In this instance, the end justifies the means. If we knew a guy was guilty, we'd both use whatever we had, right or wrong, to get him convicted."

Carolyn tried to conceal the frustration she felt. "Besides, we're talking about my money, money given specifically to put Warner in the White House. We aren't using it for any other purpose, it's still going to the appropriate cause. Hiring investigators is a necessary expense. Don't kid yourself--the other candidates are doing exactly the same thing."

Mark paused. "I guess."

"Are we talking about the money? I get the feeling something else is troubling you."

"Of course, we are," he answered abruptly. "What else would I be talking about?"

"I don't know. I was hoping you'd tell me."

Carolyn heard Mark sigh. She wondered if she'd pushed him too far.

"You need some totals, don't you?" His voice sounded flat. "I'll crunch the numbers, then courier the paperwork over to you. You can decide if you want to keep the funds in checking accounts or put them into short-term investments."

"Thank you." Not wanting to end on a bad note, she softened her voice. "Have I told you lately how wonderful you've been?"

"Carolyn, don't do this . . . I'm sorry . . . Thank you for the compliment."

Perplexed, Carolyn reluctantly recradled the receiver. His distorted sense of concern confused her. He'd talked in circles, as if the topic they were discussing wasn't what worried him. Did he have another agenda? Did he have a guilty conscience? She dismissed the thought as ridiculous.

* * *

Associated Press
January 22, 2000
YOUNG WITHDRAWS FROM PRIMARIES
WASHINGTON---Senator Richard Young announced today that he would not be running in the presidential primaries in order to devote full attention to his son's recovery. Although the primaries have not officially begun, Young was considered the front-runner for the party nomination. The driver of the hit-and-run car that injured his son has not been located. She is still wanted by the police for questioning.

* * *

January 27, 2000---Jefferson City

Ernie Weiland met Warner as he walked out of his dressing room and handed him the newspaper. "We have a meeting in fifteen minutes with Carolyn and the rest of the inner circle. So you'd better hurry."

Warner said nothing. He felt like a trained seal. He kept waiting for the moment when Carolyn would demand that he spin a ball on his nose. No matter how hard he tried, she expected more of him. She reminded him of Edmund. No, he silently amended, recently she'd become far worse. But he had a surprise for her. She thought she controlled the campaign. In a few months she'd know the truth.

Lately, her attitude had changed toward him. At one point, it seemed as if their relationship had moved to a place of truce that included trust and respect. He lived his life, she lived hers, and their mutual dream of the White House was their bond. Now, instead of a bond between them, he felt as if he was bound *to* her. With the presidential campaign in full gear, he was surrounded by people who were hired to handle his image. Or was it his behavior?

He grudgingly admitted that Carolyn had put together a brilliant election team. Due to her competence, the Council found no need to influence her choices.

Matt Carson was terrific at manipulating a story with the press in order to slant it in their favor. Like Warner, he was a master of semantics. Warner liked him as a person. He was a superior point man, who could easily assimilate himself into any situation. As the primaries drew closer, Matt set up the infrastructure of the campaign machines in each state. Warner felt certain that he could trust Matt, and with trust came the prospect of a little rest and relaxation.

He glanced at Ernie, who was also quick on his feet. With his facile mind and command of the verbal style necessary to be persuasive no matter the venue, he often articulated winning arguments for the Lane position.

When they were on the road, he and Ernie shared a suite. Back at home, Carolyn had given Ernie a room in their residence. Was that to keep him informed? Warner wondered as he browsed through the headlines of the paper, or to keep him on a short leash? Warner mentally shrugged. He was comfortable with Ernie, and that made dealing with Carolyn easier to manage.

Nick, he mused, was turning out to be the star of the campaign staff. He dissected situations, located the targets, and implemented action. Ambitious by nature, he was a sponge for every shred of information that came his way, and every detail that would put them ahead in the polls.

As an aide on the Hill, Nick had learned to locate the centers of power. He was like a baseball player who knew all of the pitchers: their strategies, their best pitches, and what they were likely to throw at you when you stepped to the plate. He memorized the specialty of every reporter. He anticipated their questions and grasped their prejudices.

"Objective reporting only exists in fantasyland," Nick once told Warner. "Most reporters don't do their own research and investigation. They're a complacent bunch, and more than willing to let someone interpret information for them. We just have to be out there to do the interpreting. I'll let you know when we run across a real reporter"--Nick had paused, his gaze locking with Warner's--"like your hometown nemesis Rudly. Then you can be blindsided. Fortunately, though, the Rudlys of the world are few and far between." Nick knew his stuff, and Warner felt well guarded by his guidance. He intended to take Nick to the White House.

Ernie sat in a chair next to the window, reading a newspaper and drinking orange juice. Warner never had a minute alone any longer. He was supposed to please Edmund. Please Carolyn. Please the people-- well, fuck them all. Granted, he could play the role, but he refused to buy into the bullshit. Everyone was out for himself. They all tried to suck the life out of him. Damn, he needed to snap out of this funk, and pump himself up. This was his year. The victory and the glory were going to be his, and he needed to keep that in focus.

What he needed was a drink, something to take the edge off the stress. Warner poured himself a glass of orange juice. He drank half of it before getting up and heading into the bathroom, glass in hand. Ernie remained submerged in the morning paper. Warner opened the cabinet door and pulled out his flask. He poured some Jack Daniels into his orange juice and drank it down. He eyed the empty cup, then refilled it with the whiskey. He tossed it back with a grimace, rinsed out the glass, and rejoined Ernie in the sitting room.

"Let's go," Warner said as he shrugged into his suit jacket, popping two mints into his mouth.

The meeting had already started when Warner and Ernie walked in. Matt, Nick, and Carolyn were all sitting around the conference table in the basement of their home.

"Nick, where are you with the new economic plan?" Carolyn asked as Warner and Ernie took their seats.

"Almost finished. My staff's working on it even as we speak."

"How about the press? I know they've been quizzing us on the details."

"Handled. I released a statement this morning saying we'd have the entire document to them in two weeks." Nick shuffled some papers. "And here's your speech on the war on drugs you asked me to review. I edited it last night. Go over it one more time, fine-tune it for your style. You don't need it until the Women in Politics caucus tomorrow, right?" He handed the loose pages to Carolyn.

"Thank you."

"About the platform issues we were discussing yesterday. I did some research, and I feel very strongly that Carolyn should stay with the war on drugs platform. The public loves it. Warner can focus on tax relief and the environment." Nick proceeded to hand them packets of information. "Here's a synopsis of my reasoning and some of the facts that back it up."

"Great job," Carolyn said. "Is there anything else?"

"One more thing. Here are the travel arrangements for New Hampshire." Nick passed out additional folders, stuffed with a variety of travel documents.

"If that's it, then we're adjourned," Carolyn announced.

Warner held up his hand. "Wait a minute everyone, I have a few comments."

They sat back down.

"You're all doing good work here, and Carolyn and I appreciate it. The New Hampshire primary is critical, and as you all know the polls show a close race. Some believe that we don't have a chance of winning. It's time to prove them wrong." Warner hit his fist on the table. He met the gaze of each person in the room.

"I want a concise message. If we're talking tax relief, then let's be specific. Apply that to the environmental issues as well. I also had a thought about Carolyn's undefeated record against drug lords and child abusers. As the polls show, her image is tremendously strong,

let's build on that. Maybe coin the phrase, the 'undefeatable team.'"
Everyone in the room remained silent.

"Edmund taught me that perception is reality. If we're perceived as indestructible, than we'll be unbeatable. The voters want politicians to save them. We need to be superheroes capable of righting all wrongs. Carolyn's abilities have already been proven. Capitalize on them, and we can 'leap tall buildings in a single bound.'"

Carolyn flushed under his praise. His assessment was accurate. She hadn't lost a single case. Still, it surprised her that he'd even noticed.

Carolyn watched Warner in a conversation with Nick and savored a glimpse of the man in whom she'd seen so much promise. The man she'd allowed herself to fall in love with; a man who walked the edge of ambition but instinctively kept his balance. His compliments felt good, like drops of rain falling on a parched traveler in the middle of the desert. She slammed the brakes on her train of thought. Only fools repeated their mistakes, she scolded herself.

The thought of their defeat during his first re-election campaign and his subsequent behavior was the splash of ice water that kept her focused. She couldn't afford to forget his history of becoming arrogant and self-destructive when he was on top. Warner's volatile pattern had been established.

He caught up with Carolyn as everyone walked out of the meeting. "I know things have been strained between us lately, but I believe this is our year," he said. "I've given up my bad habits. I'm committed to this, to us. You're my partner, my teammate. Together we're indestructible. Shit, our entire lives have been about this goal, and I haven't lost focus. Together, we'll make it happen."

Carolyn wrinkled her nose, his breath projected the bitter smell of alcohol thinly disguised by breath mints. The reminder destroyed the warmth of her earlier thoughts. He'd given up his bad habits? Right, she thought, sadness welling within her. She knew he could be a *great* man--a man capable of changing history. But he was squandering his talents with self-destructive behavior.

She shook her head, spun on her heel and walked away. It hurt to love a man beyond his faults, and to know that it wasn't enough. Nothing she did or said could protect him from himself. Her challenge lay in damage control. But could she hold him together through this campaign?

CHAPTER THIRTEEN

February, 2000---New Hampshire

They attacked New Hampshire, and the resultant campaign drew copious amounts of blood. Martin Gaston became a threat, although Senator Dave Taylor barely treaded water. The most charismatic of the candidates, however, was Warner Lane. His speeches flowed eloquently, and he charmed everyone he encountered.

The polls showed Warner as the clear front-runner. His message was simple: he was one of the hometown folks who was going to take on Washington and change the way government was run. Warner Lane cared for the people. His motto became "People Before Business." The crowds ate it up.

Warner finished a speech at a high school gymnasium in Concord late one evening. The crowd surged to a standing ovation, and he was flying on their energy and enthusiasm as he walked out into the crowd to shake hands. Matt Carson caught up with him and pulled him aside.

"We've got a problem," Matt whispered. "Our motto, 'People Before Business,' is about to be crammed down our throats."

Warner stopped walking. "What do you mean?"

"The tabloids are releasing a story claiming you own a company that's using children, in sweatshops, in Haiti to manufacture goods. Tell me this isn't true."

Warner stepped back. "Son-of-a-bitch!"

"I take it these accusations are true."

"No," Warner retorted. "They're not true. Those are Edmund's holdings. They have nothing to do with me." He felt suddenly queasy.

"Well, unfortunately, your father's business just became our business. This is bad, really bad. When this is released, you're going to look like a hypocrite. 'People before business,' will be a national joke."

This can't happen now! I've come so far. "I don't need to hear how bad it is, that's apparent. Tell me how to fix it." Warner ran his fingers though his graying hair. *I've got to call Edmund. This was so typical. Edmund had perfected the art of screwing up his life. He'd like to choke the old man with his bare hands.*

"We're working on it."

"How's Carolyn taking this?"

"She's upset, but handling it."

"Good, good," Warner said. He'd been afraid that something like this might happen. Edmund didn't care whom he devastated. This, however, was different. Edmund had a vested interest in Warner attaining the White House.

Oh God! Warner thought again of Carolyn. Fear rose like bile in his throat, the taste caustic. What if this pushed her beyond her capacity to understand? The thought of children being used in sweatshops would infuriate her. She'll know that her own agenda could be jeopardized by this family affiliation. If she thought he was finished, it would benefit her to distance herself from the Lane name. They both knew that she could be wounded and still salvage a lesser political career for herself. Fear rose in his throat. He drew a deep breath, steadying himself and collecting his thoughts.

Minor setback, he reassured himself as they headed for the cars. Matt handed Warner the newspaper article.

LANE ABUSES CHILDREN IN SWEATSHOPS
WASHINGTON, D.C.--Senator Warner Hamilton Lane, presidential hopeful, whose motto is "People Before

Business," owns a garment company in Port-au-Prince, Haiti, using child labor in sweatshops. Humanitarian activists are calling him a hypocrite whose motto should be, "the bottom line on the backs of children".

Many are asking for an investigation into Senator Lane's business affairs. Currently, he is ahead in the polls in the race for the party nomination. But will these charges end his hunt for the White House? Insiders tell us that this will destroy his chances.

Son of a bitch, Warner thought, they'd slaughtered him. Relax, he told himself, it's just a tabloid. The Council employed the resources to contain the situation. Control was key, and they possessed the control.

Once they arrived at the hotel, Warner hurried to his room and dialed Edmund.

"Son."

Warner ground his teeth at the reference. The cruel pettiness of the man would never change. "We've got a fire here. A big--fucking--fire, and it's yours."

"I'm on it already, son. Consider it taken care of."

"'Consider it taken care of.' Are you out of your mind? This is a mess."

"Lower your voice. You'll never amount to anything if you continue to let your emotions get in the way. You're acting like a woman. Find your balls, and act like a Lane. I don't give a shit whether or not it's in your blood. You're wearing my name, and I expect you to act like a man."

The desire to pull the phone out of the wall overwhelmed Warner. His knuckles turned white, as he gripped the receiver. He swallowed hard, wishing for a drink. Don't do anything rash, he told himself. You need this bastard and the Council. Relax.

Edmund must have taken his silence for submission and continued. "Here's what I want you to do. First, release a statement to the press that you are not, in any way, connected to my businesses. Then, speak out against it personally, act outraged. Directly address the plight of these people who are abused in sweatshops--say you're glad this came up, for it's a great opportunity to help raise awareness of these horrible situations, etcetera, etcetera. You know the routine.

Oh, and have Carolyn demand that these charges be investigated. Her sincerity will carry it off."

"Why the hell couldn't you have straightened this out before the campaign?"

"Shit, son, this makes things interesting. Quit being such a pussy. Besides, I said I have it handled. Within the week, the conditions at the factory will be exemplary. At which point, you'll be doing your television interview."

"What television interview?"

"The one I've set up for you and Carolyn. You'll be hearing from the producer shortly. I'll let you be surprised by my choice. It's a top rated show, I'm sure you'll be pleased. In the meantime, parade that wife of yours around in public. Her popularity will keep you afloat until we can put out the flames."

"Fine." Warner switched gears, trying to sound tough. He wasn't sure why he still tried to please the old man. "What about the Georgia primary? If we pull off New Hampshire, I don't want to lose our momentum. Call Richard and see if he can persuade Governor Hicks to endorse me."

"Richard and I have already discussed it. If we need Hick's pull, Richard can call in a marker. But Warner, if Richard does this favor for you, it locks you into running with him as your vice presidential candidate. Now that his son is recovering, he wants back in."

"We need the edge, so I'm willing to solidify the deal. Richard will look good on the ticket. He has the strength to carry the south. Shit, he'd probably beat me if he'd been able to run in the primaries."

"Is Carolyn still set to meet with Governor Hicks?" Edmund asked.

"Yes. Knowing the way she thinks, she'll also ask Hicks to endorse me."

"Good. Let her believe it was her success. She can also take the fall if it backfires."

"I know the drill," Warner said, and hung up.

* * *

That night they flew back to Missouri to escape the press and regroup. The sweatshop story had frazzled everyone's nerves.

Carolyn convened a meeting in the basement of their home, the "Situation Room." The location insured privacy. Kentucky Fried Chicken buckets sat on the table. No one ate, except Warner. Quietly he observed the group between bites.

"How are we going to deal with this?" Ernie finally asked. "Is it even possible to recover?"

"Yes, and we're going to come out swinging," Carolyn announced.

Everyone in the room stared at her. Warner watched cautiously; he refused to say anything about his conversation with Edmund. As long as Carolyn and Nick headed in the right direction, he'd remain silent. So far, the methods of the Council had yet to be detected, effective as they'd been.

They let Carolyn believe she ran the campaign. This illusion provided an excellent cover for the Council. Warner's next gift to her would be her belief that she'd convinced the Governor of Georgia to endorse him. He knew it was a done deal. Edmund and Richard would make sure of that. Yet, no one knew, and they wouldn't be told until Carolyn believed she'd orchestrated the maneuver. He took delight in predicting Carolyn's future moves and staying ahead of her.

"There are several fronts on which to attack," Nick said, picking up the gauntlet. "We've devised a strategy. First, we issue a press release denying any affiliation on Warner's part with Edmund Lane's companies. This is technically accurate, and we can produce corporate documents proving Warner and Carolyn are not stockholders. When we leave this room, Matt, Ernie, and I will be on the phone, calling every major periodical, television network, and newspaper in the country. Second, we attack the allegation on the basis of credibility. Let's face it, this is a tabloid reporter we're talking about. We'll attack him on that angle. And third, we create a diversion." Nick looked around to make sure everyone was paying attention.

"And now, for the *big* news--we've just been called by the producer of 'Barry Sears Live.' I'm not sure where the break came from, but it's a Godsend. This is our chance to make an impact. Barry Sears is the epitome of credibility. With him, we can easily fix this mess. Thank God the story broke in the tabloids. The public will be willing to accept it as a lie when they witness Warner and Carolyn's outrage on a show like Barry's."

Damn, if Edmund and his Council weren't good, Warner thought. Their reach was far and effective. His attention turned back to Nick.

"Carolyn and Warner shine when they're together, and the Sears show can only enhance their image. The viewers will see them interact naturally, speak candidly. Both of you will be offended by these accusations and demand an investigation into the charges and the factory itself."

Nick turned to Carolyn. "This is your forte, and it will highlight the causes you've been fighting for all these years. You'll come off as the heroine demanding that these poor people, and especially the children, be saved. But I have one other request, and I feel it's imperative."

Carolyn met his gaze. "The diversion?"

"Exactly," Nick said. "The country is wondering why you and Warner have no children. Sooner or later, we need to address the question. This is the perfect time to explain."

Carolyn bit her lower lip. "I have to go on national television, and say that I'm not able to conceive?"

"Yes. It'll divert the media's attention. And right now, we need that diversion. Your honesty will become the next headline. We can rehearse if you feel it's necessary."

"No. No rehearsal." Her face flushed. "If I have to do this, I'll speak from the heart." *But can I actually do it? This was personal, too personal. How much of myself do I have to sell?*

"I understand."

No, you don't. Because if you did, you'd never ask. "You *really* feel it's necessary?"

"Yes. We need this offense maneuver. Otherwise, I'd never suggest it. And, as I said, eventually the topic has to be addressed. If we do it now, we're using it to our best advantage."

God, I feel like a prostitute, selling my pain to divert the public's attention. "I don't like it. If you insist, I'll do it. But it makes me feel dishonest."

"I'm not asking you to lie. I'm just asking you--"

"To exploit a very painful, personal subject on national television."

"You're paying me to get Warner into the White House. Strategy's an inherent part of my job, and I wouldn't be doing my job if I didn't come up with offense planning. We're in a bad situation. This is my recommendation. And I believe if we handle it correctly, it may help our campaign. The best defense is a good offense."

Warner knew that Carolyn would agree. Nick's argument had merit. A diversion, especially an emotional one, was the perfect solution. 'Barry Sears Live,' Warner thought, a perfect vehicle to attack any allegation nationally. Too bad he hadn't thought of it himself.

* * *

Carolyn pulled Nick aside as they left the meeting. Her voice was low and intense. "Do you really believe this can help the campaign?"

"Yes."

"It's just so personal. I can't get comfortable with the idea of discussing it on national television."

He searched her eyes, witnessing her pain. "I'm sorry. I wouldn't ask if I didn't feel strongly about it."

"Okay." Carolyn paused. "I always hoped that our childlessness could go unaddressed, but I realize that people want to know every detail about the lives of politicians and their families. I'll do what's necessary."

"Good. It'll work out. It probably won't be as hard as you--"

She held up her hand. "Don't even go there, Nick. I appreciate your sentiment, but you have no idea how much this will take out of me." She lowered her hand. "I'm not complaining. I knew that I'd have to make sacrifices and compromises when I signed on for this campaign, and I'll follow through."

He nodded, his respect for her growing. This was probably the strongest woman he'd ever had the good fortune to meet. And she wasn't going to let anything get in the way of the greater goal, not even her personal pain.

* * *

Carolyn squared her shoulders. As the interviewer shifted his focus from Warner and the Haitian sweatshop topic to her, she couldn't help wondering if he sensed her anxiety.

Barry Sears smiled at her.

Carolyn didn't feel at all reassured. Studio lights glared, intensifying her discomfort. She released a shallow breath, and maintained a thoughtful expression.

"Mrs. Lane," the interviewer began.

She said graciously, "Carolyn, please."

"Carolyn, of course." He nodded. "Your passion for children is apparent in everything you do professionally. Our audience is well acquainted with your single-handed campaign to rectify the foster care system and fight drug abuse among our youth. And yet, you and your husband don't have children of your own. I'm confident that I'm not the first person to ask why?"

Carolyn swallowed convulsively. She'd expected this moment to be difficult, but she hadn't expected such excruciating pain to tighten around her chest.

When she didn't speak, Warner reached over and grasped her hand. She felt the sting of tears at his unexpected kindness. Oh my God, she thought, I'm about to cry on national television. Inhaling deeply, she composed herself. "Warner and I have discovered that I'm not able to have children." Her voice shook. "Despite how desperately we both want a family, it isn't possible for us."

"How very painful for both of you," Barry remarked, his tone inviting more explanation.

Carolyn took his cue. "Coming to terms with my inability to have a child has been the greatest challenge of my life," she admitted. "I'm comforted by two things. My husband's compassion, and the fact that there are hundreds of thousands of women around the world who are just like me. I've tried very hard, with Warner's support, to turn the negative into a positive. We've spent our lives focusing on the needs of the many children who fall through the cracks in our social services system. And we remain committed to all of the children of America."

"Hasn't this situation tested your marriage? How in the world have you survived this as a couple?"

Carolyn looked at Warner. "We're a team," she said. Then she gazed into the camera with unshed tears shining in her eyes. "We're a team."

The in-studio audience burst into applause.

Warner slipped his arm around Carolyn's shoulders.

Barry Sears pressed on. "What about adoption?"

Carolyn smiled at her husband. "It's a very definite possibility."

* * *

The New Hampshire primary turned into a great victory, Carolyn reflected. After their television interview, the campaign ignited. Warner received forty-seven percent of the vote, leaving a stunned Martin Gaston to wonder how he'd been defeated so soundly in his home state.

Her openness regarding her inability to have children fueled the flames of Carolyn's popularity, making her more human and approachable. The public related to her anguish. Everyday she received thousands of letters from fans and supporters, and she personally answered as many as she could. Carolyn had touched the hearts of millions.

Nick's strategy was flawless, the "Barry Sears Show" the perfect vehicle. In effect, the sweatshop story had raised Warner's national recognition, and people all over the country had tuned in to the interview.

Stan Braunson, their pollster, had come running to Carolyn, wearing an immense grin. Across the country, Warner's numbers had risen substantially, showing him as the clear front-runner. The newspapers featured Warner Lane, calling him "the man to watch." Gaston, Landon, Davis, and Taylor would be forgotten, she told herself as she drew lines through their names on a program in front of her.

Warner hammered Super Tuesday and rolled right into the Midwest. That's when they were assigned Secret Service. Every time Carolyn saw an agent, a shiver of pleasure ran down her spine. Their very presence was a tangible sign that victory danced on the horizon. With the race for the nomination going their way, she knew it was time to make her move.

Nervous about what she was about to propose, Carolyn composed herself in the hallway. She entered the Situation Room and glanced around. "Is everyone here? I have a proposition."

Matt and Ernie leaned forward in their chairs. Nick lounged comfortably in his, as was his habit. Warner sat silently, his chair rocked onto the rear two legs and his feet up on the table.

"This is a highly sensitive discussion," Carolyn began. "Not one word is to leave this room." Her accomplishments to date empowered her. She knew she could institute great change in the country, and the approval and acceptance she was finally receiving fed her soul. "I'd like to run with Warner as his vice presidential running mate."

Warner's eyes widened. He swung his feet off the table, bringing them to the floor as his chair shifted forward onto the front legs with a thud. "Are you out of your fucking mind?"

"That's right, Warner, your running mate. My popularity numbers are higher than yours."

Warner looked desperately around the table. No one else said a word. Matt and Ernie looked poleaxed. Nick remained expressionless.

Carolyn held her breath, her confidence wavering in the silence. Had she miscalculated? Fear tightened around her chest. Rejection reared its head.

She pushed on. "With that in mind, we need to send up some test balloons to measure the public's reception of this concept. Nick and I have discussed this, and we believe it's a good idea to have Warner introduce me at the next rally by saying that the country will get 'two for the price of one.' Stan will run some polls, and we'll go from there. Are there any questions or suggestions?"

Matt recovered first, his drawl emphasized by his enthusiasm. "I think it's worth checking out. I wish I'd thought of it myself. 'Two for the price of one.' I like it. Of course, we need to run some television spots that will promote the concept and test the waters, and we'll have to educate the voters as to Carolyn's qualifications. But so far the polls have shown that Carolyn's popularity has made an impressive impact."

Carolyn drew in a deep breath. She quickly lowered her gaze to hide her relief.

The room erupted into a buzz of activity. Matt and Ernie began brainstorming. Nick rapidly took notes.

Warner stood abruptly, knocking his chair over. Everyone fell silent. He glared at Carolyn, then stalked out of the room.

* * *

Warner felt as if the walls were closing in around him. He needed a breath of air to clear his head. He and the other members of the Council had not anticipated this. What had started out as Carolyn's backstage act was turning into the headliner. Granted, he'd known that her confidence would grow when she believed she was controlling the campaign. While that strategy made for a great cover for the Council, he'd be damned if his dream was going to turn into her triumph.

He made his way up the steps of the basement and out onto the back lawn, shivering when the cold air hit him. The chill felt good. He needed to think. Richard had obtained Governor Hick's endorsement, and for that favor he expected to be the vice presidential candidate. This was a mess. He needed Edmund's brilliance when it came to maneuvering Carolyn and her ideas. Ideas, Warner believed, that would cost him the presidency.

It would be so much easier if Edmund could be in the campaign meetings, Warner thought. But Carolyn hated the man, and she'd be furious at Warner's continued relationship with him. Their association was a calculated risk, but he needed the behind-the-scenes guidance, contacts, and power that Edmund and the Council could provide. Of course, Carolyn had no knowledge of the Council, and she never would.

Edmund had been right. Carolyn couldn't be allowed free reign and control. They'd pumped her up too much. What had seemed fine in the smaller state election was becoming unbearable in the national campaign.

No, Warner realized, there was no way he could bring Edmund into the forefront of the campaign. Besides, it could jeopardize the Council's anonymity.

He concluded that he would have to continue to let Edmund work behind the scenes. Edmund didn't like the situation anymore than Warner did, but he didn't have a choice. They needed Carolyn as a decoy and, even though her ego was growing immensely, their plans were jelling nicely.

If Carolyn found out that Warner was even communicating with the old man, there'd be hell to pay. The kind of hell that left a man permanently burned.

CHAPTER FOURTEEN

March, 2000--Jefferson City, Missouri

Jack slammed the phone into the receiver. The son of a bitch didn't have the balls to confront him face to face. He'd mailed the letter then gone on vacation. Typical Pat Mead, Jack thought, deliver the news and wait for things to calm down. He re-read the notice he'd received via Fed Ex from his office.

Mr. Rudly-
*Your story on Senator Lane's military history was substandard. You are hereby warned to verify your sources more carefully. You'll be expected at the National Convention, until then your assignment is to report on the campaign, **not** investigate personal issues. Management expects you to write a personal apology to the Senator. This notice shall serve as a warning. When you're back in town we can discuss this further.*
> *Signed,*
> *Pat Mead, Senior Editor*

"Verify sources more carefully," Jack mumbled. "Substandard?" *What the fuck did that mean?* Never before in his journalistic career had anyone ever questioned his reporting methods, let alone reprimanded him for inaccurate information.

Jack prided himself on being precise, and he knew his article was accurate. He'd verified all of his sources, and had authentic medical records as evidence. The facts obviously didn't matter, Jack realized; he'd stepped on powerful toes. But he didn't give a damn.

Jack crumpled the paper, and tossed it into the garbage can. *Like hell he'd write an apology. He'd done nothing wrong.*

* * *

March, 2000---Cleveland, Ohio

Weeks later, he was still smarting from Mead's chastisement as he stood with other members of the press in the back alley of a large red brick auditorium waiting for Candidate Lane to exit after a speech to the Teacher's Union. Jack glanced over at a colleague. "Hey, Dan, how the hell are ya?"

"Fine, fine, and you?"

Jack lit a cigarette, exhaling as he spoke. "I'd be better with some dinner and a beer right now."

"I hear ya." Dan was an old-timer in the business.

"What do you think about the candidates?"

"Same shit, different mouth," Dan joked, "but personally I like what Lane has to say. What about you?"

Jack shrugged. "Keeping an open mind. There're a lot of questions I'd like to see answered, but his campaign staff isn't very forthcoming."

"They're just being cautious. Give him a break. He's new to the national scene. Missouri's small potatoes compared to the market he's jumped into now. I mean, you have to admit, we're a tough crowd."

"Are we? I'm not so sure, anymore. I can't believe how easy these guys have been on Lane." Jack took a drag on his cigarette. *He wasn't prone to arguments, but damn, the lack of curiosity his colleagues were showing was frustrating.*

"I don't think anyone has been easy on him."

"What about the sweatshop thing? That was dropped like a pregnant debutante."

"Maybe the press is getting a conscience. It could be argued that journalists are trying to be more objective and not ruin people's careers just to sell a few newspapers or boost ratings. Look at the Kennedy days. The press kept his personal business quiet and it was probably better for the country."

"I don't buy it. If that were true, we wouldn't have jobs." *What's with the double standard? Suddenly the press has a conscience? Bullshit!*

"Come on, Jack, you're ignoring the facts. Warner Lane didn't own that company, his father did."

"My take is different. Maybe the press only has a conscience when it comes to politicians with ideals they agree with." Jack tossed his unfinished cigarette onto the pavement.

"I can't believe you don't like the guy. He's one of us. He's a product of the sixties, just like we are. He stands for the same things we do and his wife is a powerhouse. She'll be more than a pretty figurehead. I believe she may actually make a dent in the drug problem. Shit, she already has." Dan smacked his fist into his palm. "Their concerns are right on target."

Jack shook his head. *Dan didn't get it. This wasn't about liking or disliking Warner Lane. It was about manipulating the system and biased reporting.* "You know, I keep getting the same response when it comes to my colleagues."

"Maybe that means something," Dan commented.

"Yeah, like a lot of crack reporters have gotten caught up in all the Lane hype and forgotten their jobs."

"I call it listening to the man's message."

"I call it bullshit." Jack watched Dan walk away.

But maybe he was the one getting things wrong, Jack thought. He'd known of the Lane family for years, and rumors of trading political favors for profit had always circulated about Edmund and Warner. He'd tried to maintain an open mind, but maybe his father's theories of graft had prejudiced him. The implications in his father's files were unsavory, yet none of them could be proven. Still, the documents haunted him. And he couldn't ignore his own experience of being reprimanded for revealing Warner's military career. Someone had applied pressure to shut him down.

Jack leaned against the cool brick of the auditorium and mentally reviewed his next move. Was he being a hard ass? No, he decided, the facts were apparent. At the very least, Warner was being protected and Jack wanted to know by whom.

Time to go back to Missouri and pick up his father's investigation, Jack thought. He was not into tabloid press, but there were a lot of loose factors that didn't add up. Carolyn's relationship with Mort Fields, for one, and why Mort would expose Carolyn to Bill Rudly. This made no sense. And the reference to Winston Cain, made to Bill Rudly from Adam Miles, struck Jack hard.

Winston Cain's agency would stop at nothing to complete a job, and his father's notes implied a relationship between Cain and Carolyn. The hottest lead, Jack had followed up by visiting Cain's office in Washington, D.C. Not surprisingly, he was thrown out.

Then, there were the strict orders from the news magazine to report only the standard campaign rhetoric. They wanted him off any real story and essentially threatened his job if he didn't comply. Jack debated on how hard to tread on very thin ice.

Jack thought of his father. It must be a family character flaw, he mused, to find oneself pushing against the grain of popular opinion. He wasn't used to having his hands tied by his employer. This job might be considered the big-time by industry standards, but compromising his journalistic integrity wasn't worth any dollar amount. To Jack, journalism fostered passion and, like any other passion, it would not be denied.

He had expected support for Lane from some of the competition, like *National* news magazine. Andrea Walden was Lane's media advisor, and her father was editor-in-chief of *National.* But he didn't expect a complacent, even defensive, attitude from his own employer. Could the Lane machine have power sources that deep into the press? It had happened before, and he believed it was happening again.

Jack thought again about Missouri. He had to go back. He didn't care if his editors didn't approve. He'd chased lesser stories against greater odds. The fact was, he had a job to do, and he'd be damned if he'd let someone else tell him how to do it.

He wasn't dropping his investigation of Warner Lane. He owed as much to his father.

Jack pulled his tape recorder from his pocket and checked to make sure it was rewound and ready to record. The back door of the auditorium swung open and Warner Lane's entourage made their exit to the waiting cars. First the Secret Service agents, then the handlers, and finally the candidate. Jack found himself face to face with Warner Lane.

Immediately, one of his top aides stepped between them. The handlers held up their hands to say they were not allowing any questions.

A female reporter managed to sidestep next to Lane. "Senator, you're promising a renewed war on drugs and a tax break for all Americans. But do you really think it's possible to do all of that in one term?"

Warner Lane stopped. "I don't intend to do it all alone."

"Please explain."

"With my wife by my side leading one attack, while I lead the other, we'll accomplish all of that and more."

"So, Mrs. Lane is a large part of your campaign?"

"No. She's a large part of my life."

"Senator Lane, tell us about your affiliation with Mort Fields and Winston Cain?" Jack shouted.

Warner's head snapped around, his gaze locking with Jack's.

"Have you hired Winston Cain's agency?" Jack saw Warner's jaw clench.

"Who's Winston Cain?" another reporter yelled.

Warner flashed a grin. "You'll have to ask Mr. Rudly. I have no idea."

Quickly, Matt Carson wrapped his arm over Warner's shoulders and pulled him into the limousine.

* * *

Associated Press
March 28, 2000
LANE NAILS DOWN NOMINATION
SACRAMENTO---Warner Hamilton Lane secured the party nomination yesterday by taking California's 165 delegates. The win came as no surprise to campaign officials, who

predicted the landslide after Lane swept the Great Lake states on March 21. Sources close to the candidate say that Senator Lane is now looking forward to the convention and to squaring off against President Washman.

CHAPTER FIFTEEN

July, 2000---Washington, D.C.

"I don't care what it takes, Warner, shut her down. We have a deal. I got you Governor Hick's endorsement, and I expect you to hold up your end of our bargain." Richard Young slammed the phone into its cradle and reached for the Tums. Damn, Carolyn's escapades were destroying his digestive tract. And he had to keep Warner in line. Warner was the key to his success. He rubbed his stomach.

The aggravation was worth it, though, he thought with a smile. These little episodes served a purpose. They kept Warner off balance and caused further estrangement between him and Carolyn. They weren't problems; they were opportunities, Young reminded himself. Opportunities to shift the balance of power to himself. Richard knew how to exploit the exercise. If he shut off his support of Warner, Warner's campaign would deflate like a punctured balloon.

He gazed out the window of his senatorial office in Washington, D.C. Sitting back, he placed his interlocked fingers on his stomach. If only he'd known how quickly his son was going to recover, he'd never have dropped out of the primaries. The presidential nomination would have been his. Fucking doctors. They always painted the worst scenario to make themselves look like heroes.

He closed his eyes, visualizing the vice-presidency and beyond. He'd simply adjust his strategy, Richard thought. By the time the election came, Warner would be convinced he couldn't function without him. Carefully he plotted to make himself indispensable to Warner and ingratiate himself with Carolyn. Considering the friction between them, the challenge lay in showing loyalty to one without revealing dedication to the other.

An interesting match, Richard reflected. A loveless marriage brought together by one man, Edmund Lane, and held together by one cause, the White House. He'd done his homework and realized that Warner and Carolyn's estrangement was to his benefit. They were both damaged goods, yet possessed the skills to present themselves as the perfect couple. They had to get elected! Nothing was going to stop that process. Nothing.

Carolyn's insistence that she be the vice presidential running mate would not be tolerated. Warner would act, or he would call upon the Council. The deal was done and he intended to hold them to it. He was the vice presidential candidate. This was his shot at power, real power, and he would win.

* * *

Jefferson City, Missouri

Warner hung up the phone, Richard's angry voice still ringing in his ears. He leaned forward, resting his chin on his fists. A headache pounded behind his forehead. Damn Carolyn! Her insistence on running as the V.P. had thoroughly pissed off Richard, and they couldn't afford to lose his support. Unfortunately, Carolyn had no idea that Richard was even a factor, nor could she be allowed to find out.

But, Warner thought, Richard needed to understand that she had to be handled carefully. Her national profile was too strong. The safest way for them to deal with her was to make her candidacy someone else's concern. Nick was the perfect messenger.

Warner pressed a button on the intercom. "Call Stan Braunson, and get him in here pronto," he said to his assistant.

155

Ten minutes later the campaign pollster stood in the doorway of Warner's office. "Stan, hi. We need some information. I want a current read on the public's perception of Carolyn's reform ideas and my economic policy. See how it compares to President Washman's policies and try to pinpoint the areas where people are most dissatisfied with Washman."

Stan looked surprised. "Nick and I have already discussed this. I suggested we do a dial group."

"Run that by me again."

"It's a group of people who represent a cross-section of the population. They each hold a dial while being exposed to various information on video. When they like something they turn the dial up, and when they don't they turn the dial down. The information is compiled and broken down into age, gender and race. It can be pretty specific."

"Can we do it quickly? I want the information now." Warner realized he'd stepped into the consultants' territory, but he didn't care.

"Sure, Nick already has me on it."

"Right out of the starting block, I want to hit these areas hard"-- Warner stood and leaning across his desk, handed Stan a handwritten list-- "starting with my acceptance speech at the convention. And run some potential running mates by these guinea pigs. Include Carolyn. Let's see what the feedback shows."

"Nick's already approached me," Stan said. "He wants numbers on Richard Young."

"Good." Smart man, Warner thought, Nick knew where victory lay.

"Oh, and Stan, I want to see the numbers first. Give me the original papers, and don't make copies. Understood?"

Stan shrugged. "Am I to assume this conversation never happened?"

"You know how to stay employed."

"I'll get right on it."

"Get the numbers to me as soon as possible, but be thorough," Warner ordered.

"I can have results to you--" Stan started to say over his shoulder.

"How about Wednesday at two o'clock?" It was a directive. Warner moved past Stan and headed in the direction of the conference room. The daily two o'clock meeting was about to begin.

Warner's political savvy told him that he couldn't afford to anger Carolyn. She was too strong and too popular. He'd have to manipulate her carefully. Warner knew that maintaining Carolyn's loyalty and support could make the difference between success and failure.

* * *

Warner was the first to take his seat for the dissection of the dial group data. Carolyn was absent, speaking at a "Women In Politics" caucus. Preliminary numbers showed the Lane economic policy as well received, and Carolyn's war on drugs as their strongest suit. President Washman's foreign policy stance remained his best asset.

The voters, however, were disillusioned by Washman's lack of concern about the sluggish economy. Even though people respected his foreign policy, the data showed that they no longer cared about world affairs. Their concerns had shifted to their own economic needs and job security.

The voters wanted change; and they no longer had faith that the current administration could improve their lives. Thank God, Warner thought, for the bad economy---it was the best front on which to attack the other party.

"Well," Nick said taking charge as usual, "my sense is that we can kick the pants off Washman if we stick to economic reform by virtue of tax relief. This recession is killing his approval ratings. We emphasize supply side economics and stimulate the marketplace by cutting taxes, both individual and corporate. Simple concepts, just hit the highlights, include the environment, and keep Carolyn in the limelight with her war on drugs. Focus on her consistent record against drug dealers."

"Let's hear it for the recession," Matt cheered.

The group laughed.

Warner sat back, gauging the interaction. He allowed them to run the meeting as long as his agenda dominated.

Nick continued, "Washman's camp will keep trying to replay his foreign policy successes. The only way to address that is to

157

demonstrate that we're more concerned with the people in this country than the plight of others around the world. Stress domestic issues. Change versus more of the same."

Everyone was quiet; some were taking notes.

"What else do you have?" Nick asked, looking over at Stan.

"I asked Stan to run some numbers on potential vice presidential running mates," Warner interjected. "I feel Richard Young would boost our campaign." He'd already reviewed the numbers in private, and had made a few adjustments to the original figures.

"Has there been discussion with Senator Young?"

Warner sensed the anger in Nick's question. Nick didn't like being outside the loop. "Richard and I go way back. Let's leave it at that."

"What about Carolyn?" Nick asked.

Warner turned to Stan. "Why don't we concentrate on the numbers for now?"

Stan handed out additional data sheets illustrating the dial group's response to various V.P. candidates. The top page showed Carolyn's profile; the numbers were high. Her national popularity had increased dramatically. Charismatic, gracious, and an eloquent speaker, Carolyn had won over the public. Her one woman war on drugs had hit a national nerve, and her record stood for itself. The polls confirmed that she was perceived as a role model for both men and women, alike. A rare occurrence for a public figure, Warner mused, and possibly for the first time in the history of America for a female. He hadn't tampered with any of these numbers, knowing that the data was critical to the correct positioning of Carolyn in the campaign.

Their ad campaign was obviously affecting the polls, Warner thought. They were currently running a series of television spots in which his head and shoulders were superimposed over people and events important to the country. This gave the impression that he was in control of the very issues the viewer witnessed on the screen. He loved the image.

They'd run an ad featuring Carolyn in courtroom settings, emphasizing her background as a prosecutor who'd beaten down every drug lord who'd crossed her path. The ad went on to show her in the political arena, suggesting a battle for tough legislative reform to punish offenders. All the while, Warner was superimposed over the picture, giving the impression that he was directing the fight against these issues.

Warner pretended to peruse the information in front of him. He ran his finger down the page, searching for the data on Carolyn as a potential running mate. He stopped where the numbers took a nosedive. The last study confirmed that, although Carolyn was exceptionally popular, the public was not ready for a husband and wife team in the White House. The idea smacked of a monarchy. He bit back a smile. Before his adjustments, the numbers had reflected negatively. Now they plummeted.

Warner looked up, watching the others as they read through the data and caught up with him. Discreetly, he studied Stan's reaction. Stan smiled reassuringly. His secret was secure.

When everyone had read the information, Nick began. "We need to speak to Carolyn about this and give a recommendation on who the running mate should be."

"The numbers show clearly that Senator Young was well received, but that's not a surprise," Matt stated. "How's his son?"

"Bobby's fine. Kids bounce back quickly," Warner said.

"If he can commit to the campaign without worrying about his boy, he'd definitely add strength to the ticket," Ernie chimed in. "His wife, Dixie, is also an asset. They make an attractive couple, and they're well liked inside and outside of the beltway." Young was the obvious choice. Warner had made sure of that. But who was going to tell Carolyn? he wondered. This was an awkward situation for the consultants. Warner knew that no matter what happened, she wouldn't back down without a fight.

"This needs to be discussed with Carolyn," Matt said. "I'm sure she'll agree when she reads this data. Washman is going to be tough to beat, we need every advantage."

"When can you speak to her?" Nick asked.

"I'll speak with Carolyn this afternoon, I guess, but we need to interview Young."

"I'm sure that will only be a formality." Nick's gaze met Warner's.

Warner was impressed with Nick's smooth pass to Matt. Without intending to, Matt had caught the job of sacrificial messenger.

"Matt, tell Carolyn we're setting up a meeting with Young. I'll take care of it. We'll try for tomorrow at five o'clock. Warner, you need to stay in Jefferson City. We'll hold the interview here. Oh, and guys, try to keep it from the press."

Warner relaxed. Success, he mused, lay in the preparation.

* * *

Carolyn scanned the data. "We need to do something--run some ads to spin the idea and educate the public. We can move the perception away from the appearance of a monarchy and reinforce the democratic image."

Matt took a drink of water. "You're probably right. It could just be a matter of education, but we don't have time to find out. It would be a huge risk to put you on the ticket, and as you know, we need to announce the vice presidential candidate before the convention. We wouldn't have time to find out if an ad campaign was successful before we'd have to commit to your candidacy."

He set his glass down. "If you want to do it, I'll back you, but you have to consider the downside. We've been focused on our own party in the primaries. Now we have to focus on Washman. He's no pushover, we've got a tough battle ahead. Young brings some serious advantages. The numbers show him in an extremely strong position. Plus, it appears Warner is set on Young as his Vice President. We can't afford to have you two at odds. The campaign just came off life support from Warner's problems, and this could put us back in intensive care."

"What about his son?"

"He's on the mend. Young can commit to the campaign."

"The country's crying out for change." She looked up at Matt. "But maybe the wife of the President as Vice President is too much, too fast." Carolyn clasped the arms of the chair, struggling for composure.

God, how she wanted the vice presidency! Yet all of her efforts, her popularity, and her strong record would now go to put Warner and Richard in office. Typical, Carolyn thought. Everything boiled down to gender issues. Women throughout history had suffered the same fate. But that reality did nothing to lessen her disappointment.

160

Be patient, she told herself, your turn will come. She knew that Matt was right--they couldn't afford to be back on a respirator. She swallowed hard, still trying to choke down the unfairness of it all.

Matt's cellular phone rang, and he took the call.

Young was the best option, she knew, but he was going to be difficult to control.

Matt severed the connection and set aside his phone.

"Young is it, then," Carolyn said, forcing a confident tone she didn't feel. "He has no obvious skeletons and a good family image. His family history in politics will help with the Washington insiders. When do we interview him?"

Matt looked perplexed. "You surprise me. How do you know what Young might, or might not, have to hide?"

She dismissed his question with a flutter of her hand. She'd never admit to hiring Winston Cain.

"I'll tell Nick to set it up. Would tomorrow afternoon work for you?"

"Fine, let's get this done," Carolyn said, preoccupied with her own thoughts. She knew that all of their guns needed to be drawn when they marched into the National Convention and readied themselves for the shoot-out against incumbent President Charles Washman. But first, Richard Young needed to understand that she and Warner were running the campaign. Hence, he would be expected to take a secondary role, a role that never overshadowed Warner, and never compromised her control.

CHAPTER SIXTEEN

August, 2000

Jack stepped out of the shower. He tossed his towel onto the bathroom floor and stood damp and naked in front of the mirror. "Decision time," he said to his reflection.

The man who stared back looked frustrated, stifled, housebroken. He'd been following the Lane campaign for weeks and doing little more than regurgitating their rhetoric. He had to follow his instincts, even if it meant war with his employers.

Jack strode into the bedroom, grabbed to phone, and dialed his secretary.

"Maureen, book me to Missouri and then on to the National Convention."

Missouri, Jack thought, the Show Me State--time to live up to this motto or he'd force the issue. Maureen, thorough as usual, put Jack on the next flight to Jefferson City.

* * *

The first two days he was back in Missouri, Jack felt like one of Pavlov's dogs. Every candidate had a dark side and Lane was no exception. The figurative bell rang with rumors and innuendo, making his mouth water. The scent of a story wafted through the air, but the meat of the scoop eluded him.

His greatest frustration was Mortimer Fields. Upon his arrival, he'd immediately driven to Fields's office. Mort's assistant claimed he was out of town, and refused to say where he was, or when he'd return.

Jack walked to the nearest pay phone. "Mr. Mort Fields, please."

"I'm sorry, he's not in," Fields's assistant said. "Can I take a message?"

"This is Sergeant Leonard Rand, of the Jefferson City Fire Department. We have an urgent matter to discuss with Mr. Fields. Please tell me how to contact him," Jack said.

"I've been instructed not to give out his travel arrangements, sir. Can I take a message and pass it along?"

"This is urgent, ma'am. I believe he'd want to speak to me. His residence needs to be boarded up," Jack said.

"Boarded up?"

"Yes, ma'am, from the fire."

She gave Jack a hotel phone number in New York City. Jack called repeatedly, but never got an answer in Fields's suite. He knew it was better to catch a source off guard, so he didn't leave a message.

Sipping a cup of coffee at a local diner, Jack glanced at his list of leads. One jumped out at him: Erma Miles.

* * *

The next morning Jack went out for a jog. After forty-five minutes he slowed, turned a corner and found himself staring at the house of Erma Miles. He walked up the steps and rang the doorbell. When there was no answer he walked around to the back of the home.

Across the yard he saw a small figure, wearing a wide-brimmed hat and crouching over some flowering bushes in the garden. Gloved hands skillfully clipped and shaped the plants.

Without turning to look at him, she asked, "Who might you be?"

"Jack Rudly." He wiped a bead of sweat as it trailed down his temple.

"You're Bill Rudly's son, the journalist, aren't you?" She turned, her blue eyes sparkling with vitality.

"Correct. I was wondering if I could speak to you about your husband?"

Erma's face clouded. "My Adam passed away some time ago."

"I was sorry to hear that."

She patted his arm. "Thank you."

"I don't mean to impose on you, but--"

"Yes, you do. You need something."

"You're right. I do. I was wondering about Adam's relationship to my father. Specifically why they started meeting. Can you help me?"

"I'm not sure. Come in." She led him through the back door of her home.

"You need to be careful, young man. There are those who would not take kindly to your inquiries. Your father, God rest his soul, would have told you that." Erma removed her hat, revealing perfectly coifed white hair.

"How well did you know my father?"

"Only socially. Our paths crossed quite often at political functions. He and Adam disagreed regularly." She hung the hat on a wall hook next to the door, and continued into the kitchen with Jack close behind. "Even though they often argued, Adam always had the utmost respect for him. He wasn't bogged down in all the political hoopla. He just told it straight--very diplomatically, of course. Boy, he used to raise the hair on the back of Edmund Lane's neck. Those two were always fighting."

"I have a few questions."

"I'm sure you do. But smart folks won't have anything to say about these people. Please, have a seat. Would you like some iced tea?"

"Sure."

"Sugar?"

"No, thanks."

She poured two glasses. "People won't go on record."

"I don't understand. The man is running for the President of this country, he's got to be used to questions."

"Oh, he's used to questions. It's just that they need to be the right questions, coming from the right people. Since your father's death, there's been very little opposition here, and what little there is, has no impact. I can tell that you aren't part of that crowd, so I'm just telling you to be careful. These are powerful people."

"If it's risky to speak to me, then why are you doing it?" Jack asked.

"Well, there's nothing they can really do to hurt me anymore," Erma said, pouring the tea. "Except, of course, to kill me. But once I've spoken to you that'd be a little obvious, don't you think? In a way, speaking to the press is a sort of insurance policy. Besides, they can always claim that I'm senile." She laughed at herself. "I'm not, I assure you, batty."

Jack grinned. "Hardly."

"So, you're wondering why my husband went to your father."

"Indeed."

"Adam and Edmund Lane had been friends for over thirty years. They made their fortunes together, always backed each other up. They were inseparable. Once Edmund had accomplished his goals in business, he became obsessed with politics, especially where his son's concerned."

She sipped her tea. "For years my Adam supported Edmund and Warner. When Adam semi-retired he moved further into the world of politics, although he still sat on the boards of some local corporations. He became what the pundits call a political advisor. The fact was that Adam and Edmund had enough money and political pull to enforce their will. That's what your father objected to. But Adam objected to abusing his power. That's when the friction began between him and Edmund."

Jack sipped his tea. "Go on." *Adam's visit to his father was starting to make sense.*

"Unfortunately, Adam kept most of this to himself. He didn't believe in bringing his problems home. But from what I gathered, Adam felt Edmund had changed. He became power hungry and ruthless. Then, there was that plane crash with Ron Spietzer and his family. Adam was extremely distressed about it, but he refused to say why. After that, he and Edmund spent less time together. In fact, toward the end, Adam only saw Edmund at meetings for a political group they both started."

"What kind of political group? What did they meet about?"

"They were secretive. I used to think that was funny, these old men sneaking around. I don't think Adam ever realized that I knew about the group. But I pay attention, and occasionally I'd overhear a telephone conversation, or Adam and Edmund talking on the porch after supper."

"Why do you think they were secretive?" *How strange. He knew Edmund liked to work in the shadows, but this was more than he'd anticipated.*

"I don't know."

"Think hard. Maybe a conversation or a phrase will come back to you. This group had to be important for Edmund and Adam to be involved."

Erma paused for a moment, tapping her index finger against her lip. "Now that I think about it, I'm sure that group caused the big fight between Adam and Edmund. It was formed in order to influence Missouri politics. But I think that changed. I know Adam wasn't interested in going beyond the borders of Missouri, and I think Edmund wanted a national agenda. That makes sense, seeing as how he wanted Warner in the White House."

"Do you know what they planned to do to influence politics?"

"I just assumed it would be through contributions."

"But that wouldn't require any secrecy."

"I suppose not."

"Did this group have a name?" Jack asked.

"The only thing I ever heard Adam say on the phone was the 'Council.' Understand, this is nothing official. You won't find anything about them at party headquarters."

Council! Bingo. Jack smiled. "Did you do your own investigating?"

"A little. I just wanted to make sure my Adam wasn't unhappy at home. At times, he spent hours away. One hears of old men chasing young women. But I felt bad and confessed to Adam what I'd done. He said he was flattered that I'd think some young thing would be interested in an old geezer like him. I miss my Adam."

"I'm sure you do."

"You know, the living always betray the dead."

"What do you mean?"

"Nothing." Tears formed in Erma's eyes.

166

Jack grasped her hand lightly. "Tell me."

Erma sank lower into her chair. "Do you have a good soul, Mr. Rudly?"

Taken aback, Jack hesitated. "I like to believe so."

"I hope so, too." She looked around the room before continuing. "I was speaking of myself. You see, I've stayed silent since Adam's death, and I feel my silence has betrayed him. My husband was a man of honor. And I don't believe he died of natural causes, I believe he was viewed as an obstacle that needed to be removed."

"Who do you think removed him? And why?"

"I don't know, but about a week before his death he and Edmund Lane had their serious fight." Her voice was low.

Jack's jaw clenched in concentration. *Would Edmund Lane kill a friend? If so, as an adversary, his own father may have been in danger. No, that's ridiculous, Lane's a prominent businessman. And from his father's notes it appeared Carolyn was the problem.*

"Adam was so upset over the fight that he woke me up when he returned home late that night. He didn't give me many details, but he talked more than usual. Something about a business deal that involved Carolyn Lane."

Carolyn? That fit.

"Also, Edmund had brought in men from Washington. Men who, Adam felt, were dangerous. He didn't want to be associated with them. I knew Adam was referring to his political group, but he never said so. He just said that Edmund was selling his soul to the devil with these new 'friendships.'"

Jack's heart rate increased. "Do you know what type of business deal involved Carolyn? Could it have been with Mort Fields?"

"I wish I knew." Erma sighed. "All I do know is my Adam wouldn't do anything illegal. He was very principled."

"Who were these men from Washington? And why do you think their activities were illegal?"

"I don't know their names. Adam refused to say." She wiped a tear off her cheek. "He said that Edmund told him, 'If you're not with me, you're against me.' Adam just kept repeating that phrase. After thirty years, it crushed him that his friend would say such a thing. Adam said he just didn't know who Edmund was anymore." She sniffed.

"I think that's what finally sent Adam to talk to your father. He said there was going to be a bloody feud in the party, because he wasn't going to let the Lanes have their way. I didn't know who the other members were, so I had no idea how bad it could be. I just knew that Edmund was powerful. He doesn't sidestep obstacles; he bulldozes through them." Her voice broke, but she continued, "One week later, my husband was found dead in his office."

A bloody feud? Not too uncommon in politics. His father, however, never mentioned a fight in the party. "What killed Adam?"

Erma shrugged. "They told me that his heart stopped. 'It must have been his time,' the doctor at the hospital said."

"And you don't believe it was his time?"

Erma's gaze met his, "No. I don't believe it for one minute. He'd just had a physical. 'Fit as a fiddle,' his physician said. I should have spoken up then, but I was shocked and frightened. Edmund handled everything for me. And I let him. He was a good friend in that manner. Later, I learned that an autopsy would have been standard procedure, but the doctor had already signed the death certificate and there were no questions raised. I didn't know what to think. I was just so devastated . . . so weak." Jack could see she was fighting for composure.

He reached across the table and took her hand. "You did the best you could do under the circumstances. No one would ever fault you for that."

They both sat in silence as he gave her a moment to compose herself.

"Do you think Edmund Lane killed your husband?"

"When you say it like that, it sounds ridiculous. I just don't believe Adam died of natural causes." Sadness draped the room. "I hope our talk helps you find whatever you're looking for."

"I hope so too. Did Adam ever talk about, Mort Fields?" Jack asked as they both stood.

"Yes, now and again. I assumed Mort was part of the Council. And Adam mentioned that he, too, spoke to your father about his concerns."

"I see." *Adam and Mort were part of the so-called Council, and both had gone to his father. Their visits had to be related.*

Erma walked him to the door. "If you need any further assistance, call me," she insisted.

"Thank you. And please, if you think of anything else, I'm at the Best Western."

* * *

Walking back to the hotel, Jack felt as if he were being watched. The eerie feeling made the hair standup on the back of his neck. He turned quickly on the street, taking a few steps backward, only to find the sidewalk behind him vacant.

I must be getting paranoid, he thought, tossing his keys on the dresser after dinner at a restaurant down the street. It was seven o'clock in the evening, and he had left his room at five, two hours earlier.

He noticed his computer and frowned. He was sure he'd left his laptop in his briefcase. Now it sat in plain view on the desk, plugged in. Son of a bitch, someone had been in his room. The maid? No. She had made up the room earlier that afternoon.

Jack went through his computer files. Nothing seemed to be missing. But why would someone break in and not take anything? The bastards were looking for something. He was getting too close. Somebody was getting nervous.

He wondered if his own employer was checking up on him. That was crazy. But was it? He'd seen crazier. And he'd never bothered to find out how the magazine knew he'd been to Missouri before.

He unscrewed the phone and disassembled the light fixtures, hunting for listening devices. Then he tore the room apart looking for anything dangerous. He'd seen bombs planted under toilet seats, toothpaste laced with poison, and a multitude of maiming weapons. Three hours later, sweat dripping from his brow, he had the room reassembled as if nothing had happened. He flopped down on the bed. *Shit, I'm paranoid.*

He called the switchboard for messages. The operator told him that Mort Fields's assistant had phoned to schedule an appointment. A smile lit Jack's features. Fields was back in town. He could put the pieces of the puzzle together. While Erma had certainly given him interesting information, it was all second hand and speculative. He needed Mort to fill in the blanks.

* * *

The dimly lit parking garage was all but vacant. A small Asian woman dressed in a janitorial suit and carrying a large purse approached the last remaining car. Pausing, she glanced around to assure herself that she was alone. She moved to the side of the vehicle, looked in through the driver's side window, and found the car unlocked, the alarm disarmed. No surprise, she thought, given the amount of security she'd had to circumvent in order to gain access to the private garage.

With a slight click, the door opened. Silently, she moved around it, dropped to her knees, and leaned into the car, examining the steering column. Finding the standard construction, she set her large purse on the seat and removed her tool pouch. She unscrewed the bolts securing the steering column, and removed the structure, exposing the wiring harness for the airbag.

She found the termination of the wiring harness, made a splice, and inserted a small electrical switch completing the circuit. She threaded it to the speedometer needle, setting the strike point to seventy-five miles per hour.

This was one of her cleverest ideas, she mused. Without the benefit of a Porsche expert directly comparing factory wiring to her revision, no one would ever notice her handiwork.

Her job complete, she replaced the steering column, stuffed her tools back into her purse, and moved out of the car, closing the door behind her. As she stood beside the vehicle, she removed her gloves, shed the janitorial suit, and shoved the items into her bag. She wiped a bead of sweat from her forehead, smoothed her hair, and straightened her dress. Then, she backtracked, making her way out of the garage the way she'd come in.

* * *

Mort Fields folded his small frame into his new Porsche Carerra Cabriolet, started the engine, and put the top down. As he drove out of the underground garage, he glanced at his watch: 11:16 p.m. He'd missed the benefit dinner given to support The Arroyo Del Valle Camp for children with life-threatening illnesses.

"Damn," Mort muttered. He was always running late by this time of the evening, especially when he'd been out of town. He'd hoped to at least make an appearance.

On the freeway, he pushed the accelerator down, enjoying the feel of power and speed as the vehicle responded. The speedometer registered seventy-three miles per hour as he accelerated into a mild curve. His mood lifted as the balmy, summer night air rushed over him, and the highway stretched vacant ahead. Pushing the pedal to the floor, he let the engine roar.

The airbag exploded.

* * *

The Jefferson City Democrat
August 12, 2000
TYCOON KILLED IN CAR CRASH
JEFFERSON CITY--Local businessman, Mortimer Fields, died last night when he lost control of his Porsche Carrera Cabriolet. Apparently, the victim was not wearing a seatbelt at the time of the crash and was thrown from the car.
Recently divorced, Mr. Fields was not reported missing until the next day when he failed to make his morning appointments. His car was found in a ravine off a remote section of Highway 50. An investigation is underway to determine the circumstances of the crash.

CHAPTER SEVENTEEN

August 12, 2000

Jack stood at the edge of the ravine. The mangled body of the Porsche was crushed between two trees. Yellow crime scene tape corded off the area.

He identified himself as a member of the press. "Do you have any idea what time the crash occurred?" Jack asked the officer posted at the sight.

"After eleven last night," the police officer responded. "Real shame, too."

Jack nodded toward the yellow tape. "Do you suspect foul play?"

The officer adjusted his gun belt.

"This is off the record," Jack said.

The man shrugged. "Doubt it. But with him being a bigwig and all, we've got to cover the bases."

"You ever hear of him being in business with Carolyn Lane?" *It was a long shot, but why not?*

"Naw, but he was supposed to fly to New York to speak at the convention. That's how he was discovered. He missed some appointments, then didn't show up for the plane. I suppose that was for the Lanes."

Fields was speaking at the convention? Why? And on what topic? Jack didn't recall seeing him listed on the schedule. *Who wouldn't want Fields's to be there? Was someone eliminating Warner's obstacles, as Erma had suggested? If so, who?* Attending the convention suddenly sounded appealing.

It seemed no coincidence that the men who'd spoken to his father were dead, including his father. *But the deaths were either from natural causes or an accident-- explain that, Rudly.*

* * *

Jack ran for the gate. He never wasted time, scheduling appointments up to the last moment, and stepping onto the airplane as the door shut behind him.

"Please grab any available seat. We want to take-off on time," the gate attendant called as Jack darted down the ramp to the aircraft.

The plane was congested. Jack made his way down the aisle, spotting two free seats. Quickly, he sized up his options. With his long legs, the empty aisle seat was the most comfortable choice, but then he spotted her. Katherine Seals.

What was she doing in Jefferson City? Jack's heart quickened. *How long had it been? Years. Would she even speak to him?* She sat in the window seat, the center seat was open. Jack stored his laptop in the overhead bin, then excused himself and slid into the seat.

Katherine glanced at him. Her face flushed with recognition, but before he could speak, she deliberately turned back to her work.

So much for warm reunions, Jack thought. But what did he expect? As far as she was concerned, he'd shown himself to be the lowest life form ever to inhabit the earth. She'd never allowed him to explain. He understood why she hated him. He decided to say nothing. Chicken. No, he assured himself, only a brave man would have chosen to take this seat--or a man set on self-torment.

After take-off, someone doused his head with Coca-Cola. "Son-of-a- . . ." Jack exclaimed! He shot a look upward to see a woman giggling, her hand over her mouth. Standing behind him, talking to friends, she had spilled her drink.

Katherine was drenched as well.

"She got you too?" Jack asked, unbuckling his seat belt.

"I'd say so. Damn! My computer."

Jack pressed the overhead button for service. "Here let me help. I'll hold your computer, and you can wipe off the tray with this." Jack handed her a drink napkin. They both looked at the four-inch square tissue.

"Somehow I don't think it's quite adequate." Katherine laughed.

"I'm impressed by your ability to concentrate through all this noise," Jack said, holding her computer aloft as she did her best to blot the liquid on her tray.

"I was just getting some odds and ends done, nothing that requires much brain power."

"It's good to see you."

"Let's leave it at that."

They dried everything off as best as possible.

"We need to talk," Jack said.

"No," Katherine clarified. "You may need to talk, but I already know more about you and your methods than I care to know."

"At least let me explain."

Katherine pressed the light for service.

"What are you doing?"

"If you won't leave me alone, I'm moving."

Jack switched off the light. "Fine, have it your way."

Katherine glared at him, then she returned her attention to her computer.

Damn, Jack thought, she had it all wrong. And her stubborn streak refused to let him explain. Katherine still believed he'd sold her out in a story about her trapping a German spy who was breaking into government computers. Even though she was never mentioned by name in the article, she'd lost her security clearance and her job. She held Jack responsible for the damage to her professional reputation.

The plane landed at La Guardia. Jack turned to Katherine. "It's been good to see you." They hadn't spoken in two hours. *He felt badly. If she'd just let him explain.*

She gave a curt nod.

An expert at emotional shutdown, he surgically cut Katherine from his thoughts as he rode to his hotel in the cab. He pulled out his notebook, reviewing his notes. The delegates from Missouri and most of the Midwestern states, as well as the candidate himself, were staying at the Inter-Continental, as was he.

Jack registered, then grabbed a shuttle over to Madison Square Garden where the actual convention was being held. He noted that the usual propaganda was in full swing. Reading a program, he reviewed the schedule of appearances. Day one was packed with speeches from Kate Mills, Governor of Texas; Joseph Shiripa, Governor of New York; and Cork Mackney, Governor of California. The second day would feature speeches from various high profile activists, including Carolyn Lane. And the last day would end with Warner's acceptance speech. *Strange, Mort Fields's name wasn't on the schedule.*

Jack turned away from the stage and battled his way through the crowd. In the lobby he stood studying the faces and gauging the energetic atmosphere. T-shirts, banners, hats, and buttons all proclaimed Warner Lane for President or boasted the pride of a home state.

He spotted Katherine across the hallway, then lost her briefly in the crowd. Why was she here? Jack wondered. Computers were her life, not politics. He ran after her. "Hi, did you ever dry off?"

"You just don't give up, do you?"

"Not when I'm right."

"Right and wrong are often a matter of perspective."

"My point, exactly."

Katherine looked surprised.

"Come on, Kate. Give me a few minutes, only a few. If you don't like what I have to say, you can leave. No one will stop you. Hell, I'll even buy you a sandwich."

Katherine wavered.

Jack pushed. "Look at these lines." He gestured toward the herds of people at the concession stands. "You'll starve to death if you stay here. I'm going to head out for a bite. Come with me."

"I thought I'd just give up all together," she admitted as she laughed. "I don't feel comfortable enough in New York to venture too far from the hotel or the convention floor. It was enough of a trauma just to get here."

Jack felt immense relief. He'd forgotten how much he liked the way she laughed. "Let's go. I know the perfect place."

Jack led her out of Madison Square Garden and two blocks down to a deli, where they sat at a table in the corner.

"So what brings you to the convention?" Jack asked.

"I'm here to--"

"What can I get ya?" interrupted a waitress.

"If you'll allow me, I know you won't be disappointed," Jack offered.

Katherine smiled at his attempt at chivalry. "Thank you."

"Two pastramis on rye."

Katherine laughed. "You made ordering sound so serious."

Jack grinned. "Hey, in New York ordering pastrami *is* serious. It can be a religious experience." *God, he'd missed her.*

Katherine looked at him expectantly. How to start? he wondered. Just tell the truth. Focus.

"The notes were stolen," Jack blurted.

"What?"

"My notes. The ones on the espionage story. They were stolen."

"All this time, and that's the best you can do?" Anger flashed in Katherine's eyes.

"It's the truth."

"I--"

"You said you'd give me a chance. So, please, listen."

Katherine remained silent.

"If it had been up to me that story would not have broken until you consented. I would never do that to you. Shit, I wouldn't do that to anyone. Gregory White stole the notes out of my desk and broke the scoop as his own."

He could tell she didn't believe him.

"Think about it, Kate. If I wanted the story so bad that I'd risk our relationship, then why was my name *below* his on the byline? For that matter, why was his name on the byline at all?"

"I don't know," she whispered. "I've thought about that."

"It makes no sense. White launched his career with that story. My career was already established. I didn't need it. I've never needed to cheat to break an exclusive. I just hope you'll finally believe me." *Even if they never dated again, he didn't want her to think badly of him. She mattered; her opinion mattered.*

"I don't know." Katherine's eyes searched his face. "Give me some time. This pastrami smells delicious. Let's just enjoy lunch for now, okay?"

"Okay."

Jack and Katherine talked little once their meal arrived. She ate with gusto, Jack noted. She was unlike so many other women. Many of which, claimed that they were starved, and then only picked at a small salad. He'd decided long ago that this consistently inconsistent behavior was the eighth wonder of the world.

Finally, when the dishes were cleared, they sat in companionable silence, enjoying their coffee.

"Do you mind if I smoke?" Jack asked.

"Go ahead."

"Actually, I'm told that I don't really smoke. I tend to light them up, take a few drags and put them out. My friends tell me that I'm too impatient to even enjoy a cigarette."

"Just not happy unless you're going mach one with your hair on fire?"

He grinned. "How'd you guess?"

"Tigers don't change their stripes." Katherine glanced at her watch. "I'd better get back to work."

"Whom do you work for?"

"Carolyn Lane."

"Carolyn Lane!" *Holy shit.* "As in Mrs. Warner Lane?"

"Yes, I'm her aide in Jefferson City. We've been together for years now. She's also a good friend. Usually, I'm only involved in the behind the scenes aspect of campaigning. But after I'd finished up for her at the office, she asked me to come to New York to help. I think she was taking pity on my limited social life in Missouri. I've never been to New York before, let alone to one of these conventions. My father's spent time at them, but I never have."

Jack's mind spun. Katherine was Carolyn's friend? This was *not* good--not if he wanted to salvage their relationship.

"And, you're here to cover the convention," Katherine stated.

"Yes . . ." Jack hesitated. *Should he tell her about his investigation of the Lanes? No, he couldn't. She might think he was trying to get information from her. Not only would he forfeit any trust he'd regained, but he didn't know how she'd react. She might go directly to Carolyn.* "Just the usual political nonsense."

"How unlike you. No major stories on the horizon?"

Jack shrugged, his heart sinking.

The waitress approached with the bill. Jack paid it before they strolled back to Madison Square Garden. The minute they moved through the doors, they were caught up in the frantic pace.

"Have dinner with me?" Jack asked.

Katherine smiled. "You're pushing."

"Can't fault a guy for trying."

"All right."

"All right for dinner, or all right you won't fault me."

"All right for dinner."

Jack beamed. "I take it your staying at the Inter-Continental. After the last session tonight, I'll ring your room."

"Sounds good," she called out over her shoulder.

* * *

Jack escorted her to a late meal at an Italian restaurant on West Forty-Sixth Street. It was after midnight when they finally sat down, and they both were exhausted. They ordered, then sat drinking wine, only talking periodically.

"Did you hear about Mort Fields's accident?" Jack asked.

"Just horrible." Katherine shook her head. "The Lanes are very upset about it. They were friends."

"I'd heard he was once in business with Carolyn." *Was he actually pumping, Katherine for information? No, he was just making harmless conversation.*

"I didn't know that."

"I also heard that he was supposed to speak at the convention, but I didn't see him on the schedule."

"He was a last minute addition. His idea, actually."

"What was he speaking on?"

"Political contributions. Carolyn wasn't happy about it."

"Why not?"

"I'm not sure. He was supposed to speak right before her, maybe she thought he'd empty the house. I guess I shouldn't say that now-- respect for the dead and all that."

"There's nothing wrong with being honest."

Katherine sighed. "What a day. I am not used to all this political strategy---what you're supposed to do, what you're not supposed to do. It's mind-boggling. In fact, I think it's a genetic thing; you're either born with political instincts or you're not. It's kind of like being born athletic or not. I was definitely not born with a political gene. Even after all of these years of working with Carolyn, it's still foreign to me. I'm much better with a computer."

"Having that gene missing isn't a handicap; it's an advantage." Jack smiled. She had the most incredible green eyes. He felt like he could drown in them. He also wanted to hold her hand, but resisted the urge. Just then, their salads were served, and the moment passed.

They finished dinner at two a.m. and strolled back to the hotel. It looked like a casino, still packed with conventioneers, talking and partying as if it were early evening.

"Let's do this again tomorrow night."

"I'm sorry," she said. "I can't. There's an official dinner engagement. And unfortunately, the rest of my trip has been booked for me. Carolyn's schedule is very demanding, and I'm going to be working nonstop to keep up with her. I was lucky to get away for a few hours tonight."

"I guess this is good-bye then. I've really enjoyed seeing you again." Jack forced a laugh. "I'll miss your sanity in this crazy place."

She reached into her shoulder bag, and quickly wrote her home phone number on the back of her business card. "Call me if you're ever back in Jefferson City. I promise to take your call this time."

"I will." He reached into his pocket for his card. *Shit, where were his cards?* "I'll leave my number at the front desk for you. Call me if you ever come to Washington."

She leaned toward him and kissed his cheek. "Thanks for showing me a little bit of New York," she said, then turned and walked away.

He watched her slip into the crowd and vanish. *I should have told her about the story. Maybe she'd understand the obligation I feel to finish what my father started.*

Either way, a replay of the past hung on the horizon. The damage to their relationship would be irreversible if she found herself caught between her employer and his journalistic priorities. Yet, he had no idea of how to convince her that he didn't have ulterior motives. And until he did, he decided to keep his mouth shut.

Jack called her every day for the balance of the convention. Most of the time, he was only able to leave a message. On the last day he sent her flowers with a card telling her how nice it was to see her. Katherine called to thank him on his hotel voice mail.

The New York Times
August 16, 2000
LANE-YOUNG THE TICKET

* * *

Jack arrived back in Washington on the first airline shuttle of the morning. He tossed his luggage onto a chair in the sitting room of the two-room suite in the hotel he'd been calling home for the past few years, then placed a call to Pat Mead, his editor. Unable to get through, Jack left a message saying he was in town.

Jack booted his computer and logged onto the Internet. He quickly found the news stories regarding the plane crash that Erma had referenced. One article referred to Ron Spietzer's disagreements with Warner Lane regarding union busting. All four people on board the aircraft had been private pilots. A mechanical failure was listed as the cause of the crash. The case was closed.

A compelling story was forming, but what did it amount to? Jack couldn't prove anything yet, but Erma had given him plenty to question.

From a small plastic box that served as a filing cabinet Jack retrieved a file labeled: Rudly, Bill. The folder contained legal documents and one large envelope--the last communication his father had sent to him before his death. He read through the notes and documents again, most of which dealt with Carolyn Lane, Mortimer Fields, and Adam Miles. At the end of the notes the word *Council* was handwritten, but his father left no explanation of the group.

Jack reviewed the facts as he knew them on a separate sheet of paper, listing the players and their roles--Bill Rudly, Adam Miles, and Mort Fields. Adam and Mort had been members of the Council. Bill wasn't a member. Bill was in politics. Adam and Mort were businessmen. Bill regularly disagreed with the Lanes. Adam and Mort were initially friendly with Warner, Carolyn, and Edmund Lane. Adam had a disagreement with Edmund; Erma felt this had to do with Carolyn and some men from Washington. From the documents in his possession it appeared that Mort and Carolyn were in business together. Both Mort and Bill had disagreements with Carolyn. According to the documents, Adam Miles disapproved of Mort and Carolyn's partnership.

All of these men shared two common denominators. One, they were dead. And two, they'd had a conflict with the Lanes, specifically Carolyn Alden Lane. This is crazy, Jack thought. None of these deaths were suspicious, except possibly Fields's. But the police officer at the crash sight was confident it had been an accident. And what about the plane crash?

"Damn." Mort Fields was the link, and now he was dead. Frustration swept over him. He didn't want to let his father down. There had to be another way to unravel the truth.

He flipped his notepad to the list of questions he'd had for Mort and read through them. Tell me about your partnership with Carolyn? Why, specifically, did it end? Why'd you go to my father? Who's in the Council? What does the Council do? What's their agenda? The list went on and on.

Obviously, he needed to head back to Jefferson City. It would be easy to arrange another trip there after the convention. He smiled, his thoughts shifting to Katherine. He wanted, no, needed, to see her again.

Finally, at around four-fifteen in the afternoon, Jack received a return call from his editor. "Hey, Rudly, how ya doin'?"

"You want to explain your letter?" Jack asked. Pat Mead was the main reason why Jack had joined *Today*. Substantially older than Jack, he had taken Jack under his wing out in the field, when they'd both been foreign correspondents. Pat had left the trenches a few years earlier to become Special Projects Editor for *Today*. Shortly thereafter, he recruited Jack.

"I'm sorry for the formality. But the legal department is a stickler for employment files." Pat's voice was tight.

"I don't care about my employment file, and you know it. What I care about is the contents of that letter. My story on Lane's military service was accurate and the sources were verified. I had authentic medical and military records. So what gives?"

"You and I need to talk. Why don't you come into the office tomorrow morning, around nine?"

Jack clenched his jaw. "Spill it. I'm not waiting for tomorrow morning."

Pat paused. "The brass at the top aren't pleased with your style."

"What are you talking about? They *hired* me for my style. When I signed on, they specifically said that they needed more of my kind of reporting."

"Then you're more than they bargained for. Unfortunately I've been given the job of issuing you another warning. You've already had your hands slapped, and now this is getting serious. You need to back off, or you're going to see a drastic change in the type of assignments you receive. They've got you under contract, they can assign you to anything."

"You've got to be kidding." Jack's voice was a harsh whisper. Every muscle in his body tensed.

"I wish I were."

"And what exactly did I do to warrant this hog tying?"

"You were spotted on a fishing expedition in Missouri. You were warned before to watch your step where the Lanes were concerned."

Jack sat back in his chair, questions spinning in his mind. *How did Pat know he'd gone to Missouri? Neither he nor Maureen had spoken to the office since his trip. And why the backlash?* Finally, Jack responded, "This is outrageous, and you know it. I'm a reporter. Remember? Getting the story's my job. You, of all people, should know what I'm about. I can't believe you're going along with this."

"I know, I know. And I'm sorry. I'm not sure who the players are, but I can tell you that it came down from on high that you were to be cut off at the knees. It was all I could do to convince them you could be reeled in. The brass is about to ship your ass to Siberia. I don't want to lose you, Jack, you're the best I've got."

"Yeah, right, I'm the best you've got as long as I do as I'm told and only report what the magazine wants me to. That's the fattest line of bullshit I've ever heard. If you're going to tie my hands like this, then let me out of my contract--fire me."

"Come on, Jack. You're not being fair. You know I'm on your side here."

"If you're on my side, then talk the magazine into releasing me."

"You can't be serious. Take a few days to cool off, then we'll talk."

"I've never been more serious in my life. Let me out of my contract." Jack's voice was cool. He fumbled through his pocket for a cigarette.

"I'm sorry, but the magazine's not willing to do that." Pat's voice was clipped and hard. "If you want to quit, that's your business, but you won't be able to write for anyone else until the contract expires."

"Unbelievable." Jack snapped the pencil he was holding. "Quite an effective way to shut me down, isn't it? They tell me what I can write, or I can't write at all. And you support that? What happened to real journalism? And freedom of the press? What happened to Pat Mead? I never thought you'd ever sell out like this."

"All I can say is you've pissed off some powerful folks. And I'm doing my damnedest to save your career."

"Don't worry. I get the picture. And for now, I'll play ball." As if he had a choice, Jack thought. He'd just have to find a way around their rules.

"I'm glad you're being reasonable. You're my best correspondent, and I need you. You won't be sorry. I'll take good care of you. Let things cool down for a while. Next week I'm sending you to cover the end of the Washman campaign."

"Don't trust me near the Lane camp?"

"Very perceptive. But don't be a hero on this, okay? Stay the hell out of Missouri. Maybe later we can get you in there, but for now, just watch your back. It looks like you've made some nasty enemies."

"It's not the first time, and it won't be the last." Jack stared at the phone as he replaced the receiver. *Yes, he'd have to watch his back. Someone had used a lot of pressure to call him off, a very powerful someone. But who?*

From experience he knew that the more extreme the reaction, the bigger the story. If that theory held true, he was onto one of the largest stories of the decade. But how to handle it?

Jack had the resources to hire a battery of attorneys to deal with his employer and his contract, but a protracted legal battle was not the answer. His father had taught him that to right a wrong one should work within the system, not alienate himself from it. *No.* Jack shook his head, the choice was simple. *He'd fight his own battles.*

CHAPTER EIGHTEEN

August, 2000--Jefferson City, Missouri

"Who is Warner Lane?" President Washman asked. He stood among classroom desks, a flag hung in the background. "Is he a man we can trust with the welfare of our country? And the future of our children? His voting record in the Senate shows that he's cut spending on education, raised taxes, and invested in projects his own state didn't want. Does Warner Lane tell it like it is? Or does he tell you what you want to hear?"

Nick turned off the television. "This ad campaign is focused on Warner's first term, but the average voter won't know that. In a nutshell, he's hurting us. We've got to fight back hard. Washman can be beaten, but as the incumbent he's got the advantage."

The consultants, campaign managers, staff, Carolyn and Warner Lane, and Richard Young all sat in on the strategy session.

Nick stood with his hands resting on the back of the chair. "Andrea Walden feels strongly that Warner should appear on some of the top pop culture talk shows like 'Late Night' to appeal to the younger, more hip crowd. Other politicians have done it in the past with great success."

Andrea Walden, the media consultant, sat apart from the rest of the people gathered around the conference. Chain-smoking, she resembled an inscrutable chimney. "This afternoon we're filming the television spots with Warner, Richard, and Carolyn. We'll follow the same layout as the ads from the primaries, except this time Warner and Richard will be together, superimposed over Carolyn in the courtroom, for crime, industrial cleanup for the environment, etcetera."

Nick gestured across the table at Dave Willis, one of the campaign managers. "Dave believes that if we get back to basics and utilize a grass roots type of approach, we'll be viewed in sharp contrast to the ivory tower image of the Washman ticket."

"What do you have in mind?" Richard Young asked.

"Actually we want to revitalize an old method. A tour blitz with a hometown angle." Dave explained, "I've got it mapped out. We can do fifty cities in thirty days. We charter a few planes, take along the press, and we go out and meet the people. Face to face. Both you and Warner excel at this approach, so let's use it to our best advantage."

"What's the hometown angle?" Carolyn asked.

Nick smiled. "We fly into metropolitan areas, but drive out to the suburbs and throw big community picnics in the parks. The press will eat it up, no pun intended."

Carolyn laughed. "I can see that." She glanced down the length of the table, meeting Dave Willis's gaze. "Good job, Dave. This is an excellent vehicle for Warner's and Richard's styles."

"Let's not forget yours," Nick reminded her. "We're going to have you stumping with them."

"All right." Carolyn started making notes. "Why don't you get Braunson on the line, Nick? We'll want polls on everything. We need to know exactly what the American people want. Have him do the polls constantly, so we can adapt as the trends change. We'll review his data every day, and that will keep us up to date on what our positions should be. Matt, you'll want to call the Secret Service and notify them of our itinerary."

* * *

186

Without preamble or a fancy introduction, the hometown boy, Warner Hamilton Lane, strode onto a small stage in the town square of Medina, Ohio and greeted the masses like a rock star at a concert. "Good evening, Medina!"

A roar went up from the crowd, which was packed for a three-block radius.

Upturned faces carpeted Warner's field of vision. "I love this town--" he started, only to be interrupted by another roar. "Medina is an example of the United States at its best. A beautiful town full of hard working, law abiding citizens. Citizens who raise America's future leaders. I grew up in a town like this, a town where you could walk the streets at night without concern. But times have changed. Thieves, gangs, and drug dealers lurk in the shadows of America's finest communities. Well, I say enough! It's time to take back our neighborhoods. It's time to take back our lives--our freedom. And I'm ready to lead that fight!"

The crowd cheered.

Richard and his wife, Dixie, joined Warner on stage. Warner shook Richard's hand and hugged Dixie. Like a tag team member, Richard picked up the speech where Warner left off. "We must direct our energy to fight those who cut funding for our police forces, the programs for our youth, and those who cater to the underworld with soft prison sentences and lenient laws . . ."

Their remarks, which focused on their dream for America, their goals, and their plans for attaining them, continued for forty-five minutes. Technically the speech should have lasted thirty minutes, but breaks for applause and chanting stretched the time.

Then Warner joined in. "Now, please let me have the honor of introducing the real headliner for the evening. Our very own one woman war on drugs, my partner, my wife--Carolyn Alden Lane."

Carolyn walked onto the stage and the crowd went wild. Three minutes later, she was finally able to speak over the din. "Ladies and gentlemen," she said as she pointed at the crowd. "*You* are the heartbeat of America. *You* are the people who matter most. And *you* are why we are here today!"

Again the crowd began to cheer.

"We have a dream for a drug-free America, where children flourish, no one lives in fear or hunger, and families thrive. But as simple as this sounds, it's far more difficult to accomplish." Carolyn made eye contact with several people in the crowd below her. "The battle begins right here, in hometowns across America, where we come together to fight against drugs and crime. I've joined this battle, Warner has picked up the challenge, and we need you to finish the war. We can be victorious, we can hand America back to her law abiding citizens--but it starts with your vote!"

The crowd roared its approval and began chanting, "Lane in 2000."

Warner, Richard, and Dixie stepped forward. They linked hands with Carolyn and raised them high in the air.

* * *

October, 2000

"We've done it!" Stan Braunson stood in the doorway of their hotel room in Hutchinson, Kansas. "We've pulled ahead of Washman in the polls, and our numbers are growing."

A cheer went up in the room.

Richard Young pulled Carolyn aside. "I have to compliment you," he said as he took her hand. "Your war on drugs platform is our strongest asset." His eyes searched hers.

"Thank you," Carolyn said as she met his gaze. Now that she'd gotten to know him, she realized he wasn't at all as she had expected. Although he could be strong when necessary, she sensed a vulnerability in him, a sensitivity.

"You've got to have some of the highest approval ratings of any woman in American history," he said.

Carolyn blushed under his scrutiny. His compliment felt good.

He smiled as she blushed.

She'd never paid attention to his dimples before. He was handsome, she thought, and like Warner, the female constituency loved him.

He still held her hand in a warm but gentle grip. "I wasn't sure about our relationship in the beginning of the campaign," he continued. "But I hope we can be friends. I truly do admire you, and I think we make a great team."

Carolyn reached up and kissed his cheek. "We're already friends."
She heard a cork pop in the background.

"Champagne all around," Braunson said.

A shiver of excitement ran down Carolyn's spine. The pendulum had swung in their favor. They just needed to keep their balance and maintain momentum.

* * *

On election eve, the culmination of years of hard work ended. At eleven fifteen in the evening, activity eddied around campaign headquarters as the exhausted staff returned to Jefferson City to give one final push, then to watch Warner and Carolyn cast their votes the next morning.

"It's almost over," Matt said, slapping Nick on the shoulder. "I just want you to know, win, lose or draw, I've enjoyed working with you."

Nick extended his hand. "I'll only agree to a win, but the feeling is mutual."

"The polls are looking strong." Nick shrugged.

A phone rang in the background.

"That's mine." Nick rushed into his office. "Creed," he said, then a moment later, the color in his face drained. "You rotten son-of-a-bitch. You do that and I'll personally hunt you down and shoot you."

Matt turned when he heard the uncharacteristic fury in Nick's voice.

"You go public with that bunch of crap and I promise--and I mean *promise*--that you won't live to cash the check." Nick slammed his door shut, but his raised voice remained audible.

He emerged a short while later, his gray eyes cold. "Call Carolyn and tell her we've got a problem," he said to Matt. "Have her meet us in the Situation Room as soon as possible. You come too, Matt. Get Ernie and call Warner." Nick grabbed his car keys for the short drive to the Lane residence. "Son-of-a-bitch, it's eleven-thirty. Only a half an hour to Election Day. Why now?"

* * *

Carolyn arrived at the Situation Room last. Her face was washed clean and her hair was pulled back into a ponytail. She looked fresh, calm, exhilarated.

"What's going on? We're all supposed to be resting up for tomorrow."

"Nick received a phone call from a reporter who told him that Warner has an illegitimate child and that they're going public with the information in tomorrow's early edition," Matt said.

Warner paled. "That's not true."

Ernie grasped Warner's arm.

"You have a child?" Carolyn asked, her voice barely above a whisper.

"I swear it's not true."

"You bastard." She slapped him across the face. The smack reverberated through the room.

Warner touched the welt growing on his cheek. "Carolyn, I don't--"

She turned her back on his protests, afraid that if she even looked at him, she'd completely lose control. *They were so close she could smell the scent of Washington's cherry blossoms. Why now?* The words kept echoing through her mind. *After all of their hard work, why now?*

"Where's Richard?" she asked.

"We haven't called him," Matt said.

"He's part of this team," she said. "Get him on the line and update him."

Ernie moved into the hallway with his cell phone.

"The reporter told me that they know who the mother is and the child's name," Nick said. "They located them in St. Louis."

"But it's not true! She's lying--"

Carolyn spun to face Warner. "If you kept your dick in your pants this wouldn't be an issue. Do you have her phone number?"

Warner nodded.

She turned back to Nick. "Call her. Pay her off." Carolyn glared at Warner. "The poor woman probably needs the money. And make sure the child's well cared for."

Carolyn paused. "Then, get to the reporter. I don't care what you have to do or say, this cannot happen. An accusation like this will destroy us. If it comes out in the morning, we won't have time to react."

"The reporter didn't leave his name," Matt said. "We have no way of contacting him."

"What are you telling me? How could you not get his name?" Carolyn cried. *This can't be happening!*

"He refused to identify himself. I knew the Secret Service would have the line tapped, so I didn't worry about it."

"Call security. They can trace it," Carolyn said.

"We already did. It was a pay phone in St. Louis."

"That certainly narrows it down," Carolyn said, not caring that she sounded sarcastic.

"Not really. The reporter could be *from* anywhere."

"Think, damn it! Didn't he give you any clues?"

Warner rose. "I need a drink," he said to no one in particular. As he left the room he flipped open his mobile phone.

Carolyn registered his departure, but didn't follow him. First, she had to find a way to save them from the disaster that loomed over their campaign.

"Not one clue. I've gone over the whole conversation, but I didn't recognize his voice," Nick said. "He outlined his scoop. I went into some details of what would happen if he followed through, and then he hung up."

"I need to speak privately with Nick, so will you all excuse us for now?" Carolyn asked quietly.

A subdued group of advisors departed the room.

Less than twenty-four hours to victory. They had to stop this--no matter what. Carolyn took a deep breath and calmed herself. "Call Mark Dailey. You two coordinate the investigators. I want every one of them acting on this tonight, and I don't care what we have to do to stop this train wreck from happening. Now, please."

"I'll take care of it," Nick promised.

"I know you will," she said softly. "Make sure Richard is thoroughly briefed. He needs to know what's going on. He should have been called immediately."

"It was an oversight," Nick said.

"Don't let it happen again."

Nick nodded.

191

Warner made a confidential emergency call for help to Edmund. The resources of the Council reached far into the press. The source of the threat boiled down to a handful of major news organizations. The independent newspapers would be too small to make an impact before the electorate cast their ballots. After Cain's forces were deployed, there was nothing more anyone could do, except wait until the newspapers came out in the morning.

* * *

Each time zone meant big newspaper releases, starting with the East Coast. As soon as the latest edition arrived, Nick and Matt searched for the incriminating story. They found nothing. Finally, morning dawned in Missouri. None of them had slept. When the local papers came off the press, there still was no sign of the threatened exposé.

"Just a few more hours," Nick said. "Then we're in the clear."

Carolyn remained silent. *It seemed like an eternity.*

At seven-forty-five a.m., Carolyn appeared in a red Donna Karan dress, and Warner wore a dark gray, double-breasted Armani suit with a white shirt and a navy and red striped tie. Clasping hands, holding their heads high, confident smiles secure, they walked down their front porch steps and out to the limousine that would take them to their assigned polling place. They would be the first to cast their ballots in Missouri.

People lined the sidewalk, and camera strobes flashed as they left their car and strode over to the rope line for a few handshakes with other voters before walking into the building to vote. Carolyn walked a few steps behind Warner, bracing herself for possible questions.

* * *

The room was silent.

Nick replaced the receiver. "That's it."

Carolyn was the first to speak. "Are you sure?" She could barely breathe.

"Positive," he said. "Ohio put us over the top!"

"Oh, my God," Carolyn said. Tears filled in her eyes. "Oh, my God! We won! WARNER, WE WON!"

Everyone erupted into cheering and congratulations.

Warner leapt out of his chair, swept Carolyn into his arms, and twirled her around the room.

Richard Young grasped his wife's hand and simply smiled.

Associated Press
November 7, 2000
WARNER HAMILTON LANE, 44TH PRESIDENT

* * *

January, 2001

Warner took his place at the head of a walnut conference table in a meeting room at the Ritz Carlton in Washington, D.C. Assembled at the table with him were Carolyn, Matt Carson, Ernie Weiland, Nick Creed, and Richard Young. "The first area of business is getting together a short list for the cabinet," Warner announced. Weeks ago, he'd reviewed his selections with Edmund. With the markers they'd called in during the campaign, he had a list of favors to repay.

"I want to start promoting names in the press to build popularity and get these appointments accepted. Nick, start writing. Let's make a short list of each of the candidates for every position. We'll start with Secretary of State. My first recommendation would be Jack McPherson," Warner said. "Any other recommendations?"

"He's from Missouri, right?" Richard Young asked.

"Yes. He's an exec with Bounce Plastics, but he's had a lot of international experience."

"Still, I think Secretary of State should be a Washington insider."

"Thanks for your input," Warner said, deliberately cutting Young off. *Now that he was president, Richard needed to learn his place.* He continued on to the other Cabinet posts, then on to the White House staff.

"What about Mark Dailey?" Young asked. "I thought you were considering him for a Cabinet position."

Warner turned to him. "I said no such thing. Mark will be named as a White House advisor." *He didn't care if Mark was part of the Council. He wasn't going to be bullied by Richard.*

"I think there's a problem with that," Richard said.

"Listen to Richard, Warner," Carolyn said. "He's got the inside track."

"If I want your opinion, I'll ask for it." Warner said to her.

Carolyn glanced around the room. "Forgive me, but I thought this was a meeting, you know, a gathering where ideas are to be shared. So far, you've done nothing but shut Richard down."

Warner ignored her commentary. He felt presidential for the very first time. And he liked the feeling.

Carolyn stood to leave. "Obviously, I'm not needed here."

Richard Young glanced at her apologetically. "Warner, I'm concerned that none of these people know the inner workings of Washington," he said.

Warner crossed his arms over his chest. "Outsiders, with lower public profiles, will be less controversial. Strategically, we need to show a strong command, and having our selections questioned or opposed would indicate weakness. This is our safest and most powerful avenue. Besides, we've got Washington handled with you and Nick. You've both been on the Hill long enough. Not that I need to explain myself to you."

"Shouldn't *we* discuss these choices?" Richard asked with barely controlled anger.

"No," Warner replied. "I know what I want."

"I thought we'd work together on this."

"You thought wrong." Warner walked out, leaving the vice-president elect sitting at the table alone.

* * *

Anger flushed Richard's cheeks. He knew that Edmund had directed every name on the short list for cabinet appointments; most were his close allies. The interviews were going to be a formality. None of the selections were Richard's; he would have no power in the White House. He'd been well and truly fucked, and he hadn't even seen it coming.

He headed up to his suite, alone. He'd called in a multitude of favors to give Warner the presidency. And this was how he was repaid. Rage shook his body. Obviously, Warner intended to keep him on the outside.

He'd underestimated Warner, and this realization cut him to his core. He reflected on past conversations. Warner believed that citizens should be made more dependent on government. "This country is full of people who are not able to care for themselves," he had said. "They need a strong government to do it for them. The more dependent the people are, the more powerful the government."

At the time, Young had found the statement harmless. Now everything Warner said and did possessed a new perspective. Richard had always known that Edmund was power hungry, but Warner's ruthlessness stunned him. Clearly, his demeanor had veiled his true countenance from the public, and even his old friend.

Richard sat up abruptly. "Son of a bitch, I should be the President. This should have been my year." His stomach heaved, and he felt bile rise in his throat.

He realized, however, that they were on his turf now---this was Washington. But his options were limited. As much as he hated the realization that he'd been used, he couldn't blatantly oppose Warner. It would destroy their political party--possibly forever. By placing his cronies in the cabinet, Warner had effectively frozen Richard out. No doubt he was counting on that tactic for protection. Shit, Warner was smart. Or was this Edmund's strategy? Richard wondered. Regardless, they were underestimating him. He wouldn't tolerate their double-cross. They would pay. And they would pay dearly.

* * *

Vice President-elect Richard Young called Mark Dailey. "I've got some bad news. Warner bumped you out of a Cabinet post." *He'd fix Warner. He'd declared war on the wrong man.*

"Are you kidding me?" Mark's voice was filled with disappointment.

"I know, I know," Richard said in his friendliest tone. "I tried to get him to rethink it, but he was against the idea from the start. You'll be named as a White House advisor. I had to push hard just to get you that position. Carolyn was in on it, too."

"Carolyn? Carolyn cut my throat?"

"I know you thought you had her under your thumb, but she really stabbed you in the back, buddy. It was ugly." Richard knew Mark would never discover his lie. Divide and conquer, he thought.

"Son of a bitch," Mark hissed.

"They've already forgotten who their friends are," Richard said.

"Maybe they need a reminder." Mark hung up.

BOOK IV

THE FOURTH ESTATE

2001

.

CHAPTER NINETEEN

March 22, 2001

Pacific Rim Trade Conference, San Francisco, California

Mark Dailey sprawled in an upholstered chair, his long legs stretched in front of him, a crystal glass full of Glenlivet in his right hand. Through the walls of glass in his suite at the Mark Hopkins Hotel, he savored the glory of the San Francisco skyline. Fog threatened to blanket the city from the west, but remained a thick bank hovering over the Golden Gate Bridge.

All he could think of was Carolyn. He thought he could count on her, that she'd champion him for a Cabinet post in the White House. Shit, he'd been kissing her ass for years. He realized how foolish he'd been, how wrong. Her devotion was to Warner, and only Warner. She didn't even *know* her precious Warner, and what he was really capable of doing. Or rather, had done. Now, she'd sealed his fate with the new president by relegating him to a background position on the White House staff. The bitch.

He'd sold his soul for his career, and come up empty. Only now the country would suffer. What kind of man had he become? What kind of men were running the country? How could he have helped the

Council to create such a loathsome situation? Men were dead. Good men.

"Fuck it," Mark said aloud. "Fuck Carolyn. Fuck Warner and Edmund Lane, fuck all of them." And he knew just the man to do it. Mark looked at the telephone. Did he dare? The thought of calling Jack Rudly sobered him.

Mark stared at the phone, and the phone number he had written on a scrap of paper beside it. Rudly, like most of the press, was in town for the trade conference. It was now or never, Mark realized. He dialed.

A sleepy Jack Rudly answered, "Who is this?"

"What's deadlier to a country than war?" Mark asked.

"I don't do riddles," Jack snarled.

Mark blinked as the sound of a phone being slammed down jarred his alcohol-dulled senses.

"Son of a bitch." He dialed again.

Jack answered more quickly, "It's three a.m. Don't call me--"

"Does 202-555-1416 sound familiar?"

"Are you calling from the White House?"

"Very good, Mr. Rudly. You know a private White House telephone number."

"Who is this?"

"What do murder and the White House have in common?"

"Murder? That's a bit far-fetched, isn't it?"

"Only if I were making it up," Mark said.

"You got my attention by using a White House phone number," Jack said. "And that bought you about a minute of my time, but I don't take kindly to phone calls at three in the morning. Tell me who you are, or I'm hanging up."

"Your father would understand the morass I'm in."

"What does this have to do with my father?" Jack asked.

"An honorable man, your father. The last of the honorable politicians. A great senator. He would know what murder and the White House have in common."

"My father's dead."

"Shame, such a shame. He just wouldn't play, would he? And he paid the highest price." Mark looked toward the window. A light rain was now hitting the glass pane. "There are several good men who are dead."

"I don't know what you're talking about. My father died of a coronary. And I know he wasn't into games. So cut the crap."

"They're going to kill me now, especially now. It'll be headline news, just like him." A lump formed in Mark's throat. *Good men were dead. Maybe he deserved to die, too.* "Is he the reason you became a journalist?"

"I'm not into psychoanalysis at this hour of the night. Why don't--"

"Scotch is a man's drink, you know. Your father loved scotch, especially Glenlivet." Mark sipped his own.

"Tell me who's going to kill you."

"I know what I'm saying. You're talking to a dead man." Mark sighed. "We've deceived an entire nation, you know. Your father would never have done that. He's still a legend on the Hill."

"I don't do well on this topic," Jack replied. "Why'd you call me? And how'd you get my number?"

"I can get anybody's phone number. Whenever I want. It's one of the few benefits of the job."

"That's impressive. What's your job?"

"Not important," Mark said.

"I'll be back in Washington after the trade conference. Why don't you call me then?"

"I'm not on the Hill. I'm here in San Francisco, just like you."

"Where are you staying?"

"Trust me. You don't need to know my identity or my location."

"I think you've got the wrong guy." Jack's tone changed. "I'm interested in facts from credible sources, not some idea of a poor joke."

"This was a mistake," Mark whispered. "You make a lousy last option." His voice rose with agitation. "I thought you'd understand. You're his son, for God's sake! Didn't he teach you anything? He cared, he truly cared. How can you dishonor his memory like this? You assholes in the press are letting this happen."

"Fine," Jack answered sharply. "If this is so damned important, then meet with me."

"That's not possible. I'll be dead soon."

"You're alive now, meet me now."

"I don't believe that would be prudent."

"Then call the next guy on your list. Like my father, I'm not into games. Good night."

"Wait!" Mark pleaded. "You know the lookout on the north end of the Golden Gate Bridge?"

"I can find it."

"Thirty minutes." Mark paused. "Be careful, they're watching you. Try to stay alive, Jack Rudly. You've got a job to do. And revealing your father's murderer is only part of it." Mark heard Jack's sharp intake of breath, and continued. "You want to know how I know? I'm one of them. I helped. But I'm not helping anymore." Mark hung up.

He had rented his own vehicle at the airport, in order to maintain flexibility. He headed for the parking garage. No one noticed his progress. He wasn't important enough, he knew, for anyone to care.

* * *

The moon had long since disappeared in the fog. From where Jack stood, the Golden Gate Bridge should have been a glorious sight, but dense tendrils of mist obscured the looming structure, leaving only a milky whiteness in its place.

Jack leaned against his rental car. Three-thirty in the morning and thirty minutes since the phone call that had compelled him to the bridge. His father, murdered? My God, it made sense, it fit with his investigation, but just the thought caused him physical pain.

He peered up at the sky, noting that the stars were lost to the marine layer that shrouded everything above a couple hundred feet. He listened to the waves pounding the shore, and to the periodic moans of a distant foghorn.

Jack dug into the pocket of his worn leather jacket and retrieved his pack of cigarettes. Strange city. Desolate place. Probably not one of his brighter moves.

He sucked on his cigarette. The tip glowed orange-red in the murky darkness. The air grew still, eerie and oppressive. He shivered in the dampness and turned to get back inside his car. Headlights suddenly blinded him and a car came to a stop directly in front of him.

The car door opened, but the interior light did not go on. A tall figure exited the vehicle on the driver's side, then paused near the open door. He remained a vague silhouette behind the headlights. "State your name," he ordered.

Jack couldn't make out the man's features or what he was wearing. "Jack Rudly."

"Good of you to come. You'll understand if I ask you to remain where you are."

Jack recognized the voice from the telephone call. "It's damn cold out here. How about we go get a drink somewhere and talk?"

"I don't think so."

"Then at least tell me who you are." *Was this guy for real? God, he hoped so. He had to know the truth about his father.*

"Someday that will be evident, but for now you'll just have to trust me."

"It's almost four in the morning, and you obviously want to talk to me, but I can't trust a source if I don't know his identity." Jack wiped at his forehead as a drizzle began. It was hard to know whether it was really rain or just the moisture weeping from the dense fog.

The man chuckled. "There aren't any easy answers to this one, so you can take it or leave it. But I promise you, if you walk away now, you'll regret it. And so will a lot of other unsuspecting people."

Jack tossed the butt of his cigarette on the ground. "Tell me about my father. Or did you just mention his name to get my attention?"

"Use your head. Think, Mr. Rudly . . . murder and the presidency."

"I told you, I don't like riddles."

"Sure you do. You're a journalist."

"I'm out of here." Jack reached for his car door handle.

"Okay, okay, I'll give you a break," the man said quickly. "I know you went digging in Missouri during the campaign."

"How do you know that?" *This guy knew a lot. He was obviously connected to the power crowd, but how?*

"You're not the only one with contacts. Something was bothering you, Mr. Rudly, or you wouldn't have gone snooping around. You asked me why I picked you? Your background had something to do with it, but mainly I picked you because you weren't wrong. Listen to your gut. That something you were searching for is still there. And it started before the death of your father."

Jack's heart pounded. *Was this the break he'd been looking for?* "What does my father have to do with anything? And what's all this shit about murder? All I got in Missouri was a lot of conjecture and a handful of air. Nothing I could verify."

"You haven't looked in the right places. Neither did your father."

"You keep bringing up my father. Tell me how this involved him?"

"If I had all the answers, I wouldn't need you." An anguished note crept into the man's voice. "God, maybe this was a mistake. I've probably misjudged you. I shouldn't be doing this. I'm in too deep . . . it's too late. Fuck it. Never mind." The man got back into the driver's seat of the car.

"Please, wait." Jack stepped forward.

"Stop." A hand rose above the door.

Jack saw the outline of a gun. He extended his arms, palms turned outward. "Relax, man. You obviously thought I could help, but you're not giving me much to go on. What did you mean when you said the press was allowing this to happen?"

"Move back," the man ordered.

Jack quickly obliged.

The gun dangled loosely from the man's fingertips. "If the press doesn't report the truth, the people don't get the truth. Remember, we're only as far from becoming a dictatorship as the people we elect to represent us. Everything can be changed, and things are changing. The Council will see to that."

Council! Holy shit, he's connected to the Council. "Tell me about the Council."

The man laughed.

Jack inched forward. "Who's involved?"

"We both know who I'm talking about. I've been instrumental in allowing this to happen. Good men are dead, I should have stopped it. But I was afraid, so I pretended I didn't know. God have mercy on me." He paused. "You'll know me, Jack Rudly. One day my identity will be made perfectly clear. Just watch the front pages. The article will be like the one about your father."

Jack stiffened. *Your father was murdered. You've suspected this for some time now. You just couldn't admit it. It hurt too much.* "Why was he killed?"

"Your father liked to talk; he said a lot of things that weren't appreciated." He exhaled unsteadily.

"How about Fields and Miles? Were they murdered too?"

"You're on the right track. But I've stayed too long." The man held up an envelope, then placed it on the ground. "I'm leaving this. After I leave you can get it. But think about it before you accept this, because this note will pull you in. And once you're in, you'll either bring them down or you'll die trying."

Jack watched him drive off, then picked up the envelope and opened it. Inside was a cassette tape and one sheet of paper. Written on it was: *Cleopatra1600.com; password: Caesar.*

CHAPTER TWENTY

March 23, 2001---Jefferson City, Missouri

Jack threw his luggage on the bed and glanced at his watch: 4:10 p.m. "Shit, the day is shot." He strode into the bathroom. He would have been in Jefferson City hours earlier, but his departure from San Francisco had been delayed by dense fog. He knew he was lucky to have gotten a flight at all.

Jack filled a glass with tap water and took a sip. He stared into the mirror and the blue eyes he'd inherited from his father. Pain caught in his throat. *His father had been murdered. He should have known. It made perfect sense. How could he have ignored the obvious for so long?* Guilt weighted his heart. He'd failed to see the truth from the beginning. He'd failed his father.

He walked back into the bedroom, sat on the bed, and re-read the e-mail he'd accessed by using the password the unknown man at the bridge had given him.

Winston,

Professional as always. Payment can be obtained through the usual source. C

"C", Jack thought, stood for either Cleopatra or Carolyn, or they were one in the same. He stared at the note as if it could provide an answer. He pulled out his recorder and replayed the tape.

A woman's voice filled the room. "It's time to collect the last payment from Mort. He's going to be sorry he pulled his support." There was a pause. "Once we have that money, we don't need him anymore. I'm going to need the funds for a special project I want you to set up. If there's a way to delay paying taxes, that's the route we need to take. Pull strings if you have to."

"What's this project you're talking about? Is it for the campaign?" A man responded.

"Of course it's for the campaign," she said. "Remember the firm we used for Rudly and Fields?"

This question jolted Jack. Did she mean himself, or his father? he wondered.

"Sure," the man said.

"It's time to set up a permanent staff to investigate possible candidates for the nomination. After that's accomplished, the investigative staff will come in handy for the big campaign, in order to gather ammunition against President Washman and any of his advocates. I want you to set it up."

"You need to be careful about this. It could ruin Warner if anyone found out."

"Which is why I trust you to handle everything for us. I want the best. Contact Winston Cain again."

Jack hit the pause button. He could swear the woman's voice was Carolyn's. Her male counterpart sounded like that of the man he'd met at the bridge. Jack realized that the tape proved nothing, but if, in fact, the voice was Carolyn's it tied her to Cain. And it certainly added fuel to his questions. He pressed play, and the tape resumed.

"He can get us ex-FBI and ex-CIA agents. We'll need a lot of money to pay for the best, but I want them on retainer for us, and strictly us," she said.

"Of course, but . . ."

"No buts. Start right away. Call me if you have any problems. By the way, I've set up a private meeting room on the Internet. Here's the address."

Jack heard the rustle of paper.

"The password is Caesar. Make sure Winston Cain has it, but no one else. Either of you can leave me a message anytime, I check it frequently."

The tape ended.

He knew that the recording was meant to tie the woman's voice to the e-mail address. Proof, Jack thought, he needed proof.

He pulled a notepad out of his pocket and reached for the phone to call Maureen. A crumpled business card fluttered to the floor. He retrieved it, then turned it over, recognizing Katherine Seal's writing and phone number. On impulse he dialed her work number, but the line was busy. Disappointed, he hung up, then dialed Maureen.

She answered immediately. "Jack, where are you?"

"Missouri."

"I thought so. Pat Mead called. He told me you left the trade conference early, and he wasn't happy about it."

"I'm sure he wasn't." Jack reached for his pack of cigarettes, brought a smoke to his lips, and lit it.

"You don't sound like yourself. What's going on?"

Jack took a drag off his cigarette, then said, "I can't get into that right now, but I'll take care of Mead." He stood, taking the phone with him. He pulled the wall-cord out to its full length, and began prowling the room like a caged cat.

"I hope you know what you're doing, because Pat is going to be furious."

"Don't worry about it. I know what I'm doing." He walked back to the nightstand, replaced the receiver, and resumed pacing.

Son of a bitch, Jack thought, he was sick of being on a short leash. In fact, he wasn't used to any kind of a leash. Every other news organization he'd ever worked for loved his independent drive and lust for a scoop. They encouraged--shit--*congratulated* his go-anywhere, do-anything style, touting him as an investigative hound who didn't stop digging until he'd uncovered every bone.

Now, he found himself spending almost as much time finding a way around his employers as he did following the leads. What a mess, he thought. He hated having to sneak around, but the damned contract had him by the balls, a contract that he'd never imagined could be used to keep him from publishing his material.

Frustrated, Jack sat back down on the bed and stabbed out his cigarette in the ashtray. He wasn't giving in. Not now, not ever. He had too many questions, and he was determined to find the answers.

Jack's glance fell on the business card with Katherine's phone number. He dialed her number again and smiled when he heard her answer.

"What brings you to Missouri?" Katherine asked.

"Let's have dinner and I'll tell you all about it. I know it's last minute, but does tonight work?"

She hesitated. "All right."

Later that evening, Jack followed the directions she gave him into an older, well-developed neighborhood. Large oak trees lined the streets and towered over manicured lawns. He pulled up to a little yellow house with white trim. "The perfect neighborhood," Jack mumbled to himself, walking to the door and ringing the bell.

Jack's breath caught when she answered. Her curly auburn hair cascaded over her shoulders. And her incredibly green eyes left him speechless.

She stepped back from the door. "Come in."

He struggled to recover.

At his hesitation, she continued, "I'm not sure this is such a good idea. I mean with our past history and all, maybe it would be best if we just left things as they are."

Jack stepped over the threshold, realizing that she'd misunderstood his reaction. "No, no, it's just . . . You look beautiful."

She blushed and turned to get her coat.

They walked to an old world Italian restaurant not far from her neighborhood. Katherine looked up at the sky. "What an incredible night. I bet I could count a thousand stars if I tried."

"I'm sure you could, but that'd take awhile and I'm too hungry to wait."

"Obviously a romantic, through and through." She punched his arm, and he faked the pain.

Puffs of breath appeared in the air as they talked. Jack jogged ahead and held the door of the restaurant open.

Handsome, Katherine thought, in a rugged sort of way. He wore a fine, navy wool sweater over a white turtleneck, jeans, and a leather bomber jacket that was well worn and stylish. She remembered his

209

jacket, a faithful garment he'd relied on for years. It suited his personality, warm and durable.

As Katherine stepped through the entryway, she skidded across a spot of ice. Jack reached out and pulled her to him. She looked up to say thank you, but instead met his lips in a tender kiss.

The cold air whipped around them and gusted into the restaurant.

"I'm sorry, it just happened," he started to apologize. "I didn't mean to catch you off guard like that." His eyes searched hers.

Katherine smiled at him and touched his cheek. "It's okay."

"Please, please come in," the maitre d' said, grasping the door and struggling to close it against the wind.

Realizing that the other patrons were staring at them, Katherine felt her face turn pink for the second time that night. She stole a glance at Jack, who appeared completely nonplused.

"Table for two?" the maitre d' asked.

"Yes, please," Jack said, then waited for Katherine to step in front of him to follow the maitre d' to their table.

Throughout dinner they talked nonstop about where their lives had taken them over the years, both careful not to broach the incident which had caused Katherine to change careers.

"So, tell me, Jack, what brings you back to Missouri? Do you still have family here?" Katherine asked, then took a sip of her decaffeinated coffee.

Looking pensive, Jack skipped her first question. "No, my dad was the last of my family." The mention of his father brought to mind his real reasons for being in Missouri, reasons he didn't believe he could share with her just yet.

"You miss him, don't you?"   ·

He met her gaze, then said, "Terribly."

She reached across the table and placed her hand over the top of his. "I'm sorry."

Jack smiled and turned his palm upward in order to clasp her hand. "It's okay. He's been gone awhile now. I just haven't gotten used to the idea."

Katherine nodded in understanding.

The waiter arrived with the check. Jack quickly paid, thankful for the interruption.

An undercurrent of attraction flowed between them as they started back out into the night. The temperature had dropped, so they alternated between a brisk walk and a light jog as they hurried toward her home. They linked arms, trying to keep warm. The trip took fifteen minutes, and their teeth were chattering when they finally entered her front door.

After shedding their jackets, Jack started a fire while Katherine went to make hot chocolate.

Five minutes later, she returned to the cozy living room with two mugs of hot chocolate. He watched her as she pulled out two coasters and set the mugs down.

Jack sat on the couch, took her hands in his, and pulled her down next to him. "I've missed you."

"Me, too." Katherine stared at the floor, her hair falling forward around her face. "I'm sorry I didn't let you explain about the news story when it happened. I assumed the worst, and destroyed our relationship in the process."

He lifted her chin. "You couldn't have known. It wasn't your fault." His eyes searched hers. *He loved her, had always loved her, but the words felt stuck in his throat.*

With her fingertips, she straightened an unruly lock of hair that fell across his forehead. "Can we start over?"

He answered by pulling her into his embrace, meeting her lips in a kiss.

The fire burned low and flickered warm shadows against the walls. He continued to kiss her, and she began to unbutton his shirt.

He lifted his mouth from hers and gazed into her eyes. "I don't want to rush you. We don't have to do this."

"I've missed you, too," she said softly.

"I know." His voice was husky with desire.

She raised her lips to his, wrapping her arms around his neck and pulling him to her. Tenderly and slowly, they explored each other, making love in front of the fire and then moving to her bed when the hour grew late.

The next morning Jack woke to the smell of coffee and fresh cinnamon rolls.

"I hope you're hungry, because this batch of rolls just kept growing. I must have fifteen here." She walked into the bedroom carrying a platter. "Hey, you never did tell me what brought you back to Missouri." She sat on the bed, set the tray aside, and kissed him.

Jack rose up on one elbow. "Well, I came to look into some matters."

"What type of matters?"

Jack took her hand. He could hear his own heart beating. "I believe my father was murdered."

"My God, Jack, that's horrible. I'm so sorry. Why would anyone want to kill your father?"

"I believe it was politically motivated."

"How awful." Katherine shook her head. "It doesn't make any sense. Your father was one of the most well-liked and respected men in the state."

"It appears that someone didn't like him."

"Do you have any ideas who?"

He looked into her eyes. "The Lanes."

"What?" Katherine pulled her hand from his, as if his touch scorched her. "The Lanes? So, that's why you're here. How stupid could I have been? I trusted you. My God, I slept with you! And you're here to get information out of me. Again!" She tried to jump off the bed, but he restrained her.

"No, no, I'm not. Damn it, listen to me." He tried to hang onto her, but she pulled away. The rolls scattered across the floor.

She darted across the room, her eyes snapping with anger. "You must have thought you'd hit the jackpot, at the convention, when you found out I worked for Carolyn."

"It's not like that."

"Don't insult my intelligence. You fooled me once, so you figured I was good for another go. I want you to get out"--she pointed toward the door--"this could cost me my career. Another career."

In one fluid motion, he stood before her. "Kate, please." He placed one hand under her chin, trying to make her look at him. "I don't want anything like that from you. That's not why I'm here with you. Please, believe me."

"Just leave, Jack." Katherine turned and walked out of the room as the tears spilled down her cheeks.

She batted at her tears, went to the kitchen and poured herself a cup of coffee, then carried it to the living room. Don't get emotional, she told herself as she sat down on the couch. Be rational.

Katherine bit the side of her mouth to stop the crying. *How could she have been such a fool? Twice.* Be an adult, just end it. She bit harder, fighting the pain and humiliation that threatened to overcome her.

After dressing, Jack walked into the living room. Katherine huddled on the couch, and clutched a cup of coffee. Her hands began to shake, so she set her cup down.

"Kate, I, I . . . love you."

She held up her hand. "Don't even . . ."

"I would never use you. Please. You've got to believe me." He sat down next to her and grasped her shoulders, trying to turn her toward him, but she jerked free, surged to her feet, and stepped back.

She met his gaze, her own angry and accusing. "Then why didn't you tell me right away what you were here for? Why did you wait until after we'd slept together?" Her lashes glistened with tears.

"It just happened that way." He stood and approached her, his voice and eyes pleading. "It wasn't intentional. Please, believe me, I'm not lying to you." He caressed her cheek. "I wanted to tell you, but I was afraid of your reaction--this reaction."

She ducked away from his touch. "I don't buy your excuses, Jack. There were plenty of opportunities to tell me before we made love. What was the plan? Wine me, dine me, a little romance, and then I'd happily succumb to your charms. Maybe even become your inside source?"

"No! Katherine, please . . . ."

"Just go. Please." She stared at the floor. "I'm not interested in a replay of our sordid past."

Jack tried to hand his hotel telephone number to her, but she refused to accept it. When she turned away, he placed it on the table next to her and left.

CHAPTER TWENTY-ONE

March 24, 2001---Jefferson City, Missouri

Jack got into his rented Ford Taurus, and pounded the steering wheel with his fists.

"Boy, did you blow that one, Rudly." *But how to fix it? He didn't have a clue.*

Jack shook his head and started the car. He drove in circles for forty-five minutes. When he passed the same convenience store for the fourth time, he stopped to get his bearings.

"Damn it, Rudly, time to get with the program. You can't fix it with Katherine right now. So, move on." He needed a plan of action, he thought. He could no longer put off the inevitable. He'd come to Missouri for a reason. As painful as it was, he needed to focus on his father's death.

Mort Fields had died before he'd ever gotten to interview him, but maybe his staff would have some information on his partnership with Carolyn. It was worth a try, Jack decided as he pulled away from the curb.

Thirty minutes later, Jack parked in front of the Fields, Inc. office and got out of the car. With Mort no longer at the helm, a board of directors kept the company running. Jack walked into the elaborately decorated reception area that appeared to be deserted except for the multitude of fish that occupied a full-wall aquarium.

"Hello," Jack called.

"Be right with you," said a voice from the back. Finally, a stout woman, dressed in blue jeans and a T-shirt, appeared. She held out her hand as she approached Jack. "Please excuse the mess, but we're in the process of moving the offices. I'm Rachelle Watkins."

Jack shook her hand. "Jack Rudly, we've met before."

She smiled at him. "Yes, we have. And I should be angry at you."

Jack feigned ignorance. "Why? What did I do?"

"Does Sergeant Leonard Rand of the Jefferson City Fire Department ring any bells?"

Jack took a deep breath. This was just his luck. Of course he'd have to run into Mort's personal assistant, whom he'd tricked by using a false fire claim in order to get Field's phone number in New York. "I'm sorry, but it was urgent that I speak to Mr. Fields, and you were doing such a good job of screening my calls . . . anyway, do you forgive me?"

She shrugged her shoulders. "I don't think it matters much now."

He looked around. "Place looks empty."

"Well, since Mort's death the company has slowed to a crawl. It's just not the same without him, even though the board is doing their best. Mort was an incredible force and really kept things hopping. We're consolidating office space with another business."

"If you have a minute to talk, I'd really appreciate it. I never did get to speak to Mort."

"Sure. I don't know how much I can help, but I'm willing to try," Rachelle said.

"I understand that Mort and Carolyn Lane were in business together."

Rachelle looked at him, her smile fading. "You don't mess around, do you?"

"I'm not into wasting anyone's time," Jack replied.

"Well, there are certain things I wasn't privy to. Mr. Fields was a very private man, and certain aspects of the business were handled exclusively by him. What I can tell you is that we did receive a lot of phone calls from Mrs. Lane, but that could have been legal business. I believe he consulted her on several legal issues."

"But she was a county prosecutor, not a corporate lawyer. Doesn't seem logical, does it?" Jack asked.

Rachelle shook her head and said, "I have no idea. I wasn't a party to those calls. The only thing I know is that it became apparent that a strain in the relationship had developed when Mark Dailey started calling on her behalf."

"When did this happen?"

"I'm not sure, exactly. I think it was about the time Edmund Lane and Mort began spending a lot of time together. It coincided with a shake-up in the partnership. Mort was in a terrible mood for weeks. I would have been happy to look up the paperwork for you and tell you exact dates, but unfortunately I don't have it anymore."

"What do you mean?" Jack's heart skipped a beat.

"Well, the night Mort died, we also had a break-in. Oddest thing, they didn't take anything of value like paintings or state of the art business machines. Instead, they helped themselves to records, a bunch of files, and all of our computer disks that backed up the paper trail. Most of it pertained to the computer company."

"Did you tell the police?" Jack knew he looked shocked, but he couldn't help himself.

"Oh, sure. The minute I got to the office and saw that someone had broken in, I called them. It was before we knew about Mr. Fields. God, what a day." Her serious expression accentuated the lines around her eyes. "It was really amazing that the thieves got around Mr. Fields's security system. He was always a bit paranoid about security and had had an elaborate system installed. But whoever broke in marched right past it and never set off a single alarm. Boy, would that piss off Mort if he was still alive."

"What did the police say?" Jack asked.

"Well, they did quite a bit of investigating after they found Mr. Fields's body, but they determined the two events weren't linked since Mort's death was obviously an accident. The person most upset over the whole thing seemed to be Mark Dailey."

Jack frowned in confusion. "Mark Dailey?"

"Yeah, he came to do some investigating right after Mort was found. He kind of blew a gasket when he learned that files were missing. I never did understand why he wanted them. I guess it was just part of his job as a district attorney."

216

"Yeah," Jack responded absently, "I guess so."

Jack half-listened to Rachelle go on about how Mort loved his Porsche, and what a shame his death was, but his mind was occupied elsewhere. He finally excused himself and left. He wanted to know who had taken those files? Why they were so important? And why had Mark Dailey wanted them?

* * *

Later that night, Jack sat in his room and reread his notes. All of his documentation rotated around Carolyn Lane. Mark Dailey, however, was a new piece to the puzzle. Dailey had worked with Carolyn Lane in the county prosecutor's office for years and was now part of the White House staff.

Jack lay back on his bed and rubbed his eyes. Could Dailey have the answers? He glanced at his watch, which read midnight. He doubted that Dailey would talk to him. "You're not trying hard enough, Rudly." He rolled onto his stomach to continue studying his notes.

Where to go next? Jack wondered with a yawn. As he lay on his bed, he heard a light tapping on his hotel room door. At first, Jack thought he was imagining it and ignored the sound, but then he heard it again. Cautiously he stood. He silently slid to the door and checked the peephole. There in the late night shadows of the hallway stood Katherine.

Jack threw the door open.

"We need to talk," Katherine said, entering his room.

Jack stepped aside, afraid to crowd her, and not wanting to scare her away.

"I need to apologize."

"No, you don't."

She held up her hand. "Please, I need to finish. I'm moving to Washington to work with Carolyn, and I don't want to leave without clearing this up."

Jack nodded.

"I've been going over our time together, and I realized that you never once asked me about my job or Carolyn. I accepted your explanation of what happened before, and it's unfair for me to drag that up again. I know you have an impeccable reputation in journalism, and I believe that you've never had to lie, cheat, or steal to get a story. It's just that I got so stung the last time we were together that I lost it this morning. It was wrong of me to think the worst of you. I'm sorry. I believe that we can balance professional discretion with a personal life. So, what do you think? Can you forgive me?"

He pulled her to him. "Can I forgive *you*?" He put his hand under her chin, tilting her face upward and looking into her eyes. "It's *my* fault. I've been over this a million times in my mind, and I know I should have told you immediately. I'm the one who's sorry, Kate."

"Can we start over?"

Jack kissed her lips. "We already have."

They spent the night together in his room. It was a reunion that fed both of their hearts. Jack was the first to wake up, and he sat contemplating the news Katherine had given him. She was moving to Washington to work for Carolyn. He should have guessed that it was the natural next step for her. And he'd love having her in D.C., but he feared that his investigation would somehow compromise her safety. It appeared that she worked for some very dangerous people. Jack decided to broach the subject as Katherine awoke.

He nuzzled her neck, and she rolled over to kiss him. His intentions of speaking to her immediately about his concerns were good, but he found himself distracted as she snuggled close to him, kissed him passionately, and began stroking him.

After they made love, they enjoyed a hot shower together.

"Kate, are you sure you want to take this job in Washington?" Jack sat back on the bed, watching her brush her hair.

"Why would you ask such a question? You should be happy for me. Besides, I'll be closer to you." She met his gaze in the mirror and smiled.

"I know, but I doubt if your employer is going to be very happy about our relationship."

"Why would she mind? Carolyn and I are close friends. She knows she can trust me."

"I'd be careful about that," he cautioned. "Don't tell her about me right away, wait and get a feel for Washington first."

"You look so serious, Jack. What's wrong?"

218

He knew he couldn't accuse Carolyn of anything illegal without proof. It would only jeopardize his relationship with Katherine. "I just don't think Carolyn would be happy about you dating a journalist, particularly me."

"What do you mean?"

Jack told her about the meeting at the Golden Gate Bridge with the drunk.

"Jack, these people are my friends and you've got them all wrong," Katherine stated, turning to face him. "I can understand that having someone tell you that your father was murdered would upset you, but this doesn't make any sense. I'm sure the police investigated everything thoroughly. The guy you met in San Francisco was probably a disgruntled drunk with an overactive imagination. You probably know better than I do that the world is full of them."

"I also know the Lanes," she added, setting her hairbrush down. She walked over to him. "Carolyn is like the big sister I never had. She's a wonderful, caring person. I've worked with her for years, and yes, she's an intensely driven, very focused person, but that's only because she believes so strongly in what she's fighting for."

"Just be careful." Jack reached out and took her hand, pulling her into his lap. He could tell there was no changing Katherine's mind. "And for now, don't tell them about me. Not at first. I don't want our relationship to adversely affect your career."

"I think you're being overly protective." She kissed him. "But I won't say anything about our relationship if it'll make you happy. The bad news is that Carolyn expects me immediately, which means I leave the day after tomorrow, and I have a ton of packing to do."

Jack frowned. He loved having her in Missouri with him. "I guess I'll get more done with you in Washington, but I'm sure going to miss you." He kissed her nose.

The next two days with Katherine were frantic as he helped her pack and prepare to move. Most of her things she put into storage.

On the last morning, Jack drove Katherine to the airport. He held her tight and kissed her as she was about to board the plane. "I'll be back in Washington soon. Take care of yourself," he whispered. Jack felt a profound sense of loss, and he didn't understand why.

"Hurry," she said. "I like having you around." Katherine kissed him once more, then turned and, without looking back, boarded the plane.

* * *

Jack struggled to focus on the investigation, but Katherine's image intruded on his every thought. How could he have fallen so hard? he wondered, smiling as he walked to a nearby drugstore to buy more three-by-five index cards.

Not for the first time, he felt as if someone was watching him. Looking over his shoulder, he recognized a man he'd seen repeatedly. Jack scolded himself for being paranoid, and reasoned that Jefferson City was a small place with a population of about thirty-five thousand. It wasn't unusual to see the same people in the same neighborhoods.

Jack returned to his hotel room, knowing he was overdue to call Maureen. He'd now been out of touch with the magazine for over a week and knew there'd be hell to pay. Hopefully, they weren't being too tough on Maureen.

He placed the call from his room, and Maureen picked up immediately.

"Jack, why haven't you called?" Maureen asked.

"I'm sorry. I've been busy. Have you heard from the office?" Jack asked.

"Have I heard from the office? Are you kidding? They've been ringing my phone off the hook for the last three days. Pat is convinced you're in Missouri. I keep telling him I have no idea where you are and that you haven't called. He doesn't believe me, though."

"Did he say what was so urgent?"

"No, but he sounded very stressed." Maureen's voice took on a worrisome tone. "And the last phone call was rather unpleasant."

"What do you mean, 'unpleasant'?" Jack asked.

Maureen hesitated a moment before speaking, "He said you were . . . fired."

"Son of a bitch," Jack muttered. "Are they going to let me out of my contract?"

Maureen paused, then said, "I'm sorry, Jack. You know I don't know much about these things, but he did say that if you so much as tried to publish an article in a high school newspaper, they'd sue the shit out of you. Forgive my language, but that's what he said."

"Don't worry about it, Maureen. It'll all come out okay. And don't worry about your job. I'll cover you financially."

"I'm not worried about my job. I'm worried about you."

"I'll be fine. Just hang tight and I'll stay in touch." He replaced the receiver and stared out the window. The sun cast bright rays of light through the glass and warmed the room. He was definitely beginning to feel the heat, but it wasn't the kind of heat that came from the sun. He slammed his fist against the desk. He'd be damned, he decided, before he'd stop his search for the truth about his father's death.

Throughout history, Jack realized, politicians had tried to influence the press. The Kennedy administration had been very accomplished at manipulating the media, successfully keeping Jack's extramarital affairs far from the public eye. But this was different, he reflected. This situation brought to mind the Nixon White House and the intense pressure *The Washington Post* suffered during Bob Woodward and Carl Bernstein's pursuit of Watergate. The difference here, Jack thought as he laughed bitterly, was that *The Post* had stood behind Woodward and Bernstein.

Was he so far off base that the magazine was determined to sabotage him? No, Jack decided, the pressure was coming from higher sources than the magazine. His employers, or former employers, were just succumbing to pressure. The magazine had no idea of what he was really onto. In fact, even *he* wasn't sure about the true scope of this story. But somebody out there knew the stakes, and that somebody, or group of somebodies, was doing a hell of a job of trying to stop his investigation. The opposition alone was proof enough that he was onto a major scoop. Given the radical reaction he'd already evoked, Jack knew he must have been cutting too close to the truth.

Maybe he was just being paranoid, Jack thought, shaking his head. But the words of an old mentor reverberated in his mind--- "Just because you're paranoid, doesn't mean that they're not out to get you." It was his old friend's way of saying, watch your back.

Well, Jack thought, I'm watching my back, and it looks to me like someone has successfully stuck a knife in it. Knife or no knife, he didn't care. He wouldn't back off. He'd never backed off before, and he wasn't going to start now.

* * *

The next day, Jack drove over to the Cole County Courthouse. With Mark Dailey's White House position just recently confirmed, Jack knew that Dailey was probably in Washington, but he hoped to talk to someone about Mort Fields's death and the missing files.

Jack sat for over an hour on an uncomfortable, straight-backed chair in the lobby. When he had shifted his weight for the fifth time and finished thoroughly perusing the local newspaper, he rose and walked over to the receptionist's desk. "Could you please check to see when I might be able to speak to someone?"

The receptionist held up her index finger, signaling him to wait as she listened to her telephone headset. Then she dashed off a note in her message book before looking up at Jack. "Well, sweetie, if you want to make an appointment, you won't have to wait. But if you want to see Mr. Dailey, you're just going to have to be patient. He's only in town for a few hours today before flying out tonight, and with the amount of work he has to tie up before moving permanently to Washington, you'll just have to stand in line."

Jack looked at her in surprise. "Mark Dailey is here?"

Her brow furrowed. "Of course. That *is* who you're waiting for, isn't it?"

"Yes. I just wasn't sure that he'd be here." Jack sat back down with renewed enthusiasm. He'd wait all day to see Dailey. Jack couldn't help but smile. His luck seemed to be turning around.

Finally, a secretary appeared in the reception area and ushered him into a standard government office. "Mr. Dailey will be right with you," she said as she left Jack standing alone in the room. He walked around, examining the decor. Contemporary prints hung on the walls, alternating with diplomas and certificates of achievement. One of the commendations was from the Supreme Court. Jack remembered his father telling him about Mark Dailey's success with the case.

"How can I help you?"

Jack turned away from reading a plaque with a flash of recognition. *He knew that voice.*

"Nice art work," Jack stalled, pointing to a painting on the wall.

"My wife picked it out for me." Mark Dailey gestured to the seat across from him as he sat behind his desk.

Jack noticed the empty oak shelves, once full of books now crated in boxes that cluttered the floor. A bottle of Glenlivit scotch sat surrounded by highball glasses atop the credenza behind Mark Dailey. *Scotch. Oh my God, the bridge. He was the man from the bridge. The pieces fit.*

"Getting ready to move to Washington, I see." Jack took the seat across from Dailey's desk.

"Yes, and as I'm sure you can appreciate, I'm very short on time. So, how can I help you, Mr. Rudly?" Dailey blinked rapidly and clasped his hands in front of him.

Bingo, the way he rolled his r in Rudly was a dead give away. Dailey had been the man he'd met at the Golden Gate and, no doubt, the man on the tape. "I appreciate your agreeing to see me, although, I have to say I'm a bit surprised."

"My secretary told me that you wanted to discuss Mort Fields's death." Mark sat behind his desk.

Jack hesitated for a moment, determining the best course of action. *Stay cool. Relax.* "That's right. I also want to know more about my father's death."

Dailey blinked rapidly again and hesitated, then said quietly, "I don't know what you're talking about."

"Yes, you do. You called me in San Francisco and met me at the Golden Gate Bridge. I know it, and you know it. So, let's stop playing games. You wanted me involved. Now, I'm involved. I want answers." Jack slammed his hand down on Dailey's desk. "Who killed my father?" *So much for staying cool.* His body trembled with pent-up rage.

Dailey jumped to his feet. "I'm going to have to ask you to leave."

"Not until I get answers. If you're in danger I can help, but you have to tell me what's going on?" Jack stared into Dailey's eyes. He'd hit a chord, he could see it in Dailey's expression. The atmosphere crackled with the undercurrent of unspoken words.

"I'm very busy." Mark did not back down from Jack's stare.

"Let me help you." *Son of a bitch. Dailey had the answers. Jack knew he was right.*

Mark pressed the button on his intercom.

"Don't," Jack said, feeling Daily waver. "You came to me for a reason."

"Please call security. Mr. Rudly needs some assistance with his departure."

* * *

Mark reached for the bottle of scotch and poured himself a drink.

"Looks to me like you've got a bit of a problem."

Mark startled at the sound of Edmund Lane's voice. "How'd you get in here?"

"I'm Carolyn's father-in-law, remember? People know me around here. I come and go as I please." Edmund sat down, uninvited. "You know, I warned Mort Fields about playing two ends against the middle. But it seems he died before he learned that lesson."

Mark sat back and eyed the man. In the many years he'd known Edmund, his appearance had not changed. He couldn't remember Edmund ever looking young, yet he still did not look typically old. His thick, white-gray hair and cold blue eyes gave him a distinguished air, but it was his arrogance that made the energy around him sizzle. "Is that a threat, Edmund?" *How much of his conversation with Jack had Edmund overheard?*

Edmund laughed, then said, "Take it as you like. The Council doesn't forgive traitors."

"I would never betray the Council," Mark said. "I'm in this all the way, and you know it."

Edmund's eyes narrowed. "Is that so?"

Mark nodded, unsure of where Edmund was headed. If he'd heard Jack claim they'd met on the bridge, then Mark knew his days were numbered.

"Prove it. E-mail Cain through Carolyn's address. Jack Rudly needs to be eliminated."

Stunned, Mark stared at Edmund Lane, speechless.

Edmund walked around the desk and turned on Mark's computer. "Do it."

Mark swallowed hard, then began to type:

Cain-

Rudly's in Missouri.

Mark stopped typing.

"So, you met Rudly on the Golden Gate Bridge?" Edmund's tone was ominous. "It's either you or him. You decide."

Eliminate the problem.

C

Edmund nodded. "Wise choice." He turned and left with the same quiet menace as he had arrived.

CHAPTER TWENTY-TWO

April 2, 2001---Washington, D.C.

"Katherine, how wonderful to see you." Carolyn walked around her desk and gave Katherine a big hug. "I'm so glad you're here."

"It's exciting to be here," Katherine responded, smiling.

"Well, welcome," Carolyn said, hugging her again. "I've missed you terribly. The place just hasn't felt organized without your touch." Carolyn released her. "How do you like your new town home? I picked it out myself, you know."

Katherine beamed. "I love it. That was so nice of you, but you really didn't have to spend the time. I could have done it."

"Oh, nonsense, I enjoyed looking. It gave me a chance to see the neighborhoods in Washington. I found it amazing that those buildings were built in the late 1890s. And that street is so quaint and cozy. The minute I saw it, I knew it would be perfect for you. You can even walk to work, so you don't need to worry about having a car." Carolyn knew she was speaking quickly in her excitement, but she couldn't help herself.

"It *is* perfect, and I love it. Thanks, Carolyn--I mean, Mrs. Lane--" Katherine laughed nervously. "Now that we're standing in the White House, I'm not sure what to call you."

Carolyn smiled gently, then said, "Carolyn, please. My God, you're my closest friend. I know that these walls and this city can be intimidating, but I'm still me. Okay?"

"Of course, I'm sorry."

"Don't be. We both have to learn how to navigate these new waters. I wouldn't admit this to anyone but you, but there are times when I wonder what I'm doing here. Can I handle this immense responsibility? It feels very daunting." Carolyn lowered her voice conspiratorially. "So we'll just stick together. Deal?"

Katherine relaxed. "Deal."

"Why don't you take a seat, and we can talk about how we're going to handle this job." Carolyn shut the door behind her, then walked to her desk. "We have a large staff here, and you, Katherine, are going to help me run it. I consider you my right hand. The rest of the staff will report to Maggie Wyndon, my Chief of Staff, but you and I are going to work together as a team."

"Just like the old days."

"Of course." Carolyn grinned. "My war on drugs platform was so well received during the election, I've decided to make it my signature cause. You and I are going to write new legislation to attack the drug problem and reform the social services system. Warner's given it a rubber stamp, so my task force will have as much funding as we need to achieve our goals."

"My God, Carolyn, with the U.S. Treasury to back your platform, we can't lose. This is what you've always wanted." Katherine's eyes sparkled with excitement. "Can you believe we're actually here, in the White House, doing what you dreamt about?"

"You mean, 'what *we* dreamt about.' You and Warner were always a big part of this dream."

"How is Warner?"

Carolyn hesitated a moment, her smile fading. "He's fine. Great, actually." Her gaze met Katherine's.

"Is everything all right?" Katherine asked, concern etched in her features.

"Warner's a brilliant man who's going to do wonderful things for this country. I'm thankful to be a part of his legacy."

"But you want more."

Carolyn shrugged. "We always want what we can't have."

Katherine could see the pain in Carolyn's eyes. "I'm sorry."

"Oh, don't be. It's my own fault."

"I don't understand."

"Someday we'll talk, but not now." Carolyn waved her hand and forced a smile. "I certainly didn't mean to unload on you during your first day. I'm sorry."

"Just remember, I'm always here for you," Katherine offered.

"Thanks, that means a lot," she responded.

* * *

April 3, 2001--- Washington, D.C.

It was after midnight when Katherine returned to her townhouse. When she found no message from Jack on her answering machine, she called him at his hotel in Missouri, but he didn't answer. Odd, Katherine thought, hanging up. She took a quick shower and tried calling him again, still with no luck. Exhausted she dropped onto her bed, and fell sound asleep.

Morning came and Katherine awoke to the pre-dawn light. She made herself some coffee and picked up the phone. Glancing at the clock she realized that although it was 5:35 a.m. in Washington, it would only be 3:35 a.m. in Missouri. She hesitated, then dialed, knowing that her day at the White House would be busy, and this would be her only chance to talk to Jack. She let the phone ring ten times, then dialed back to the hotel operator to make sure she was connecting to the correct room. Still, there was no answer.

* * *

Carolyn rose from her desk when he entered. "I wondered if you'd come." She knew what he had come for. It was only a matter of time, or so she had hoped.

He wrapped her in an embrace. "I couldn't wait any longer," he searched her eyes. "Tell me you feel the same."

She nodded, unable to speak.

He kissed her neck. "God, you smell good," he whispered.

A small sigh escaped her lips. Throughout the campaign the tension between them had built, but neither had dared to act upon it. Now, the White House was theirs, and their privacy insured.

Without releasing her from his embrace, he took a moment to lock her office door.

"Are you sure about this?" he asked.

She wound her arms around his neck. "I've never been more sure about anything."

His lips covered hers.

She responded hungrily.

His hands traveled over her body, lingering, worshiping, then moving on until she grew breathless from desire.

Carolyn felt herself spiraling into a beautiful, warm light. A light she had longed to see and feel for far too many years.

Without breaking their kiss, he scooped her up and carried her to the couch opposite her desk. He gathered her into his arms as they lay together.

Gently, slowly he made love to her. Carolyn felt as if she would burst from joy as he used his hands and mouth to bring her pleasure again and again. She reached for him, wanting to reciprocate as she savored his tenderness, but he refused her.

"This is about you," he whispered. "Only you."

CHAPTER TWENTY-THREE

April 2, 2001---Jefferson City, Missouri

That night Jack put on his leather jacket, shoved a few bucks into his right pocket, grabbed his pack of cigarettes, and stuffed them into his left pocket. After turning off his laptop, he started out the door. Realizing his room key was still on the dresser, Jack backtracked. He retrieved the key and, remembering the package he wanted to mail to Maureen, picked it up and left the hotel room. He decided he'd head to the post office before going to the diner.

Jack, a creature of habit, ate supper every night at the same diner. The food was homemade, and the place was comfortable. He patted his pockets, checking for all of the necessary items as he exited the hotel.

The diner was a short walk from the hotel, but he headed to the post office first. Jack enjoyed the fresh air. He mailed his parcel and then backtracked to the diner. As he entered the place, Jack bumped into an exiting patron.

"I'm sorry," Jack said. The guy never looked up, just kept walking. That was weird, Jack thought, as he continued over to the counter.

Dismissing the encounter, Jack took a seat and read the menu. He always looked it over, although he never ordered anything but his standard cup of coffee and the house meatloaf special. Jack loved meatloaf with mashed potatoes and gravy, and he felt the diner did a fair job at preparing it.

Deciding to read the local newspaper, Jack got change from the waitress. He walked over to the newspaper dispenser, dropped in his quarter, and pulled one from the stack.

Jack began reading through the front section. Nothing earth shattering in the headlines today, he thought. His food arrived, and Jack enjoyed the warm meal. When he finished, he asked for a coffee refill and began to read another portion of the paper.

Jack reached into his pocket for his cigarettes, but they were gone. Damn, he thought, he must have dropped them when he'd bumped into the guy at the entrance to the diner. Jack walked to the door and looked around, inside and out.

"What'cha lookin' for?" asked a burly man who sat a few stools down from Jack at the counter.

Jack did a double take. It was the same man he'd seen numerous times on the street. "My cigarettes. I must have dropped them."

The man stood and walked over to Jack. "No matter, have one of mine." The man pulled out his pack of cigarettes. "What do ya smoke?"

"Usually Marlboros, but I'm not particular."

The man shook the pack until a tip appeared. "Your lucky day, guy. I smoke 'em too, help ya' self." He held out the pack to Jack, who took the tallest tip.

"Thanks, I appreciate it."

"No problem," the man said. He lit Jack's cigarette for him. They sat back down at the counter, and the man picked up his own newspaper and started reading.

Jack sipped his hot coffee. He took one drag off the cigarette and started to read the sports section. He took another drag, but it didn't taste very good. Even so, he initially ignored the acrid flavor. Then, very definitely aware that the smoke smelled odd, Jack stopped reading, put the cigarette to his lips, and inhaled again. This time he felt a slight tingling sensation in his mouth, so he put the cigarette out.

Why do I bother? Jack asked himself. *I must waste a small fortune on half-smoked cigarettes.* Jack looked around for the waitress. He needed a glass of water, but she wasn't there. Suddenly he felt dizzy. *Wow,* Jack thought, *I haven't gotten a buzz from smoking a cigarette since I was twelve.*

The walls started to spin. The room was going in and out of focus. Jack tried to rub his temples, but the movement threw him off balance, and he toppled over, landing on the floor. His throat felt swollen. He could barely breathe. *What was happening to him?* he wondered frantically.

He thought he called for help. No sound came from his mouth. Thoughts floated around inside his head, like pieces of confetti tossed in the air. *Where was he?* Confusion engulfed him as he struggled to focus and fought to remain conscious.

He saw Katherine and felt immediate relief. Katherine. He loved Katherine. She would help him. He called her name, but she didn't hear him. He tried again. She continued to ignore him. With every ounce of strength left in his body, Jack reached his hand out to touch her, but she vanished an instant before darkness engulfed him.

CHAPTER TWENTY-FOUR

April 4, 2001

Jack woke to consuming darkness. Wind whipped around him, freezing his naked frame. He lifted his throbbing head and spit blood. His stomach churned. He vomited. His entire body ached from injury and exposure. Jack struggled against the ropes that bound his wrists and ankles. Pain exploded like flashbulbs behind his eyelids.

Scraping the side of his body on rocks and underbrush, he inched over to a large oak tree and rubbed the rope that bound his wrists against an exposed root. He wore down much of the bark on the root as he slowly shredded the twine and the skin on his wrists.

His fingers, stiff from lack of circulation and the cold, touched his face and felt something crusty---dried blood. His right eye would barely open, and his cheek was swollen underneath.

He reached to untie his ankles, but his breath caught at the pain stabbing his ribs. He held still and took a shallow breath. Then another one. *Someone beat the crap out of me,* Jack thought in confusion. He laid back and carefully probed the damage to his ribs. *Shit, the last time I felt this bad was the day after that barroom brawl in Turkey, and the only thing that made that bearable was knowing the other guy had been hospitalized for weeks.* Jack laughed, but pain lanced through him like a knife blade, silencing him.

He licked his lips and tasted more blood. He was obviously in a game of hardball, and someone else had wielded a heavy bat. Jack strained, trying to recall what had happened. He knew he'd gone to the diner. After eating, he'd read the newspaper, then . . . he didn't know. The trail of his memory ended.

Jack heard an owl screech. *Where am I?* He inched himself up on his elbows, dead leaves and twigs snapping beneath the weight of his body. He tried to focus in the dark. He heard another shrill scream in the distance.

With each passing moment, Jack's thinking became clearer. His adrenaline started to flow. All his instincts told him to get the hell out of there. *But where was he?*

Jack's eyes adjusted to the darkness. A cloud moved past the sliver of illumination offered by the moon. Dense forest surrounded him.

He grimaced as he forced himself to a seated position. Jack's body felt heavy and weak, as if he'd been drugged. *Where the hell were his clothes?* He untied his ankles, then gingerly shifted to his knees. He straightened, trying to stand. *Oh, God.* Pain sliced through him. He wrapped his arms around his chest and curled into a ball. Tears welled in his eyes. *Not good, Rudly, not good.*

He knew he needed to get up and start walking.

The howl of coyotes floated on the sharp wind. Jack clenched his teeth and forced himself to his feet. A wave of dizziness rolled over him. He steadied himself against the tree. His arms and legs felt weak and rubbery.

Shit, this is not good. Jack looked around---he saw no sign of his shoes and clothing. *They dumped me in the middle of nowhere like a snack for ravenous animals.* He glanced up at the sky, trying to get his bearings. Clouds obscured the stars, making it impossible to determine his location or the direction he needed to pursue.

Was it before or after midnight? Maybe some time before dawn? Just get moving, and keep moving.

He hobbled forward. Jagged stones tore at the soles of his bare feet. His body throbbed from the beating. Leafless branches whipped at his arms and legs.

He peered through the darkness for a landmark. *Where the hell am I?* He could see nothing in the periodic flashes of moonlight, other than trees and shadows. His left eye was focusing better, but his right eye was almost swollen shut. The smell of rotting leaves and decaying underbrush assaulted his senses.

I bet I'm an attractive sight, he thought as he lightly touched his bruised face. *Boy, I must have really pissed someone off.* He'd obviously been beaten beyond unconsciousness? *Nice crowd.* He rubbed his hands together. His feet tingled in the aftermath of numbness. Jack rubbed his sides to warm himself, then flinched from the pain. He tried to increase his body temperature by jumping around, but his body wasn't up to being jarred that way. Jack looked back over his shoulder, hoping he wasn't traveling in circles.

He had no idea how long he walked, or how much ground he covered. He suddenly spotted a road. Jack approached cautiously, fearing that his captors might still be nearby.

Hearing a car in the distance, Jack ducked into a cluster of bushes. He prayed that poison ivy didn't bloom until late spring. Once the vehicle passed, he followed the road, staying in the brush and ready to dive into the low growing shrubs if necessary.

He had to find someone to help him, he realized. If he could find a home, he could wake up someone and ask for help.

At that thought he gave a short laugh. *Right, I just walk up to a door in the middle of the night, naked, with a bloody, distorted face, and ring the doorbell. I'm sure the residents will be delighted to assist me. In fact, when I tell them I'm Jack Rudly, they'll probably ask for my autograph.* Jack shook his head.

He needed to develop a feasible plan of action: first, establish his location; second, clothe himself; and third, get the hell out of there. Jack continued through the brush, branches smacking his face and arms, the cold accentuating his pain.

Jack stumbled upon an old gas station, closed for the night. There must be a way in there, he thought, longing for the warmth it could provide. The front doors were padlocked. Jack walked around to the back. He studied the rear door, which had the old push-button type lock.

He knew what he needed to do, although he couldn't summon much enthusiasm for the task. Damn, he wished he wasn't so sore.

Still, he didn't have much of a choice. Jack stepped back, held his breath, then threw his shoulder against the door. He gasped, clutching his side as he doubled over in agony.

"Shit, shit, fucking shit!"

Tears formed in his eyes. When the pain subsided, he looked up and watched the door swing open. Jack stepped over the threshold and ventured into what appeared to be the garage office. The warmth of the building provided him with instant relief. He sat on a chair and began rubbing his feet. He felt the urgent need to formulate a plan, and then move on.

Jack got up and began to explore. In the garage portion of the gas station, he found a blue work suit, stained with oil and grease, hanging on a door. He grabbed it and put it on. The suit was huge, but he felt immensely better with clothing over his entire body.

Jack continued to rummage around the shop. He didn't want to turn on any lights and risk drawing attention to himself if a car happened to pass by the station. Far in the back corner, among a pile of old tires and cans, lay a pair of rubber boots. They too were large, but at least they promised protection for his feet.

Jack walked into the office and sat at the desk. There was a telephone, but whom could he call? He assumed he was still in Missouri, but barely knew anyone anymore. Who could he trust?

Erma Miles. Wonderful Erma, the lady who had told him the story of the people killed in the plane crash. She lived alone. In his heart, he knew that she would help him. Jack dialed information, got her number, and called her. Even though it was the middle of the night, Erma sounded alert when she answered the phone.

After a quick hello, Jack described his location.

"You're just outside of Jerome, in the Mark Twain National Forest," Erma said. "I know where that gas station is, we used to vacation there."

"I'm really sorry to ask, but can you pick me up?"

"Sit tight and I'll be there as quickly as I can," she said. "You know, I told you to be careful. Doesn't sound like you listened."

"I'll tell you the whole story when I see you, but please hurry. I'll be waiting about a half-mile closer to town on the right-hand side of the road, hiding in the trees." Jack explained. "I can't risk staying put.

Someone may show up, and I'm not feeling real sociable right now. How long will it take you to get here?"

"About an hour this time of night. You just keep your head down, and I'll look for you. I'll be driving a yellow Ford Zephyr with an orange styrofoam, Union 76 ball on the antenna."

"I'll be watching for you," Jack replied, "and, Erma, thank you."

"Don't thank me until we get you out of there, it's bad luck."

"Okay, see you soon then." He hung up the phone and headed out the rear door, pushing in the lock as he left. He shook the handle of the door to be sure it was secured. The doorjamb was slightly cracked, but the lock held. There was no obvious reason for anyone to suspect he had stopped there.

Jack made his way down the road. About a half-mile from the garage, he hid in a cluster of bushes to wait for Erma.

The minutes crawled by. He shivered in the cold, the sound of the gusting wind his only companion. No cars passed by. He crossed his arms and leaned back against a tree.

What if Erma was being watched and now they'd caught her? What if--? Stop. He knew the late-night hours were a haven for paranoia and exaggeration. It hadn't been much more than an hour since he'd spoken to her. Besides, she was an old lady, and old ladies didn't drive fast.

At that moment, he heard the sound of a car engine.

He peered up over the large clump of bushes. It couldn't be Erma, he thought. The car was coming too fast, at least seventy. *Damn, they knew he'd gotten away.* He wondered if the thugs who'd drugged and beaten him were returning to make sure the animals had finished what they had started.

Jack ducked down, concealed behind branches thick with leaves as he observed the vehicle. The car slowed. The orange ball glowed on the antenna. Erma. He straightened up.

Erma rolled down the window, took one look at Jack, and just shook her head. "What a sight you are."

"This is an upgrade. You should have seen me before I found the gas station."

Erma chuckled, then leaned over to unlock and push open the passenger side car door. "We should get you out of here."

Jack climbed in and rolled the window back up.

"Buckle up." She stomped on the gas pedal as she spoke.

Jack grabbed the armrest as they tore off down the road. So much for the idea of the elderly being conservative drivers, Jack thought. Erma's foot reminded him of solid lead.

Erma drove Jack to her home and immediately sent him to the shower. She placed some of her deceased husband's clothing in the guest bedroom for Jack. "The clothes on the bed will be a little short, but they'll keep you decent," she shouted over the sound of the streaming water.

When he finished cleaning up and dressing, he walked down to the kitchen. Erma applied antibacterial ointment to the cuts on his face, arms, and feet. "You really should be seen by a doctor."

"Thanks, but I'm fine," Jack said. He could smell the aroma of her cooking.

"No, you're not. You've definitely got some broken ribs and probably a concussion. How many fingers am I holding up?" Erma raised her hand, extending two fingers.

Jack smiled feebly. One of his eyes was swollen shut, his head throbbed, and his vision, if not double, was certainly not very clear. "I appreciate your concern, but I don't think it would be wise for me to turn up in a hospital emergency room right now."

Erma frowned. "You're probably right. Whoever did this to you definitely didn't want you to be found. You're not the first person to disappear without a trace into the Missouri backwoods, and you're one of the few to survive the experience."

"I may have survived, but living to tell about traveling buck naked through the woods could have its downside."

"How do you mean?"

"Well, is poison ivy a problem this time of year?"

"I don't think so."

"Thank, God." Jack met Erma's gaze and they both laughed. Jack held his ribs in an attempt to lessen the pain.

"Time to feed you." Erma served him chicken with dumplings, followed by hot cocoa and the apple strudel that she'd made the day before.

"Erma," Jack said, "I'm in heaven. This is the most delicious food I think I've ever eaten. I feel like I'm at my grandmother's house.

You really didn't need to go to so much trouble. It was nice enough of you just to pick me up."

"Oh, don't be ridiculous, Jack," Erma said with a wave of her hand. "You look thin as a rail, and I won't be having anyone go hungry in my home."

While he ate, Jack explained what had happened, at least as much as he remembered.

"You've been through an ordeal, young man, and you should eat." Erma dished up more strudel.

He consumed the strudel with gusto, but his body throbbed with pain and ached for sleep.

"What day is it?" Jack asked, assuming it was Wednesday.

"Thursday morning," Erma told him.

He'd lost a day. That meant he must have been poisoned at the diner Monday evening. Jack put his fork down and stared at the wall. Either he'd eaten something, or the cigarette he'd bummed had been laced with a toxic substance. He reviewed the sequence of events and decided it must have been the cigarette.

Thank God, he hadn't finished the cigarette. If he'd smoked the whole thing, he'd probably be dead now. How stupid he'd been. He knew to be careful, but he hadn't paid attention, instead he'd been negligent.

"I have something for you," Erma said, walking into the living room.

"I couldn't eat another thing."

"It's not food. I was going through my husband's things and found these files. I don't know if they're important, so I thought I'd let you decide. I was going to send them to your office at the magazine." She lowered the box to a spot on the floor next to him.

"I'm glad you didn't. What's in them?" Jack slowly reached for the box.

"Oh, no, you don't." Erma pushed the box out of reach with her foot. "You get your rest first, then you can get into these."

Jack stood up from the table. He didn't feel much like arguing. "Can I use your phone? It's long distance, but I'll pay you back."

"Go right ahead and don't worry about it."

"I don't know how I'll ever repay you for all you've done, Erma."

"You can repay me by keeping your fanny out of trouble." She shook her finger at him.

Jack walked across the kitchen and gave her a hug. "Thank you, you saved my life."

Jack picked up the receiver of the wall phone. He was concerned about Katherine. He knew she would worry if she couldn't reach him. She might even try checking with the magazine if she thought he was in trouble. He needed to stop her. If they found out she was associated with him, she could be in grave danger. He didn't know the identity of the person who'd masterminded his abduction, but he didn't want to take any chances with Katherine.

He glanced at the clock on the stove. It was four o'clock in the morning in Missouri, five in Washington. When Katherine answered, she sounded wide-awake. "Kate, this is Jack."

"Where've you been? I was *so* worried. I haven't been able to reach you for days. Are you all right?"

"Yeah, I'm fine. I don't want to stay on the phone too long, so listen carefully."

"What's going on?"

"I don't want to discuss it on the phone." Jack decided not to take any chances. He didn't want to endanger Erma, either. "I'll see you very soon, but first I need you to do me a favor."

"Sure, name it."

"I mailed you a package Monday night. Did you get it?"

"No, not yet."

"You'll probably get it today or tomorrow. Katherine, it's a critical package, and what I just went through proves it. Please watch for it. When it arrives, I want you to take the tapes out of it and hide them. Would you do that for me?"

"Certainly. What's on them?"

"Important documentation." Jack was never so glad that he'd mailed off his work early. He still needed some of the tapes transcribed, and he'd debated whether to wait, because he also hoped to get additional interviews, but he'd finally decided to ship the package.

Unfortunately, he hadn't mailed the cassette he'd gotten from the man at the bridge. Damn, that recording was his only solid piece of evidence. He knew that going back to his hotel room for the tape would be a fool's errand. No doubt, it was history.

By now, whoever had tried to kill him would have gone through his room and taken everything. He'd bet that there wasn't a trace of him left in Missouri, except, of course, for his somewhat dented anatomy.

"I'll explain everything when I see you," Jack added. "Just know that I'm safe, and I'll be there soon. And, Katherine, do not under any circumstances tell anyone that you know me."

"Jack, this is crazy."

"I know." Jack paused. "Oh, and Kate."

"Yes?"

He turned away so that Erma couldn't hear him. "I love you." He noticed that the words were coming more easily.

"I love you, too. Please be careful."

"I will."

They hung up and Jack turned back to Erma.

"What are your plans?" Erma asked. "We need to get you someplace safe."

"I'll get a couple hours of sleep and then head out of Missouri."

"That's good---you need to get away from here quickly. If they realize you made it out of the woods alive, they'll be looking for you. But, for the time being, you'll be okay here."

"You're right. I'd better assume they know I'm alive--the airport is out."

"I've got an idea." Erma seemed to be enjoying this little game of espionage. "Tonight, when it's good and dark, we're going to dress you up with one of my wigs and send you off in my husband's old car. I drive it periodically to keep it running, and people will just think you're me. Tonight's my Bingo night, so if anyone recognizes the car, they'll see the gray hair and just think I've left Bingo early. Of course, you'll need to scrunch down a bit, since I'm not as tall as you are."

"Erma, you've done enough. I can't take your car."

"It's all right. You're just borrowing it, and someday you'll get it back to me. I don't need it anyway."

"You're incredibly generous, but I'm worried they may find out you helped me. I'd better not take the car."

"I'm not afraid of these people anymore, Jack. They can't do much to me now. I've lived my life, and I want to help you. I have a suspicion that you just might be able to expose these crooks, and if I can make a difference, I will. You take the car. I also have some money here at the house you can take. You shouldn't use credit cards. Those television movies always show people getting caught when they use their credit cards."

"Erma . . ."

She stopped him by holding up her hand. Erma obviously didn't intend to take no for an answer. "Now, you head off to bed and get some sleep."

* * *

Thirty-five minutes after midnight, on Friday morning, Jack crossed the Missouri state border and began to whistle. A slow smile spread across his face as he stripped off the disguise while still driving. Then he relaxed behind the wheel.

Traveling across the country through the night in a 1979 blue Impala was more enjoyable than Jack would have ever guessed. The large car allowed for plenty of legroom, and he could stretch out as he drove virtually straight through to Washington. Traffic was heavy on the Beltway for a Friday evening. Darkness had fallen by the time Jack pulled up to Katherine's new address in the seventeen hundred block of Swann Street.

Jack hobbled up to the front door, still sore from the beating and stiff from sitting so long. He rang the bell, praying she would be there. Jack hadn't told Katherine over the phone when she could expect him. Now, he wished he'd called her while on the road. But he'd been in such a hurry to get there, he'd stopped as infrequently as possible.

After a few minutes, Jack turned to walk back down the steps when the door finally opened. Katherine wore a short white terrycloth bathrobe, her hair dripping wet.

"Jack." She flew into his arms. "I thought I heard the doorbell, but I was in the shower."

He grimaced at the impact of her body against his, but ignored the pain. "So you always answer the door so scantily dressed?" he asked against her lips. Then he kissed her. "I missed you," Jack whispered and kissed her again.

"I missed you, too." She reached up to clasp his face between her hands. "Look at you. What happened?"

"Later." He led her inside, then closed and locked the door behind him. "I can't have the whole neighborhood gawking at this beautiful woman standing half naked for all of Washington to see."

Katherine looked down at herself and started to laugh. "Beautiful woman? I look like a drowned rat."

"A very beautiful drowned rat." Jack kissed her as he picked her up and carried her up the stairs to what he assumed would be the general location of the bedrooms. He walked into the largest one. He gently lay her on the bed.

"Jack, I have so many questions . . ."

He silenced her with another passionate kiss as her robe dropped away.

They made love and fell asleep in each other's arms, the first sound sleep for either of them in days. Jack awoke at five a.m. It amazed him that he slept so soundly when he was with Katherine. She seemed to be his cure for insomnia. He had never slept so well, not even with his wife.

He quietly got out of bed, then went down to the kitchen. Fifteen minutes later, he'd made coffee and a huge omelet to share with Katherine. As he walked back to the bedroom with his spoils on a tray, he heard her call his name.

"Jack?" Sleep still weighted her eyes.

He set the tray on the bed and carefully slipped in beside her, pulling the tray over his lap. As she sat up, he handed her a steaming cup of coffee.

"Good morning." He kissed her, and then he cut off a piece of omelet with his fork and placed the large bite into her mouth.

"Umm, I didn't know you could cook. Boy, did I hit the jackpot."

Jack laughed. "This is the extent of my culinary skills, I'm sorry to say."

"That's okay, I can live on omelets." Katherine took the fork and cut another piece.

Between bites of omelet and sips of coffee, Katherine asked Jack to explain the events that had taken place in Missouri. He told her what he remembered, blaming himself for not being more aware of what was going on around him. He didn't tell her what he couldn't prove---that Dailey was the man at the Golden Gate, and that he believed Carolyn was involved in illegal dealings that might include his father's death.

"Who did it, Jack?"

He shrugged. "I don't know. The last person I talked to was Mark Dailey, and you know the rest."

* * *

Richard crossed his legs and relaxed in the chair opposite the President's desk in the Oval Office. A fire burned in the fireplace, giving the room a soft glow. He stifled a yawn, and then glanced at the door, which remained closed. His watch read 8:26 p.m. Warner had scheduled this meeting for eight sharp, but, as usual, kept him cooling his heels.

The office door opened and Edmund Lane strolled into Richard's view. "Good evening, Richard. I'll try to keep this brief."

Surprised, Richard leaned forward. "What do you mean, you'll 'try to keep this brief'? My appointment is with Warner. What in the hell are you doing here?"

Edmund sat down behind the President's desk, opened the top drawer, and pulled out a pen and pad of paper. "Warner's running late. He asked me to get your recommendations for the Supreme Court."

Face flushed, Richard stood. "I'll come back when Warner can attend to his own appointments."

Edmund set the pen down with an amused expression playing across his features. "Richard, sit down."

The Vice President's eyes narrowed as his jaw clenched.

"I mean it, son. Your treading on very thin ice, and you're smart enough to know it. If you want any input into this administration, I recommend you show me some respect. Otherwise, you can walk out that door and kiss your political future goodbye." Edmund spread his hands wide. "Your choice. I really couldn't give a shit."

Richard hesitated. He wanted to scream, "FUCK YOU and your asshole son!" While he pummeled Edmund Lane's smug face.

Instead, he sucked in a deep breath, clamped down on his emotions, and returned to his chair.

"Now, about the Supreme Court," Edmund continued.

"Brandon Ross," Richard said.

Warner chose that moment to walk into the office. "Good choice, Richard. I see you've done your homework."

"He's the most qualified," Richard said, standing to shake the President's hand out of protocol rather than courtesy. "And the most moderate of any candidate for the post."

"I agree that he's qualified," Warner said. He looked at Edmund, then glanced back to Richard. "We're done here. I need a few moments with Edmund, and I'm late for another appointment."

Richard shook his head as he walked to the door. "I don't know why I bother."

"If you don't like it," Warner shot back. "I'll accept your resignation at any time."

* * *

Carolyn strolled through the White House residence toward her bedroom. Down the hall, she thought she heard a giggle. She turned and followed the sound.

Secret Service Agent, Martin Riggs, stood in front of Warner's bedroom door.

"I thought I heard someone laughing," Carolyn said to the agent.

The agent shifted on his feet, his expression pained.

Carolyn held up her hand. "Thank you for not lying to me." She took a step toward Warner's bedroom.

Riggs blocked her path. "I'm sorry, ma'am. But the President has requested his privacy."

She met the agent's gaze. "I don't care what he's requested. I'm still his wife."

"I'd rather you didn't, ma'am." Riggs searched her eyes. "For your own good."

Carolyn moved past the agent and flung open the door. Shock held her. She blinked, not wanting to believe the tableau before her.

Warner sat naked on the bed. A stunning blond paused in the midst of her striptease at the interruption, while a nude redhead continued to massage Warner's shoulders.

"What the fuck--" Warner said, turning to the door.

Carolyn thought she was ready for anything, but her vision swirled in a wave of dizziness at the sight of Warner's debauchery. "What's become of you, Warner?"

He laughed. "I'd have invited you, Carolyn, but this just didn't seem like your style."

Agent Riggs caught Carolyn by the elbow as her knees buckled. He guided her out of the room, holding her steady until she whispered, "Thank you."

"I'm sorry, ma'am."

She squared her shoulders a moment later and walked away with all the dignity she possessed. And as she walked, she vowed to repay Warner for the humiliation he obviously enjoyed dispensing.

CHAPTER TWENTY-FIVE

April 9, 2001---Washington, D.C

Jack spent most of the weekend in bed, sleeping and healing. On Monday, Katherine reluctantly left him to go to work. Jack dragged himself out to Erma's car and unloaded the box of files she had given him from her husband's office.

Sitting at the kitchen table in Katherine's town home, Jack reviewed file upon file. He grew increasingly frustrated when nothing regarding the Council was mentioned. He was about to quit when he noticed a small book hidden beneath the folds of the bottom of the cardboard box. At first glance, it appeared to be some sort of journal.

Jack skimmed the meticulous written pages. Apparently, Adam Miles had begun this journal six months before his death. He had logged daily events. Jack smiled when he read funny anecdotes about Erma. Jack doubted whether Erma had read any of this. He knew she hadn't been able to bring herself to dispose of Adam's clothing, and he doubted that she'd delved into his records.

Adam revealed a great deal about his businesses, thoughts, plans, and concerns in his notes. As Jack read a story began to unfold of two friends, Adam and Edmund Lane. The two men had been very close, but their differences eventually ruined their friendship. Jack read on.

Edmund is furious at Mort for having taken on Carolyn as a business partner. He feels it's dangerous. Dangerous for whom? Jack wondered.

Winston Cain is becoming a regular fixture, and Carolyn is using him now. Jack's heartbeat quickened. The "C" signature on the e-mail to Cain must have been Carolyn.

Jack set aside the book and went to Katherine's computer. He logged on and pulled up the outgoing mail file from the e-mail for Cleopatra1600.com. Jack inhaled sharply.

Cain-

Rudly's in Missouri. Eliminate the problem.

C

* * *

Carolyn sat on a couch in the Oval Office across from Warner. She forced the image of the most recent humiliation she had suffered at his hands from her mind, determined to concentrate on her goals. Katherine sat next to her, providing support without being aware of the depth of Carolyn's pain.

"These ideas may seem extreme, Warner, but we're losing our war on drugs. Stricter laws and enforcement help, but I believe we need more than that. We need to cut the drug lords off economically, just as we would any country with whom we were at war," Carolyn said. "I believe we have devised a way to limit the economy of the drug trade."

Warner leaned forward. "So what you're proposing is to eliminate, or at least limit, the market available to the drug trade by drug testing."

"I know we get into some constitutional issues with this approach, but we are *way* beyond a crisis in this country. We need to address the greater cause--if we truly want to stop drugs in America." Carolyn took a sip of water. "This program would also deal with problems in the welfare system and even foster care."

"It's really no different than employee drug testing," Katherine said.

Warner's gaze never left Carolyn's face. "This is brilliant. It's simple, yet brilliant. Unfortunately, we'll have to shelve it for now."

"What?" Carolyn gasped, feeling as if the wind had been knocked out of her. "You can't do this."

Warner stood and turned to Katherine. "I'm very impressed with your work. Hopefully, we'll be able to come back to these issues someday." He shook her hand.

Struggling for control, Carolyn stood as well. "Please excuse us, Katherine."

Katherine shut the door behind her.

"Someday? Someday, Warner?" Carolyn shouted. "There's a press conference scheduled for this afternoon."

"So, give the press conference. Then we'll let the program die a silent death." Warner walked to the door, a condescending smile on his face. "The polls just don't support it."

"That's a lie, and you know it." *My God, the bastard is enjoying this.* "I won't let you get away with this, Warner. I swear it."

"You don't have the balls to fight this war. And, Carolyn, like you said, it is war."

* * *

Jack paced from one end of Katherine's town home to the other. He couldn't prove that Carolyn had issued the orders to have him beaten, or that she'd had anyone else killed, but the evidence against her continued to mount.

How was he going to tell Katherine? He believed she was in danger, and needed to quit her job. She was going to be furious when he told her that he suspected Carolyn was behind these reprehensible deeds. She probably wouldn't believe him, Jack realized, but he knew he had to try.

One thing was sure, he had to distance himself from Katherine. Jack headed for the bedroom to pack his few possessions. Every minute he stayed with her jeopardized her safety. Carolyn, or whomever, wanted him dead. He feared that if Carolyn and her cronies connected him to Katherine, she might become another in a long list of casualties.

* * *

Carolyn's hand shook as she reached for the phone on her desk.

She held her breath until she heard the sound of her lover's voice. "What's wrong?"

"He shut down my program." A sob broke her voice. "I swear he planned it all along. I felt like a trapped fly watching my own wings being pulled off. And he enjoyed it, he actually enjoyed it."

"I was afraid this would happen," he said.

She rubbed her forehead with the fingertips of her free hand. "My God, it's everything I've worked for, my life's commitment. The entire reason I've stayed married to the son of a bitch. Now, I have nothing left. Nothing."

"Will you finally agree to let me help you?" he asked.

"How?"

"You let me worry about that. Do you still have access to treasury funds?"

"We'll be doing our final invoices for the task force in the upcoming weeks," Carolyn said.

"Perfect."

CHAPTER TWENTY-SIX

April 9, 2001---Washington, D.C.

"What's going on, Jack?" Katherine asked as she walked through the front door and encountered his luggage on the entry floor.

Jack came out of the kitchen, drying his hands on a dishtowel.

"Taking a trip?" Katherine put down her briefcase, not meeting his gaze. He could tell she was trying desperately to hide her hurt.

He shook his head. "We're taking too big a risk. If they find out we're involved-"

Her eyes wide, she said, "What are you talking about? If who finds out?"

"I'm not sure. But I think your boss has something to do with it."

"Carolyn?" Her voice rose in volume. "Are you out of your mind?"

"Please, sit down," Jack said, "and we'll discuss this."

"I'm fine where I am. I'm not sure what you think Carolyn has done, but I can assure you she would never do anything to hurt anyone." She stood, arms akimbo, her chin set at a defiant tilt.

"Kate, I know she's your friend, and that may be the very reason you aren't seeing the truth."

"Can you prove these accusations?" Anger resonated in her voice.

"Not yet. But I have substantial evidence." He walked to the desk, and showed her the e-mail to Cain signed with a C. "And, I have Adam Miles's journal that links Carolyn to Cain." He didn't bother telling her about the recording that he'd gotten at the bridge. Without the tape, he'd never prove it was Carolyn's voice.

"I don't believe any of this," Katherine said. "There has to be a logical explanation."

"Maybe there is. But until this is resolved, we should live apart."

"You're not responsible for me. I can make my own decisions."

He sighed, then approached her. "I'm afraid I'm putting you in danger," he said softly. "In fact, I *know* I'm putting you in danger. Regardless of who put out a hit on me, I can't, in good conscience, expose you to this kind of danger." He pulled her to him, but she stood stiff in his arms. Putting his hand under her chin, he lifted her face so he could look into her green eyes. "Okay, I should have talked to you before I packed. I apologize."

She met his gaze. "I'm afraid, Jack."

"Afraid of what?"

"Afraid that you're irrationally obsessed with this whole thing. First, a complete stranger meets you at the Golden Gate, and you take his word as gospel. Then, you're convinced it's Mark Dailey."

"I know it all sounds odd."

"Odd? It's more than odd. And now you're pulling up e-mail messages from an address that could belong to anyone, and you're telling me it's the First Lady communicating with a mercenary."

"Katherine, do you know how many investigations I've done in my years as a reporter?" He didn't wait for an answer. "Thousands. And most of them started out with much less to go on than this."

"I'm not doubting your professionalism. I just think you're too personally involved because of your father."

"Oh, I'm personally involved, all right," Jack said. "And I've got bruises all over my body to prove it."

"You're on the wrong track. Carolyn is a great person. I won't stand by and watch you attack my friend. This is wrong, Jack, very wrong."

"Is this a deal breaker for our relationship?"

She stepped back. "Maybe. I'm not sure."

Jack started to speak, then stopped. His gaze locked with hers, he clenched his jaw as he fought his emotions.

"The break will do us good. We've been moving fast, probably too fast. We both need time to think."

"You think that's what this is about? That I need time to think?" Jack asked.

"It makes more sense than the alternative," Katherine said.

Jack shook his head. "I don't deserve this. I've never been anything but straight with you. And I'm getting sick of being accused of underhanded behavior. I don't care if you think I'm off base on my investigation, but I do care that you doubt my integrity. I don't use words like *love*, lightly. And I do love you. Try not to forget that, Katherine, while you're thinking." He picked up his bag and walked out the door.

* * *

Carolyn walked toward the Oval Office. Her footfalls echoed in the evening quiet. She'd given a lot of thought to Warner's rejection of her War on Drugs proposal, and decided that she just needed to reason with him. Her program could build his legacy, a legacy she knew he cared about preserving. She intended to point out that killing her task force, to satisfy a personal vendetta, would only hurt his presidency.

She stopped in front of the Oval Office door, took a calming breath, then knocked.

"Come in," Warner said.

Carolyn swung the door open, then gasped.

Edmund Lane pulled his cigar from his lips. "Good to see you, Carolyn."

Warner leaned back in his chair, set his feet on his desk, and crossed his ankles. "How can we help you?"

Cigar smoke hung thick and dense in the air. "Can I speak to you alone?"

"No."

Carolyn met his gaze. "I wanted to discuss my press conference and your presidential legacy."

Warner reached in his pocket and handed Edmund a dollar bill.

Edmund laughed as he took it. "You should never underestimate my knack for predicting human nature. She's right on schedule."

Carolyn felt the blood rushing to her face.

"You win, again." Warner shrugged.

Edmund sat back and sucked on his cigar.

Carolyn stood silent. Humiliation tightened around her throat.

"Do you think she gives a shit about my legacy?" Warner asked.

Edmund smiled back. "Only if it saves her precious program."

Warner swung his feet off his desk and stood. "Although I admit your press conference went remarkably well, I really see no point in having this discussion with you. My decision is made. Please excuse us, Carolyn." He walked to the door and held it open for her.

"I can't believe you're doing this," she whispered, finally regaining her voice.

"If you don't like it, divorce me," he said as he shut the door behind her.

Carolyn stared at the door unable to cry, unable to scream, unable to feel anything but the rage of a trapped animal. He knew she couldn't divorce him without sacrificing everything she'd ever worked for and cared about. If this was war, she'd lost another battle. *But I'm still standing, she thought, and as long as I'm standing I will fight.*

CHAPTER TWENTY-SEVEN

April 13, 2001---Washington, D.C.

Jack sipped his beer. He hated spending Saturday nights alone.
Sitting in a bar wasn't his style, but he refused to wallow in self-pity.
So, he'd forced himself to go out, only to discover that surrounding
one's self with strangers only magnified the loneliness. Unfortunately,
he hadn't realized his mistake until after he'd ordered his meal. He
resigned himself to eating quickly, then leaving.

What had happened to him? he wondered. He'd always been a
loner, and he'd even enjoyed himself. Or had he? Regardless, he
realized that that was before Katherine's return to his life and before
he admitted to himself that he loved her.

He stared at the photograph on the front page of the Washington
Post. Katherine stood off to Carolyn's right at a press conference that
had taken place the day before at the White House. Even in newsprint,
Katherine was stunning.

Jack re-read the headline.

Crowd Cheers First Lady's War On Drugs

He'd known that Katherine and Carolyn were working on some
major reforms, but with his policy of not mixing work with their
relationship, he'd had no idea of the impact. He read on.

First Lady Carolyn Alden Lane is beating her own previous record as the most popular woman in history with numbers that surpass any other person in recorded time.

Even John F. Kennedy did not enjoy such outstanding popularity. Her latest attack on the drug trade is being touted as a brilliant plan with the kind of teeth that could end the reign of drug lords for years to come.

"By eliminating the market for drugs versus trying to eliminate the pushers, we are bringing this fight onto our own battlefield," Carolyn Alden Lane said. With the polls climbing, legislators are quickly jumping on board to support the First Lady's plans.

Jack knew that the fate of his relationship with Katherine relied on him. He'd been the one to walk out. *Was he irrationally obsessed?* No, too much evidence existed. He sipped at his beer, theoretically piecing the puzzle together. His father's paperwork, Adam Miles's journal, the tape, and the e-mail all tied Carolyn to Cain. Even though her investments with Mort Fields appeared to be legitimate, his father's files implied impropriety. And suspiciously, Jack realized, his father's last known business appointment had been with Carolyn.

Jack knew his father opposed Warner's reelection to the Senate. And with the death of Bill Rudly, Warner had not only claimed the Senate seat, but had also become the *senior* Senator for Missouri, thus positioning him for his presidential bid.

Throughout history people had been murdered for less. Power. Money. Love. The three main reasons people resorted to killing. But could Carolyn have ordered Cain's men to murder his father? Jack wondered. What about the deaths of Adam Miles and Mort Fields? It certainly appeared that she'd ordered his elimination.

The whole scenario sounded ridiculous, Jack thought. Maybe Katherine was right. Maybe in his desperation to deal with, and solve, his father's death, he was grasping at straws. He finished off his beer and ordered another. Regardless of what this investigation did to his relationship with Katherine, Jack knew he owed the truth to his father's memory and to himself. And he'd uncover it, or die trying.

* * *

Any decision was better than no decision, Katherine thought, standing in her office. She stared at the copy of the e-mail message that Jack had shown her. This couldn't be from Carolyn, but she had to admit, she believed it was Carolyn's personal e-mail address. There had to be a logical explanation.

"Only one way to find out," Katherine said to herself.

Katherine strode into Carolyn's office. The drapes were pulled back. The sun's rays streamed into the room, causing Katherine to blink as her eyes adjusted to the bright natural light.

Carolyn looked up from her desk. "Good morning. How are you today?"

"Well . . ." Katherine felt her face flush as she sat across from Carolyn. This was much harder than she'd expected.

"What's wrong?" Carolyn asked.

"I have to show you something, but you can't ask where I got it."

Carolyn nodded.

Katherine handed the e-mail to Carolyn.

Carolyn quickly read the message. "Who wrote this?"

"I was hoping you could tell me."

"Katherine, you need to tell me everything you know. Starting with Jack's well-being."

Katherine blanched. This wasn't what she had planned. But now, she knew, she was committed to a complete explanation. She just hoped Jack would forgive her.

* * *

Vice President Richard Young walked beside the President as they made their way to a luncheon with the congressional leadership in the East Room.

"This is a good opportunity to float Brandon Ross as a candidate for the Supreme Court appointment. I think a soft approach---"

Warner stopped and turned to Richard. "I would have thought that after all your years on the Hill, that you'd have realized that how you approach these guys doesn't matter. It's all about what they want, negotiation. And by the way, I'm not going with Ross."

"I thought we had agreed he was the best choice," Richard said through clenched teeth.

"No, you wanted Ross. I simply agreed that he was qualified. I'm going with Carl Rembrandt."

Richard shook his head. "He's too controversial and extreme. This will bite us in the ass. I can't endorse that man."

"When I want your opinion, I'll ask for it," Warner turned and strolled into the room.

* * *

Richard hid his rage behind a practiced smile. Warner had made a habit of freezing him out, and showed no signs of thawing. He took another bite of filet mignon as he watched the interaction of the President and the Congressional leaders. The topic was an energy conservation bill that was destined to hit the President's desk within the month.

"I think we need to take this up on the golf course," Warner said.

"Only if you carry a pen in your golf bag," Speaker of the House Jonathan Daniels said with a laugh. "In fact, you sign off on this bill, and I might consider letting you win the round of golf, Mr. President."

Everyone in the room erupted into laughter. Richard forced a smile.

Warner's gaze lifted from his plate and his eyes locked on Richard's. "Richard, I'm sure everyone is interested to hear about your recommendation for the Supreme Court opening." All of the attention in the room turned to the Vice President.

"The Vice President is recommending Carl Rembrandt for the post," Warner continued. "Please expound on your reasoning."

Richard caught his expression one beat before it slipped to shock.

A slight smile played on Warner's lips. He had him by the balls and knew it. In fact, it was obvious to Richard that Warner was thoroughly enjoying this moment.

Son of a bitch. Warner's sniper shot hit the bulls eye. He should have seen him taking aim, Richard thought. Warner's set up had been perfect. The depths of his ruthlessness amazed Richard. In all of his years in politics, he'd never met a man so able to bend the rules to his will and repeatedly get away with it.

Now, he faced a no win situation. Contradicting the President in public would be considered an unforgivable offense capable of destroying his political future.

Publicly supporting Rembrandt for the post would lock him to the radical judge and tarnish his Boy Scout image. He didn't have much choice in the situation, Richard realized, the latter was the least of the two evils.

Warner's machinations were brilliant, Richard thought. He'd set him up to take the fall if Rembrandt was rejected as the next Supreme Court Justice, and if he was approved, then Warner got his way. A win/win for President Lane.

Richard set his fork down, regained his composure, and began, "Carl Rembrandt is a brilliant judge with a distinguished legal history."

CHAPTER TWENTY-EIGHT

Carolyn stormed into the Oval Office.

Warner turned to her as she entered. "I'm in a meeting. Check with one of the secretaries to see when I'm free next."

"You're free now." Carolyn looked pointedly at the men, two senators, the Speaker of the House, and three cabinet members, who sat with Warner. She refused to play by Warner's rules, even if it meant suffering his humiliation from time to time. "Or we can air your dirty laundry in front of them?" She waved the sheet of paper she held. "Your choice."

Warner's jaw clenched. He nodded toward the door and the meeting dispersed.

Carolyn watched them exit. When she turned back to Warner, his face was crimson.

He stood, walked to his bar, poured himself a double Jack Daniels, and belted it down.

Not his first for the day, Carolyn was sure.

"Don't you ever pull a stunt like that again." He set his glass down, and moved toward her. "I won't tolerate it."

"And I won't tolerate this." She threw the paper at him. "How the hell did you get my e-mail address and my password?"

He laughed. "Don't you mean, who did this? And why?"

Carolyn shook her head. "That's your problem, Warner, you've always underestimated me. I know who did this. And I know why. I want to know how?" She knew she'd been betrayed. But she wasn't sure by whom. All of the arrows pointed to Dailey, but she struggled to believe it was true. She hoped Warner's ego would force him to gloat, providing her with the answer.

"All you need to know is that you've been set up, and set up well. You'll march to my tune now, or I'll see you arrested and claim you're mentally unfit. The deeds you've set in motion are horrendous." Warner shook his head. "And the smoking gun is so hot, it appears to have been used in a shoot out."

"So, Mark came up with this on his own?" She played her hand.

"Dailey couldn't come up with shit on his own. He had help."

"You son of a bitch." Her worst fears were confirmed. Now, she knew she couldn't give Jack away by mentioning Adam Miles's files. It would be like issuing his death sentence.

"I like to think so." Warner smirked. "Some of your crimes may be forgivable, the heat of a political battle and all that, but when you went after Young's boy. Well, no one will ever forgive an attack on a child. Especially when it's ordered by a woman who claims to champion children's causes."

He'd hurt a child. He'd almost killed Richard's son. And he'd done it in her name. Carolyn felt something snap in her mind. She remembered screaming, "You bastard, you bastard . . ."

And then she flew at him, unable to control her rage.

Warner wiped at the blood that trickled down his cheek. "You bitch! You fucking bitch! You scratched me."

A Secret Service agent held Carolyn away from Warner.

She took a few deep breaths and turned to the agent. "You can let go of me." She could see sympathy in the embarrassed faces of the agents, and it made her feel worse.

The agent immediately released her.

Carolyn smoothed her fingers over her hair, then straightened her clothing.

"Don't you ever touch me again," Warner hissed, his nose four inches from hers. An agent handed the President a tissue. Warner stepped back, and pressed it against the scratch. "She is not allowed past the outer office. Do you understand me?"

"But she's—"

"I don't give a fuck who she is. She isn't allowed in the Oval Office again. Am I clear?"

"Yes, sir."

Tears stung Carolyn's eyes, but she refused to let them fall. Head held high, she spun on her heel and left the Oval Office with all the dignity she could muster.

CHAPTER TWENTY-NINE

April 23, 2001---Washington, D.C.

Carolyn shivered as she sat quietly in a private waiting room of the hospital. She wished she'd worn a sweater. Why, she wondered, did hospitals always feel so cold?

Secret Service agents stood outside the door, giving her privacy, but their thoughtful consideration felt more like solitary confinement. Carolyn clasped her hands in her lap. There was nothing to do but wait. God, she hated being here, but protocol demanded her attendance as soon as she'd been notified, especially since Warner was delayed on Air Force One.

An hour and a half later, Warner sauntered into the room. A Secret Service agent shut the door to the waiting room, intensifying the trapped feeling that threatened to overwhelm her. A current of animosity surged between them.

"Worried about the love of your life?" Warner asked as he sat across from her.

"He's *your* father," she responded, surprised that he'd even speak to her.

"But he was your lover." Anger flecked with pain sparked from his eyes.

Carolyn froze. "Warner--" What could she say? she wondered. Nothing, she finally realized. Absolutely nothing. The truth she'd always feared had come back to haunt her. She slumped in her seat, the weight she'd been carrying for so many years finally crushing her.

Warner leaned back on the couch and crossed his arms over his chest. "Come off it, Carolyn. Edmund told me everything. The affair, his baby--you remember--the reason you had the abortion. All of it," he ground out through an obvious wall of hurt.

Now, she understood his hatred, his reason for striking out so cruelly time and again. She stared at her hands. "When did he tell you?"

"It doesn't matter," Warner said, shrugging. "I don't give a damn, anyway. You've served your purpose."

The emotion in his voice betrayed his words, giving evidence of how much he really did care, of how much these facts had destroyed him. That realization hit her like a clenched fist to the temple. Her head throbbed violently. "It was before I knew you." Why was she bothering to defend herself? Nothing she could say or do would repair the chasm between them.

"Not according to Edmund." Warner laughed. "Of course, that bastard's about to burn in hell with the rest of them. He served his purpose as well. His time was up." He leaned toward her. "This is a lesson you should take to heart, Carolyn. No one tries to control me."

Her eyes met his. "Warner, tell me you didn't cause this--"

Warner glared back. "This what? Heart attack? Don't be naïve."

"My God, he's your father."

Warner's eyes narrowed. "That son of a bitch is *not* my father!"

"What are you talking about?"

"My mother had an affair. Seems to be a recurring theme." He arched an eyebrow at her. "So you see, I'm really a bastard. I've never been anything to Edmund other than the bane of his existence. A reminder of my mother's failure. An imperfection in his life that he tried to dress up for his own gain."

She shook her head in disbelief.

"All along, I've been Edmund's pawn. If not me, it would have been someone else. I was simply convenient."

"I'm sure he loved you in his own way."

Warner laughed, the sound bitter and harsh. "Don't kid yourself."

"I understand your hatred of me. But I don't understand---"

"You understand perfectly. You said it yourself, Carolyn, politics is war. Edmund will be joining all the other casualties of battle."

"Casualties? You act like you've had a hand in this."

Warner's jaw clenched as he gave her a knowing look. Then he said, "And you're acting like a novice. You need to catch up, Carolyn. Stupidity doesn't become you."

"How many have you killed?" Her voice was a whisper.

"Don't be ridiculous. *I've* never killed anyone."

Carolyn knew he deliberately meant to hide behind semantics. Of course, he'd never *personally* killed anyone, but he didn't deny issuing the orders. He wanted her to know the truth. "Your *precious* Council is a pit of vipers. You even turn on one another."

"Politics is survival of the fittest. It eventually had to come to this, him or me. And it wasn't going to be me." Warner laughed. "Your problem, Carolyn, is that you're too fucking naïve, too fucking innocent."

"Go to hell," she said.

He ignored her response as he rose and opened the door. "Can I get some company in here?" he asked the agents who guarded the door.

* * *

The sound of footsteps echoed in the corridor outside the waiting room.

Warner nodded toward the door, then said to the agent reading a magazine beside him, "It's show time."

Moments later, the doctor walked into the room. "They told me you'd arrived, Mr. President." He extended his hand to Warner. "I'm Dr. Jacobs."

He turned to Carolyn. "Mrs. Lane." She accepted the doctor's handshake.

"I'm sorry, sir, but your father has passed away. Once he started having problems, it was like a chain reaction. All of his vital organs began to shut down, and we were unable to stop it. Finally, his heart gave out."

"Do you know what caused his organs to fail?" Carolyn asked. Only she could see the hostility in Warner's gaze when she spoke.

"No, unfortunately, we have no idea. We can order an autopsy if you'd like."

"Yes," Carolyn said.

Warner shook his head as he turned to the doctor. "No, that won't be necessary. My father lived a full life. It was his time. My wife's just upset." His expression was the epitome of grief. Only Carolyn recognized the relief in Warner's eyes.

* * *

Katherine met Carolyn at the entrance to the White House. "How's Warner's father?"

Carolyn felt out of sorts, confused, and numb. Lately, she felt as though she existed in a continuous state of shock. She forced herself to focus on Katherine's question. "He's gone."

"I'm sorry," Katherine said.

"Thank you."

"What can I do?"

Carolyn shook her head. "I just need to rest. To be alone for a few minutes. Please ask the Navy mess steward to bring me a cup of almond tea in the Garden Room." ·

"Certainly."

Carolyn walked to the elevator and rode it up to the Garden Room of the White House. Nothing was as it seemed. She'd been duped. The men in her life had made a career out of using her and others for personal gain. At least, Warner had the balls to be blatant about it.

It was Mark who shocked and hurt her most. He'd double-crossed her for years, using her as stepping stone to his own career, yet pretending to love her. She'd deal with him later, she decided. Fortunately, she'd had the foresight to align herself with another powerful player.

The Navy steward appeared almost immediately, carrying her tea on a tray. "Sugar or cream today, ma'am?" he asked, setting down the tray and then pouring her a cup.

"No, thank you. Plain is fine," she responded. He handed the beverage to her, then turned smartly and left.

Carolyn took a sip, then sat, putting her feet up on a wicker stool. Sun streamed through the windows, warming her body but evading her soul.

She heard a door open. "I don't want to be disturbed."

"It's only me." He walked in, taking a seat across from her.

"I'm so glad you're back from your trip. Edmund has died."

"I know." He leaned forward. "I came to see how you're holding up. Was everything all right with Warner?"

Carolyn set her teacup down. "It couldn't have been any uglier."

"I'm sorry." He took her hands in his.

"He, Edmund, and Mark Dailey made a career out of eliminating any opposition." Her voice was flat. "I've been set up. Mark Dailey screwed me royally. He's been working with Warner all along."

"I suspected as much." His gaze held hers. "How did you find out?"

"Jack Rudly. He told Katherine that a man met him late one night at the Golden Gate Bridge and gave him my e-mail information. She, in turn, returned it to me along with Jack's suspicions that the man was Mark. It was a short hop in deductive reasoning to figure it out. Dailey's the only one who had access to my e-mail and password. Shit, I gave it to him myself. Warner confirmed it all."

"I can no longer ignore what they've done to you, to me, to so many good men, and to our country. It's time to act."

Carolyn hesitated. "What are you going to do about it?"

"Do you trust me?"

Her eyes searched his. Then she nodded.

"That's all you need to know."

CHAPTER THIRTY

May 9, 2001---White House, Washington, D.C.

Mark Dailey nursed a scotch while surveying the Roosevelt Room. The reception was small, but with a distinguished guest list. From his vantage point he witnessed many powerful people in quiet, but intense conversations. He realized that no one really noticed him. His position in the White House, despite his title of senior adviser, was a known joke. Even his assistant filled in at other offices because there was virtually nothing to do at his.

Mark took a swallow of his scotch. He was sick of the backstabbing bullshit. Sick of what he'd done to facilitate this administration. And quite frankly, he was sick of himself.

The approach of Vice President Richard Young interrupted his sour thoughts.

"Mark, great to see you." Richard shook his hand and patted him on the back.

"Mr. Vice President," Mark said with a nod.

Richard pulled him outside onto the balcony. "Enough of that Mr. V.P. crap. We've known each other far too long."

Mark took another sip of his scotch.

"I'm concerned about you, buddy. I understand Warner's got you wasting away in the basement of the West Wing."

Mark grunted in disgust.

Richard lowered his voice. "Don't feel alone. He's not treating me much better. But I plan on correcting the situation. First off, I've got you hooked up to fly to California with Warner to consult on his speaking tour. This will give you a chance to get out of the basement and back into the limelight."

Mark raised his glass to Richard. "Thanks, I really appreciate having you in my corner. I won't forget this."

"Actually, it was Carolyn's idea."

Mark smiled. "Tell her thank you for me."

"Be happy to. In the meantime, I need a favor from you."

"Sure," Mark said. "What's on the agenda?"

"First, let Cain know it's time to take his South American vacation, then deliver this envelope for me." Richard pulled an envelope out of his breast pocket and discreetly passed it to Mark.

"What's in it?"

"A bank account in the Caymans."

"What are we paying for?"

"We're paying for a remedy to our problem."

"Usual spot? Asian woman?" Mark asked.

Richard smiled.

* * *

May 11, 2001---Santa Clara, California

The sun glistened off the water in the San Francisco Bay as President Warner Hamilton Lane and his entourage, including senior adviser Mark Dailey, arrived in Silicon Valley forty-five minutes late. Lane stepped out of the helicopter followed by Dailey. They were greeted by four corporate executives at the landing pad on the office building rooftop and then were escorted to an elevator, which took them one floor down.

Lane turned to the corporation's vice president of operations. "If I understand correctly, not only is your company recycling chemicals for further use, but you're also doing it in the safest, most efficient way."

"That's correct, sir. We're very proud of our operation here. As one of the largest chemical repackaging companies on the West Coast, we employ over five hundred people."

Warner nodded as they walked into a private conference room with a large oval mahogany table, plush leather chairs, and aerial photographs of the corporate campus lining the walls.

He had insisted that his tour include a state-of-the-art chemical recycling facility because he knew it was the wave of the future. Visiting this high-profile plant at the end of his trip had been a brilliant move, he thought. The polls showed a public outcry for political support of environmental issues. The hell with Carolyn's war on drugs. He intended to be the poster-boy for the environment.

Dailey approached Lane. "It's all set up, Mr. President. After the guided tour, you'll address the employees with full media coverage. Are you ready?"

"I'm ready. Let's get this show on the road." Lane's voice rose in excitement. Taking on environmental issues would insure his place in history. He stood taller, enjoying the feel of control and power.

After a brief presentation, given by the corporate executives, about the facility that Lane was about to visit, the tour began in the main offices. The President was photographed shaking hands with workers. Media representatives lined the walls with cameras, microphones, and tape recorders.

He smiled when an Asian woman with long dark hair stepped forward to present him with a single red rose. "Thank you, it's beautiful," he said. "Just like you."

She bowed.

Progressing into the manufacturing portion of the plant, they all put on hard hats and goggles. Four Secret Service agents, three corporate executives, and two media people accompanied Dailey and the President.

They advanced through an inventory area and up onto a walkway in order to view the entire facility from above. As they stood over large tanks containing volatile chemicals, the plant engineer explained how the processes worked and most important, how the chemicals were treated and recycled after use.

As they stood above the vaults, the journalist and cameraman recorded the presentation on air circulation. The plant engineer explained that most of the chemicals were toxic and that fresh air had to be constantly replenished in the facility to protect the workers.

"How fast does the air circulate?" the President asked.

"The air in this room is completely turned over every three minutes."

"And when you say 'toxic', will these chemicals make you ill or worse?"

"After a matter of mere seconds of exposure, disorientation takes place and then rapid death. That is why compliance with OSHA is critical."

When they moved to the next room, where the reprocessing was done, the engineer said, "At this time we ask that the media stop filming, because this process is a proprietary trade secret." The engineer pointed to the next walkway. "Step right this way, and we'll move on to a filmable portion of the tour."

As President Lane reached the middle of the pathway, a small beeping alarm sounded.

The Secret Service agents looked around, trying to determine the origin of the beep.

Wide-eyed, the plant engineer spun to face them.

Warner took a hesitant step, unsure of whether to continue. Then, he regained his confidence. He was Warner "Fucking" Lane, President of the United States. What did he have to fear? Nothing.

"What's wrong?" Dailey asked.

"My vapor sensor's going off. Get the President out of here."

Immediately, Warner felt his eyes begin to water and his chest grow tight.

"Mr. Pres--" The plant engineer tried to speak, but a coughing fit choked off his words.

Two Secret Service agents grabbed the President under the arms, knocking the hardhat from his head, as they pulled him backward toward an exit. A few steps later, they dropped him. Hands to their mouths, the agents collapsed, coughing blood.

Dailey folded to the ground, curling into a ball at the president's feet.

Warner tried to speak, but the words wouldn't come. He tore the goggles from his face. He felt as if a vacuum had devoured the oxygen from every pore in his body. Throat aflame, he reached for the railing. He clung to the metal, mouthing a silent plea. Then he slid to the deck of the catwalk. He seized convulsively.

Warner sucked desperately for air, fully aware that he was suffocating. He clawed at his face and throat frantic to relieve the pressure building in his head. His eyes bulged, feeling as if they were going to explode. Noxious fumes seared his nostrils and dehydrated his lungs, prohibiting the oxygen from penetrating the delicate mucous membrane tissue. He writhed in agony. Blood trickled from his nose, and ran down the back of his throat.

Next to him, a third Secret Service agent dropped to his knees, then fell forward in a spasm.

A high-pitched ringing began in Warner's ears. It escalated to a thunder in his head. He felt someone dragging him toward the exit. Blackness obscured his vision. His body burned for oxygen. His mind begged for relief. Even death. If the pain would just stop.

Suddenly alarms pierced the air. Huge fans sprang to life, ventilating the vapor-choked area.

CHAPTER THIRTY-ONE

Washington, D.C.

Three days later, Carolyn stood quietly in the Oval office. She had just returned from the hospital where the President had been transferred. Bright light streamed through the bulletproof windows. The tragedy at the chemical plant seemed surreal, she thought.

Carolyn walked around the Resolute desk. Like so many presidents before him, Warner had chosen to use the beautiful antique in the Oval Office. The light scent of lemon oil wafted around her.

She carefully sat down on the leather chair. Lightly, she ran a finger over the smooth top of the desk, then gripped the arms of the chair, feeling the leather give beneath her touch. Carolyn closed her eyes. Compromise had become a way of life, a method for survival.

She twirled in the chair, letting her shoes slide off her feet as she spun around. Her skin prickled in apprehension as the chair came to a stop facing the windows. Carolyn peered out onto the lawn from the highest office of the land. Tears ran unchecked down her cheeks. She'd compromised so much that she wondered if she'd finally lost her soul.

"Forgive me, Father, for I have sinned," she whispered.

* * *

273

Richard Young strolled toward the Oval Office. He smiled. Soon he'd raise his right hand and repeat the oath of the office of the President of the United States. And the beauty of it was that the taxpayers, and the United Stated government, courtesy of Warner's rubberstamp on Carolyn's War On Drugs task force, would pay for his final rise to the presidency.

My God, it had been so simple. He'd had his own private army, thanks to Edmund, Warner, and the Council. Now, he was the only general left standing. Soon to be the Commander-In-Chief.

Without knocking, Young entered the Oval Office.

* * *

Carolyn felt a kiss on her neck. She closed her eyes while wiping the tears from her cheeks. "Now you're the Acting President," she said.

"Acting President?" he murmured against her skin. "For the moment. By tomorrow at noon, I'll *be* the president." He kissed her shoulder between sentences. "A written declaration from myself, the Speaker, and the Senate leader has already been submitted to Congress."

"Will the doctors be done testifying?"

"They'll be done by midnight tonight. No one can realistically expect Warner to recover. Once his condition is confirmed, the vote will be expedited. I expect it at eight tomorrow morning. Plans are underway for my swearing-in at noon."

"Are you ready for this?"

"Am I ready?" he asked. "Of course I'm ready. I've been planning this since Warner took office."

She stiffened with apprehension. *Didn't he mean, planning this all his life?* The hair along the back of Carolyn's neck prickled. She could no longer suppress the suspicions that had been plaguing her since she'd learned of the chemical release. Suspicions that caused Richard's words to keep replaying in her mind, "It's time to take care of the problem." And, "Do you trust me?"

Carolyn spun around to face her lover, his breath touching her cheek as she did so. "Constitutionally--"

"The White House lawyers are following the letter of the law. After this hearing it's up to Congress to decide if the President can perform his duties. The answer is obvious."

She eyed him thoughtfully. Gauging her words, her questions. Wanting to know the truth, but afraid of the answer. If what she suspected was true, what *would* she do? What *could* she do? "It doesn't matter to you how you've achieved the office?" She knew she was bating him, but she couldn't help herself.

He held her gaze. "Why should it? I would have been president if Warner hadn't caused my son's accident. I owed him on two accounts. He injured my son and, by doing so, he stole the presidency from me. This was my destiny, not his. Mine." He lowered his voice. "He got what he deserved."

As vice president, Richard had possessed the necessary inside information, the kind of access to pull off the murders. Her worst fears confirmed, Carolyn's breath caught. "But to kill--"

Richard placed a finger over her lips. "This is a conversation we are not going to have. Not now, not ever."

She hesitated. Fear gripped her.

Richard placed his hands on the tops of her arms. A lock of his dark hair fell across his forehead as he glanced down at her cleavage, then at her bare feet. He reached for the button on her shirt. "Looks like you started the job. Let me finish it."

"Was this the only way? I . . ." Panic rose in her chest. With her palms, she pushed lightly against his chest.

He leaned back and gazed into her eyes. "You aren't new to this game. The greater the prize, the higher the risk. I assure you that Warner understood the rules. Hell, he defined them."

"I've never thought of this as a game," she said, stalling for time. How could she have thought that she loved this man?

He shook his head as if scolding a wayward child. "You'll feel better when I nominate you as vice president."

Shock coursed through her. "What?"

"You're the most popular political figure in our nation's history. And Warner's situation has turned you into an icon. I've turned you into an icon. And I can turn you into the first woman vice president of this country. I've already mentioned the idea at my earlier press conference."

My God, is he serious?

"You'll be able to write your own ticket. Mark my words. By tomorrow when your name is posed for the vice presidency, the country will go wild."

"I take it that you're spinning the 'carrying on my husband's legacy' rhetoric?"

"Exactly." He smiled as if she finally understood.

Kissing him suddenly seemed abhorrent. He was a murderer. No different from the rest. *What did you expect he was going to do?* she asked herself for the millionth time. *You let him do this. You encouraged him.* But she never dreamt he meant murder, even when he said he was going to "take care of the problem." She understood machinations, but not murder. Naïve, she was too fucking naïve, just like Warner had said.

He pulled her close, pressing her cheek to his chest. "We're a team now."

She forced herself to relax in his arms, while her mind reeled. What was she going to do?

* * *

The Washington Post
May 12, 2001
PRESIDENT WARNER HAMILTON LANE NEAR DEATH!
SAN JOSE---President Lane was critically injured Tuesday morning while touring the Sycon Chemical Repackaging plant. During the visit, toxic vapors were released causing an exothermic reaction. Ten others were killed during the accident, including Senior White House Adviser Mark Dailey.
Unofficial sources state that the President has not regained consciousness. Hospital doctors have refused to comment.
Sources have confirmed that the emergency exhaust ventilation system at Sycon responded but that it started seconds too late. Sycon's emergency response team entered the facility to find an unconscious President and Mr. Dailey wedged in a doorway between the chemical storage room and the reprocessing facility. Rescuers report that it appears that

Mr. Dailey pulled the President out of the contaminated area shortly before succumbing to the chemicals himself.

Four Secret Service agents, three corporate executives, and two members of the media collapsed on a catwalk where they died.

The area where the release occurred is under investigation by Fed OSHA. The cause of the accident is still unknown, but investigators have focused on the valve seals for the process piping. The facility has been closed until the exact cause can be determined. FBI sources said that this investigation will probably take weeks, if not months.

Congress will hear testimony regarding the prognosis of the President. If it is determined that he is unable to execute the duties of his office, then Vice President Richard Young will be sworn in as the 45th President.

While President Lane is comatose, Richard Young is the Acting President in accordance with the constitutional line of succession.

CHAPTER THIRTY-TWO

Carolyn closed her eyes and leaned her head back against the seat of the Secret Service Suburban. The smells of fresh leather and plastic told her that the truck was new.

Lightning lit up the night sky. Thunder cracked. She shivered. While watching the testimony to Congress regarding Warner's condition, she'd suddenly become certain of what she must do. But she had no idea of how it would all come out in the end. She was ready to place her own life on the line, but what concerned her was the other lives she knew she must involve.

As the vehicle turned onto Swann Street the LCD display on the dashboard glowed the time: 1:17am. Only street lamps and the Suburban's headlights lit up the dark neighborhood at this early hour. The driver pulled to the curb in front of a townhouse. Carolyn had called thirty minutes earlier. She hoped they both were there, and that they would help her, for tonight was her only chance to correct the course of history.

* * *

Jack arrived at Katherine's home within minutes of Carolyn's call. They hadn't spoken in days. Her eyes met his when she opened the

278

door. He could see the hurt etched in her features, although he knew she'd never admit to it.

They sat in living room. Even the cozy blue and white overstuffed couch and chairs couldn't dispel the combative air of the room. Katherine sat across from Jack, her posture straight and unyielding.

"I can't believe you told Carolyn everything," Jack began in a low voice. "Do you know that the Secret Service ransacked my hotel room, took all of my files, and my tapes?"

"I'm sorry, but I didn't think we had a choice." Katherine cocked her head to the side. "Face it, Jack. You got what you wanted."

"And what was that?"

"You wanted me to believe you. Well, I did. And I think we're about to find out exactly how right you were."

* * *

A Secret Service agent opened the car door and stepped aside. Carolyn hurried from the truck to the front door, praying the black night would cloak her arrival. She rapped twice, and the door swung open.

Jack pulled her inside and quickly shut the door.

Katherine stood beside him. "Take off your coat. I've got tea on."

Carolyn handed Katherine her wrap and moved to a chair in the living room. The curtains were drawn against prying eyes.

Jack sat across from Carolyn. Katherine set the tea service and cups on the coffee table, then joined Jack on the couch.

"I need your help." Carolyn looked at both of them. "And after you hear what I'm asking, I want you to feel free to say no. This is my fight. I realize it's not fair that I even ask for your help, but quite frankly, I don't know whom else I can trust or turn to."

Katherine folded her hands in her lap.

"What's going on?" Jack asked.

"It's more of a question of what has already gone on," Carolyn said. She explained that she'd discovered that Richard Young had orchestrated the accident causing Warner's critical condition and Mark Dailey's death. That he, too, was a member of the infamous Council.

Katherine paled. Jack's brow furrowed in concentration. They both remained silent.

Carolyn explained how she had been set up and revealed her own mistakes along the way, including her affair with Richard Young, her use of Winston Cain to investigate various candidates, and her partnership with Mort Fields. Finally, she revealed her suspicions and how she had come to know of Young's involvement. She ended by telling them how guilty she felt for not recognizing Richard's meaning when he'd told her that he was going to "take care of the problem."

It seemed pointless to mention that Young had offered her the vice presidency, a place in history like no other—the first woman to hold the second highest office in the land. They would hear about it in the press tomorrow, she thought, but by then she would have destroyed that opportunity. So, she left it out.

"I could have prevented these deaths had I understood. Now, I feel I must do something to make this right." Carolyn paused. "I've made a lot of mistakes, horrible lapses in judgment." She fixed her gaze on Jack. "Katherine told me that you suspected I was involved with these crimes."

He stared back. "That's true."

"That's why I asked you here, Jack. I believe I can prove not only my innocence, but also show who's guilty. But I need your help—and Katherine's. I'm being completely honest in revealing my own faults because I don't feel I can ask for your trust without giving you all of the facts to consider. If you have any questions, I'll answer them as best as I can."

Jack sat for a moment searching Carolyn's gaze. "You've done a pretty thorough job of explaining the situation. And, I have to say that my gut tells me to believe you."

"I'm stunned," Katherine said. "But I believe you're telling the truth."

Carolyn breathed a sigh of relief. When she formulated this plan, she'd realized that gaining their trust would be her greatest hurdle.

"I do have a couple of questions, though," Jack said.

Carolyn met his gaze.

"Why not go to the attorney general?"

"For the sake of the country, this has got to be taken care of before tomorrow's Congressional vote. His hands are tied by the rule of law; he won't be able to act quickly enough. If Richard Young becomes president, he will have the power to potentially squash this investigation."

"You've got to be kidding," Katherine said.

"Unfortunately, I'm not. I've seen worse happen. More than likely, Richard would come up with a way to neutralize me. So, we've got to preempt his ability to strike."

"I'm too cynical to question your reasoning." Jack shook his head in disgust. "I assume you have a plan for exposing Young."

She nodded.

"What do you hope to achieve?"

"As a former prosecuting attorney, I don't believe that we'll be able to come up with the evidence necessary to actually convict Young. I do believe, however, that we can keep him from the presidency and remove him from office."

"He deserves to go to jail," Katherine said. "If not worse."

"I agree," Carolyn said. "But Richard's a smart man. I doubt that there's any direct evidence linking him to the murders. Also, once we make this public, this case will be tried in the media. It will not be a matter of right and wrong, or of finding justice, but a popularity contest that will depend on the talent of the spin-doctors and the attorneys. It'll be a three-ring circus. The best we can hope for is to ruin his political career. That's where Jack comes in. He has to be the voice of reason in the press."

"I don't think I'll be much help. I'm under a contract that's not allowing me to publish anywhere."

"I'm aware of your situation, and by tomorrow afternoon I'll have it handled."

Jack nodded.

"I've given this a lot of thought," Carolyn said. "In my professional opinion, the only way to beat Richard is to hit him with a surprise blow. Knock him off balance. He can't have any time to react. And for the country's sake, this must be done before he's sworn in tomorrow."

"This will tarnish Warner's legacy," Jack said.

He was too polite, Carolyn thought, to mention the damage she would also suffer. She smiled slightly. "No doubt. But I can't worry about that now."

"What do you need from me?" Katherine asked.

Jack stood, walked to the window, drew back a corner of the curtain, and looked out onto the street. "Katherine, you have no idea what you are signing up for. Carolyn and I can handle this. It's not your fight."

"That is such sexist bullshit," Katherine said. "I don't need a protector, so knock it off. I'm in, and I will not discuss it further."

Jack's jaw clenched, but he remained silent.

Carolyn leaned across the coffee table and put her hand on Katherine's knee. "I'm relieved to hear it, because you are an integral part of our success."

The tea remained untouched between them.

"How many Secret Service agents came with you?" Jack asked, while still watching the street.

"Only one."

"Can you trust him?"

Carolyn nodded. "Martin Riggs is the only one I do trust. Speaking of which, Martin has the files the Secret Service confiscated from you."

Jack turned from the window. His eyes narrowed.

"Before we leave tonight, he will bring those in for you," Carolyn said.

Jack nodded as he returned to his seat. "So, what's the plan?"

CHAPTER THIRTY-THREE

Carolyn led Katherine through the White House and up to the private quarters. She glanced at her watch. It read 3:16 am. A shiver of apprehension ran down her spine, as they walked through the residence.

They moved to the Treaty Room, which Warner had made his home office. Dark greens, burgundies, and navy wove through the furniture and draperies. Normally, the rich upholstery provided a warm and comforting environment, but tonight Carolyn's world seemed black and white. "As a precaution, we'll use Warner's computer."

Katherine sat at his desk. Carolyn locked the doors. Painted deep red, the walls provided a masculine backdrop for the mahogany and cherry wood furnishings. Katherine logged onto the Internet.

"You're sure you can retrieve deleted messages from my e-mail?" Carolyn asked.

"Positive."

"I have to warn you." Carolyn paced in front of the desk. "I don't know the contents of the e-mail you may find on my account. I just know that Warner, Richard, and Mark were undoubtedly using it. These messages may be gruesome."

"I can handle it," Katherine said, while typing on the keyboard. She worked diligently for twenty-five minutes, then sat back while staring at the monitor.

"What's wrong?"

"Nothing. I'm just waiting for the machine to catch up. I'm almost in." She smiled. "Bingo." Katherine hit the print icon. The machine whirred to life.

Carolyn pulled the first sheets of paper off the printer. She read the text. "Son of a bitch."

Katherine moved to her side. "What is it?"

She handed her the e-mail documents, each issuing instructions regarding various deceased individuals, and even one ordering Jack's beating. There were separate messages that appeared to arrange for payment. "They're *all* signed with a 'C' as if I initiated these orders. Is there any way we can prove that I didn't?"

Katherine hurried back to the computer and began to type again. "My specialty."

"What do you mean?"

"I can track the originating computers as well as the message destinations. It all comes back to the IP addresses. Even the firewall programs can be circumvented. That's why experienced hackers will try to bounce off other computers to hide their identity, but I spent years with the NSA tracking such culprits."

"The German spy?" Carolyn asked.

"Exactly." Katherine continued typing. "And our guys *aren't* experienced hackers. Odds are they didn't believe they could be tracked," she said. "Cain might have known, but he doesn't strike me as the type to be terribly protective of his clients."

"Cain is only protective of his money. Richard and Warner would have considered themselves above suspicion."

Half an hour later, Katherine printed a listing of her findings.

Carolyn's smile grew as she read the document. It tied Cain, Warner, Richard, Mark, and Edmund together using her e-mail address by identifying the addresses of the computers where the damning messages had originated.

"Now, if Jack can use his files to correlate these messages with all the pertinent dates, we're on our way to building a case." Carolyn dialed out on her private cell phone. "Here are the numbers you need to match," she said to him before listing the dates of the e-mails. Anyone eavesdropping on the call would have no idea the meaning of the numbers.

"Who do you believe actually did the killing?" Katherine asked, when Caroline hung up the phone.

"Winston Cain and his firm," Carolyn said. "But I can't prove that."

"But someone had to pay him. And if those bank transfers were done electronically they may be on one of these computers."

"You're brilliant." This was just like the old days, Carolyn thought, when she and Katherine had worked together in the prosecutor's office.

An hour later, Katherine stood up to stretch.

Carolyn looked up from the documents she'd been reading. Her heart stuttered. "Can't get in?"

"Relax." Katherine sat back down. "I'm in Richard's computer now. It's just that my eyes are sore from scanning all of his data. Most of it doesn't apply. I wonder how much trouble I could get into by accessing the vice president's personal computer." She glanced at Carolyn, who wasn't smiling.

"You don't want to know. That's why we're on Warner's computer, and I wanted you here with me when you did this. Anyone comes in, I'm the one online."

"But--"

Carolyn held up her hand. "On this, I won't negotiate." She looked at her watch. "Besides we're running out of time. It's after five."

A few moments later, Carolyn heard the printer turn on. She glanced up from her work and found Katherine grinning from ear to ear. Carolyn jumped up from her chair. "What is it?"

"Seems Richard has a penchant for bank accounts in the Caymans. But that's not the worst part. It appears he invoiced your War On Drugs task force in the name of Winston Cain's firm for two million dollars. He deleted the document, but I found it anyway. I also reconciled it to the task force's ledger. It was processed. Since Warner rubber-stamped the budget for over five hundred million, it seems he had no problem getting paid. Guess where I found the funds?"

"The Cayman account?"

"You bet. It was withdrawn the day after the chemical release. I had to hack into the bank's computer system to verify it."

Carolyn raised an eyebrow.

Katherine smiled. "Don't worry, I jogged around a bit using some old tricks. They won't track us. Unfortunately, there's no way for me to know who actually withdrew the money."

Carolyn stepped back and then folded into her chair. "This is incredible."

"It's not a smoking gun," Katherine said. "But it should be enough to finish Young."

"We'll see," Carolyn said. "It all rides on how we handle matters from here on out." She picked up the phone and dialed. "I'm sorry to wake you, Mr. Speaker," she began.

CHAPTER THIRTY-FOUR

Speaker of the House, Jonathan Daniels, stood before the joint session of Congress. His rotund presence commanded silence. "Before we take this historic vote, I have been asked to allow a very special speaker to take the floor. Due to the extraordinary circumstances we face today, I do not believe that any of you will object. Ladies and gentleman, without further adieu please join me in welcoming First Lady Carolyn Alden Lane."

A roar of applause thundered through the Capitol as the entire audience rose to their feet.

Carolyn entered the room from the back and moved down the main aisle to the podium. Members of Congress shook her hand and kissed her cheek, offering words of sympathy as she progressed.

It felt like an eternity ago when she'd spent her days speaking in courtrooms, arguing before judges and juries, condemning the guilty, enforcing the laws. And although she had immense experience, with a reputation to back it up, no closing argument could have prepared her for this moment. She found herself again charged with the job of condemning the guilty, arguing for justice--only this time the forum had changed, and the stakes affected her country.

She stood before the lawmakers themselves, a group of men and women who were about to radically change the course of history, even though they didn't know it. Yet.

Carolyn adjusted the microphone to her height and looked out at the packed house.

* * *

Richard Young sat alone in his office at the West Wing. Security demanded that leadership separate during joint sessions so as to preserve the chain of command in case of an attack. Even most of his staff was absent, as they worked furiously over at his Ceremonial Office in the Executive Office Building, preparing for his rise to the presidency.

Volume cranked up on the television, feet resting on an ottoman, he sipped a cup of coffee while waiting for the Congressional vote-- the vote that would make him the next President of the United States. When the Speaker of the House introduced Carolyn he slid his feet off the ottoman and leaned forward in his chair.

What the hell was going on? Why hadn't Carolyn told him that she planned to address Congress?

My God, he thought after a moment, *she's brilliant*. To speak in front of Congress before this historic vote, while her husband lay near death, was nothing short of heroic. The pundits and the public would view this as an incredible act of courage. After this, her vice presidency would be a shoo-in. Her astute political strategy impressed the hell out of him. Adrenaline coursed through him as he waited excitedly for what he knew would be a remarkable speech.

* * *

The applause seemed deafening. Carolyn took a deep breath. She'd given up her entire life to reign as First Lady, and now she was about to destroy it all.

To some it would have been easy to accept Young's bribe to be the first female vice president. And although she had compromised a lot to get where she stood today, nothing was worth selling her soul for, not even the second highest office in the land. Before her lay the opportunity to redeem herself in her own eyes, to reclaim the person she'd once been, and wanted to return to, with pride.

Carolyn held up a hand to quiet the crowd. "Thank you. Thank you," she said. "Please--I don't deserve this. Please—sit down. Please. Thank you."

The room quieted.

"In many ways our country is like a growing child," she began. "Each of us loves this child dearly. And our electorate has charged each of you with parenting this child, and like all parents we do our best along the way, but even our best is not perfect.

"The child, undoubtedly, makes mistakes, fails and falls. The parents make decisions for the child, and like the child, we make mistakes, fail from time to time, and also fall down on our job for we are only human. Painfully, I must say that this is one of those moments."

Carolyn cleared her throat. "Today, you are the guidance for this child, our country. Today, you will make a history-altering decision. Each of you accepted this responsibility when you took your oath of office. And the people of this great nation depend on you to act in the best interests of our country."

She took a deep breath. "It is a fact that my husband--" her voice broke. She paused for a moment to collect her composure. "My husband, Warner Hamilton Lane, will not recover from his injuries. This is a blow to our nation and the world. But it would be an even greater blow if I allowed you to vote, in accordance with the Constitution, on the chain of succession without all of the facts."

She gripped the podium as if to fortify her will to continue. Carolyn knew that Richard would be watching, so she gazed into the television camera and concentrated on directing her words to him. "Richard Young cannot be allowed to take the office of the President of the United States."

A hush fell over the congressional floor. Shock held everyone riveted.

Carolyn lifted the key documents above her head. "I hold in my hand evidence that implicates Mr. Young in a tragic conspiracy of many years. A conspiracy of such magnitude that it took the life of Senator William Rudly, the men who died in the chemical release event days ago, and many others."

A collective gasp traveled through the room.

289

Strobes exploded. A roar of noise rolled over her from the congressional chambers as the members grasped her meaning. Pandemonium reigned as reporters, completely out of order, shouted questions.

Jonathan Daniels stepped to her side. He cracked the gavel on the podium, quickly redeeming order. He nodded for Carolyn to continue.

"As you all know," she went on, "I spent many years as a prosecutor. Today, I bring these skills to you, our lawmakers. Obviously, this must be investigated. Congressional hearings must take place, possibly a Grand Jury convened, and maybe even a trial. But until this matter of national security is resolved, the party in question cannot lead our country.

"It is with a leaden heart that I reveal this horrific news. But it is with the full measure of my confidence that I ask you to act in accordance with the demands of our Constitution. You must provide this country with the leadership she deserves. The leadership of the next man in the line of our constitutional succession, our Speaker of the House, Jonathan Daniels."

* * *

"You BITCH!" Young screamed. He jumped to his feet, at the same time flinging his coffee cup into the wall. The bone china shattered into a multitude of tiny pieces. How could she have done this to him? He grabbed the phone.

The door to his office opened, and his assistant stepped into the room. "You have visitors, sir."

"I'm busy right now," Young said without looking up.

"Put the phone down, Richard."

Young raised his gaze to the familiar voice.

Attorney General Jeffery Briant stepped into the room followed by three gentlemen in dark suits. Richard recognized them as FBI agents.

CHAPTER THIRTY-FIVE

Katherine stood in front of Jack on the sidewalk of Pennsylvania Avenue. Together they had attended Carolyn's speech. He'd covered the event for the *Today* news magazine. True to her word, Carolyn had cleared the roadblock for Jack's journalism career. She'd even committed to giving him an exclusive interview regarding her role in the historic vote.

"I guess this is it," Katherine said.

"It doesn't have to be," Jack responded.

"I thought you were furious with me."

"How can I be? When, as you said, I got my way---you believed me."

Katherine shrugged. "I don't know, Jack. We seem destined to keep repeating the mistakes of our past."

"I think that's a copout," he said. "We're both mature adults. I don't buy the idea that we can't learn from our mistakes. Granted, we have some work to do, especially regarding trust--"

"Some work to do? I think it'll take a team of therapists--years."

Jack paused.

When he said nothing, Katherine turned to walk away.

He grabbed her hand, forcing her to stop. When she finally met his gaze, he said, "So, we'll hire a team of therapists. I've got the time. How about you?"

She laughed. "Years?"

"If that's what it takes. I can't think of a better way to wile away the hours."

"You really mean it, don't you?"

He answered her with a long kiss.

* * *

July 25, 2001---Washington, D.C.

Standing on the steps leading from the White House terrace out to the Rose Garden, Carolyn glanced over at President Jonathan Daniels.

"Are you ready?" he asked.

A smile lit up her eyes. "Absolutely."

"Let's go," he said. "The press awaits."

The President walked out onto the lawn and up onto the dais. Carolyn followed. A soft summer breeze carried the sweet smell of freshly cut grass. Once on the stage, Carolyn stood slightly behind and to the left of the President.

"Ladies and gentlemen," he began, "it is my honor to present to you a courageous and unselfish patriot, who time and again has put the interests of the nation ahead of her own needs. She is the first woman to hold the second highest office in the land--Vice President Carolyn Alden Lane."

Carolyn stepped up to the podium. Bright sunlight glinted off the television cameras before her.

With thundering applause, the members of the press rose to their feet.

"Thank you," she said. "Thank you."

After a few moments, the crowd quieted.

"Today, as I stand before you, I'm humbled by the opportunity to serve this great nation. Our country faces a bright and shining future. A future led by a man of character, integrity, and honor. A man who looks to the future with vision and wisdom. A man I'm proud to stand

292

beside as vice president. Our President--Jonathan Daniels." Carolyn met the gaze of President Daniels as she joined the crowd in applause.

The President smiled and nodded in response.

"I want to thank you, Mr. President, for trusting me with this awesome responsibility. I will not let you down." Carolyn stepped toward the President and shook his hand.

She turned back to the members of the press. "Now, I'll be happy to take your questions." Carolyn pointed to a journalist.

"Madame Vice President, now that your appointment has been confirmed, what will be your first course of business?"

Carolyn beamed. Finally, her goals would become reality. "To institute the War On Drugs program and reform the social services system."

The End

ABOUT THE AUTHOR

Kathleen Antrim has won numerous awards for her writing. She has been a columnist for the ANG Newspaper Group in the San Francisco Bay Area. Residing in Northern California with her husband and two daughters, Kathleen is currently at work on her next novel.

For more information, please visit her website at: www.kathleenantrim.com

Printed in the United States
752100002B